SECOND CHANCE MAGICK
A MONSTERA BLUFF NOVEL
BOOK TWO

KATIE HAYPENNY

Copyright © 2026 Katie Haypenny

All rights reserved

The characters and events portrayed in this book are fictitious. Any similarity to real persons, living or dead, is coincidental and not intended by the author.

No part of this book may be reproduced, or stored in a retrieval system, or transmitted in any form or by any means, electronic, mechanical, photocopying, recording, or otherwise, without express written permission of the publisher.

ISBN-13: 978-1-968941-03-1

Edited by: Kate Seger

Cover art by: @linda.noeran

Interior art by: @lanabanana.art

Author portrait by: @willdahlias

Library of Congress Control Number: 2025927179

Printed in the United States of America

No AI was used in the writing of this book.

CONTENT WARNINGS

Be aware of spoilers below!
This steamy, plot driven novel includes:

*Assault to FMC while in a dangerous situation
*Discussion of parents' deaths
*Discussion of depression
*Explicit sexual acts between consenting adults
*Discussion of breeding and pregnancy

PROLOGUE
ADA

The night is too quiet. Only the hum of my old Wagoneer's engine from where it sits on the driveway reaches my ears. No revelers nearby noisily heading home from the Samhain festivities. No buzz of insects or leaves rustling in the breeze. It's as if the world around me is paralyzed with fear, holding its breath in hopes of going unnoticed by the fae. As I run toward the carriage house, the magick cast around it overwhelms me to the point I choke on it, like breathing in a cloud of cloying perfume.

I pull back to avoid it, feeling its sticky strength against my skin as I slide on my feet. Giving a wide berth, I skirt around the building with urgent but silent steps.

"What in the blue blazes?" My hands fly to cover my mouth, but not in time to catch my outburst. Behind the carriage house, a dark figure shambles toward the woods, almost like something undead out of those old human horror films. It turns its head fully behind it to look at me while its body remains walking in the other direction. The vertebrae in its neck pop like gunshots in the oppressive silence. Swirling yellow eyes pin mine in a sinister stare. I'm frozen in place as I watch them bulge too big for the head they're contained in. And like an eggshell cracking—the sound it makes not dissimilar—its body sheds and withers to the ground, a shadowed entity spewing from the husk of its skull.

This is my first glimpse of a fae. All Whispered Folk know of them. As children, we'd spin yarns to frighten each other, the more outlandish the made-up tale, the better. Yet the spine-chilling reality is worse than we imagined. Inky black coils frame the over-bright eyes, now as big as dinner plates, illuminating the space between us. It grows into a shadowed, incorporeal giant, an embodiment of pure magick. The most dangerous and powerful of the Malefic Folk. It's unfathomable that someone let this foul thing through the town's wards. I wouldn't believe anyone would do such a thing, except the evidence is staring me in the face.

My eyes dart to the discarded body. An unfamiliar human-looking male. Thanks to Mother Earth it's not Cara, but that doesn't mean she's safe. Quite the contrary. Something is happening to the carriage house, and she's most certainly trapped inside. I try to push that thought from my mind as I summon the full strength of my magick—what's left of it after performing the Samhain rituals, anyway. I must slow down the fae until help arrives. There's no room for error.

"You've come alone, Mayweather heir. Think you can save that pesky little bird all by yourself? How amusing. This shall be fun. What secrets will I steal from your mind while you eagerly wish for death?" It has no discernable mouth, no vocal chords. Yet its deranged, hollowed out masculine voice is ear-splitting, surrounding me from all sides, stabbing at me like a knife.

I can't let the taunts distract me. A glib response would be a waste of breath. I won't beg for my life, but I will fight for it.

"Shield my body and mind, no cracks for the fae to—" I falter midcasting as banshee-like shrieks and moans that don't belong in this realm of existence bellow from behind me, sending a heart-pounding frisson of fear through my veins. Both the fae and I are caught off guard, turning our attention to its source. A line of figures appears behind me, standing like phantasmic sentries, magick swelling around them. Their otherworldly voices cast spells strong enough to make the hair on the back of my neck stand on end.

Whoever they are, their appearance isn't crisp, almost like they're covered in a fine, flickering layer of static from an old television that blurs around the edges of their forms. Their movement isn't quite right either. Sometimes too quick, sometimes too slow. But their magick is certainly tangible.

Trying to keep my wits about me, I study their faces to figure out who they are. Oh, moon and stars, those are my own violet eyes gazing at me in a face all too familiar. I see it in the mirror more clearly with each passing year. My mom, so graceful even in this liminal state. And next to her, a slim, tall figure with a mop of dark red hair with a white forelock, curling so roguishly at his forehead. There's no mistaking my dad, still looking impossibly clever. I never thought I'd see them again in this life.

My parents, gone fifteen years now, stand closest to me. Followed by grandparents and others in my lineage, generations of Mayweathers, from long ago who I never met. I'm knocked for a loop, right when I need to fight for my life.

A high-pitched whine rises from behind the lump in my throat.

"Mom. Dad. You've returned to me," I gasp, as a shuddering sob pushes its way out of me. Tears blur my vision, and I nearly sink to my knees in front of them. I don't know how they're here. Unless the ward has brought them to defend me and our family land? Has this Samhain night really blurred the line between our realms so completely?

As I'm drenched by a tidal wave of grief, my mom's arms raise high and I feel a warm tingle around my body just before a sharp push unsteadies my feet. The spell, cast in a voice so different than the one locked in my memories, shields me, cushioning the blow from the fae's attack while I'm distracted. It startles me into action. Like an innate choreography hidden deep in my subconscious, the steps of which I could never recreate, magick flows from me.

I need to direct the wind, push against the fae, compress the oily, coiling tendrils trying to reach me. Instinctively, it's clear I shouldn't let it touch me. But despite all I do, those yellow eyes never dim, their strength never wavers.

Changing tactics, I cast spells to wildly swing the temperature surrounding the fae, determining whether extreme heat or cold has any effect. Pulling water out of the humid night air, freezing it on contact, I attempt encasing the fae in ice. The nebulous inky cloud is too quick for me to contain and manages to slither out in a way a physical form couldn't. When that doesn't work, I try to use physical barriers to deflect the magick. I pull the ground out from under the fae, creating a tall berm between us. The fae magick blows holes through it soon enough.

The ghostly emanations behind me continue their onslaught, though they seem focused on blocking the fae magick from reaching me. Sometimes enclosing me in a protective barrier, sometimes hitting an opposing spell straight on like an arrow, knocking it off its path. Despite their effort, sometimes the fae magick grazes me, like a lick of fire to my skin. Mostly it's only a momentary sizzle but at times it's so excruciating, like lava injected into my veins, that it pulls the breath from my lungs, forcing me to start my spell over after it passes.

A loud crash of breaking glass pulls me out of the trance of casting powerful magick. My eyes flash toward the carriage house beside this impromptu battlefield. Flames burst through the roof near the front of the structure. Even though the fire is on the other side, waves of heat roll off the smoldering building. Sweat drips from my forehead into my eyes. I rub the sting away as fast as I can. The coven should be here any moment. I can't think about what's happening there. I need to hold on just a little longer.

My voice chants a recitation of a long and ancient verse, but the words aren't my own. The ward has morphed into this living entity, a new consciousness that I'm borrowing from. Generations of knowledge and experience flood into me. My magick ups the ante, trying to disrupt the cellular structure of the fae, to force it into a solid state of matter, anything to paralyze or contain. Not knowing what that murky form is composed of makes it even trickier. But I try to target any natural elements that may occupy space along with its magickal essence. It's hard to pinpoint, but I strike at what I can. The fae staggers with each surge of magick but regroups swiftly, its form swirling into new and puzzling shapes.

As I pull deeper from my dwindling magickal reserves to cast even more potent spells, I'm shoved backwards by a wall of sound, like a sonic boom. My arms flail as I regain my balance, catching myself before I fall. A bubble of silence surrounds me, though the action around me hasn't stopped. I do my best to cast spells as before, but my voice chokes in my throat. The fae has muted me, as well as blocked my hearing. This presents another obstacle; one I'm not sure I can overcome.

I slow my breath and attempt to clear my mind, summoning my magick without the aid of my voice to focus its power. I rarely practice this, as it takes considerable mastery to be as effective. It'll be next to impossible to center myself when all I want is to turn around and catch any glimpse of my parents while I still can. It may be dumb luck they were spared this silencing spell. Their magick still swirls in the air around us.

There's a sudden rush of movement around me. Members of my coven enter my peripheral vision. Finally. They're here. Mayhap I'll survive this night after all. As another spell to fight off the fae plants itself in my mind, a particularly powerful blast hits me square in the chest. I'm horrified to look down at a long, inky tendril punching right through my sternum.

I crumple to the ground landing hard on my hip, jarred by the impact of that final crush of fae magick. A hole has been blown through my chest. Is this what it feels like to die? Will my parents escort me into the next realm? I struggle to lift my weakened arm to place my hand to my injury, expecting the smear of oozing blood and viscera as I touch it, to hold my heart during its final few beats as I expire from the land of the living. Certain of my impending death, it's an utter shock to discover my body is intact. There's no physical damage from the blow. I hold out my trembling hand in front of my disbelieving eyes, clean beyond a scuff of dirt. But the staggering pain is real. And I'm so exhausted.

With black edges narrowing my vision, I force my gaze one last time to my beloved mom and dad, whose lives were cut too short, still standing at the ready behind me, casting spells to protect me and my fellow witches.

I love them so much. I always will.

"Don't go without me," I beg in a final burst of strength before I succumb to the darkness.

"Come back! I need you!" I gasp awake, my voice a high keening wail in my dark bedroom. That nightmare repeats itself every night since. Each time I wake up their loss feels fresh, a vicious cycle of torment. Whether or not it was them in any conscious form or simply a strand of the ward's long memory, I've come to see that night as their final act of love for me. Ashes, the very notion tears my heart wide open.

Only silence answers me as I sob into my pillow. My mom and dad, my grandparents, returned to the far reaches, the realm of the dead, that night after dozens of coven members arrived and finally restrained the fae. I wish I had been awake to say goodbye to my parents, like I've always wished I could.

I'm no stranger to grief, but I'm not sure how to move forward. One doesn't just walk away from a fae and I'm no exception. My voice and hearing returned when I woke up at the healers clinic, just under a week ago now. But I was alarmed to discover that my magick was gone. Something happened when the fae speared itself through my chest. No one has answers for me yet.

A shallow emptiness remains there, even though the lancinating pain from that night is long over. I sit up in bed and attempt a simple spell to smooth the creases in my nightgown. "With my warm hands I press all wrinkles from this dress." But the pull of my magick still feels dimmed, like a candle wick that won't catch the flame.

I cover my face with shaking hands and press them tightly over my eyes as I fall back on my pillow. A tremor racks my body as I stifle a scream of frustration. Lying there, fully awake for the next few hours, I wait for the sun to rise, replaying the encounter with the fae endlessly in my mind. My parents and grandparents. Generations of family. The absence of my magick is palpable, separating me from that long Mayweather heritage that came to my aid that night. My connection to them, and even to my coven, severed for now, maybe forever. I've never felt more alone.

CHAPTER 1
NORRELL

"A fae attacked where?" I roar, causing my irksome cousin Torman, the bearer of this news, to take an involuntary step backward.

"Monstera Bluff. I was told it was an inside job, a group of warlocks invited in a fae to get rid of some human they did not like. *Idiots*. All of them. The New York City coven took over the investigation of that evidently incompetent settlement and reached out for *our* help. Asking us to join some assembly. Only the blue hag of winter knows why they thought our clan would care. I told them right where they could put that invitation. They should clean up their own mess and not bother us again. We have no need to get swept up in their trivial business. But I know you have spent time in this place, so I thought you would find it amusing," he relays with a smug grin on his face, not seeming to understand the gravity of the news.

His obliviousness is either a mark of stupidity or a blatant show of disrespect. Not that I would expect otherwise from him. I have covered for his uselessness time and time again, at great personal expense. And this is yet another situation I must mitigate.

Even if it happened somewhere other than Monstera Bluff it would be beyond callous to dismiss the situation. I was raised by my parents, both noble hunters, to be in service of this clan and to all Whispered

Folk through our commitment to defend the powerful magick of the True North from the scourge of Malefic Folk. We all were. But Torman's and my interpretations of that are markedly different. He would have us all stick our heads in a snow drift and pretend that no other Whispered Folk exist. If the world melted around us, he would not notice until he was face-deep in a puddle. He takes after his father, our former clan leader, in that belief. Thus, I have as much esteem for him as I do his intolerant and dogmatic father. None.

"Fire of the frost, your shortsightedness is astounding. How dare you make that judgment without my authorization? And then insult the most respected coven in the world, on top of that? You are acting out of turn, cousin, as if any of this was your choice to make. If you wanted the perks of leadership so badly, you could have done *something* to earn it. Do not *ever* speak on my behalf again. Get out of my sight, or I will show you exactly why the Arctic wraiths fear me!" I seethe, my face twisting in disgust.

His expression is dumbfounded, like he cannot fathom that I would not have the same heartless antagonism toward an appeal for help. Turning on his heel, he flounces out of my office, clearly thrown off balance by my reprimand. He has always coveted my role as leader of our clan despite being completely unsuited for it, wanting all the glory without putting in the hard work.

I never wanted to lead the clan, but his laziness as a young hunter left him woefully unprepared, so it fell to me. As the son of our last leader as well as my cousin, he was forced on me as an advisor. It is just another means for him to wield his incompetence. I catch him pushing boundaries where he can. But this is a step too far. I must take matters into my own hands, it seems. I cannot trust anyone else in my clan to take this seriously. They made me their leader, demanded it of me. Now they get to live with the consequences. While I agree we need to keep our autonomy, we do not have to ignore serious struggles within the Whispered Folk world to do so.

There is a balance to strike. It will not be easy, but it is possible. We yetis are not hairy oafs, lumbering single-mindedly around snowcapped peaks and icy tundras, striking down any Malefic Folk we cross. We serve a noble purpose, one that has given us a near mythical status among the

Whispered Folk. Why not use that to our advantage instead of a reason to further isolate ourselves? The extent of our abilities does not need to be common knowledge, nor how we repurpose the Malefic's twisted, violent magick. Many in our clan believe that if our unique abilities became widespread knowledge, we would be treated like a threat rather than a faraway self-governing community. The irony is lost on them that this mindset is borne from the same fear and prejudice they want to avoid. It will not be a popular decision, but we are uniquely positioned to help in situations like this where the stability of the Whispered Folk world is in question. We will answer their plea, one way or another.

Working my jaw back and forth, I think on the best course of action. There is no trusting my cousin to cooperate on this matter. Whoever he spoke with may not entertain a call from us again. I should reach out to someone at the witch academy I visited so many years ago. At the time, I had not wanted to leave the clan, but the elders insisted I learn what I could from the great library they amassed over centuries. It changed the course of my life. I never would have crossed paths with my mate otherwise.

I kept in touch with one of the deans, a canny witch named Esmeralda Jurado. She showed herself to be an ally when the school was approached by my clan to gain entrance to me. Her guidance when I arrived, organizing a discreet curriculum for my studies, made my time there productive. But it was Ada who made it unforgettable. I shake my head clear before more vivid memories parade across my mind. Dean Jurado will give me the full story and help coordinate my assistance if it is truly needed.

Time may be of the essence, so I call her immediately. She picks up after the first ring. "Norrell, I thought you may have lost my number. What a pleasant surprise to hear from you after so long," she chastens me without any real sharpness.

"Greetings, Dean Jurado. I would never do such a thing. But I apologize for not checking in sooner. It has been a few years since we last spoke," I express regretfully.

"Call me Esmeralda. You have not been my student for a long time, so no need for formalities," she reminds me.

"If you wish, Esmeralda. I only want to show you the respect you are due," I acknowledge, remaining deferential to her ongoing role as a mentor in my life.

"That's very thoughtful of you, but I hope that we have been friends long enough that we can skip the titles. Though I'm happy to call you Huntmaster of the True North if you'd prefer it," she cajoles.

"Your point is made. I try my best to forget that title," I grumble, failing to keep a bitter note out of my voice.

"It's an important one, though I know what it cost you. You are the leader your clan needs," she sympathizes.

"Sometimes I believe the clan has completely ossified," I confess. "They remain in a dark age, unable to be convinced we can thrive around witches and other magickal Whispered Folk. It is such a long-held conviction that I do not know how to prove otherwise to them."

"If anyone can, it's you and your brother who will change their hearts and minds. I know there's a lot of clan history you can't tell me, but the Whispered Folk, especially witches, understand that your fight against the Malefic helps us all. They are a menace even without the dangerous boost of power from the wild magick that concentrates at the poles. Ah, but I don't need to *witch-splain* that to you. I just want you to know that you will have support from us. How ever your people stop them, we won't interfere," she promises.

"I believe you. But this obvious logic has not swayed them," I vent, my voice overloud. I take a deep breath, not wanting to take out my frustration with my clan and my cousin on her. When I compose myself, I continue, "They barely tolerate contact with Whispered Folk who have no whiff of magick. Like proximity alone taints our community. My life, everything I have given up for the clan, will be a waste if I do not succeed in changing this."

"There must be some consolation, some measurable progress you've made. They will follow your lead when the time is right. But you're correct that you gave up... someone... very important. Ada, she is..." Esmeralda pauses, like she is mulling over her words. She exhales a shaky breath before she speaks again. "Norrell, I'm not sure how to tell you this. She was gravely injured by the fae that entered Monstera Bluff. She's alive, physically uninjured, but her magick... it's gone and we can't figure out why. She fought off the fae almost single-handedly. The protective ward around her family home manifested itself in the strangest way, as members of her family, casting spells through them. It helped her as much as it could. But the fae was much more powerful than it should have been. It managed to touch her and drain her magick before her coven finally weakened and contained it."

My blood runs cold as I listen to Esmeralda describe what happened to Ada. Her magick is gone—the very thing that alienated her from my clan. My poor ember in the frost, it must have been terrifying. I remain mute, silently stewing over Ada's suffering, as Esmeralda goes on to recount the events in Monstera Bluff leading up to the attack. The deception of three power-hungry warlocks who unleashed evil in an apparent attempt to take control of the town. Ada thwarting their plan, nearly by herself. She is even more remarkable than I remember. It is a miracle that she lives.

Even if the fae only drained her magick, it should come back after a period of rest. It is not quite the way of the yeti, but the coincidence is too great to ignore. We drain magick, but from a distance, nullifying spells, and eventually weakening Malefic Folk like fae, wendigos, wraiths, and banshees until they are unable to defend themselves. Then we strike them down if they prove too stupid or determined to turn tail and run. Most are. It could be the fae placed a curse on her. Knowing them as I do, it will be something as nasty as it is powerful.

The days of the North Clan eschewing their involvement in the Whispered Folk world are officially over. Wild work of frost, if this is not a clear sign, I do not know what is. As Esmeralda mentions leadership and experts from across the Whispered Folk world joining a so-called safety council convening in Monstera Bluff, I interrupt her, "There is much I know about fae magick. I should be there representing the North Clan. Who must I speak to about this?"

"I hoped you'd be stirred to action. The council needs you and your experience with Malefic Folk. Ada may not know it yet, but she'll need you too," Esmeralda advises.

She puts me in touch with the New York City coven, mayhap even the same witch who was harassed by my insolent cousin earlier. My attendance is confirmed. They will arrange my long trip to Monstera Bluff. The clan's council of elders will balk at my plan, but my attendance is not up for debate. I am their leader. It is my call to make despite their disagreement. I will arrange for my younger brother, my most trustworthy ally, to stand in for me while I am away. Finally, I may be able to push us to a brighter future and do right by my mate in the same turn.

CHAPTER 2

ADA

Life handed me lemons but forgot the sugar to make lemonade. It's turning me into an insufferable sourpuss.

The sun has only just risen, and I'm already sitting on my front porch glumly watching the bustling and downright noisy activity on my lawn. I can feel the pout in my lower lip. It's stuck in place. Several members of my coven, assisted by a construction crew, shovel the final, grimiest layer of charred debris from where my carriage house formerly stood. Now it's a big old mess. The volunteer clean-up effort has been at it for a few days. Using their magick, the witches condense and shrink the burnt wood, remnants of furniture and appliances, roofing tiles, and everything else that was destroyed, piling it all into a dump truck provided by Guardian Construction.

Each shovelful makes me wince as it clunks into the bed of the truck. One of the crew notices me staring while he's at it and gives me a friendly wave. I lift a hand and twist my lips into something resembling a smile to try to act like a normal person who isn't obsessively watching part of her home getting carted away. The construction company is now owned by my friend Ben Garde-Pierre, Cara's mate, who freed her from the carriage house and flew her to the healers clinic just in time. He's at home recuperating with her, but his dad Nicolas, who retired from the business just a few years ago, flies overhead. His long leathery wings beat unhurriedly as he lands near the truck to inspect their work. Nicolas stretches those great wings behind him before neatly folding them along his back. The gargoyle has stopped by every day during this process.

"Good morning, Ada! Looks like we'll be done this afternoon!" he calls out to me as he cheerily waves.

"Thanks!" I respond, faking a similar level of enthusiasm. "I have coffee and oatmeal bars inside if you want any." Luckily, there are still a few left after the rest of the group swooped in to devour them when they arrived.

"I had breakfast already with Lillian but thank you for the offer. I'm only here for a few minutes. Do you still want this area seeded with grass?" he asks.

"Yes, please." I confirm the original plan. "I still don't know what I'll do with it."

Nicolas nods sympathetically, witnessing how hard I took the news earlier this week when he told me the structure wasn't salvageable. He's been so kind that I've tried to be stoic in his presence to spare his feelings.

The last several grueling days were spent sorting out its burnt hull, recovering as many of Cara's belongings as possible to give back to her, getting the damage assessed, and ultimately, choosing to tear it down. Clancy Evermane, the mayor and a close friend, was with me through a lot of it, making decisions and directing work when I could barely get out of bed the first couple days following the attack.

Losing the carriage house gutted me, though I'm trying to keep that to myself while these friends and neighbors are hauling it away for me. They don't need me weeping over every burnt scrap. I haven't given up on *all* sense of propriety just yet. It was built at the same time as the manor house. A piece of my family's history is lost with it. But I'm the only one left to care. The end of the Mayweather line in Monstera Bluff. I don't know if I'll ever rebuild it, considering what happened. It may be time to do something else with that space.

Nicolas looks busy with his crew, so I force myself to stand up from the porch swing with an unladylike grunt and head inside. It's early November and even here in coastal Georgia there's a chill in the morning air a little too cold for my liking. Anyway, there's a lot to tackle today, though I'm jonesing to crawl back into bed.

First thing on the list is to check my email. Even though I was thoroughly exhausted last night, I finally sent an invitation to the contingent traveling for the safety council, a group of representatives from around the Whispered Folk world. I will provide housing for five of those guests in my home. The first to respond would reserve those spots—the fairest way I could think of to offer it. I didn't want to promise anything before the construction was over, so my email came after several other community members with large homes and extra bedrooms did the same. The inn will soon be full as well. In all, there will be at least fifty convening here, if not more, helping us deal with our town's situation as well as planning for more robust security measures for their own communities. It's a lot of distinguished guests to host at once for an extended period—at least a few weeks, maybe longer for some—so I will take in as many as will be comfortable.

Same as I've done the last couple mornings, I sit at my kitchen table after fixing myself a pot of my favorite English breakfast tea to work from my laptop. The kitchen is the coziest room in my home, always warmer than the grander rooms on the main floor. It's situated at the back of the house, with tall glass doors that lead to the back garden. I spend a lot of time here.

Without magick, the simplest tasks, like brewing a pot of tea, have proven tedious. I never knew how true it was that a watched pot never boils. Well, eventually it does, but it's slower than a Sunday afternoon. Usually, I'd instantly heat up water inside my charming ceramic teapot using a miniscule amount of magick, a blip really, but I can't even muster that anymore.

Luckily, Walt Sutton, my honorary uncle, came to my rescue the other day after witnessing me losing my vertical hold. Impractically, I tried boiling water in a much too big pot on the stove which I proceeded to spill more than pour into our mugs, almost burning both of us in the process. Lo and behold he returned a couple hours later after running some errands with an electric tea kettle among other items I haven't needed until now. As a human, he had a good sense of what I'd need to get by until... if... my magick returns. Even though I thanked him profusely, I was being so ridiculous and morose. He took it in stride like he always does. But I'm still upset at myself about the way I acted. Like I was complaining I had to live like *him*, Mother Earth forbid. But he knew I didn't really mean it. My fear and sadness got the better of me.

"I'm just plain useless, Walt. I'm not cut out for life without magick!" I whined to him that afternoon as we finished sorting through the shopping bags.

"You are a capable young woman. I'll teach you how to use all of this. Heck, I've got Acton using an immersion blender and a juicer at home to make his plant food. All of this will be a piece of cake for you. You'll be whizzing around the house like you used to in no time." His voice had a smile in it the whole time, not holding my petulant mood against me.

Acton's plant food has been a long-running joke between all of us. As a dryad, a forest sprite, Acton's diet is quite different than ours. He used to tease me about trying it when I was a little girl. I'd always laugh and shriek and run away. It became a game between us throughout my childhood since it was all in good fun. *You'll sprout the most bountiful blooms from your ears!* Or my favorite, *Your flatulence will be scented of the sweetest roses!* It got me every time.

"I'm no spring chicken. Haven't been for a while now." I sure was pissing and moaning something fierce.

He laughed good-humoredly at me the whole time. "I just call it like I see it. You have a long life ahead. Whether it's with magick or without, you'll do just fine. Trust me on that."

"What if I get too accustomed to not using magick? I might jinx myself and it'll never come back." I wanted to sound defiant, but my quivering chin gave me away. I was just so embarrassed by those superstitious thoughts.

Walt looked shaken up by my admission, but he quickly pulled me into a tight hug. "It'll all come out in the wash, my dear. You'll see." He held me while I cried on his shoulder and didn't let go until my tears stopped. I'm the luckiest witch in the world to have him as my uncle.

Despite Walt's constant reassurances when he and Acton checked in with me daily, the gravity of my situation feels like being mired in quicksand. I'm not sure which moves to make. If they'll sink me even further or lead me to safety. So, I've gone the scaredy-cat route and have been lying low, not wanting to go to my shop, Mayweather Potions and Panacea, or to town hall more than is strictly necessary. It's too hard to keep up appearances. Sunny, my apprentice, is more than capable of taking on the extra responsibility while I'm away. She's already gone above and beyond while I'm holed up at home, wallowing in peace.

I'm tired of answering the same questions and hearing the same condolences. I'm pinned down by their near universal pitying eyes and overflow of sympathy, all but broadcasting their inner appraisal of so much power and potential lost. The doom of the once-great family who founded the town. It's not meant to be malicious, but I still see it, feel it. It was non-stop the one day I attempted to work at the shop this week, overwhelming me while I was already so fragile and self-conscious. But that's small-town living. Gossip is the town currency.

While I'm home, I continue to work on organizing for the arrival of those coming to help us. Making sure we have meeting spaces and plenty of food and caffeine on hand while they're here deliberating. I'm basically in full event-planner mode. Fresh off organizing the town's Samhain festival, I'm in my element.

My cats, two British shorthair brothers named Vanilla Paws and Earl Grey, keep trying to walk across my laptop on the table. They're very playful in the morning. I've already tossed around their catnip toys and waved their feather wand, but they still demand my attention.

After a few failed attempts to walk over my keyboard, persistent enough that I had to block them with my arms and gently scoot them back, they finally give up. Vanny, who is all black except his white paws that make him look like he wears kitty-sized socks, jumps to the floor and struts away haughtily, as if telling me he didn't really want anything to do with my laptop anyhow. *How dare I suggest otherwise?* Earl Grey, regal and gray like his name suggests, lounges on a chair next to mine to take his first nap of the day. He's a prolific napper. They seem thrilled that I've been home so much this week, though I wouldn't go so far as to say they nursed me back to health. They're in it for treats and a warm lap.

They excel at the art of distraction, but after a few sips of tea, I'm ready to buckle down even with Earl Grey nearby. I'll have a full house in a couple of days, and I still have to clean and prep for them. I'm curious who has taken up my offer to stay at my house. Mayhap I should have only offered it to a smaller, curated group, but I wouldn't want anyone to feel unwelcome. After draining my cup of fortifying, highly caffeinated tea, I muster the energy to check my email inbox reserved for town council business. I'm met with a flurry of responses to the message I sent right before I went to bed.

The tea instantly curdles in my stomach as I open the first one. "*Fire burn it to ashes!*" I curse loudly, earning me a sidelong glance from my cat who then promptly falls right back to sleep. It's as if the stars above have turned their back on me. *Again.* Out of the massive group of recipients, the first to claim a spot in my house is none other than Norrell Snowstrider. My former mate. The most unforgettable male I have ever met and the one I most wish never to see again.

Eighteen Years Ago

I don't bother stifling my yawn as I sit in the academy library late at night, completely alone, poring over yet another tome on the alchemical properties of precious metals. Their value in the human world is truly a reflection of how complicated and exacting it is to magickally transmute them. I have created so much fool's gold—and the equivalent in silver and platinum—it boggles the mind.

As I'm nearly ready to lay my head down on the increasingly blurry page, I startle awake by the sound of the entry doors creaking, followed by their latch loudly crunching shut. I must not be the only night owl who likes the peace and quiet of a late-night study session. That jolt is enough to keep me up a little longer at least, so I focus on the book again, picking up where I left off.

Heavy footfalls thud across the library's stone floors. Strangely, they sound like they come from something bigger than a witch. Of course, there are other magick-wielding Whispered Folk at the academy, but I wonder who this is and why they're here so late. The footsteps move toward the stacks, presumably to retrieve a book and leave, so I may not get to see their source tonight. No matter, I probably spend equal time here and in the experimental magick lab, so I'll likely run into them eventually, though my curiosity is piqued in the moment.

Minutes go by without another sound. Mayhap they already left without my noticing. So it goes, I guess. I should probably do the same. I'm about to nod off. There's nothing in this book that can't wait until tomorrow.

I close the book with a thump, cut off my reading light, and start to gather my belongings. I'm not silent as I do so, but I also don't try to draw attention to myself. The sound must carry far enough that my fellow night owl hears me. The footsteps resume, steadily growing louder, heading toward the long reading tables where I'm still sitting.

Somewhere in the back of my mind, it occurs to me that if I were outside the academy walls, encountering a stranger late at night while alone in a darkened building might mean I'd be in for a little trouble. But not here. This stranger is more of a novelty. I wonder what book would entice them to come in so late.

Moonlight cascades through the tall windows, creating long pools of light that paint stripes across the floor, shelves, and tables. It's bright enough that I can still see what I'm doing as I get ready to leave. The footsteps grow closer but slow down, taking their time. They might also find simple joy in being alone in the library. Well, I won't rob them of that. As I stand up from my chair, I finally catch sight of who it is.

The stranger... he... is stunning. He glows like a specter as he steps through those stripes of moonlight. He's shirtless, allowing me a glimpse of his physique. His light blue skin—what's not covered in a thick layer of glistering silvery-white pelt—looks lustrous in the nocturnal spotlight. I have no idea who he is. What he is. I've never seen anything like him in all my years living in a diverse community of Whispered Folk.

He pauses, standing still, assessing me just as closely. Mayhap he thought he was alone, that I'm just a lonely apparition haunting these halls on an endless search for a book she'll never find.

"Hello," I venture, softly, as we are in a library.

"Hello." His impossibly deep voice rolls through me. I can feel it as much as hear it.

"I didn't think anyone stayed up reading as late as I do. I think more clearly alone, working into the night. Tonight though, my book seems to be putting me to sleep faster than any nonmagickal remedy I've tried. So, you'll have the place to yourself as soon as I put it back," I tell the stranger, feeling inexplicably bashful.

"That is a pity. I would not mind sharing a table," he responds, sounding faintly disappointed.

"Oh, I guess I can stay for a little while longer then," I offer, my curiosity about him a compelling enough reason. Sitting back down, I switch on the lamp again and put my notebook and pen back on the table.

He sits facing me, though at the other end of the table, leaving ample space between us. Carefully opening the aged book, which he must have just plucked from the shelves, he scans a page near the front and then his large, clawed hands deftly leaf through the pages to an interior chapter. His gentle handling of the book mesmerizes me. Watching him from the corner of my eye is much more engrossing than my own book. I only scarcely pretend to continue reading it, instead focusing on him in my peripheral vision, angling my book for a better view. His harsh, masculine profile and the delicate way his claw curls under each page are riveting.

"What is your name?" he asks unexpectedly after some time has passed, not looking up from the book, as if he's only half-listening.

"Ada Mayweather. What's yours?" My eagerness shows.

"Norrell Snowstrider," he states, finally looking up at me. I do the same.

I repeat his name slowly. "Do you come from somewhere north?" I wonder, trying to piece together who he may be.

"Yes, far from here, where very few humans dare go." It's a clue, but I still can't be sure.

"This is the coldest place I've ever been," I remark without exaggeration. I finally summon the courage to fully meet his eyes. The icy blue stare pierces me.

"It is very cold here in the dead of winter," he agrees.

"What brought you to the library?" It might not be any of my business, but I'd regret wasting this opportunity on a discussion about weather, so I attempt to steer us back. I need to know more about him.

"It is peacefully empty late at night. I am asked fewer questions when alone." His resonant voice sounds warm, like he's teasing me.

"Oh," I breathe. "I see. I suppose I should recognize a fellow night owl and respect his wishes."

"A night *yeti*, not owl. This place has made me more nocturnal than usual," he discloses, a smirk tugging at his tusk-framed lips as he returns his attention to his book.

A thrill runs through me as he volunteers this information, even though I suspect he's intensely private. Why a yeti would be at the academy in the first place is anyone's guess. His kind is rare. I've heard of them, but beyond that I know very little. They are secretive, withdrawn. They purposely live away from others, in the coldest, most desolate parts of the world. If others here knew a yeti was in their midst, the gossip would spread like wildfire, and he'd be a spectacle. It would probably drive him away. His secret is safe with me, though. I won't spoil it for him. But I hope this isn't the last I see of him.

"As a witch, I also prefer the ambience of the library after nightfall. It gives the illusion that this place is full of secrets to be revealed. That I'm uncovering hidden knowledge with each chapter I read. It isn't nearly so romantic in the light of day," I muse, running a hand over the unread page. My blatant curiosity must be written on my face. But I should be wise, hold my tongue, try not to get off on the wrong foot.

Quietly, I close my book, deciding that I should end our chance midnight encounter while everything is going so well. It's the most beguiling night I've had in my years at the academy, maybe in my entire unremarkable life. Plus, he really did come here to read, so I don't want to be a distraction. Standing up from my chair, I gather my things and look over at Norrell one last time.

"Goodnight," I whisper, a wistful smile on my lips, as I move away from the table.

"Until tomorrow." The invitation hangs in the air between us. I look at him in confusion for a moment until I comprehend his meaning. He wants to do this again... on purpose. He chuckles softly as I gasp my surprise.

♡ ♡ ♡ ♡ ♡

The memory of the night we met flashes in my mind. He swept me off my feet, and it made me a fool for him. But the bookends of our relationship were such contradictions. Fool me once, as the saying goes. There's no second chance after what he put me through. Hurling my mug across the room would be so very cathartic, but I hold back because it would upset the cats. And it's too pretty to break just because of *him*. He's broken enough in my life as it is. I'm so angry at myself. I should have known this was a possibility. I've been wrapped up in so many other issues, it simply didn't occur to me he'd ever travel here.

He certainly wasted no time claiming a spot in my house. His response arrived mere minutes later according to the time stamp. The gall of this male to show his face here again. Clearly the invitation wouldn't apply to him. He lost all goodwill when he walked out on me while my parents were still fresh in their graves.

What in all that's magickal is the meaning of this? On the surface, this play looks like it's meant to torment me, kick me while I'm down. No doubt he's heard about my latest misfortune. If I was more generous, I'd say it was because he knew my house well. No, he's a cold-hearted male. He's up to something.

Searching for hidden meaning between the lines, I read aloud his brief response, "Thank you for your generous offer to host guests in your home. I roundly accept the invitation and will arrive the day after tomorrow. I look forward to reacquainting myself with Monstera Bluff."

I blow an angry raspberry at the screen, vexed by his stupidly polished message. Like we're distant acquaintances. Well, I guess that's close to the truth nowadays. It's the first I've heard from him in nearly fifteen years. But the tone annoys me beyond measure, as irrational as it is. I can't believe I've invited him back into my home, even if it was inadvertent. I'm a glutton for punishment, apparently.

I should tell him no. Emphatically. Unequivocally. Deny him access to me and my home. How dare he do such a thing when he knows I wouldn't want him here? But then he'd know he still gets under my skin. He and the fae share equal status as villains of my story. If I'm forced to live a life without wielding magick ever again and possibly face a future without my coven or my family's shop, it would do me good to thicken my skin. I can't face the fae again, but I *can* face Norrell. Isn't that what you're supposed to do? Face your fears?

Everything I hold dear is in jeopardy. Cohabitating with an ex-mate for a few weeks on top of all that will be easy-peasy, right? I owe him nothing beyond fulfilling the obligations of this invitation. One I won't revoke... *for now*... so he has nothing to hold over me. All I need to do is tamp down my discomfort around him and go through the motions of hosting. Eventually he'll leave. And I'll have proven to him and myself that I've moved on. After that, I'll make sure I never see him again.

What I would pay for a spell to erase him from my memories... Especially of the day he decided he didn't want to be with me any longer and left. End of story. End of *our* story, anyway. One misfortune in my life and he's gone, off to do his own thing. Time has given me some clarity, though. In hindsight, I see now that even if my parents hadn't died, his priority was never going to be me. That's a lowering thought in and of itself.

It did a number on me. If the love of my life could leave me to twist in the wind right when I needed him most... may love never find me again. I'd have been better off without it. He ripped my already broken heart straight out of my chest and stomped on it with all his might. Ground it down with his heel for good measure. Fifteen years is a long time to resent someone. But I try not to let it show. A Mayweather picks herself up, dusts herself off, and keeps marching forward. Still, behind closed doors, I drift alone in my oversized ancestral home, haunted by the ghosts of old heartache.

If nothing else, his unwanted invasion of my home will show me and everyone else what a small, contemptible male he is indeed. There's not much worse he can do to me beyond mocking my hardship. Or rubbing a new mate in my face. A family that could have been mine. It's been long enough. There's no doubt he moved on. Every possibility ran its course through my mind a million times since he left. But maybe after this he won't live rent-free in my brain for the *next* fifteen years. Honestly, I should hand him a bill the moment he steps through the door.

I never begged him to stay or tried to find out about his life after he returned to his clan without me. It's best not to know. A break should be clean. He'd made his decision. I'm truly in the dark about what he's been up to, especially since information from his clan is sparse. It's not my business anyway. He can do as he pleases.

My eyes prickle, a sure sign this good-for-nothing male is going to make me cry again. I pour more tea into my mug and then absently scratch Earl Gray under his chin until the sensation passes. Forcing my attention back to my laptop to get some work done, I note the names and contact information for the next four so I can confirm their accommodation at my home. Carefully, I compose a response to the thread confirming that Niven Whitehall—my old friend—Cyrinda Ariti, Tallie Sureheart, Aurelia Woodrum... and of course, begrudgingly, Norrell Snowstrider... are the lucky winners, so to speak. I write back directly to a few others who weren't as quick on the draw to let them down gently. There will be more options sent around today to make sure everyone is accommodated. They won't be left stranded.

The message makes it official. Norrell will be here in two days. And I'll be the talk of the town all over again. I drink the last dregs of my tea in one long hot gulp. A bad idea. It burns all the way down. The mug clatters on the table as I set it down with shaky hands. It conjures the memory of Cara's arrival, telling her that everything turns into a tempest in a tea pot here. If only I could take a vacation until this passed.

I'm about to get up to place my mug in the sink when my cell phone rings, Clancy's name on the screen. My centaur friend always has his finger on the pulse of the community. "Good morning, Mayor. Who do you want to gossip about this fine morning?" I drawl facetiously, guessing the nature of the call.

"Fire and ashes, Ada. I just read your email. Did that scoundrel really take you up on your offer? Are you okay with this? I have a mind to tell him exactly where he's welcome..." Clancy scoffs, sending me into a fit of ringing laughter that ends on a sigh.

"You could have knocked me over with a feather, I won't lie. If I knew he was even part of this, I'd have added the disclaimer, 'Not you, Norrell. Kick rocks with a stubbed toe.' Imagine if I had, what fun that could have been. Alas, he wrote back lightning fast, like he wanted to make sure I'd be forced to share space with him. It's confounding why he'd do this when he could stay anywhere else in town. Surely, he heard about what happened to me. I would rather not see him again, but it's done. I won't go back on my word, especially as a town council member. If he behaves badly, all the better to get over him," I declare, despite the deep sense of resignation churning in my gut.

"And he damn well knows you wouldn't. That's why he did it. You lead with your heart, and he took advantage of it. Well, he is persona non grata around here. Believe me, memory runs long in these parts. So much so, he'll mistake us for a big ol' herd of elephants. Everyone remembers what he did and they'll make sure he knows it too. It's a shame we don't have an elephant shifter around here to *accidentally* stomp some sense into him. Now that would almost repay him in kind," Clancy muses, wrenching one of the few genuine smiles from me all week.

"In another era we could have blamed it all on a rampaging elephant broken out of a nearby traveling circus. It's almost too perfect, no doubt the scheme would have gone off without a hitch," I joke, breaking into dry laughter. I hold the phone away from my face when it borders on unhinged.

"He is just plain lucky I don't have any stray cousins who ran away to join one. It would really come in handy for plotting our revenge by elephant right about now," he bemoans with a sarcastic flair. "Now let's think outside the... tent. How do we feel about lions? With nary a tamer in sight? If we're considering lions, there are some favors I could call in..."

"Well, if we're talking about revenge plots, let's focus on less maiming and more shaming. Send him home with his tail between his legs, if he had one that is. I think that would be most satisfying to witness," I suggest playfully.

"Now that's an idea I can really work with. I think you're on to something. Ashes, he has got to be up to something, though. I don't like it. I'll keep a close eye on him. Everyone else will be doing the same. If you're out and about today, why don't I take you to lunch? You've been spending too much time alone this week. It's not good for you," he coaxes.

"No, not today, but thanks for the offer. I'm not ready to face more scrutiny. And I have so much work to do at home to get ready for my guests. I'm not above dropping a few fire ants into you-know-who's bed. If you hear any complaints, it's purely coincidence," I quip, steering the conversation back to irreverence.

"Are you sure you can't make it? I excel at running interference. Hanging out with me is like having a fifteen-hand busybody barrier at your beck and call." We both chuckle. I can always count on him to make me laugh. "You know I can spot them a mile away. They've got that hungry gleam in their eyes, like they've been offered one of those delicious Pearlhouse Pastries cakes they only make at Yuletide. How do I know that? I see it every time I look in the mirror. Takes one to know one. And if someone starts acting too outrageous, we'll feign some important town business, and you can just hop on my back. I'll skedaddle us on out of there."

"I'm sure you would, *pony express*. Soon. We'll go soon. But not today," I answer, trying to mask my melancholy with some giggles.

"Okay, Ada. But call me if that answer changes. Or if you need anything at all. You're one of my best friends and I hate that I can't do more to help you. This week has been tough. After everything that's happened to you, and to Ben and Cara, we need to stick together, now more than ever."

"I will. And thank you. You do way more than you give yourself credit for," I assure him.

After we hang up, I slump low in my seat, scrubbing my hands up and down my bare face, surprised to find my cheeks damp. I exhale a drawn-out breath. Absently, I comb my fingers across my scalp and through my long hair, pulling apart a few knots while I think about what Clancy said. It was a good conversation. A necessary one. He feels so deeply troubled that his friends were hurt, that they are still hurting. But I don't have the luxury of time right now, nor do I want to face the town just yet.

This house hasn't seen this many overnight guests since my parents' funeral. So many loved them and came to say goodbye. They were happy to sleep on sofas or on the floor when the bedrooms were all claimed. It didn't matter where they slept. They just wanted to be here. I should check the linen closet to be sure there's enough sheets and towels for everyone. And I'll order groceries to be delivered. If I get started today, I'll be ready for everyone when they arrive.

When I finish answering all the emails that need my attention, I finally place my mug and teapot in the sink and head upstairs. First thing, I open the windows in the spare bedrooms to let in fresh air. In one of the rooms, the pretty blue feldspar charm I use to attract particulate matter needs magickal recharging. We call it a "dust magnet" at my shop, selling different sizes and strengths of enchanted charms. This small one should be coated in dust and cat hair, but it's not. It's perfectly clean, meaning all that dander is collecting elsewhere. I'll have to thoroughly clean this room today. Another thing to add to my long list. Normally I would recharge it myself, a small zap would have it as good as new. Now, well...

I pick it up, holding it between my thumb and forefinger, staring at the innocuous little stone. My instincts emerge, ready to pour a tiny amount of magick into it. My skin tingles lightly, a familiar remnant of my magick. Then it fades to nothing.

I blink hard and suck in a shuddering breath. I squeeze the now useless rock tightly in my hand, a jagged edge biting into my palm. A welcome distraction to keep me from losing it. Before I end up in tears, I slip it into my pocket to bring to the shop with me later this week for one of my staff to recharge. I should check the other ones too. I wouldn't want witnesses to my dusty house I seem unable to take care of in my magickless state.

CHAPTER 3

ADA

A knock on my front door echoes from the high-ceilinged foyer. Mother Earth in all her glory, please do not let Norrell be the first to arrive. I should have asked Walt or Clancy to be here with me just in case. Even my thoughtful friend Thea, who has been checking in on me since she healed my physical injuries after the attack, would drop everything to help.

My footfalls tap much too loudly as I cross the room toward the front door. The foyer makes a grandiose statement when someone enters the house, but right now it feels like the walls are pressing in on me. I wipe my clammy hands down my dress. When I reach the door, I peek through the eyelet. My tension releases into a noisy exhale when I see it's not *him*. Mayhap he won't show up. No, that would require luck that abandoned me long ago. While slowing my breathing, I smooth my hair and dress one last time. When I open the door, a stranger and a friend wait at the threshold.

Greeting them both with a genuine, relieved smile, I usher them and their luggage inside saying, "Welcome to Monstera Bluff. And to my home." Thrusting my hand out to the stranger, a capable-looking bear shifter in her late fifties from Upstate New York, I greet her, "I'm Ada. You must be Aurelia?"

"I am. Good guess. I'm thrilled I snagged a spot in your house. I'm not a fan of cramped spaces. The inn just seemed like it would be too busy for such a long stay," she answers, blunt but not unfriendly, as she firmly shakes my hand. Her ruddy, tanned skin and the sturdy hiking boots she wears tell me that she spends a lot of time outdoors.

"Well then, I'm very pleased you're here. The woods are not far, either. Our wolf pack will get you acquainted," I assure her.

I finally get a good look at my old friend. He's noticeably matured since I've last seen him in person. His dark hair hangs long enough that the ends curl. He always dressed well, but his slacks and collared shirt looked pristinely tailored. He holds himself confidently, having aged out of that cockiness of youth. He looks every bit the part of lead investigator of major crimes committed in the Whispered Folk world, a position earned through his hard work and uniquely powerful magick.

"Niven!" I cheerfully address him, reaching up to hug his tall, lean frame, clutching his unexpectedly broad shoulders. "I'm so happy you accepted my invitation. It will give us time to catch up while you're here."

"I couldn't pass up an opportunity to spend time with you." As he steps back from the hug, his hands grasp mine, holding them between us in a comforting gesture. "From the bottom of my heart, I am so sorry for what you're going through. When your clinic contacted us looking for a healing spell or a cursebreaker that could help you, I could scarcely believe it. I won't rest until we find it," Niven vows. His voice is deeper and gruffer than I remember.

"I know you won't." I sigh. "It's been difficult. The attack... and then my magick... It's probably like losing a limb, phantom pain and all. But I'll adjust someday. If I have to." I chew on my lips to stop rambling.

"You lost a considerable piece of yourself. No one expects you to just get over it. It was a singularly traumatic event," he reasons, his green-eyed gaze holding mine, welling with sympathy.

I look away when tears sting in my eyes, his compassionate appraisal almost too much to bear. Letting go of Niven's hands, I slide back into my role as hostess, an easy way to distract from myself from turning into a sad sack.

"I don't want to bog you down with my issues when there's so much else to worry about. Let me show you both to your rooms. Then I'll give you the full tour. It must have been a long trip from New York," I stammer, gesturing toward the grand staircase to the second story that wraps around the back wall of the foyer.

Aurelia's face lights up as she says, "I only had to get myself to New York City. The coven transported all of us coming from the tri-State area through their portal. Like pushing your way through a closed curtain charged with static electricity. I've never felt anything quite like it!"

"It's been quite a long time since I traveled through it, but that strange feeling is unforgettable. I always pat myself down to make sure all of me made it!" I agree.

Due to the warlocks giving a travel amulet to the fae, the coven has been vetting all arrivals at our outpost, a building just outside the ward enchanted to look like a decrepit, dirty gas station. It really is a gas station, as well as a post office for mail to and from the human world, and a neutral meeting place. Our coven also maintains our travel portal there, connecting to many other key locations around the world. The high cost of magick spent opening it on both ends requires a good reason or an expensive fee. Well, this qualifies. Some of those coming here will be taking this shortcut, so to speak, and avoid human-made forms of transit, which often require uncomfortable glamors to avoid detection. Aurelia and Niven were born under a lucky star to forego that burden today.

Though I ask out of courtesy, neither Aurelia nor Niven need help carrying their bags. Both are visibly stronger than me. "Go ahead and hop on my back. I'll carry you too!" Aurelia jokes as she starts walking up the stairs.

Niven, still standing at the base of the stairs with me, quirks his mouth like he finds her amusing. On the surface, they're a seemingly odd pair to become fast friends, but they clearly get along. Based on my first impression of her, she's brash with a strong, though not domineering, presence. Niven is more of a chameleon. He can blend into the background or, if you're the focus of some of his more particular magickal abilities, he's all you can see.

I asked him to try it on me for fun once, his ability to extract the truth from anyone, no matter how unwilling. It was an unsettling experience I wouldn't want to repeat, even though he went very easy on me. He had been self-conscious about it since it's a form of mind control, not wanting to frighten me or do something to fracture our friendship. It took some cajoling, but I managed to convince him by providing a couple benign questions to ask me. When he began, my awareness of the world shrank, confined to just his voice and authority. There was no opportunity to veer from the truth. I folded immediately and divulged my favorite pizza topping and the best book I read that year. If those simple questions were imbued with such intensity, I can't imagine what it's like for suspects he interrogates. Mayhap because I knew Niven so well, it didn't scare me. I trust him not to abuse that power. But I learned I'd never want to be on the receiving end of it in any other circumstance. If criminals knew what they were in for, it would be quite the crime deterrent.

I'm probably one of the few friends he would humor with that experience. Some find it unnerving—I've personally overheard other witches talk about it with callous ignorance, saying it's dangerous and unnatural—but I think it's fascinating. If that magickal ability had to manifest in someone, he's the best one for it, though I would never underestimate its burden on him. He has done such good work for the Whispered Folk world, though. I hope he's found fulfillment in it.

He wouldn't hesitate if I asked him to be a buffer from Norrell. Maybe I could convince Niven to find out exactly why Norrell left. The thought nearly causes me to snort out loud. I won't do that to Niven. Norrell, yes, in a heartbeat. He deserves to squirm. But Niven's magick is in demand for much more important work.

Niven motions for me to go ahead of him, following Aurelia up the steps. I show her to the room she'll be sharing with Cyrinda and give her a quick rundown of the room and the nearest bathroom for her to use. Then I lead Niven to another room down the hallway, nearest to mine.

"I hope this won't be too cramped. It used to be my father's study. I thought you'd like to have a desk to work at in your bedroom. I tried to declutter, but I may not have done a good enough job. If you need more space, I can box up some of these books and knick-knacks," I offer, my voice upswinging into a question as I motion my hand toward the large, antique desk.

"This is exactly what I hoped for. Thank you for allowing me to use it," he answers graciously as he rolls his suitcase just inside the doorway.

"I haven't changed much. I still think of the room as his, even after so many years. Not that it's a shrine to him or anything so sacred. I've just wanted to preserve this little space he spent a great deal of time in. I can still picture him sitting in the chair, his head in a book or writing in his journal," I reminisce, nostalgia washing over me.

He scans the room as I speak. When his attention returns to me, there's a wistful smile on his face, matching my own. "Your father was an impressive witch. Both of your parents were."

"He'd be happy someone was doing such important work at his desk. He'd have been honored," I quaver.

"I think he'd be proud that his daughter fearlessly confronted a fae and held her own until most of her coven arrived to capture it. *That* was important," he stresses, taking my hand and squeezing it when I blush and look away. It brings my gaze back to him. "Your quick thinking saved the town, Ada. If the fae was allowed to get away, who knows what worse could have happened?"

"Clearly I wasn't very successful," I argue, waving my free hand toward myself.

"Victory isn't only measured by coming out of a battle unscathed. The most important battles are rarely won easily. You were courageous, you didn't flinch when everything was on the line, including your life. And you turned the tide for all of us because of it. Your battle wound is a sign of your bravery. You're still standing, still helping, even at such a great cost to yourself," he commends me, his weighty tone brooking no argument.

Staggered, I nod, the lump in my throat leaving me unable to speak. Sometimes it's hard to accept praise, even from a friend, especially knowing I went into the fight on a wing and a prayer. I didn't have any notion of courage or bravery or any of these pretty words he used. I did what I had to. There wasn't any other choice for me.

I turn my gaze again to my father's desk, breaking eye contact with Niven. He still watches me for a quiet moment. With one last comforting squeeze, he drops my hand. I wipe the wetness from my eyes and cross my arms over my torso, taking a few ragged breaths to gather myself.

"You know I saw them that night? My parents. My long-gone family. They were there. They protected me and the rest of the coven too when they arrived. I wouldn't be here without them. Probably shouldn't be," I whisper hoarsely, my throat still tight.

"They're a part of you. Their magick is a part of you. And always will be. They did all they could to save you through the ward." He exhales deeply, like his own words are affecting him as much as they are me. "I'm here to talk if you need to, anytime. I'm never too busy for you. Okay?" There's an uncharacteristic gentleness in his voice.

"Okay." With a brittle smile, I add, "Well, I'll let you settle in."

Before I thoroughly embarrass myself and blubber like a baby in front of him, I turn on my heel and walk back downstairs to the comfort of my kitchen.

There's a lull while my first two guests unpack. I need it after that unexpectedly sentimental talk with Niven. My hands shake, slowing me down, as I slice lemons for the pitchers of sweet tea and lemonade I made earlier. I push the cutting board away from me as a jumble of memories from that night rush through my brain. Turning around, I lean against the kitchen counter and wrap my arms around myself, willing them to go away. Soon enough, Aurelia and Niven chat animatedly as they descend the stairs. I wipe my face and hurry to meet them in the foyer so I can show them around.

They must have finally piqued the cats' interest because Vanny and Earl Grey tear around the corner, racing toward our new guests like they've been dipped in tuna. Earlier, I'd given them strict instructions to be on their best behavior. Clearly it was in one ear and out the other, as they batted at and then rubbed against the accusing finger I had pointed in their direction until I gave them scritches.

"Who are these two munchkins?" Aurelia coos as she picks up Earl Grey and scratches under his chin.

A snort of laughter bubbles out of me at how adoringly they stare at each other. "These lover boys are Vanilla Paws, or Vanny as I call him, and Earl Grey," I say, gesturing at each. "They're brothers and best friends. This is their house and I'm just living in it."

Niven bends down to run his hand along Vanny's back and up his tail. After walking in circles, rubbing himself on Niven's pantlegs, Vanny lays down at his feet stretching out on his back for belly rubs, which Niven immediately obliges.

"Well, I see they won't have any trouble with strangers invading their space," I jest. "But I will warn you they have no sense of propriety or boundaries. What's yours is theirs."

"I see no problem with that. I think we'll be as thick as thieves," Aurelia remarks, making me chuckle at this ridiculous love fest.

"We'll bring them on the house tour. Too bad they can't lead it themselves. I'm sure they know all the best spots to nap. First, would you like sweet tea? Coffee? Lemonade?" Both opt for coffee.

Leading everyone into the kitchen, including Vanny who hops along closely at Niven's heels, I pour their coffee into mugs to bring along. Since this will be a very long, stressful day, I take a mug as well.

"The kitchen is fully stocked with groceries and even some new kitchen gadgets, so feel free to eat or use anything here. You can go out to the garden through these doors whenever you please, there's plenty of seating out there," I tell them as I point out the various elements.

The tour continues as we walk through the succeeding doorways into the richly painted terra cotta dining room and dark pine green living room. Wide-plank antique wood floors run throughout. I point out the wide, light gray marble double-sided fireplace that sits between them that I light during the short chilly season.

Exiting the living room into the foyer, matching double doors on the opposite side of the house lead into the salon, an over-sized formal entertaining room painted a dark, muted blue that runs almost to the back of the house. It once held balls and dances, but now it only serves as a meeting space for the coven. Tucked away at the back of the house is a workroom stocked with everything needed to make potions and enchantments. The attached short hallway with the downstairs powder room and a butler's pantry leads back to the kitchen.

"This house is something! No wonder these two act like little princes," Aurelia remarks.

"Just like me, the kitchen is their favorite room. As you can tell, they love to eat," I joke as Vanny lopes between my legs toward his food bowl.

"There's nothing wrong with enjoying a good meal, Earl Grey," Aurelia whispers into his ear, making all of us laugh. He could not care less about our conversation as he contentedly purrs in her arms, oblivious to anyone but her.

Stepping back into the foyer, I take them upstairs once again to point out all the bedrooms and bathrooms. Luckily, they'll only have to double up on bathrooms. And everyone will have their own room except Aurelia and Cyrinda, who I learned are close friends.

"That's about everything there is to see. I do have a musty old attic, but I'll spare you. It's a lot of old furniture collected over the generations. Who knows, maybe someday I'll go through it," I say with a shrug.

"I had no idea your house was so impressive," Niven remarks as we head downstairs again.

"It was built by my family in the mid-nineteenth century, many decades after they founded the town. There's so much history here, and I love every inch of it." I sigh, and my smile slips a little. "But it's a lot of house for just me, if you can't tell. And upkeep just got a little more *hands-on*," I add wryly.

"You mentioned it at academy, but I guess I didn't pay enough attention. At the time, if it didn't revolve around New York City, I wasn't that interested," he confesses with a chuckle. "Clearly I wasn't at all a snob."

"Well, if it's hands you need, we've all got them. You didn't think we were going to make you slave away cleaning up after us?" Aurelia accuses, pretending to look offended.

"No, no. You're all guests. You wouldn't have to do much if you were staying at the inn. Besides, I've considered hiring a housekeeper since everything... happened. It's the smart thing to do." It's a serious consideration I mulled over while getting the house ready. Staying on top of everyday upkeep will be too much, even after everyone leaves.

While refilling everyone's coffee after we make our way to the kitchen again, Aurelia suggests we sit outside. After bribing the cats to stay in the house with some treats, I take us to the front porch in case new guests arrive. Aurelia and I sit on the porch swing and Niven stretches out on a nearby chair.

"Why the light blue on the ceiling? It doesn't match the shutters," Aurelia questions as she points out the two different shades of blue.

"Haint blue," Niven replies.

"Exactly. It's the color of water, something feared by haints, as some called them. This isn't warded, but it's a nod to the lovely tradition that some regional witches developed to protect their neighbors' homes. The enchanted paint tricks some of the lesser Malefic into thinking they can't cross into a house. Maybe I needed to splash more of it around the carriage house." My gaze wanders to the plot of dirt where the carriage house used to be.

"I don't think the fae cares about shades of blue," Niven notes.

"No, it didn't care about much," I confirm.

"Ashes, they sound like vicious buggers. I'm glad they're rare. I've never seen one before and I want to keep it that way," Aurelia remarks with a wince.

"I hadn't either. It was the single scariest thing I've ever seen. A real-life bogeyman. I don't think I could stand to look at it again," I divulge. I rub my forehead, as if I could scrub the image from my brain.

"You won't have to," Niven assures me.

"Thanks for looking out for me." I reach over and pat his arm.

"How long have you known each other?" Aurelia asks, eyeing me and Niven.

"We met at the Sparklight Academy in Maine, where it's too cold most of the year to do anything but study. Or find your own mischief. We're the same year, so we were stuck in a lot of classes together. Friendship was sort of forced on us," he jokes with an impish smile. "Once we began our apprenticeships there, our studies diverged but we still socialized. Not as much as we should have, but that's how it often goes."

"I'm convinced the thing he liked most about me was that I had so many pretty friends he could impress with party tricks," I quip.

"Absolutely. It's what made those early years at academy tolerable," he declares.

"Do all witches go? Doesn't your coven help you train your magick?" Aurelia asks.

"Covens do work with young members to teach them how to use their magick, and eventually most do attend one of our academies," I clarify. "Not all apprenticeships take place there. I have an apprentice in my shop currently and she is about to surpass me in almost every skill we use there. But intensive specializations require guidance from experts. My parents encouraged me to complete my apprenticeship at the academy. It was the closest place I could study transmutation, which is turning one substance into another. Plus, I already knew most of the faculty."

"I thought my life was over when mine forced me to leave New York City for Maine. I was such a little terror because my magickal ability manifested at a fairly young age. They were in over their heads with me. But they were right. I needed to go. To be humbled a little. It opened a lot of doors and put me on this path," he recalls.

"You? Humbled? Mother Earth bless your heart," I chide him with a grin. "But I wholeheartedly agree it was the right place for us."

"Don't *bless your heart* me! I remember what that means," he grumbles, faking a scowl.

"Ooh, she's pulling out the big guns," Aurelia goads.

"You'd never believe she was the shyest of our cohort when she first arrived," he teases. "I was trying so hard to impress her to get her to like me, but I quickly realized that there was no need for pretense with her. She's one of the most genuine witches I know. Maybe I can appreciate that more than most, given my... talents. The rest of her friends, on the other hand, they were a tough crowd."

"I didn't really know how to make friends when I first got there. Everyone already knew who I was in this town, being a Mayweather and all. Not that I wanted that extra attention and automatic acceptance. It put me at a disadvantage when I left since I never quite needed that skillset here," I reveal with a self-deprecating chuckle. "I think that put you at ease with me almost instantly. I was also fumbling at making friends, so I wasn't being too picky at the time." I punctuate my affectionate burn with a wink.

"Fumbling!" he repeats incredulously. "Neither of us were

fumbling, exactly. That's rewriting history. You made a close circle of friends right off the bat. And then sometimes you'd deign to hang out with me."

"You dated enough of them that you were a pretty regular fixture, if my memory still serves," I deadpan.

"Were you two ever an item?" Aurelia cuts in.

"No, I saw right through his best pickup lines," I answer with a sly grin.

"I barely used any on you! And certainly not my best ones," he protests, bringing his hand to his chest in mock disbelief. Turning his attention back to Aurelia, he adds, "No, we never did. Friendship with Ada is something special. I didn't want to spoil it."

As we laugh over stories from our academy days, a large automobile pulls into the circular driveway in my front lawn. I hold my breath as the back doors open. I nearly cry in relief when a faun and an orc emerge. It must be Cyrinda and Tallie.

"Who said this party could start without me?" Cyrinda demands playfully, standing with her hands on her hips.

"We're just warming up! What took you so long?" Aurelia cheeks back as Cyrinda sashays up to the porch. Tufts of fur and her polished cloven hooves stick out from the bottom of her designer jeans. Her steps rhythmically clop on the sidewalk.

Tallie grunts, hauling luggage out of the trunk. "As soon as you think there's a party, you leave me hanging, Cyrinda? Aren't you forgetting something?"

"Nope. It gives you the perfect opportunity to show off those biceps. You're welcome," Cyrinda remarks tartly from over her shoulder. Tallie exaggeratedly flexes her biceps exposed by her sleeveless shirt as she takes out the last piece of luggage.

"It's a pleasure to finally meet both of you. Can I get you anything to drink? Tea or lemonade? I have a pot of coffee on…"

"Sure, if that's all you've got, but I do always carry my own flask with me. The sun isn't so high in the sky anymore. How about something a little stronger?" she suggests with a smirk as she pats her hand over something solid in her jacket pocket. "Considering the next few weeks, we should celebrate our last night of freedom."

She's not wrong. Tomorrow, the first day of safety council meetings, will be rough, with testimony and timelines given by witnesses including me and my friend Ben. He fought to keep his mate Cara out of these meetings. Clancy and I agreed it's the right call. They'd needle every disturbing detail, making her relive those horrible moments in the carriage house. It's unnecessary. Between everything Ben and I can tell them, along with the coven members who were there that night, we have it more than covered. Cara and Ben are convalescing at home, though healing quickly with magickal aid. Ben told us he wants everyone to see his not-yet-faded scars, along with photos of Cara's injuries when they were new.

"I do have a few options." I chuckle at how Cyrinda's entrance has, in fact, livened up the vibe to something more celebratory. "Why don't I show you to your rooms and then we'll break into the good stuff?"

"Be a dear and make sure my bedroom is next to *tall, dark, and handsome's* over there," Cyrinda requests as she waggles her eyebrows at Niven.

CHAPTER 4
ADA

By the time Cyrinda unpacks and freshens up from her and Tallie's journey from the West Coast, the rest of us, including the cats, have moved into the kitchen nearer to the snacks and drinks. At Cyrinda's request, I set out wine and spirits. Beer is in the fridge. Dinner tonight will be roast chicken and vegetables, so I start spatchcocking the whole chickens and rough chopping root vegetables. I bought a blackberry pie and fresh bread from Pearlhouse Pastries, a local bakery, so all I'll have to do is slice those. It's an easy dinner, just more than I usually prepare at once. Niven offers to help but I wave him away.

When I begin wiping off the counter after setting the oven timer, there's a knock at the door. My throat constricts, forcing me to gasp for breath. My guests' chatter stops abruptly when they hear me. He's finally here. The last one to arrive. A sudden dizzy spell overtakes me. The chef's knife I had picked up drops from my hand, clanking onto my work surface. I grip the kitchen counter for support as the edges of my vision darken. A chair noisily scoots back and rapid footfalls cross the kitchen floor. A warm hand wraps around my shoulder, propping me up and forcing me to blink up at its owner. Niven stands beside me, a deep-set grimace stamped on his face. My head snaps toward the direction of the door again at a second set of knocks, more tentative this time.

"Do you want me to answer the door? You shouldn't meet him out there alone," Niven asks, his tone on the edge of menacing. He knows what happened, of course.

"I don't think I could bear an audience for our reunion," I murmur, my voice strained.

"Okay, bring him back here as soon as you can. We'll keep him away if he starts bothering you."

I nod silently and then force myself to calmly walk out of the kitchen into the foyer. I push my hair from my face and smooth it as best I can. Alarmed at my close call, I realize I'm still wearing my apron just in time and swiftly pull it off, tossing it over the banister at the base of the stairs. Only a few feet and a door separate me from Norrell, the male who shattered me. Who I think about nearly every day. Who often stars in my dreams, whether good or bad. It's time to put an end to that.

I take one last breath to compose myself and blank my expression, steeling my nerves. I need to be that brave and courageous Ada who can take on anything. Slow and steady, I open the door. Norrell stands there, shirtless as he always preferred, looking almost the same as I remember. The version of him burned into my mind.

But not quite.

He's changed in ways that make me realize the male I loved doesn't exist anywhere but in my memory. He's aged. We both have. There are more lines on his face, maybe a little too deep for his years. His eyes look colder, harder, yet their ice blue gaze alights on me with something like apprehension. His lips are pressed thin, almost frowning. I remember them. One point slightly higher than the other on his top lip. A small scar carves into his cheek. Something new that part of me wonders where it came from. I absorb every detail, catalog every difference, while I'm frozen, mute, my brain hijacked by the opposing needs for self-preservation and to swoon in his presence.

Maybe we're both stunned in place, neither of our brains cooperating. Maybe he truly wasn't expecting this plan to work, even though he's the one who masterminded this messy scene. The jagged, painful tension rises between us the longer we both stare silent and still. But I refuse to make it easier on him. I can't, in the moment, anyway. His throat visibly bobs, drawing my eyes to it and the strain in his jaw, his look of discomfort.

Finding the will to move again, I swing the door open a little wider. "Norrell, it's been a while. Why don't you come in." I hear my voice, sedate, quiet, not giving anything away, saying these words of its own accord.

As he steps past me into the house, I get an even better look at him. He's as towering as I remember. I'm a tall gal, but the top of my head barely reaches his chin. He's bulkier now, somehow having gained a broader musculature. Not that he was ever anything but strong, but not like this. His coloring is as striking as ever, meant to blend into the snow and ice of the Arctic. His skin looks almost glaucous in its bright cast of pale blue-gray. He wears a beard now and the white hair on his head hangs a little longer, too. The equally silvery-white pelt covering his chest, arms, and shoulders is fuller. It suits him, it's just different. Reminding me he's different. A stranger.

"Ada. You look..." he starts, then his voice tapers off. His mouth lifts into a feeble smile. Feigned. Like it came out wrong. "Thank you for allowing me to stay here. It is generous of you. More than generous. More than... I deserve from you." His voice, a low rumble, like the start of an avalanche, sounds too self-assured for this to be a true attempt at an apology.

I shrug. This *is* more than he deserves. He's simply stating a fact. I'm not going to refute it out of some misguided convention of politeness. "Your room is the third on the left. Dinner will be ready in an hour," I inform him as I push the door closed and walk back to the kitchen.

As I round the corner, you could hear a pin drop. Clearly, they were eavesdropping, but I can't blame them. This is top shelf drama. Ex-mates are rare. Meeting again under such onerous circumstances and after so many years... unheard of. Norrell had to make sure there's an audience of VIPs present to witness this shitshow, so I guess I'll give him what he wants.

"Our final housemate has arrived. Mayhap he'll join us for dinner," I report back to them as I check the oven. Everything looks good, so I pour a glass of wine for myself and sit with them at the table. I've felt

Niven's eyes on me this whole time, so I give him a thin smile to let him know I'm okay.

"I can't believe the North Clan sent a representative. I don't think I've met any of them before. If I didn't know better, I'd find it hard to believe yetis really exist," Cyrinda notes with a snort as she pets Vanny, who has made himself comfortable in her lap.

"He may as well be a unicorn," I remark, detached, not addressing anyone in particular.

"*Unicorn!* Humans have such wild imaginations," Cyrinda snorts.

"You never met his family?" Niven asks tentatively.

"We talked about it. But… it didn't work out that way," I respond after taking a long sip from my glass.

"You didn't need to show him to his room? Give him a tour of the house?" Tallie asks, sounding confused. She must not be caught up on the gossip.

"He knows his way around," I answer too fast, almost cutting her off.

Tallie's eyebrows fly up to her hairline. "Oh, that's why…" She doesn't finish her thought. I nod as she connects the dots.

"And he decided he wanted to stay *here*? Is he crazy? Ashes, why didn't you tell him to stick his tongue on a frozen polar bear's ass and shove it? Make him sleep outside! Or better yet, on your most uncomfortable couch so he has a backache for the next three weeks," Cyrinda exclaims, sounding gratifyingly irate on my behalf.

"I didn't intend to invite him. But since I did and he accepted, I felt I couldn't revoke the invitation because of my role on the town council. What if I did and then he decided not to attend? I will set aside my feelings. It's just a few weeks, I'll manage," I attempt to clarify, my excuses sounding feeble as everyone stares at me, skepticism written plain on their faces.

"I agree with Cyrinda. You're being too nice. He's up to no good," Aurelia pipes up, pointing accusingly with the hand she isn't using to scratch under Earl Grey's chin.

"Bullseye. Exactly what I was thinking. I knew I liked you for a reason," Cyrinda jokes, winking at her. Aurelia rolls her eyes like she's used to her antics.

"Has he contacted you at all? Asked if you'd be okay with this?" Niven questions.

"Not once. I haven't spoken to him since he left. This was a surprise I didn't need, considering everything else," I respond honestly.

"Can we ice him out? Pun intended." Cyrinda snickers.

I huff a laugh and shake my head at her joke. "I wish, but no we shouldn't. We're lucky anyone from his clan agreed to help. They are no strangers to the fae living so far north. I don't want to compromise that, if it turns out his help is somehow conditional on him staying here."

Sensing him before I see him, I look over as Norrell strides through the doorway. Hopefully, he wasn't listening to us, but it's feasible given his superb hearing. Even if he heard, I only spoke the truth. I'd say it again to his face.

"Good evening, everyone. I am Norrell Snowstrider," he introduces himself as he steps toward the table.

"We figured," Cyrinda retorts, apparently not taking my plea to heart.

Niven stands up and extends a hand to him. "I'm Niven Whitehall, a representative from the New York City coven and a lead investigator in the hunt for the three fugitives. I'm also an old friend of Ada's from our academy days."

Norrell seems to size him up but shakes his hand in a friendly manner anyway. "I do not know if I remember her mentioning you, but I am glad she has a friend here," he answers in a way that feels too territorial for my liking.

Niven's eyes dart to mine with suspicion, and he sits down again as Tallie and Aurelia introduce themselves. "Tallie Sureheart. I hail from Alder Glen in the Puget Sound, and I'm the top advisor to our chief."

"Don't forget he's also your father," Cyrinda interjects with a smirk.

"I already regret telling you that," Tallie says with a sigh.

"I'm Aurelia Woodrum, chief of the Catskill Mountains Bear Clan. Our community Sky Mountain is made up of more than just bear shifters and werebears, but we account for much of the population," Aurelia says. Side-eyeing Cyrinda, she adds, "You may even spot a faun there on occasion."

"Only when I get bored of New York City, darling," Cyrinda remarks flippantly.

Aurelia ignores her comment. "And if you haven't figured it out yet, this is Cyrinda Ariti, self-proclaimed faun-extraordinaire, professional pain in the ass, and a renowned member of the Whispered Folk Congress of Los Angeles. How anyone gave her a position of power is beyond me."

"Charmed, I'm sure," Cyrinda deadpans with a sniff aimed vaguely in his direction. While I enjoyed her sweet sass earlier, it makes me nervous she'll cause trouble for me.

As he looms over us, I realize there isn't anywhere for him to sit at the kitchen table. We only ever had five chairs at the table for family dinners. One for each of us. Me. My parents. Walt and Acton. It was the perfect number.

"Why don't I bring in a chair from the dining room," I offer, striving to remain an impeccable hostess.

"I would stand for now, if you do not mind," Norrell responds as he leans against the kitchen island.

"Maybe she doesn't want you hovering and is too polite to say anything," Cyrinda digs into him. Niven and I shoot each other an uneasy glance.

"It's fine," I assure everyone with a tight-lipped smile. "There are plenty of seats at the dining room table where we'll eat dinner. He can stay where he is."

"Fine." Cyrinda sounds dubious.

Cyrinda has amused me up to this point, but right now, I need her to stick a sock in it. "Does anyone need a refill? I know I could use another glass of wine," I offer the group, catching her eye with a pointed look.

Everyone's glass looks full, so no one takes me up on it. I stand up and walk to the counter where I set out the drinks, giving Norrell a wide berth to discourage him from interacting with me. To my chagrin, he sidles up to me, looking at the collection of bottles I've set out.

"That is the scotch your father used to drink," Norrell observes.

"It is. Feel free to help yourself," I respond with a bland tone, unable to bring myself to look at him.

He watches me pour more wine into my glass. Sounding mindful, he declines, "There is much I aim to accomplish. I should refrain from anything heavy tonight, so I am not sluggish in the morning."

I subtly roll my eyes at his sanctimoniously timed statement. But it's a good point, I suppose. I decide that this will be my second and last glass of wine. I don't need to risk lowering my defenses around him, anyhow. "There's iced tea and lemonade in the fridge, if you'd prefer," I mention, gesturing toward it.

Luckily, Cyrinda mellows and conversation flows, covering more benign topics. Norrell remains at the fringes of the conversation, but he makes me nervous. I've caught him observing me, but he unhurriedly looks away like there's nothing odd about it. Like his arrival doesn't upend any modicum of peace I've found during the last fifteen years of my life.

I'm relieved when the oven timer blares. It gives me something to focus on other than Norrell's imperious, unnerving presence. The two roast chickens look crispy and golden brown, and the vegetables are caramelized, so I pull them out to cool for a moment. As I quickly slice the loves of sourdough bread and set the pieces into a basket, Norrell slides on my oven mitts and lifts one of the pans of chicken and vegetables.

"Where should I put these?" he asks, an impassive expression on his face.

I gape at him for a beat before my mouth moves. "Put it on the table runner, please. There are platters out there for the food," I answer briskly, the domesticity of the scene rubbing me the wrong way.

He returns empty-handed and takes the second pan out as well. I set the table earlier, so all that's left is to bring serving utensils and bread to the table. I linger for a moment, waiting for him to come back out, but he doesn't. Fire and ashes, he isn't going to make this easy. "Get your drink refills, dinner is just about ready," I call out to the group at the kitchen table to try to hurry them along.

Dreading being alone with him again, I walk into the dining room, where Norrell makes short work of neatly carving up the chickens. I hadn't noticed him grabbing the knife and carving fork. He finds the joint to cut away the thighs and then separates them from the legs.

Removing the wings, he then slices through each side of the breast, cutting those into smaller portions. He looks well-practiced.

"Oh," I breathe, surprised to see what he's doing. "Thank you. I'll bring a plate for the leftovers."

"I am at your service," he answers enigmatically, finishing up the remaining chicken.

The others begin streaming into the dining room, chatting with each other, commenting on how good the food looks and smells. When I return with a large plate, Norrell places the carcasses from the cut-up chickens on it and, to my annoyance, follows me into the kitchen where we're once again by ourselves. I'm tempted to shoot my mouth off, tell him to back off, but I hold my tongue. Mother Earth only knows how I manage it. But it'll only cause me more grief to show him any emotion. I need to remain unflappable, so he'll lose interest in being around me.

"More lemonade?" I ask dryly, keeping my eyes ahead to avoid looking at him, as I finish pouring myself a glass.

"Please." He slides his glass next to mine. "Your lemonade is still the best I have ever tasted."

"Oh," I hum. Well okay then. I guess he remembers it's homemade, not that it matters. "Thank you."

Are we trying to out-polite each other? Doesn't he realize that Southerners are known for their hospitality? Even among the Whispered Folk? This is getting on my nerves. It would be easier if he was an asshole so I could kick him out. I don't like him being so... nice.

I spin around, still not having looked at him at all, and return the lemonade to the fridge before I walk to the dining room. Once again, he follows me like a shadow. The group has arranged themselves around the table so that two seats are open apart from each other. I could kiss them, I'm so happy they planned this. Hopefully it will unglue him from me for the time being.

Taking a seat between Tallie and Niven, I spear some chicken and vegetables onto my plate before the breadbasket and butter are passed to me. Norrell ends up next to Aurelia. Thankfully, Cyrinda is on the other side of her, so hopefully she won't have too much opportunity to pester him.

"Excellent dinner, Ada," Niven compliments me. Everyone else chimes in their agreement.

"Did everyone make it in today?" Aurelia asks the table. Since I wasn't part of coordinating their travel, I'm not in the loop.

The group lists who they ran into and any stories they heard. Norrell stays quiet until everyone says their piece. "I was among one of the last groups. The nocturnals are still on their way. A dragonkin will be flying in late tonight as well. He should be the last to arrive," he informs us.

"Wow, everyone's coming out of the woodwork for this, aren't they?" Cyrinda barbs as she leans around Aurelia to give him a fractious look.

Moon and stars, this female needs to hush up. Donning my peacekeeper hat once again, I remind them, "Well, I'm glad everyone is taking this seriously. Even those who often do not involve themselves in Whispered Folk politics. The fae didn't just happen to come across our sleepy little town. It was brought here by some of us willing to join forces with it. That night would have turned out very differently had any one of us there arrived on the scene even a minute later. If this could happen in Monstera Bluff, it could happen anywhere."

Cyrinda has the good sense to look sheepish. "You're right, Ada. I know what this cost you. The same thing could be happening under our noses in Los Angeles. Probably is. It's hard to keep track of such things in a large human city," she acknowledges.

I smile graciously at her to let her know there are no hard feelings. Everyone's eyes remain fixed on me. Without intending to, mine dart to Norrell's, and sure enough, they seem to search mine, pulling me in with their intensity. He knows what happened. It's why he's here in Monstera Bluff. The only explanation as to why he's sitting *here* at my dining table is to see it for himself. The witch whose magick was stolen by a fae. The cautionary tale parents will tell their children for generations to come. With that realization, I wrench my gaze from his and onto my plate, where I move food around with my fork, trying to escape his scrutiny.

"This investigation will last far longer than our meeting here. There will be much to uncover," Niven remarks. After absently taking a bite of food, I look up in time to watch his expression darken. "It was far too easy for the fae to waltz in here and wreak havoc. As Ada said, it could have been far worse. But what has transpired is already a calamity."

"Well, the good news tonight is that we still have pie. I think we could all use a slice right about now," I drawl to break the tension. My chair scrapes noisily as I scoot back from the table, drawing their attention to me again. I suppose it's practice for tomorrow when I'll be Exhibit A, dissected and analyzed. Just the thought frays my nerves, so I hustle to the kitchen.

I lean against the counter, just breathing, enjoying these precious seconds alone. It's all I can do to pull myself together to get through the rest of the evening. This may be one of the lowest points in my life, but they don't need to see it. As I open a drawer to dig out a pie server and knife, I sense eyes on my back. Whirling around, my heart drops. Norrell stands in the doorway, taking up most of its space. Fire and ashes, this male is dogging my footsteps something fierce. He walks toward the other end of the counter and places a stack of dirty plates next to the sink.

"Much appreciated," I respond automatically, sounding more stressed than intended. Hoping he'll go away if I ignore him, I get to work slicing the pie, working carefully on the first piece since it's always difficult to cut and lift cleanly.

"May we speak for a moment?" he asks in a soft rumble.

"We've been speaking all night. Why don't you take this back to the table with you?" I insist, as I lay the pie slice on a small plate.

"No, Ada, we have not," he keeps on.

"Well, then I guess there isn't much to say," I deflect, though my voice sounds thin as I slide the plate toward him.

"I disagree. There is much that should be said. That should have been said a long time ago," he persists.

I consciously, carefully, set down the knife as I turn toward him. I'm trying not to choose violence today. "Well, you can't have your *pie* and eat it too. So please, take your plate and leave the kitchen. You may have access to my house, but that doesn't give you access to *me*," I hiss with bared teeth. My glare should be angrier, but it's shaped by too much grief. His body betrays a faint wince, as I'm finally pushed far enough to lash out. Sadness reflects back at me in his widened eyes. As if he has the right to be.

I sniffle, my emotions coming to the fore. Swiftly turning back to the pie, I continue slicing it in silence as he stands there. Tears well in my eyes, but I don't dare acknowledge them. Slice by slice, I work my way through the pie until finally he sighs, sounding resigned.

"Mayhap tonight is too soon for the discussion that we need to have. But it is necessary. I know I have made mistakes. I treated you unfairly. But I am not your enemy, Ada," he attempts to pressure me, still without an apology in those empty words.

"No, I'm not interested. Now if you'll excuse me, I need to deliver these to the rest of my guests," I answer, voice only wavering a little. I take two plates and walk away.

As I set the plates in front of Cyrinda and Tallie, they both have questions in their eyes, but don't say anything about Norrell. When I return to the kitchen for the rest of the plates, he's gone, presumably to his bedroom. Finally. Good riddance.

After everyone has their slice, we dig into our dessert.

"Delicious! Did you make this?" Tallie asks enthusiastically around a bite.

"I'm no expert pie baker. It came from Pearlhouse Pastries. You'll love it. I'll take you there this week," I offer.

She hums her enthusiasm while chewing a bite.

As the five of us eat and talk, Norrell's absence is the elephant in the room. But everyone's tactful enough not to bring it up to me right now. It's a welcome reprieve. Tallie, Niven, and I clean up the dining room table and the kitchen after we're finished. I run the full dishwasher and leave the remaining dishes soaking in the sink.

My guests aren't ready to turn in yet, so I suggest that the living room or the back garden would be good places for a nightcap if they're interested. While they discuss the merits of each, I drag myself up the stairs. I'm bone tired, physically and mentally. It makes me consider whether hosting anyone in my house, Norrell or not, was a terrible idea. I should have listened to Clancy and Walt. But as a Mayweather and a town councilwoman, it's my duty. Still, I could have left it to someone else who isn't already an organizer as well as an exhibition wrapped up in one messy, overworked package. The witch I used to be would have taken it all in stride. The not-quite-witch I am now can't keep up with burning the candle at both ends.

Barely mustering the energy to change into pajamas and wipe the makeup off my face, I finally fall into bed, nearly delirious with exhaustion. My last swirling thoughts are of those ice blue eyes, seeing too much. Wanting more than I have to give.

Eighteen Years Ago

In the weeks Norrell and I met in secret at the library, we've gradually drawn closer from the opposite ends of the long study table where we started without ever acknowledging it. Tonight, like usual, he arrives after me. He likes to challenge me to focus on my own awareness of sound, so much duller than his, so I listen for anything out of the ordinary. His footsteps aim toward the stacks, far back it seems, to select a very old book, mayhap from the archives, which he was granted special access to support his study of old magick. They draw closer, louder, swifter, like he's impatient as he approaches our table.

Tonight, he takes the chair right next to me. Our shoulders nearly touch. A first. His body heat radiates into mine. Hot enough to keep him comfortable in Arctic weather. Every so often he feeds me a tidbit of information like this about himself. He usually focuses on me, instead. Despite my attempts to draw more out of him, he keeps me at arm's length, in every sense. This sudden closeness is an intimacy with him I haven't yet enjoyed. Without saying a word, he delicately opens an impressively old tome with a fine touch and flips to a page within.

It's too dark for me to see the text, and we're not near enough to a lamp for it to be useful, so I whisper, "Hang a light that's cozy but bright so all that's written is in sight." A small golden orb appears and floats above us. Its soft glow gently illuminates us. I didn't intend for the lighting to add to the romance, but I'm not upset about it.

Norrell turns to me and smiles coyly, a short tusk catching his upper lip. It makes him look incredibly sexy. Butterflies seem to have taken up residence in my stomach, my chest, my head. Everywhere. "Does it have to rhyme?"

Blushing, I pretend there's something I need to erase in my notebook to give myself an excuse to look away. "No, but I like it. It feels right for my magick."

"All of your spells are little poems?" he asks quietly, undemanding but curious.

"Speaking them helps set the intention of the magick. The words focus me. Some can just imagine the spell in their head, but I'm not good at that. Each witch finds their own way to a spell. That's just how I find mine," I answer with a bashful smile, my gaze meeting his bright, watchful eyes again. He's shifted in his seat to better face me.

"I never witnessed magick like this until I arrived here. The Malefic Folk are... different. Their magick is unruly and destructive. Meant to harm. Yours... is beautiful. Full of life. Something to be treasured. You are too, Ada. That is how I see you." His voice is unusually coarse.

My stuttering pulse beats loud in my ears. After so long, building it up in my head, I can hardly believe this is happening. The thrill of the moment almost blanks my mind. "I... I felt connected to you since that first night, and it's only grown deeper," I stammer.

He takes my hand from the table, our first physical contact, and brings it to his lips, brushing kisses along my palm and wrist with surprisingly soft lips. I must be head over heels because I've never been so aroused as I am now with this chaste touch. Warmth pools low in my belly. I exhale, slow and shivery.

Norrell smirks at my reaction, though affection brims in his eyes. He lifts my hand to place it on his shoulder and then takes my other one and does the same, gently twisting me so I'm also facing him in my seat, embracing him as he leans in closer. I don't waste the opportunity to stroke my hands along his arms and up to his shoulders again, running my fingers through the pelt that covers both. A growl burns in his throat as I grab onto his shoulders, drawing him into me.

His large hands gently hold my face, the pads of his fingers a rougher texture than the rest. My skin tingles beneath as he brushes my hair aside with his claws, runs his thumb along my lips, traces the contours of my face. A low moan of anticipation escapes me as his palms then settle on my jawline, tilting my head up toward him.

"These nights have come to mean a great deal to me. I have never felt more at peace than I do with you. And you remain in my heart when we are separated, an ember always burning bright. I need more of you, Ada. I need all of you. Open yourself to me," he purrs as he closes the distance between us.

His lips crush mine, firm and in control. He nips at my bottom lip with a ticklish scrape of sharp teeth, sending a fresh zing of arousal through me. As my pleasure hums, his tongue sweeps through to caress mine in alternating shallow and deep strokes, like a hypnotizing dance between us. His short tusks frame our lips, and he lets out a hungry groan as I glide my tongue along his bottom lip and lick up one of them, making sure to avoid the pointed edge.

It's like he instinctively knows when my need for him becomes nearly too intense. He breaks the kiss for only an instant as he drags both of our chairs away from the table. Lifting me out of my seat, he lays me across his lap with my legs dangling off one arm of the chair. I wind my arms around his neck to better touch and explore. His burly body heats me up like a furnace. The long outline of his arousal, hard and ready, bulges beneath me. Stars above, he's big. But he doesn't pay it any mind. Instead, he rubs and kneads along my hips, butt, and thighs over my clothes, learning me as he molds me to him tightly.

No part of him I can reach goes untouched or unkissed by me. His stubbled cheeks, pointed ears, strong jaw. His chest rumbles as I discover the spots that arouse him most, so I return to them frequently, purposely drawing out those fervid growls that vibrate through me deliciously, heightening my own pleasure.

He's intrigued by the sensitive skin of my neck behind my ears, where he licks and softly drags his tusks, driving me to gasps and moans. Our hungry urgency never wanes during our first night as lovers. Long hours of kissing and caressing, savoring each other, but only that. He doesn't take it further, and the way he keeps me on his lap prevents me from doing so either. Clearly, he is a male who takes his time with *everything* he does. It's still undoubtedly the most erotic night of my life.

♡ ♡ ♡ ♡ ♡

Jolting awake, the real world comes rushing back while I still hear Norrell's deep, sexy rumbling in my ears. I can't escape him now, not in my house, not even in my dreams. It's an unwanted reminder that being with him almost felt like a dream. Until it didn't.

Unable to fall back asleep, I lay in bed until the sky lightens, mulling over how differently my life turned out than I thought it would. After such a restless night, there isn't a snowball's chance in summer I'll remain composed today as I talk about the fae and my faded magick. The big group of strangers will expect me to relive every sordid second of that night. It's their job, since any tiny detail could be important. I've made peace that rehashing it will be a death by a thousand cuts. I'll be bled dry by the time they're done.

Finally, I peel myself out of bed. While I shower and get ready for the long day ahead, my spirit feels smaller, like a piece of me was left behind yesterday. My reflection in the bathroom mirror doesn't show me any clue of what could be wrong. It's troubling, but there's not enough time to dwell on it this morning.

I may as well be dolled up while I have a come-apart in front of the safety council. I dry my hair, smoothing a cream-based potion through it that adds gentle waves, and then apply makeup, including a spelled mascara that tears won't run. I slip on a simple, dark green A-line dress with a fitted bodice that flares at the waist. I pair it with a cream-colored cardigan, pinning one of my mom's brooches to it. I want to keep a piece of her with me today.

When I walk into the kitchen, my jaw drops as I see the sink, now empty of dirty dishes. Checking the cabinets, it seems that someone already washed, dried, and put them away. The dishwasher is emptied as well. Huh. Someone must have woken up terribly early to do this. It was incredibly thoughtful. I find myself smiling a little as I start brewing the first batch of coffee for my houseful of guests.

CHAPTER 5

NORRELL

Relief courses through me as I rip the accursed glamor off my neck. The pressure surrounding my body, like being a sausage stuffed too tight in a casing, suddenly gone. It was necessary during my long journey to Monstera Bluff through overcrowded, abysmal human airports. If I could not hide how pissy and uncomfortable I was, most humans would not give it a second thought. They looked about the same. Soon after my final flight landed, a witch from the coven picked up several of us from the airport in a van, driving us straight to the gas station just outside the town's ward, the first safe place to show my true form.

Glamors and magickal identification are among the select few enchanted items my people will abide by when it suits them. The clan will purchase them from witches and warlocks in the region but hold their noses while doing so. Then they go on believing all magick wielders are untrustworthy and threatening while still using their enchantments.

As bothersome as glamors are, the discomfort is a small price to pay to finally have the chance to atone for all I put Ada through. We only had three years together and I still do not know how I walked away from my mate, my fiery ember in the frost. Why I let others dictate my time and attention for so long. Has it really taken forty-seven years to get my priorities straight? Life rarely grants us such gifts. And I squandered mine the first time. That will never happen again. I am not naïve enough to believe that it will be easy between us after so much time has passed. But come what may, I will prove to her how deeply sorry I am.

We wait an endless time for our escort through the wards, though it is an extra security measure I approve of. But I am anxious to keep moving. The rest of the group chatter endlessly. I listen in case there is any information useful to me but do not join in. Instead, I take in my surroundings. Little has changed since the last time I was here. Eyeing the now-dark travel portal, I cannot help but think how differently life could have turned out for me and Ada if one of those connected reasonably close to my home. But there is no sense dwelling on it overmuch. There was no alternative but to leave her behind. For her sake.

As the minutes tick by, my nerves ratchet up. I will lay eyes upon my beautiful, perfect mate for the first time in fifteen years. She will hate me, mayhap curse at me in her delicate lyrical voice, and I will deserve it. But I will see her healed before I leave, and I will make sure to leverage this opportunity to drag my clan kicking and screaming into this world. If I do not, it means that I fucked up my life, and more importantly Ada's life, for absolutely nothing. I have not felt like myself since I returned to my people. This is not who I wanted to become. Cold, solitary, and bitter. I was more myself when I was with her than I ever was without. I should have held on tighter and never let go.

Seventeen Years Ago

Ada's reflection winks at me in the mirror as she brushes her teeth in my bathroom. Her mouth foams with the magickal toothpaste that she has me using. It not only cleans but also repairs cavities. I admit it is much better than regular toothpaste or the baking soda I sometimes used when my clan's supplies bought from the nearest human settlement ran low. It is one of several magickal upgrades she suggested I try. When our relationship turned intimate, she procured me a birth control potion effective until I take the antidote. I knew some of this existed prior to arriving here, but the everyday usefulness of magick, available to any Whispered Folk, not just those who wield it, has turned much of my perception on its head.

As she wipes her mouth and rinses off the brush, I close the distance between us, squeezing her hips and nibbling down the long slender curve of her neck as she raises her head from the sink.

"How did you sneak out of the dorm tonight, my ember?" I whisper low into her ear before nipping at it with my teeth. She shivers and pushes her panty-covered bottom into my already tenting groin, rubbing it enticingly.

"Wouldn't you like to know? Well, tonight everyone went into town again, but I said that all my late-night study sessions caught up with me. I needed to turn in early. They may have doubts, but they didn't give me too hard a time. I *did* hang out with them twice already this week, one night of which they deeply regret as I am known in my hometown as a bit of a pool shark. It's not my fault they didn't ask if I grew up with orcs and shifters who like to play. *Oops*. I forgot to tell them until I took all their money," she mewls as she bats her eyes innocently.

"My naughty little ember, that will teach them to underestimate you."

She breaks into a fit of giggles as I tickle her sides for being so wicked. Smacking at my hands playfully, she begs me to stop.

When she catches her breath, she remarks, "One of these days they'll see through my excuses and figure out I'm sneaking off somewhere. Dollars to donuts they're taking bets on it being a member of the faculty. *No thank you*."

I chuckle at the repulsion in her voice while softly biting the curve of her shoulder.

"I better make it worth your while then," I purr as my hand searches down her stomach and dips into the top of her panties with a fully filed nail. As careful as I try to be, I never want to risk nicking her. All are filed down now.

She gasps as I part her labia and draw circles around her clit. Her head falls back against my shoulder, watching my ministrations in the bathroom mirror with her half-lidded violet gaze. I kiss up and down her exposed neck, sucking at the base of her earlobe and rubbing behind it gently with my tongue. She holds my hips behind her and grinds into my swollen cock as I play with her clit. I still wear my sweatpants, but I could come from the exquisite friction alone.

With my other hand, I pull down a cup of her lacy bra to expose the round globe of her breast and pinch and twist her sensitive nipple—so reactive to my touch. It is red and puckered, ready for me. I love to play with her breasts. If I pluck and suck on them long enough, the smallest brush against her clit sets her alight. Tonight though, I plan on being buried deep within her as she comes on my cock.

"What do you want, Ada?" I murmur into her ear.

"Please make me come," she begs sweetly. Her shaky breath tells me she is already close.

"Want your yeti to fuck you through it?" I growl, tweaking her nipple a little harder to make her moan her response.

"Yes," she cries out.

"Good girl. Now take off your panties for me." She hooks her fingers in the waist band and pushes them down her thighs, so they drop the floor.

"The bra too," I instruct her, gently kissing the top of her head as she unclasps it. While she pulls her arms through it and tosses it to the side, I move my other hand down to her pussy and spread her labia so I can see it in the mirror. Dew coats her puffy lips, ready to take me.

"So wet already. Have you been thinking about me all day? About how you want me to take you tonight? Will it be slow and gentle or hard and fast?" I ask as I stroke along the entrance of her core with two fingers, sliding in only the tips to tease her.

"I always think about you. About your cock," she whines, moving her hips trying to notch me in further.

"That is the right answer. You will get your reward now. Exactly what you have been waiting for all day." A rumble rolls through me. I am as eager as she is.

I shuck my pants and my swollen cock springs free, already leaking thick come. I rub it along my tip and shaft for extra lubricant. My cock's numerous veins are extremely prominent to keep it warm in Arctic temperatures, giving it a more corrugated look and feel than is usual, according to Ada. It drives her into a frenzy sometimes when its texture rubs deep inside her.

Presenting to me, she bends forward and holds onto the sink for leverage. I nudge her legs wider, exposing everything to my eyes. Her pussy glistens as she wiggles her lusciously rounded butt cheeks in anticipation of being filled. I angle my hips forward, rubbing the tapered head of my cock along her pussy, collecting all her moisture, letting the head slide against her clit to push her to the brink.

"Oh Norrell, I need to be fucked," she pleads, canting her hips so my shaft rubs her even faster.

"What do you want me to fuck you with?" I demand playfully, aware I am driving her mad.

"Your fat beautiful cock," she drawls out from low in her throat, watching me in the mirror with hazy eyes.

"Then take it all like a good girl." My voice turns guttural as I line up and push my cock into her. It slides right in coated with our shared fluids. Being inside her nearly robs me of my ability to speak. A primal creature looks back at me in the mirror. I growl uncontrollably as she moans in relief.

Gripping her hips, I thrust deep then quick, over and over, rocking a fast rhythm into her tightly clenching pussy. My balls slap against her labia and clit, the motion feeling like a tug, further drawing out my own pleasure. Her channel grips me harder like a fist, and I know she quickly reaches the edge. I grit my teeth to hold back my own release until after hers.

I rub a few tight circles around her clit as I thrust even deeper, nearly lifting her off her feet. I hold those thrusts inside her a little longer, so she takes every inch of me. She shrieks, babbling my name as she reaches her peak and tumbles into pleasurable abyss. I fuck her through it, pushing through the rhythmic squeeze around my cock. When she relaxes in my arms, my restraint vanishes. My cock jerks, for what feels like ages, as my come streams deep within her.

Rumbling in satisfaction as I catch my breath, I wind an arm across her shoulders to hoist her upright, so she is standing again. She smiles sleepily at me in the mirror and declares, "That's exactly what I needed."

She turns her head to the side while I embrace her, so she looks up at me directly. I kiss her deeply, my tongue seeking hers just as passionately as I made love to her. I only stop when my come begins to leak out of her onto our pressed-together thighs. I grab a small towel and hold it to her as I pull out my softened cock. After wiping away most of it, I toss it in a hamper to deal with it later.

Before she can pick up her discarded panties, I lift her up, and she instinctively wraps her legs around me. I walk us to the bedroom and lower her onto her side of the bed. She keeps her legs hooked behind my back so I hover over her. She cups her hands around my face, peppering it with soft kisses. I run my hands up and down her sides, relishing the dips and curves of her body.

"Lie down next to me," she whispers and pats the bed.

I climb over her to do as she asks. She rests her head on my shoulder while I pull her into me. She twines her fingers through the pelt on my chest lazily. I lightly scratch her back with my dull nails. We rest for a time, appreciating each other's quiet company.

This year with Ada was the best of my life. There is no doubt she is my mate, though we have not spoken those words. She has been unbelievably generous in her tolerance of the secrecy and resulting complications of my preference to remain undisclosed here. The academy upholds this accommodation for rarer and more solitary visitors. But I see how hard it is for her, and I appreciate everything she sacrifices for me. I knew when I revealed myself to her that night in the library that I would not regret it.

She lifts her head and scoots over so that it rests on the pillow, facing me. I continue to scratch her back, occasionally kneading a muscle to give her skin a break. After a few minutes, she murmurs, "I love how warm you are. I wish I could stay all night."

I hum in agreement. "I wish you could too. I will be glad to shed the yoke of this secrecy. It grows more difficult each day."

I extended my stay to coincide with the end of Ada's studies. I did as much of my own research as I could here, though this extra time has been useful. Some deans and other faculty approached me to assist their own research on Malefic and wild magick, which I am happy to do since they have been so obliging of me for nearly a year. Though it takes up more of my free time recently than I would prefer, time I could devote to Ada.

"When my apprenticeship is over in a couple months, you should come with me to Monstera Bluff. You wouldn't have to lay low. There are so many Whispered Folk that your presence wouldn't make waves. No one would look at you twice unless it's because you're so hot," she proposes. She bites her lips nervously as she waits for my response.

"You want me to come with you? That sounds serious," I say in a light tone. "What will you call me when you introduce me to everyone?"

"I'll call you my yeti of the night," she quips.

"I would prefer if you called me your mate," I say affectionately, honestly.

"Really? Oh, Norrell. I love you. I was hoping..." Her words are cut off as she throws herself on top of me, kissing me deliriously.

My anticipation of seeing my mate makes the drive down this long road into town seem never-ending. My thoughts turn to those happy early days. At the academy and at our apartment when we first moved here. Though life became heavy after Ada's parents passed, we still loved each other fiercely. That was the last time I felt any real happiness. It makes me wonder if I ever will again.

When a sudden bout of restlessness has me fidgeting in my seat, the van finally turns into the circle drive in front of Ada's house. She had only just inherited it and moved back in when I left. It looks largely the same, aside from the missing carriage house, mayhap more overgrown now. But knowing her, it is purposeful, her small rebellion against expectations. Plus, she has always liked things a little untamed.

I pull my duffel bag from the back of the van. It drives off as I stand on the sidewalk, leaving me alone to gather myself before I go inside. Walking up to the front porch feels surprisingly familiar, even though my feet have not stepped there in fifteen long years. This should have been my home. With Ada. A different life. And certainly a happier one. This thought does nothing to calm my nerves.

The rap of my knuckles on the door sounds too abrupt, but I cannot take it back now. With any luck, she will be on the other side of that door. I will witness her candid reaction to me. Maybe there will be a spark between us still. But that is wishful thinking. She would be better off if she moved on, found someone else who had the courage to stay. Part of me hopes she has.

After some time has passed, I knock again, softer this time. The footsteps inside sound halting, unsure. They must be Ada's. I readily admit I blindsided her, forcing her hand by accepting her invitation. By the bluest glacier, I do not regret it. I would hate myself even more if I passed up this opportunity.

The steps in the foyer pause at the door. She may be just as nervous and hopeful for this reunion. No, it is too one-sided for that. This intrusion. I have longed for this for so long. And now she stands nearly within reach. She will be so exquisitely beautiful it will hurt. It already does.

When the door finally creaks open, loud in the quiet night, her presence nearly staggers me. It is nourishment for my withered spirit. She stands rooted to the spot, unmoving, except for her large violet eyes blinking rapidly in disbelief. Long, dark, garnet red hair with streaks of white in the front falls over her shoulders as vibrant as ever. Pale, opalescent skin glows in the light of the chandelier hanging high above. She looks exactly as I remember. Like my memories have been recorded and broadcast to this very moment.

Only her dazzling signature of magick is missing, replaced by the stain of a complex fae spell, its threads woven deeply through her chest. It concerns me, buried so deep inside her, pulsing strange and powerful. I do not trust I could disrupt that spell without causing her further damage. I try not to let this unfortunate discovery show on my face.

Being in her presence again is like experiencing the first glimpse of sunlight after polar night. She still shines more brightly than most, but there is an undercurrent of pain in her bearing that is partly my doing. The reality of my decisions crashes over me. What she meant to me then and still does now. Who I chose my clan over and regretted it every day since.

Long seconds pass as we stare at each other. "Norrell, it's been a while. Why don't you come in," she drawls, spoken in her slow and lilting song, a sweet soothing melody. The lullaby that I hear as I fall asleep and the same one that croons me in my dreams.

Even now, when she is so clearly unhappy with me, it is all I want to hear. No doubt she is composing a symphony of curses against me in that incredible brain of hers. I would welcome it coming from her winsome lips with her talent for infusing meaning in the most innocent and innocuous words in colorful and pleasing ways. Life has been washed out without it.

When she abruptly marches away after a chilly message about dinner, it leaves me some time to myself in her grand manor home again—her family legacy. I could navigate this place blindfolded. It throws in my face the irony that I chided my infuriating cousin for being short-sighted, yet I am by far the guiltiest of it.

I knew I could not take her away from this place. She belongs here, with a life full of beauty and magick, but I should have figured out how to make it work even when my hand felt forced. No matter, I did not stand up for us or for her like a mate should. I was an impressionable coward, doing exactly as the clan had trained me as a good little soldier, the best actually. It left me an incomplete male in return.

CHAPTER 6
NORRELL

Only birdsong and the whisper of trees in the breeze hang in the air in this early hour. Ada needs space from me after I pushed too hard at dinner, so I will give it to her this morning. Her message to me last night was clear.

I know the way to town hall from her house, but there is ample time to wander and reacquaint myself with this treasured place. The low morning sun puts a soft filter on her tree-canopied street, where most of the largest and oldest houses in town are situated. I wonder if the same neighbors live here. Some that I was well-acquainted with, a gregarious family of barghests who run the local inn, lived down the block. They talked me into helping them fix their fence after a large fallen branch collapsed a section of it. They were worried their dog would get loose. I always thought it was funny that these barghests, who were big black canine beasts in their shifted forms, had their own dog—a small yappy one at that.

The fence needed mending on a weekend that Ada wanted to go kayaking through the tidal rivers. But they needed my help and at the time it felt like a neighborly thing to do. I am unsure exactly why I agreed. Maybe I was trying to prove myself in this community. No matter, I see it differently now. Someone else could have stepped in to help. My plans with Ada were more important.

My entire walk is filled with similar memories. A beach weekend pushed off to help with an art show. Digging out a garden plot for a different neighbor when I promised to help Ada with holiday preparations. Showing up to our anniversary dinner late after covering an extra shift at the hardware store. The list is long for having lived here only two years. As my mate, I should have put her needs first. Not that mates do not help others, of course they do. But I was often in service to the community at her expense, even when none of these situations were urgent. Fire of the frost, I was old enough that I should have known better, but I was not wise enough to recognize the pattern.

The hurt shone in her eyes each time I let her down, yet I kept doing it. I treated this town like my new clan because I did not realize there was another way. In my settlement, service is critical to our survival. Our individual wants are secondary to the clan's needs. That dire dichotomy does not exist here in the same way. But I was still too sheltered to see that in those days. I put her through so much, and then I left to lead my clan without her, my final and worst transgression. I long ago came to terms with the fact that my supposed selflessness was a continual act of selfishness for which Ada always paid the price.

Strolling down the sleepy streets, I realize I have missed the trees, towering and majestic, providing plentiful shade over much of the town. Bright flowers bloom continually, painting the scenery in bright pinks and purples. The endless greenery is not even entirely magickal. There is no real winter here, and the days swelter in the summer. It was a shock at first, but not entirely unpleasant. The "Be Cool" charm from Ada's shop kept me from overheating.

The nature surrounding the town is rugged and untamed compared to its pristine and beautified streets. Pine forests, salt marshes, coastal features like natural beaches and long inlet rivers that flow into the ocean. So much wildlife. Now when I traverse the vast ice fields and rocky, mountainous terrain, bare of most vegetation in the far north, it seems desolate in a way it never had before coming here. My people stay above the northern tree line for a reason. Malefic Folk are not attracted to beauty in the way that Whispered Folk are. It would be like expecting a shark to admire the vibrant hues of the coral reef it swims around.

This town offers more to its residents than I could imagine. It speaks to the strength of the community and its diversity of Whispered Folk. The small cinema, grocery store, restaurants and cafes, more shops than I could dream of. I learned a new way of living here, less focused on survival and more on enjoyment. It marked the longest time I spent away from my clan and the most pivotal. Including my time at the witches' academy, it was only three short years out of my long forty-seven.

In the North Clan settlement, our amenities are limited living in a vast underground network of caverns in northern Canada. It functions like a town with homes, shops, and restaurants, but with very little variety. More functional than whimsical, out of necessity. We are much smaller too, only two thousand to Monstera Bluff's twelve. We have satellite internet and phone communications, of course. Like most Whispered Folk communities, over the years we developed means, often magickal, to move through the human world when needed, earning their currency through passive means, and buying their goods and services as necessary. But the glaring reality of what our settlement lacks rings anew now that I am back here.

Although today's safety council meetings will certainly have food and drink, I enter Pearlhouse Pastries, one of Ada's favorite spots. I do not recognize any of the employees behind the counter. They look rather young and were probably children when I lived here. Who would guess the family of tarasque would be such prolific bakers with their paw-like hands and leonine sensibilities. They do not wield magick, but their creations could be mistaken for it. I got to know them when I lived here. I remember them fondly and miss their friendship.

The bakery still has their popular raspberry and chamomile frangipane croissant on the top shelf of their display case. Ada would usually end up ordering it, even when she promised herself she would try something new. I ask the young male at the counter to box up half a dozen and then order a black coffee for myself.

There is no sense in delaying the inevitable, so I head in the direction of the town hall building situated at the very end of the main street as if it is watching over the beloved business district, the crown jewel of the town. There are no vacant store fronts, and it seems to have grown since I last saw it, though I remember many of the establishments. Few are open this early, so there are not many pedestrians out yet. The boulevard street is wide enough for a median accommodating mammoth live oaks that look like they are trying to reach out and touch the buildings on each side.

The town hall building itself is grand and striking. A tall, three-story limestone structure with an exterior more ornate than practical. The shady square situated in front of it invites you in, with benches and lush landscaping, offsetting the otherwise dramatic appearance. I wonder if that old centaur is still the mayor. He used to insist on greeting nearly everyone who stepped inside when he was not in a meeting, whether the visitor was there for him or not. He cornered me and gave me his entire pitch on the town right after I moved here.

The building is quiet as I follow the posted signs and head upstairs, no nosy old centaur or anyone to be seen. The layout of the large meeting room, where this first safety council meeting will be held, feels too much like a tribunal for it to simply be a day to interview witnesses and victims. A chair and table are set far apart from the rest, the focal point of the room. Only a group of constables and other law enforcement representatives are here, talking amongst themselves while setting up the tables, which might contribute to its unfriendly configuration. Still, Ada, or any other witness, should not be made to feel uncomfortable. I worry it will add to Ada's stress. She was tense last night, much of which was caused by my arrival, but certainly not all of it. This surely loomed large in her mind too.

Niven, who will be leading today's meeting, arrives right after me. He studies me, a guarded expression on his face. I wait impassively while he approaches. I do not want to make an enemy of him if I do not have to, even if I do not care for how overly solicitous he was of Ada. She needs friends in her corner, but it looks too comfortable coming from him. Still, I may be able to use it to my advantage in this situation.

"Norrell Snowstrider, you're here early." Niven's unexpectedly scraping voice is at odds with his sophisticated demeanor. "I didn't want to bring this up at dinner, but our group of friends wondered who claimed so much of Ada's time that last year at the academy. When we finally learned about you it was a bolt from the blue, to say the least. A yeti among us for an entire year. She kept your secret, you know. She was true to you. And then you did the unthinkable and left her. You didn't have to come back here, and you certainly have no business expecting a room in her house. There are plenty of other places you could stay. Ashes, if you were a decent male, you would have sent an advisor. Do you find sick pleasure in blowing up her life?" he accuses with an unnatural calmness.

"I did all of those things. But the situation was not as simple as you say. I care more about her than anyone else in my life," I counter.

"Most of the time it *is* that simple. You're bad for her. Don't make things worse. Everyone is watching," he replies, never breaking his cool stare.

It would be a bad look to start an argument with him before I speak with Ada, so I do not let him bait me.

"Is Ada up first?" I ask, motioning a hand over to the lone chair. The unrelated question does not faze him. His hard expression remains in place.

"Yes, even though her testimony falls last in the timeline. Our other big interview today, Ben Garde-Pierre, is here representing himself as well as his mate Cara Bishop so it will be a long day," Niven explains, the tone of his voice turning strictly business.

"Mayhap that chair needs to be somewhere more comfortable for her," I suggest, with a tilt of my head toward the long tables. "Like over there where she is part of the group instead of opposite them. She will feel too exposed."

"Good point," he agrees, though he gives me a piercing look like he is trying to get a read on me. "This isn't a questioning; it's a collaborative effort. I'll move her."

By the tone of his voice, it sounds like he is done with me for now, so I say my piece while I still can. "Give these to Ada when she gets here. They are her favorite. Mayhap do not say they are from me."

He nods curtly as I hand him the bright pink Pearlhouse Pastries bag. He looks inside, as if checking whether they are tainted, then strides toward the chair and drags it closer to a different table. He drops the bag onto it. Crossing his arms, he examines the set up. I leave him to his own devices and walk to the edge of the room where I lean against a wall out of the way. Before long, he enlists help to move the tables into a friendlier grouping. I hope the other witnesses appreciate it too.

An older female cervitaur rolls in a cart with coffee, water, and other beverages, along with stacks of paper cups, plates, utensils, and napkins. She is followed by a much taller golden-blonde-coated centaur with chin length blonde hair tucked behind his ears, maybe a decade younger than me. His human-like torso is donned in a crisp dress shirt and a vibrant purple tie, the color not unlike Ada's eyes. His presence fills the room, even more than his size. Mayhap they traded in the mayor for a younger model. The centaur sets down the boxes he carries. Some familiar pink ones on top of plain brown bulkier ones. As he helps the cervitaur arrange the table, I take this opportunity to introduce myself. Get it out of the way since he must know Ada well through their respective elected positions if he is indeed the new mayor.

As I approach, they look over and both of their expressions sour. The centaur's tail swishes sharply. Ah, my reputation has preceded me.

"Here he comes," the silver-haired cervitaur murmurs. The centaur snorts and continues unpacking the boxes.

When I stop next to him, he twists his human torso toward me, looking far down his nose to remark, "I'm not going to pretend I don't know who you are and that I don't have a very low opinion of you."

I nod in understanding, looking between the two of them. Both narrow their large, deep brown eyes at me, giving me no quarter. "Are you related to the centaur who was mayor about fifteen years ago?" I ask decorously, not wanting to test them further, though still needing to appease my curiosity.

He jerks his head. "I am. He's my father, the former mayor. I'm the current mayor."

"He was Byron Evermane?" I pull the name from the back of my mind.

"That's right, he is. And I'm Clancy." He finally identifies himself. "And this is Madge Feverfew, my assistant. She's worked with both of our administrations."

"Was it the fae or was it Ada's misfortune that brought you back here to darken her doorstep? I have my eyes on you. I don't care if you're a big shot somewhere. You upset her and you're out!" Madge shakes her finger in my direction as she dresses me down.

"You're as bright as the night if you think that's an empty threat, yeti. Ada doesn't need you rubbing salt in the wound. I reckon you should keep clear of her as best you can," Clancy warns me.

"Noted," I acknowledge. "I am only here to offer her and this council assistance."

"She doesn't want your help," he states with flat finality. Both return to their task at hand, effectively cutting off the conversation.

Walking away from them, I circle the room, surveying the growing crowd as I return to my previous spot. Another stray, seemingly the dragonkin I heard about, saunters toward an empty space along the wall near me. The gleaming indigo scales covering his neck and the edges of his face while in his unshifted form give him away. His long black hair is pulled into a knot high on the back of his head. He inadvertently imitates my pose, leaning against the wall with his arms crossed, though fidgeting a tad too much. He may be counted as one of the Whispered Folk *coming out of the woodwork*, as Cyrinda put it last night.

"Seems like a lot of fuss over one fae," he complains, sounding unimpressed.

"Did your leader send you here?" I guess from his criticism.

"My father. He did not want to lower himself to attend, so he sends a venerable prince in his stead." He huffs a hollow laugh, flashing his bright golden serpentine eyes in my direction. "I am here strictly to observe and report back, using as much eloquent evasion as necessary. He forbade me from making any promises that would bind him to this community, but he wants me to do so in a way that upholds his reputation as the dragonkin ruler. Thus, I will stay in the back and let the size of this crowd work in my favor."

I chuckle, understanding the difficulty of that mandate. "It seems our roles are in reverse. I lead the North Clan and I attend against their wishes. They will be assisting as I see fit."

"Bold move to go against the ways of your clan. I am impressed. You may have a struggle on your hands when you return," he observes.

"I welcome it," I respond, my eyebrow raised in challenge. "At least your father was courteous enough to send someone. Most of my people would not care how this community suffers. They likely believe it is what magick wielders deserve."

His jaw drops open. "Ashes. I thought we were cold-blooded..." If only my people knew their disregard could shock a dragonkin. He shakes his head incredulously before turning his attention back to the room.

After several minutes, his impatient body language betrays his boredom. "I have never seen such a hodgepodge collection of Whispered Folk in one place before," he mumbles.

A knowing smile crosses my face. "I lived here for a time and I agree this is... a lot. The nocturnals are not even here. I heard they will be briefed tonight and shown the recordings of today's proceedings. For the rest of the week these meetings will be shifted around so everyone can attend."

He sighs loudly. "I should have claimed a sunlight allergy."

Ada appears well after the tables were reconfigured, none the wiser to their original arrangement. She spots the centaur, Clancy, and joins him and Madge. Madge pulls her into a tight embrace, fiercely whispering into her ear and then patting her cheek lovingly. Ada responds with a watery smile. As long as they are warm to her, it makes no difference how cold they are to me.

Niven joins them momentarily, then motions for Ada to come with him. He speaks with her the entire time, their faces close, as he leads her to a chair at the tables, now arranged in an oval. Her seat is still a focal point, but it is flanked on both sides by other chairs. When she sits, he points to the pink bag. Taking out the box within it, she opens it on the table. Her eyes widen and then scan the room suspiciously. Finally noticing me, her face pinches, but she leaves the open box in front of her. Someone, probably a witch, brings her a cup of coffee along with a notebook, pen, and box of tissues.

"Everyone, get your breakfast now and then head to your seat. We'll begin momentarily," announces another witch standing next to Niven. He leads this investigation, so I hope he will ensure everyone is respectful toward Ada. But if anyone starts pestering her for answers she cannot give, and Niven does not step in quickly enough, I will not hold my tongue.

Despite Ada realizing I was behind the croissants, she takes one out and starts eating it with a distracted look on her face. Nearly fifty have crowded in already. Several others approach Ada, including the rest of her house guests, offering her encouragement. Hopefully, the pastries along with her friends' support will provide some comfort this morning.

Niven takes his seat across the oval from her and begins the proceedings. After thorough questions about her observations of three fugitive warlocks' actions while on town council, one of Niven's assistants prompts her to recount her interaction with the fae. It takes her a moment to collect herself. She presses a tissue to her face, her eyes unfocused like she is stuck in the memory.

She describes the incorporeal vaporous creature, how it seemingly spoke through magickal means. It cast powerful, sophisticated spells she was completely unfamiliar with, something I could have told them from my own encounters. Ada's testimony becomes even more riveting when she mentions the ward shared its knowledge with her while also slinging its own spells through the representations of her family. The interviewer asks her to describe the experience in greater detail.

"In the moment, I knew ways to try to attack the fae or to counter incoming spells," she attempts to explain, sounding dissatisfied. "The ward didn't speak to me, per se. It isn't cognizant like that, as far as I know. I also couldn't understand the... figures... behind me. But an instinct emerged in me. My magick became both a shield and a weapon. There was clarity in those spells that I shouldn't have had. But everything was happening so fast, I didn't have time to question it."

"Has the ward ever been activated to that extent before?" the interviewer continues.

Ada pauses, tilting her head. "No, I don't think so. But this ward is old, maintained since the founding of the town. I'm not aware of any incident in town history like this. There aren't any family stories about it either."

"Have you retained that awareness?" she follows up.

Ada subtly shakes her head, her eyes downcast. "No, when I woke up at the healers clinic it was already gone. I wouldn't be able to replicate half the spells I cast. I barely even recall them."

The interviewer writes a quick note, and then continues, "Did that awareness seem invasive? Like it had another aim?"

"It kept me alive, didn't it?" Ada bristles. "But it couldn't outsmart the fae. When one of my spells managed to inflict damage, the fae changed strategy just as quickly. It was so powerful, so seamless in its spellcasting. My magick reserves were already running low after the Samhaim rituals earlier. I couldn't find a way at the time to subdue it on my own."

"Tell us about when the fae made physical contact with you." The interviewer fixates on Ada's response in a way I do not appreciate.

"The pain convinced me it stabbed a hole in my chest. I had no idea it damaged my magick. It just...felt like... dying. And I thought maybe I'd finally be with my parents again." Ada's voice fizzles.

I struggle to breathe as she answers each question, detailing how that revolting excuse of a creature harmed her. It will not leave this town alive.

"Did the fae also attack the ward?" the interviewer presses.

"I'm not sure, but it mostly seemed focused on trying to hurt me. One moment, the fae was gloating about killing the last Mayweather in Monstera Bluff, like it knew about me and my family. The next, we were both caught off guard when the figures appeared behind me. The ward brought my mom and dad back to protect me," she rasps, her voice cracking at the mention of Estelle and Whitt, her parents. She wipes at her tear-streaked face before she continues. "More of my family was there too. My grandparents, great grandparents, everyone whose magick built the ward. They saved my life."

Her grief is palpable as she weeps into her tissue, unable to resume for the time being. Her parents were kind and loving, exactly like her. They would have done anything to save her, even from the next realm. I knew this would affect her deeply, dredging up the sharp pain of their loss that she obviously still feels so keenly. Watching her now, overcome with sorrow, breaks something inside of me. I feel as low as that fae.

Seventeen Years Ago

"Do you want to go first?" Ada asks, bouncing on her heels, as we stand in front of the travel portal at the academy. Before our eyes, the dark portal stirs to life with milky white swirls that make me uneasy.

"Mayhap you should since your parents will be waiting," I answer carefully.

"Alright. But Estelle and Whitt know all about you. They can't wait to meet you." She has worn a beaming smile all morning, excited to finally introduce me to someone. That it is her parents has her buzzing.

When I told my clan—well, more accurately, when I asked for permission from my clan elders to move to Monstera Bluff—they were not pleased. Their investment in me studying old and rare tomes on Malefic Folk did not take into account that I would find a mate. And a magick wielder at that. I was told to keep this quiet, that it stays only within the immediate family, who happen to be quite supportive of me, unlike my uncle and the elders. They insisted it would not be a good look for the nephew of the clan leader to be tied to a witch.

Now that I have been away from them for just over a year, their dislike of witches and others with magickal ability seems foolhardy. Even in my lifetime, they dug in their heels, taking an already hardline stance to an extreme. My uncle and his father—my grandfather—heavily influenced this thinking. My own father never agreed. Maybe my uncle thought of sending me to the academy as a punishment, probably something my cousin—his presumed next in line—refused to do, when in fact it freed me from this backwards point of view. I cannot thank them enough. Part of me wonders whether the elders' agreement to let me move permanently was also my uncle's doing, making sure I do not compete with my spoiled cousin.

Choosing to go to Monstera Bluff with Ada effectively cuts me off from them, a tradeoff I am willing to accept. As long as I am with her, I do not care where we are.

We are leaving the academy now that she has wrapped up her apprenticeship, and she is anxious to go home. Mayhap much of that is in anticipation of us living a more normal life together. She already rented us an apartment in the downtown business district. By the bluest glacier, it will be strange to live among so many Whispered Folk. But likely no one will care, as she says. It is a matter of course for them.

"You'll have to push yourself through. It'll exert a little pressure on your body, like swimming through deep water. Keep a tight hold on your luggage," she reminds me as she starts to step through. "See you on the other side!"

I have little beyond clothing and some books I collected over the year. Ada has much more, spending many years here as a student in an advanced program. She spelled our items to near weightlessness so they pass through the portal easier.

The portal swallows her up as she steps through. The sight makes me nauseous. My brain insists she must be in danger, but I try to keep her assurances about the safety of the magick in mind. Holding my bag firmly, I step a heavy foot into it, encountering an unusually oppressive force pulling me in. I propel myself ahead using my strength only to swiftly fling out the other side.

It takes a moment to get my bearings, but I am indeed in a different location. I look back at the portal instinctively, but it only shows the same white cloudiness as on the other side. When I turn my attention to Ada, she exudes giddiness, waving me over to her and two older witches, who are no doubt her parents. She looks so much like them both. A younger version of her mother with her father's distinctive hair, the white streaks included.

Her parents' smiles brighten as I walk over. "Norrell, meet my parents, Estelle and Whitt. Mom, Dad, this is Norrell," she introduces us. I extend my hand to shake Estelle's and she lunges at me, wrapping her arms around my middle in a crushing hug instead.

"We're so happy our Ada has found her mate. We've been over the moon about it and couldn't wait to meet you," she exclaims into my shoulder. Both Ada and her father chuckle at my wide-eyed expression. When Estelle lets go, Whitt shakes my hand, saying, "Welcome to the family. We can't wait to get you settled in. You're going to love Monstera Bluff."

Ada squeals when she notices that her parents picked us up in her beloved automobile, an old Jeep Wagoneer that she has missed so much while away. While we put our luggage in the back, her parents hand me an amulet to pass through the wards surrounding the town. The scenery while we drive in is unlike anything I have ever seen. The coastal water running along the road has vegetation growing in it. Ada calls them salt marshes. Once we arrive in town, after passing a forest of tall pines, everything is green and lush.

"Your apartment is almost ready for you to move in, but I thought you might want to stay overnight at the house tonight, so we don't have to rush through dinner," her mother chirps from the front seat.

Ada turns her gaze to me. "Would you mind sleeping at my parents' house tonight?" she asks, sounding unsure.

"I want to see the home where you grew up. There is no need to rush our move into the apartment," I assure her.

"Okay, that'll be nice," she breathes, visibly relieved. I take her hand and kiss her palm to soothe her.

We arrive at their property and park near a smaller house painted the same white with bluish gray shutters as the large main house. Ada's father takes her luggage so she is free to walk me around the exterior of the house. She calls it a two-story Greek Revival. She points out the front porches on both stories and the tall columns running the full height that support the overhanging roof. The blue of the doors and shutters is called French blue, just a color preference her ancestors had, and the lighter shade on the porch ceilings is haint blue, a regional tradition to ward off Malefic. She clarifies the paint on this house is not enchanted as a ward, only so that it does not peel and fade.

A tall, elegant cast iron fountain stands inside the circle drive in front of the house. Water flows pleasantly down its three increasingly larger tiers designed to look like blooming hibiscus flowers, with their large petals draping downward. A large marble circular pool at the bottom collects the water.

"It's a lot, I know. It's been here almost as long as the house. Luckily, it's enchanted to be self-cleaning and self-repairing. We are so glad we never have to do anything but top up its magickal charge from time to time. My dad made it my chore when I was old enough to learn how. He said if I forgot to check it every week, I'd have to clean it myself by hand when it's full of slimy leaves. I never forgot." She laughs lightheartedly.

We head inside and all three give me the grand tour of the house. Their love for its history and connection to their Mayweather heritage is clear. After we deposit our luggage in Ada's bedroom, we head downstairs to talk while her parents prepare dinner.

Estelle chops vegetables while Whitt stirs something over the stove. Ada and I sit at the kitchen table to keep them company while they work after they refused our offer to help. From her place at the counter, Estelle keeps flashing her sparkling eyes at us and grinning. I cannot recall if I have ever witnessed someone radiating this much happiness.

"We were so glad Ada met someone while studying. She didn't have much interest in anyone here, but we knew there had to be someone special out there who would be perfect for her. It seems like fate you crossed paths while both of you were so far from home. Ada is very determined when she sets her mind on something. If she had her eye on you, I'm not surprised you're sitting here in my kitchen," Estelle titters, poking some good-natured fun at her daughter.

"Mom, you're coming on a little strong. Let's not scare him. That's not even what happened." She groans, embarrassed, watching for my reaction out of the corner of her eye.

I grin at her, feeling my bottom lip stretch around my tusks. "I knew I would follow her anywhere after the first time we met."

"Now you're embarrassing me too!" she squeals, pretending to act indignant.

She giggles wildly, breaking the act, as I scoop her onto my lap and plant a comically loud kiss on her cheek. "I state the truth," I whisper into her ear.

"It better be," she replies with a wink. She pecks me on the lips before sliding off my lap and returning to her chair next to mine.

Her parents join us at the table while dinner cooks. They look exactly as a family should. They love each other, and they obviously enjoy each other's company too. It makes for easy conversation.

"Did Ada tell you she was named after her great-grandmother? We couldn't have known it at the time, but it really was the perfect name for her. They are so much alike. So smart, so responsible, with the perfect dollop of feistiness. I wish they could have known each other," Estelle says with a wistful smile. She quickly wipes her violet eyes and then uses her fingers to comb her long, dark brown hair away from her face.

"I did not know that. But that does sound exactly like her," I agree wholeheartedly.

Eyeing Ada, she says, "You know sweetheart, you don't have to return to the shop. It was never your father's dream to work there. But I always loved it." Estelle turns her attention back to me. "I apprenticed there before her father and I mated. It's how we met and got to know each other. My family is from a community in North Carolina. So anyway, when the time came, I happily took it over."

"But don't you want my help?" Ada protests.

"I have plenty of help and we're doing just fine. Plus, I don't intend to retire for a good long while. You'll be sick of me by then! Take some time to figure out what you want to do. Travel while you're young. There's a wide world out there waiting to be explored. You spent so many years studying. I don't want you to feel like you're going to waste it," Estelle insists.

"Mom, I love working at the shop. My entire time at Sparklight Academy was spent thinking about how I could use this knowledge to expand our offerings. There are so many new alchemical services I can add. I have some ideas for the coven too," Ada gushes.

"Speaking of the coven, they wanted to throw you a welcome home party tonight, but I asked them to wait a couple days so we don't overwhelm you. I don't know how long I can keep them at bay now that you're both here. They've been excited to meet you, Norrell. Sorry we spilled the beans on you. I heard you were keeping a low profile at the academy. But when we found out you were moving here, we couldn't resist," Whitt confesses.

"Everyone was bound to find out anyway. It is good to be out in the open again. I am happy to meet all of them," I say graciously.

"They do love a reason to throw a party. Don't be surprised if they serve snow cones to try to make you feel at home," Ada jokes.

"No. Would they? Yes, they probably would," Estelle considers.

"They did ask me to find out if yetis like maple syrup," Whitt chimes in.

"Well, trees cannot grow that far north to harvest it. But I tasted it once," I tell him.

"That's what I thought. I'll let them know. But don't be surprised if you see some maple flavored whiskey or maple bars there. Once they have an idea, they like to run with it," he muses.

"Your coven sounds lively," I observe, grinning at the thought of their misguided menu.

"They are. We have a friendly group here. We're too big to meet all at once on a regular basis outside of our holidays and rituals. There's a few hundred of us. So, they love opportunities like this. Believe me, you're doing them the favor," Whitt assures me.

"Yes, plenty of other witches around here to help me around the shop," Estelle reminds Ada with a wink.

"Mom, I told you! Mayhap I'll consider starting my own business, but I'd base it out of the shop anyway. You act like you're trying to get rid of me!" Ada huffs.

"Never. It will be so lovely working with you again. I just don't want you to feel any pressure or hold you back from bigger and better pursuits," Estelle reiterates, squeezing Ada's hand. They share an affectionate smile.

"If you do not work at the shop, what is your vocation, Whitt?" I ask. Ada told me a little about it, but his magickal talent seemed difficult to comprehend.

"Well, I work in sort of a specialty field. I have proficiency in languages as well as codebreaking. My magick works well in translations between human languages as well as those spoken or written by some Whispered Folk. Sometimes I'm called away as a translator for lesser spoken languages. Nowadays I'm also working on enchantments for books, paper files, and even digital files to make them indecipherable should a human find them. Like encryption, but through magick, making it hack-proof," Whitt explains.

"Did you have to learn how to write code to do this?" I wonder aloud.

"What's a few more languages?" he jests.

"Have you ever studied the native language of yetis?" I ask, genuinely curious.

"I never did. I'd love to learn a little from you if you don't mind," he requests. "Do your people speak it as well as English?"

"Yes, we all learn it in school, but it is not spoken much. The language is shared across our people, but we all have our own dialects from when our clans split apart long ago. Well over a century ago, our clan leader at the time decided we should learn English fluently to get by more easily as our contact with humans became more frequent. We needed to blend in better. Since then, English is the main language of the clan. It was a wise decision. Our native language is ancient and limited. It would not be useful in today's world anyway. Words do not exist for many commonplace items and ideas," I explain.

"That's fascinating." His interest sounds genuine. "It will be an honor to have the opportunity to learn it from you. A rare privilege for a language nerd like me."

"Norrell, we would be happy to inquire around if there's any work you'd like to try. But there's no rush. We want you to get to know the town. And of course, you two need to have a nice long honeymoon first. You both deserve it after studying so hard," Estelle suggests.

"That is very generous, Estelle. I will think about it and let you know. I am sure something will appeal to me. My training as a hunter may be too specific to be of use here, but I am a fast learner," I assure her.

Whitt's face lights up. "Ada said you loved to read, especially historic texts. No wonder you met in a library. After dinner, come up to my study with me. I have so many books I think you'll be interested in," he says enthusiastically. It is an offer I cannot refuse.

I am honored to have known Whitt and Estelle. They were special, and I cared for them deeply. From the first time I met them, they treated me like a son, embracing me as a full-fledged member of the family. Losing them was devastating in a way I had never experienced up until that point. Ada was inconsolable. The well of her sadness was deeper than I could fathom. Grief was her shadow in those months before I left, ever-present, following her even when she did not realize it. I fear it still is.

Mercifully, Niven ends the interview and calls for a break. Taking the pastries with her, Ada walks out of the room with controlled steps, but from her stiffness I can tell she struggles not to run out. Clancy and Madge trail closely behind. The loud sudden scraping and clattering of chairs disrupt my reverie. Her parents were my family once too. For a short time, anyway. I do not know what they would think of me now, had they not died when they did. Their disappointment and sadness would have shamed me even more. I know that much to be true.

Needing some air myself, I step into the hallway. I'm also curious if Ada is still nearby, but it is empty except for a few others milling around who exited the room right before me. I am unsure if I would say anything to her if I saw her, but I need to know whether she is alright. Growling in frustration at my powerlessness, I pace the long hallway for a couple minutes, figuring out what to do. I should give her something special to make up for her terrible day. The nearby shops should have something.

A pair of shifters, whose eyes are a striking shade of electric green, converse near me in the hallway. I do not intend to eavesdrop, but my hearing is too sensitive to fully ignore them.

"Did you ever hear about that fae who was caught at a school playground in Boston trying to trick young witch children into injuring their classmates with a dangerous spell? Somehow breaking their bones? Pure evil. It happened about a decade ago," one of the shifters says, sounding disgusted.

"I did." The other shifter shudders. "It hid in the shadows, away from the adults. Another kid saw something moving in the dark and alerted a group of magick-wielding teachers who chased it off. Who knows what would have happened if it wasn't caught?"

"Knowing what horrible things they're capable of, why would anyone bring one here? How could anyone want to spoil this place with violence? It's a little slice of paradise," the first one remarks.

The second one snorts. "Ashes, it's always these crusty old warlocks making trouble for everyone. That male, the really speciesist one, threw his fool hat in the wrong ring. He could have been the hero of Monstera Bluff, warning them of a fae threat, leading the charge to protect his town. Moon and stars, they'd have thrown a parade in his honor! Put his likeness in front of town hall!"

The first one chuckles darkly. "Nah, they're all the same. A warlock isn't going to save anything. They choose to be villains. His cronies fell into step because they're the same breed of hateful little malcontent. They'd rather watch the world burn and then try to rule over its ashes."

Their offhand remarks hit home. This town was close to ruin. It was a stroke of luck that there were no casualties other than the town's innocence. The shock will fade in time and townsfolk will feel safe again. But Ada will not be able to move on until her magick returns. I need to see that she recovers with my own eyes. I do not care about these meetings beyond seeking justice for her.

I will make sure that fae gets exactly what it deserves after I work out how to restore Ada's magick. There will be no mercy. I will not leave until both are done. On instinct, I stretch my claws wide, ready for the fight. But now is not the time. By the bluest glacier, I will be ready when it is. My resolve is ice cold. And that damned disgusting fae will rue the day it came to Monstera Bluff.

CHAPTER 7

ADA

My damp cheeks dry in the sun as I walk away from town hall. I need to put all of this behind me, in every sense, because crying in front of an audience wasn't the least bit cathartic. Ashes, emotions are overrated.

Walt and Acton invited me to lunch today. I suppose there's no point in hiding out anymore, so I agreed. After a few blocks of distance between me and that hurrah's nest I left behind, I finally send a text to them saying I'll be at The Roaring Wood a little early and there's no need to rush out the door if they're not ready yet. Lately, Acton is planting a veritable rain forest on their property. Even for a dryad living in a humid subtropical climate, it's proven challenging to achieve his exacting vision. Walt texts back that Acton is just finishing up outside and they'll leave in a few minutes.

My eyes roll when I realize I'm still carrying those croissants from Norrell. I'm tempted to drop them in a garbage can along the street, but I don't have the heart to do that to these edible flaky masterpieces. Walt may want one. They're absolute perfection as always except for the fact they were purchased by a heartless excuse of a male. He deserves to go in the trash, not the croissants. I won't let him taint my favorite breakfast.

The Roaring Wood is already bursting at the seams with a lunch crowd. But I appreciate how lively it makes the place. The interior always cheers me up, which I sorely need right now. Living vines and branches weave across the ceiling, and the tables are cut from wide logs showing their rings, resembling stumps in the ground. Colorful details like boldly patterned pillows on the wicker chairs and bright murals on the walls provide playful touches. The hostess, Talullah, a nereid who lives along the beach, runs out from behind her podium and throws her arm around me in an overly tight hug me.

"Oh, Ada. You're a sight for sore eyes. I wasn't sure if I should call you, but I didn't want to seem like I was sticking my nose in your beeswax," she exclaims. She abruptly releases me and steps back to look me over with probing eyes. "How are you feeling? You look good. But I know that may not mean anything. Well, we were all just so devastated that you and your human friend were attacked by that fae. I would never have fathomed one of those things showing up here. You are so courageous for fighting it off."

Offering a dazed smile, I respond, "Thank you, Tallulah, truly. I'm feeling just fine but I'm still dealing with the loss of my magick. It's been a long week. And those meals you and the team sent over were just wonderful. The last thing I wanted to do was cook, so they were exactly what I needed."

"I'm so glad to hear that. Let us know if you need anything else. I mean it. We care about you," she insists.

"That means a lot, thank you." And it does. Everyone here is so gracious.

"Listen to me rattle on. You're here for a reason. Let me take you to a table," she titters melodiously as she ushers me through the restaurant that's reminiscent of a whimsical picnic in the woods.

She leads me to a table that will be the perfect size for the three of us. I settle into my tall wicker seat and close my eyes for a minute. The chatter of everyone around me, going about their day, calms me in a way I had been craving. Holing up in my house all week, with only a few exceptions, maybe wasn't my brightest idea, but it was the best I could do at that moment. Sometimes grief makes irrational decisions.

"Who do we have here? Why I believe it's sleeping beauty!" Walt's voice proclaims from next to the table. I grin toward the direction it came from and dramatically blink my eyes open.

"My princes are here! I won't lie and say I wasn't close to nodding off," I admit as I stand up and hug them both. "Sleeping almost won out over lunch, so you know I'm exhausted!"

"Let's order you a coffee, then," he frets, looking around for a server.

"I'll be okay but thank you. Do you think you'd want some raspberry chamomile croissants for later? I have extra from this morning." I dangle the pink bag on my finger. He seems hypnotized by it.

"Well, I may take one or two for the road," he answers demurely.

The three of us sit down and a server comes over to fill our water glasses and take our order. We dine here frequently enough that we only need a cursory glance at the menu just to see the specials. The staff remember our preferences, which often comes in handy like when they delivered a few meals to me last week.

Walt leans in close, studying my cardigan. "Is that Estelle's brooch? I remember her wearing it long ago. It looks stunning on you."

I move my fingers across it. "I wanted her close to me today."

"How did it go this morning? Did your old friend take it easy on you?" Walt's expression looks concerned.

"He tried." I sigh loudly. "I was going to cross a mine field regardless. I can still barely breathe a word about it before the waterworks start. I drink calming tonics every day, and they've helped. But seeing my parents and grandparents... or images of them...whatever they were, it's really shaken me up. Made me realize you two are my only living close family. Everyone else is gone."

Walt shakes his head. "Nobody thought badly about you showing emotion. And if they did? That says a lot about them. Grief dulls over time but never fully goes away. No one would ever confuse you with a robot, as vivacious as you are. They certainly don't expect you to act like one now."

Acton's willowy voice chimes in, "Take solace in knowing that their magick, fed into the ward for so many decades, made them your protectors that night. It is their way to take care of now that they are gone." His downy soft moss-covered hand settles gently over mine. Some of the vines that grow along his skin curl lovingly around my fingers.

I brush wetness from my eyes with my other hand. "You're right, I don't know why I'm beating myself up. With Norrell here... Ashes, he saw everything." A wry laugh escapes me. "Mother Earth, I need to catch a break"

Walt looks livid. "He has no right to come back here and hassle you now. He should be ashamed of himself. When you were together, you barely asked anything of him. Hell, you even offered to go with him to that frozen wasteland and stay there as long as he wanted," he argues.

"I wanted to meet his family and see where he lived." I shrug. "Maybe he never took me there on purpose so he could plan his escape from me. What could I do, drive a snowmobile around and hope I run into another yeti to give me directions?"

"Exactly," Walt agrees, his pointer finger stabbing the table in emphasis. "So instead of appreciating all the generosity and compassion you showed him, he saved his worst traits for you. But for me? Acton? Any random person off the street? He'd show up for us in a heartbeat and give his full attention and energy. I remember how it affected you. Your parents never really caught on to that. They loved him like a son so maybe they had blinders on. Maybe we should be glad about that, at least. It would have broken their hearts had they known he was hurting you long before he left."

"I haven't forgotten," I huff. "That's what I get for falling for the mysterious type. Turns out I barely knew him. Intentional or not, he'd commit a huge chunk of time to someone else on almost every special occasion and holiday. There was never an emergency, but he always treated it like it was more important than our time together. I don't think he really wanted to be my mate anyway. It makes sense he didn't try very hard." I try to shrug away the heartache.

"What is going on at the house? I know you didn't want to make waves with that group, but someone should have stepped in and made him switch," he asserts, sounding upset on my behalf.

With my elbows on the table, I put my head in my hands and groan. "He was trying to be helpful last night. I guess I'm finally getting that infamous special treatment now that I'm not his mate. Regardless, I don't trust it. He tried to talk to me, but I shut him down. Hopefully he'll be gone in a week or so and life can return to relative normalcy."

Our server returns with our meals, and we delight in how delicious everything looks. My crispy chicken salad is hearty, with juicy chicken that's indeed quite crispy. I needed something a little healthier to balance out the two croissants I ate earlier. Walt seems to be enjoying his vegetarian curry dish. Acton delicately sips from a bowl of flower nectar with colorful petals floating on the surface. Walt leans into him and uses his thumb to rub a stray drop off his mossy lips.

"Thank you, my bluebell," Acton trills. Walt's striking blue eyes sparkle at the endearment. Acton closes the distance between them and presses a kiss to his lips. They share a loving look before returning their attention to me.

"Ada, our experience partaking in this meal together would be incomplete without an offer to share. Mayhap you could dip your chicken in it?" Acton asks, holding out the bowl to me and giving me his version of puppy eyes.

I bark a loud laugh in surprise. Acton hasn't made a plant food joke in a while. It sends a bubble of warmth through me, reminding me of happier times.

"Almost as good as honey mustard sauce, I imagine," I quip. Walt squeezes his mate's shoulder affectionately.

After a few more bites of food, Walt's face grows serious again. "Did he bother you during the interview?"

"No, other than bringing me these." I gesture toward the bag. "Something puzzled me, though. When I described the fae, I happened to glance in his direction and he looked thunderous, like he could have gone on a rampage in the room. I had never seen that expression on him before. I don't know what to think about it."

Walt looks dubious. "He's had a long stretch of years to reflect on his behavior toward you. He probably feels guilty as hell. Or he's looking for a way out with a current mate," he theorizes, rolling his eyes.

"Could you even imagine?" I guffaw. "Don't worry. I learned my lesson the first time with that good-for-nothing male. I'll never settle for being second place again."

We split up after lunch. Walt and Acton head to the gardening store in search of their next breakthrough in Acton's landscaping project. Before they left, Walt took pity on me and relieved me of the pink bag, making me breathe a little easier. I couldn't even finish my salad, so I'm bringing half of it home with me.

My feet walk me in the direction of Mayweather Potions and Panacea out of instinct. It's my second home, after all. But what will I do while I'm there? Sunny has it well in hand. She's been so kind to contribute more of her magick to me and the shop than she should. When she visited me last week, she even went around the house to top up any charms and enchantments she noticed might be running low. I also had her check the fountain. That task has been ingrained in me since childhood. Just the thought of leaves falling into it fills me with dread. But it isn't fair to her to overcompensate because I'm now lacking. I plan on tallying that extra work and pay her accordingly along with her weekly wage. For as many weeks as I must.

The door chimes in its familiar fashion as I open it. Sunny's glowing caramel-complected face lights up when she sees me. "Ada! You're back! Let me show you what I'm working on."

She takes my hand and tugs me toward our workstation where we concoct potions, which have a range of consistencies depending on the use. "One of the London covens is doing incredibly advanced work with cosmetics. They've inspired some fresh ideas that I've wanted to try out. My friends and I are having so much fun with it," she gushes. Her hair looks particularly glamorous today with long flowing curls in a shimmering purple tone, resembling tinsel. Usually it's straight and dark, pulled back in a high ponytail while she's working.

Gesturing to her hair, I ask, "Is this your handiwork? It's gorgeous."

"Yes!" she replies in an energetic burst. "I developed so many shades. Even some balayage options. They turned out even better than I hoped. Would you mind if I sell them here?"

"Of course not," I assure her. "Everyone will go crazy for them. Keep track of the amount we sell, and I'll add that to your paycheck. Keep creating new items and we'll add them to the shelves."

"Thank you! I have so many ideas!" she squeals.

Sunny's magick has always shown exceptional artistry. Her spell-weaving creates unusually compelling results. She's taken over most of the shape-changing and aesthetic work in the shop. She possesses an innate talent for it I could never replicate. While we already sell items that change hair color, they are not nearly as complex as hers based on the example she's currently wearing. It seems like she found a passion project, and I'm more than happy to support her.

Since I'm here, I tackle some work that doesn't require magick. After checking over inventory, I finish the shift scheduling for the next few weeks. Luckily, no one is taking any time off until Yule. Grasping the nettle, I mark myself down for my normal working hours. It'll force me back to reality, and I'll always hold myself accountable to my staff. Though I may be cursing my current self in the future.

Some young coven members come in, striking up a conversation with me and Sunny. "Did you feel those ward disturbances last night? It doesn't make sense. Like someone was poking at it," mentions Cash, a male close to Sunny's age. I didn't know since I can't feel the town's ward any longer. It's like a light buzz of awareness if something crosses it that shouldn't. It grows stronger if the ward doesn't expel it soon enough.

"Yes! It woke me up," she grumbles.

"A bunch of us checked out the spot right afterward. It didn't look like anyone had been there," Reed, a friend of theirs, remarks with a shrug. While I'm glad to hear it was nothing, there's something unsettling about our ward being set off right now.

During a quiet moment in the shop, I fold myself into a seat in the little lounge full of cozy chairs near the oversized windows at the front of the shop. My eyes roam the long, narrow space with antique dark wood shelves reaching the tall ceiling constructed well over a century ago. The shelves, filled with jars of ingredients, charms, amulets, potions, and much more, look almost as good as new. The rolling ladders attached to the top still slide along their tracks as smoothly as ever. I wonder if I should paint the deep eggplant walls a lighter shade. Maybe my mood is affecting my opinion today, but it feels too dark. A new paint color would fix that. So would new lighting. The old Moroccan lanterns were a later addition to the store. Those might need to go.

"I'm being ridiculous," I mutter quietly to myself after daydreaming even more updates. If I'm not careful, I'll gut the place without realizing it. I need to curb this line of thought for now. But I'll revisit it later. I shouldn't be afraid of change. I can't wallow in the past any longer. If I want to do something, I'll do it. No one can hold me back except myself, even if my magick is never restored.

Getting up from the chair, I light a fresh stick of incense, one of our customer favorites. It has calming properties that soothe without causing sleepiness. We offer a few scents, but orange blossom is my favorite. It smells exactly like a freshly bloomed flower on the tree.

After making a few calls and setting up vendor payments, most of my tasks are finished. An hour, then another, passes by quickly, always a pleasant surprise when working. When there's not much else for me to do that doesn't involve magick, I wave goodbye to Sunny and begin my stroll toward town hall where I parked my Wagoneer this morning.

As soon as I step onto the sidewalk, the hair rises on the back of my neck, that telltale sign of unease. My head twists around, but nothing looks unusual. It might be paranoia; it's hard to tell. Still, the feeling sticks with me as I reach the next block. Other pedestrians pass by on the sidewalk, none the wiser to this nagging feeling that something isn't right. Am I being followed? My steps pick up speed, propelling me until I'm nearly jogging. My breath is loud in my ears at the effort and my heart pounds uncomfortably against my chest. If I can just get to town hall, I'll be safe. There's a crunch on the pavement behind me and I yelp in fear, lunging forward to cross the street to its front plaza. I'm so close. I just need to sprint to the door...

The breath whooshes out of me as something hooks me around the waist, hauling me backward. A deep growl emanates from behind me as an automobile speeds by scarily fast down the sleepy street. The vicious sound fires up my instinct to fight with all my strength. "No!" I screech, alarmed by the dangers both in front of and behind me. I struggle against the tight hold, jerking my body to break free. I survived the fae once, I'll do it again!

"Ada!" My name breaks through the haze, but I can't stop thrashing against the restraint. "Ada! Stop! You will hurt yourself," the roaring but flustered voice vibrates through my body, calming me enough to regain control of myself. The blind panic bleeds away and my struggle slows against the loosening band around my middle.

I force myself turn around and face the thing that's been watching me, chasing me down the street, and scaring me half to death. *Unbelievable*. Norrell's frowning mug peers down at me, only inches away. Reflexively, I shove hard against his chest. Though my strength is no match for his, he moves back to put some space between us.

"You scared me half to death!" My voice chokes. "Are you here to finish what the fae started?" I can't seem to catch my breath.

"Of course not!" he bursts out, looking horrified. "I wanted to make sure you were okay, but you started running down the street not paying attention to traffic."

I shake my head in disbelief while staring daggers at him. "Fire burn it to ashes, Norrell. I'm *fine*. Leave me alone!" My chest is still tight with fear. He's the whole reason why I was running. He can't turn this around on me.

"You did not look fine this morning. And you still do not," he replies, a thread of concern laced in his voice.

"And I wonder why," I seethe, emphasizing each word. "It'd be just peachy if you'd *kindly* stay out of my way for the remainder of your time here." I twirl around and cross the street, this time looking both ways to make sure it's clear.

"Ada, wait! There is something I must say," he calls out from the spot where I left him. With ample space between us, I'm feeling a little more generous toward him.

"Fine. Spit it out," I demand, crossing my arms over my chest.

"You will have your magick back, if it is the last thing I do. I know you do not trust me, but believe that if nothing else," he portends, his voice jagged but earnest.

"Whatever lets you sleep at night," I sneer, my voice like acid. I expel a long, rankled breath. His presence is so exhausting. I don't believe a word of it, but he can go on pretending he'll be the hero of my story, all noble and full of righteous anger. Maybe it will keep him busy and out of my way.

His icy blue gaze bores into mine a few moments longer before he finally turns on his heel, departing in the opposite direction. I'm still frozen in place, watching him as he goes. The ghost of his arm lingers around my waist. His hold was brusque and efficient. But it still stirs a glimmer within me that's incredibly uncomfortable to ponder. I try to shake it off as I finally tear my eyes away from his retreating form and angrily stomp the rest of the way to my automobile.

When I get home, all is peaceful and quiet. Moon and stars it's a relief to have the house to myself right now. There's no sign Norrell followed me again. The rest of my guests are still at their meetings and they're on their own for dinner later. I head upstairs to change and put away my mom's brooch. Before I return it to its box, I run my thumb over it and then impulsively bring it to my lips. Wearing it brought me closer to her today. Reluctantly, I set it in its box and close the dresser drawer where I keep it.

I slip on a pair of linen pants and a fitted cotton shirt and head downstairs. I haven't set foot in the workshop since Samhain, but I find myself drawn to it right now. Opening the door, there are no great surprises behind it. The room is neat and orderly, unlike when it was my mom's. Most of the supplies and equipment here are useless to me now. Maybe I'll ask Sunny if she wants to use it while I can't. Her apartment is on the small side, so she might appreciate making a mess here instead of her kitchen.

Wandering down the hall, I fill the electric kettle for tea and grab my favorite mug. The boys trot in behind me looking for dinner now that I'm home. Vanny paws at my leg as I lean against the counter, trying to hurry me along. Earl Grey sits in front of his empty bowl and stares at me with unblinking eyes.

"I know what I'm good for," I quip as I raise an eyebrow at them. Still, I obey their command and pull two cans of food from the cabinet. They meow demandingly as I walk over to fill their bowls. I'm instantly forgotten as they gobble down their meal.

The kettle is done and I pour water over the tea bag in my mug. I bring it with me and exit the back door to the garden, plopping down on a patio chair. It's the only time I've had to myself today, without work or incessant questions or well-meaning but overprotective uncles. Now that I'm alone, there's nothing to distract me from so many lingering painful memories that busyness keeps at bay.

Everything that felt alive in my house, that connected me to my parents, is now just switched off. Mayhap that's why I wore the broach today. There's no enchantment in it. It was simply a pretty piece of jewelry my mom loved. I do too. The whisper of their magick still drifting around the house, and even the shop, is lost to me. The family manor is now just a drafty old house. Their belongings are just objects collecting dust. Their remaining essence is gone.

If my magick is truly gone for good, I'll sell the shop. The house, too. Maybe I'll finally travel like my mom always encouraged me. There would be nothing holding me back. And I'd be more or less human anyway, so it would be easy to navigate their world. As the last of the family line in town, there's no one left to judge what I do but me.

I'm sure my parents would understand if I left behind everything generations of my family held dear. Mayhap well over two centuries in Monstera Bluff is a good enough run for the Mayweathers, even as its founders. The tears welling in my eyes blur the garden in front of me as my mind weighs this heavy choice. A visit to their graves may help me decide.

Fifteen Years Ago

Branches catch my ritual robe, abrading the fabric as I stumble through the woods. I can't bring myself to care. My parents aren't here to see it anyway, only their remains. They weren't even old yet. Still so full of life with big plans for the future. But death doesn't care about any of that.

My dad was asked to travel to Norway to translate between groups of Whispered Folk in a dispute. There were enough languages involved to make translations complicated. My mom joined him since she had never seen that part of the world. They were looking forward to a long vacation afterward. They traveled via portal to Oslo and then flew to a smaller airport far north in the country to catch a private plane to the meeting site. They never made it. The plane crashed on the way. A mechanical error, the authorities said. Until their remains arrived, I thought it was a mistake. I couldn't believe they were gone.

Somehow, one of the most painful parts for me is that my parents never got to experience those places they had been so excited to visit. It was going to be so special for them. My dad hadn't accepted work like that in a while. This was a rare opportunity. They were supposed to be gone a month. Now they're gone forever.

I trip over a tree root, and Norrell's hand steadies me as my legs move of their own accord. I can't see where I'm going. Tears blind my vision like a mask. He'll guide me if I walk the wrong way. There's a path in the woods, but it was too crowded. I need space. Voices in the distance let me know we're close to the graveyard, hidden in an enchanted copse of pine trees where the coven buries our dead. A new tree is planted above the remains of each witch, and a plaque is attached to its trunk so that the tree grows around it like its frame. There are many generations of witches buried here. Now it's my parents' turn.

Norrell's arm slings around my shoulders as we get close, holding me into his side. He slows our pace as we approach the large crowd already gathered. There must be a thousand people here, not all of them witches. So many friends and acquaintances from town are paying their respects. Norrell guides us to Walt and Acton, who sweep me into an endless embrace. Walt's shirt is wet under my face. I don't know if I'll ever stop crying.

One of the elder witches begins the funeral rites. I stare at the big hole already dug into the ground with two wooden boxes in it. It's hard to pay attention to the rites when this is the last time I'll be this close to my parents. Norrell squeezes my hand, letting me know he's here. It pulls me out of my spiral in time to hear the most important part of the ceremony.

"May the ancestors claim Estelle Mayweather and Whitt Mayweather. And lead them on from step to step through the veil into the quiet and deep everlasting peace of the next realm where they will spend eternity. May we carry their love and wisdom with us until we are reunited again," the witch recites.

A sob wrenches from me as the readings end. Norrell hauls me into his chest, running a hand soothingly over my back. I stay there inconsolable for a time. Eventually, he tries to get my attention.

"Ada, my ember, it is time for the gifts," he murmurs. He gently pulls the items we've brought with us from a bag over his shoulder. We will place them in the grave to bring with them through the veil. That's the sentiment anyway.

"Family is invited to bring their gifts first," the witch requests. Walt, Acton, Norrell, and I step forward first. Each of us lightly toss our gifts into the grave. I brought a bag of my mom's favorite tea and a small bottle of my dad's favorite scotch. Norrell adds cuttings from the garden for my mom and a book on ancient languages for my dad. Extended family members follow behind us, coming from out of town. We greet each other as we pass. It's clear we're all in a daze, still shocked by their untimely deaths.

The witch continues, "Everyone else is now welcome to gift Estelle and Whitt with beloved objects to bring with them into the next realm." Slowly, over the course of the next hour, friends and acquaintances who have joined us to mourn my parents place their offerings inside. A few gifts are elaborate, but most are something simple like a freshly picked flower or a trinket. We then watch as the graves are filled over with dirt, leaving space for planting the tree they'll share. Walt, Acton, and I decided they would like that. The sapling is held steady until its roots are covered and packed down with the remaining dirt. It's elevated by all the gifts left beneath.

After the grave markers are magickally bound to the sapling, the presiding witch hands the four of us watering cans to be the first to offer it nourishment. It's said the tree will grow taller the more deeply the loved one is held in our hearts. Theirs will be as tall as a redwood.

Countless people approach us to give their condolences when the ceremony ends, but I can't manage much more than "thank you" in return. It's hard to talk through tears. I can't even see their faces sometimes. My ability to respond renders to nothing more than silent nods after a while. Finally, Acton uses his serene tone and poetic words to soothe any hurt feelings as we cut off the line forming around us. No one can stay upset at him for long.

The four of us start the long walk back into town from the woods. We remain quiet, each of us lost in our own thoughts. Their deaths are undeniable now. It's not a mix up. They're not still on their far-flung vacation having the time of their lives. Later today, there will be a celebration of life at the beach. Walt and Acton planned most of it for me. They've been so helpful, even though they are deep in their own grief of losing their best friends. Still, I almost dread going to it, even though I wouldn't miss it for the world. There will be nowhere to hide there. I'll have to greet family and friends, acquaintances and strangers. Somehow keep it together while I uphold my role as the last Mayweather in Monstera Bluff, something I never even fathomed. I'm only able to do it with Norrell at my side, as we've waded through this nightmare together.

When we reach my parents' house... my house now... All of us embrace one last time before Norrell and I head inside and Walt and Acton continue walking home.

When the door closes behind us, I collapse into Norrell's arms. He picks me up and I wrap my legs around his waist and bury my face in his neck. He takes us upstairs to my old bedroom and sets me gently on my feet. Crouching, he unties my boots, tapping my foot to get me to lift one and then the other as he carefully pulls them off. He raises the robe over my head and lays it across the back of a chair. He removes his formal dress shirt and jacket as I mutely watch. When he's bare-chested and magnificent, he tugs me close again and just holds me, like his brawny arms can shield me from everything that hurts. We stand there, wordless, until guests start streaming into the house. The din of it stings my ears. Hasn't the world stopped for them too? What is there to say when nothing will ever be the same again?

Voices pass along the other side of the door, with more joining in the chorus as the house fills up. The inn is full and I offered up the extra beds and sofas in this big, now vacant house. Some even brought their own mattresses to sleep on the floor, using their magick to shrink them small enough to fit in their suitcase. I hadn't realized how noise would fill the house even more quickly than the people themselves.

"Can you soundproof the room?" Norrell whispers into my hair. I nod into his chest.

"A quiet room permits no sound so inside tranquil peace is found," I rasp, my throat sore from crying.

He moves us toward the bed, where we lay down together, my head on his shoulder, curled into his side. Unmoving and trying to blank my mind, I stare at him, his face, his neck, his broad chest, as he lightly grazes his hand along my neck and back. Occasionally he lightly runs his blunted claws across my scalp. I don't know how much time passes as we lay there, but it feels like hours.

The spell is only broken when he murmurs, "We should start walking to the beach, my ember."

I want to tell him no, I'm not going. They're not at the beach; they're here in this house where they belong. But instead, I let him help me put the robe back on and guide me there, holding my hand tightly the entire time while I speak with everyone who approaches with their condolences and memories. It feels like a haze I can't shake out of. He takes over when words fail me. He insists we take a break and eat some food and have a drink. I'm fully untethered. I'd float away without him steering me. Without my parents, I've forgotten how to live. How can you relearn when nothing makes sense anymore?

Fifteen years on I could still feel them here, especially in those places they loved most. Their magick lingers almost viscerally. In frustration, I try to summon my magick to touch the ward. I do this every day to the same effect. It's fleeting, like turning a radio dial past a station, only to not be able to find it again. And then that tiniest vestige of magick left in me blinks out. Being separated from it feels like my parents' second death. The cold hard truth of it rings through me. Maybe one day, when even that little spark is gone, I'll be anchorless. I could end up anywhere.

When the sky darkens, I go inside my still empty house. I'm not even hungry for dinner, so sleep will win out over food this time. In the foyer, there's a basket sitting just inside the front door. Confused, I take a closer look. Is it for one of my guests? I'll put it in their room.

Oh, it's a gift basket. A small card attached reads "For Ada" in handwriting I don't recognize. No indication of who sent it. I pick it up and take it upstairs to my bedroom. It can wait until I get ready for bed. As I wash my face and brush my teeth, I mull over who could have sent it. Walt has been buying me gadgets, but he's always brought them over himself to show me how they work. Plus, he'd want to see me open it. He lives for that. Acton would have consulted Walt about gifts, so the same would apply. It could be from Clancy and Madge, but they would at least call me to tell me to expect something. Especially Clancy, since he can't contain his enthusiasm for gift giving. I have several close friends in the coven, especially Thea. But it doesn't seem like it's from any of them. I'm certain I warned off Norrell strongly enough he wouldn't risk it.

Stumped, I leave the en-suite bathroom and stand by my bed to stare at the basket some more. Lifting the products out, I examine each one. There's a silk sleep mask. A pair of plush socks. A high-tech white noise machine. A lavender scented body scrub and lotion. And lastly a heated neck wrap. I look at the card again and notice a discreetly embossed logo on the cardstock of a gift shop in town. I'm acquainted with the owner. She may have sent it. But if so, she'd likely have written more on the card.

This is quite a mystery. I received a lot of gifts of food in the past week, which is always appreciated. A few bouquets of flowers too. But no gift baskets like this. I wish I knew who was responsible, so I could express my gratitude. I don't want them to think I'm being ungrateful. But I suppose it doesn't matter right now. This is exactly what I need tonight.

Plugging in the white noise machine, I click through settings until I find a calming tone. While wearing the neck wrap, I meticulously rub lotion on my arms and legs and then pull on the socks. Once I'm in bed, I turn off my bedside lamp and place the sleep mask over my eyes. The constant ambient sound lulls me into sleepiness. I could have used this last week. Better late than never.

CHAPTER 8

ADA

A ray of sunlight slashes across my face, radiating through a tiny gap in my curtains. I must have pulled the sleep mask off at some point in the night. I turn over in bed, shielding my face, the blinding light too shocking to my slowly awakening senses. Combing away long strands of hair stuck to my cheeks, my fingers locate the mask tangled up in my hair. I slide it the rest of the way off and set it on the nightstand, stretching a little further to turn off the white noise machine. Scrubbing my eyes, orange bursts appear behind my eyelids from my sunshine wake up call. They're dry and scratchy, like grit settled in them overnight. Losing my magick must have given me hay fever. One more reminder of magick's considerable impact on my life and well-being. Sunny restocked seasonal eye drops in the shop last week. I'll have to snag a bottle for myself.

Pans clang in the kitchen loud enough for the sound to reach the bedroom. Someone must be busy down there. That would have woken me up if the sun hadn't done so first. Forcing myself out of bed, I groan as I stretch my stiff limbs, trying to shake off their sleepiness.

Not wanting my guests to see me in my night clothes, I change out of my modest pinstriped pajamas. As a representative of the town, I'd be mortified to be caught in something as messy as a baggy t-shirt or

Mother Earth forbid anything even remotely revealing. Especially by *him*. So, my few pajama sets will be in heavy rotation while the house is full.

As I slip a fitted navy V-neck sweater over my head, there's a knock on my bedroom door. "Yes?" I ask tentatively toward the closed door, as I hastily pull my arms through the sleeves.

"I made breakfast for everyone. Come down if you're hungry," Aurelia intones from the other side, laced with an enthusiasm for the day I don't share.

"Thanks, I'll be down shortly," I answer, my voice imbued with false cheeriness, attempting to match her energy. I choose a white knit blend wide leg trouser from the closet and pull them on. I add a belt that's drawn tighter than usual to hold them up. My lack of appetite must be catching up with me. Not even Aurelia's divine cooking sounds appetizing. That's unusual for me.

I freshen up in my en-suite bathroom, making sure I look put together before heading downstairs for breakfast. As I step into the hallway, a mighty "mrowrrr" sounds from behind me along with an ungraceful gallop of oversized cat paws. I'm unsurprised to see Vanny, such a giant boy, barely swerving around me as he hoofs it downstairs for his morning meal. Maybe I'll give him some of mine when no one is looking.

Aurelia and Niven are in the kitchen, standing next to each other by the stove. She must have recruited him to help. It looks like they have several dishes going at once. Earl Grey and Vanny sit impatiently by their food bowls, their tails whipping around. As usual, they chow down the moment the food hits their bowls. Aurelia comes over and gives them some good scratches, cooing, "Save some room, boys! I made a sausage just for you to share." We both laugh as they start to purr at the mention of sausage.

"What a nice wake up call," I say as I peek at the food. "I'm sure everyone will be coming downstairs any moment. It smells amazing."

"I tried my hand at your dad's biscuit recipe in the book you showed me the other night. I don't have much experience with biscuits, but we'll see how they taste!" she cautions me as she pulls the baking sheet out of the oven and sets it over two potholders on the counter.

"Give yourself more credit! They look exactly as they should. Perfectly golden."

"Aurelia, you're spoiling us," Niven proclaims as he steps toward the stove again, taking a big whiff of the biscuits as he passes.

"I put him on gravy duty. He's pretending he's not a decent cook himself," Aurelia teases.

"I'm much better at eating than cooking," he replies with a wink.

Figuring it's only a matter of time until the aromas wafting from the kitchen lure everyone else downstairs, I quickly set the table. We're still one chair short, but I'll just eat at the counter. Sure enough, heavy steps mingled with the staccato of dainty hoof clopping descend the stairs.

"Grab your plates and serve yourselves!" Aurelia calls out to Tallie, Cyrinda, and Norrell as they shuffle into the kitchen. She spears a sausage out of the pan and sets it aside on a small plate. "Don't want the boys to get burned," she comments to me over her shoulder.

I wait while everyone serves themselves biscuits, gravy, and sausage. There's also a fruit salad on the table. Norrell tries to gesture for me to go first, but I wave him ahead. The coffee pot is drained, so I brew another for the group. I cut up the cats' sausage into tiny pieces and set it on the table so anyone can feed them if they wish. The moment I do, the boys race over and both hop onto Norrell's lap, jostling for position. I seal my lips, so I don't tell them to get down, not wanting to make a scene. The betrayal churning inside me is irrational. I know it comes down to him having a large and very warm lap.

"Are you leading that emergency meeting today?" Tallie asks Niven before shoving a huge bite of biscuit into her mouth and humming her appreciation to Aurelia.

"I am. Until this, we had no reason to believe the warlocks were still nearby. It would not make sense for them to stay so close. We expected them to put as much distance as possible between them and Monstera Bluff before going into hiding. But they're up to something. *Again*," Niven says balefully.

Can they sneak back into town? Are they trying to get revenge on me and Cara? My heart is in my throat. I need some distance from this conversation. I'm glad I'm not at the table. The counter I'm leaning against isn't far enough. I lower my head and focus on my plate so they can't see my reaction. A biscuit, a sausage, a little gravy. That's more than I can stomach right now.

As the others speculate about the warlocks' plans, Norrell offers little pieces of sausage to each cat between his own bites of food. The little turncoats look like they're on cloud nine. It keeps me from enjoying my breakfast.

"What is there to discuss? Go get them and interrogate them like you do. As drawn out and painful as possible. And if you break their minds a little? All the better," Cyrinda fumes, a steely edge to her voice.

"That's the plan," Niven responds, unflappable. "But we'll need to coordinate with the constabulary and send out tracking teams to apprehend them. We don't know exactly where they are yet."

"Can we all join in to kick some warlock ass?" Tallie jumps in gesturing excitedly around the room with her manicured green hand.

"No, not all of us," Niven clarifies, and a look passes between them. He means me. I'm magickless and defenseless. And I wouldn't be interested anyway. The fight with the fae was out of necessity, not choice.

Norrell watches me throughout this exchange, still slowly feeding the cats as they purr and rub their cheeks on him.

"Of course. What was I thinking?" Tallie shakes her head, giving me a sheepish smile.

As I pick at my plate wishing I was invisible, Norrell clears his throat and offers, "Ada, would you like my seat? The cats can move to another spot."

I force out a lukewarm response. "No thanks. I'm done anyway." I walk over to the garbage with my half-eaten plate and slide the food into it. The coffee finally finishes brewing so I fill a mug for myself and then walk around the table for refills. Honestly, coffee is the only thing that sounds palatable right about now.

"This meal is delicious, Aurelia," Norrell compliments her. "I have not had biscuits like this in a very long time."

"Oh, in about fifteen years?" Cyrinda drawls. Norrell looks at her curiously.

Aurelia elbows Cyrinda, who makes a face at her. "I appreciate that. The recipe is from Ada's father," Aurelia explains. Understanding dawns on his face, and he fixes his gaze at me with an unreadable expression. I look away, busying myself with the coffee pot again.

"After this, I'll be making some dessert for the meeting. We aren't needed until later, so I figured I'd bake," Aurelia adds.

"Delightful. We'll dine on cupcakes while we talk about getting the drop on those weaselly little warlocks," Cyrinda snorts.

"I'll get the drop on you, if you don't watch your mouth," Aurelia warns her, pinching her arm playfully. Cyrinda smirks back at her.

"This seems unimportant in light of everything, but did any of you give me that gift basket that was downstairs last night?" I wonder, eyeing everyone sitting around the kitchen table.

No one knows anything about it. When I narrow my eyes at Norrell, he shrugs and blinks up at me completely unruffled.

"You don't know who sent it?" Niven's eyebrows raise in question.

"Not yet," I answer, still dubious that no one claims responsibility.

An hour later, I stand inside the homey little gift shop, hands on my hips. Unsurprisingly, I spot a few of the gift basket items sitting on neat white shelves. The tinkling piano music playing on the speakers grates my nerves during this frustrating interaction.

"What do you mean you were asked not to tell anyone?" I say a little indignantly to the cashier at the gift shop. With no leads on the mysterious gift giver, I arrived as soon as it opened.

"We know our customers like to surprise their loved ones, so we abide by their wishes," she answers primly like that explains anything.

I fight the reflex to roll my eyes. I don't want to have to play this card, but I am fit to be tied, and she leaves me no choice. "As you may have heard, I was attacked recently by a fae. Mysterious gift giving is not exactly welcome right now. I recommend you tell me who it was or I'll have to take this matter to the constabulary."

It's such a waspish threat, but Mother Earth needs to grant this female some common sense.

She blanches, finally understanding her blunder. "Of course. I'm not sure about his name, but he was tall with light blue skin and white hair with a voice as deep as the ocean."

She says that last part a little too appreciatively.

I grumble out loud in frustration. Apparently, I wasn't clear enough with that pompous jerk yesterday and he lied to me to boot. Just shows I still can't trust him as far as I can throw him.

"Much appreciated," I reply curtly before marching out of the store.

The gift basket with all its contents sits obnoxiously in the passenger seat of my Wagoneer. I brought it with me after some doubt about it sprung up in my mind this morning. Now I want it out of my sight. Cara could make use of it. She will enjoy these items meant for relaxation. That ship has now sailed for me. After I drive to her place and drop it on her front porch, I send her a quick text letting her know the details about it. She'll be more than happy to take it off my hands.

I've felt achy and exhausted since I woke up this morning. Nights of poor sleep are catching up with me. More caffeine is a must, so my next stop is Midnight Mystic for a monster-sized coffee, pun intended. The large twenty-four-hour café is an unofficial social center. Tables fitting every size of Whispered Folk fill the space. Artwork on its walls changes regularly to showcase local artists. When I step inside, my friend Thea waves me over to her table with Zinnia, another good friend from the coven, and Selene, a shifter in the local wolf pack.

"I just happened to come in here during my break and ran into these two. And now you're here? What a treat! Come sit down!" she exclaims.

"Absolutely! I'll be over after I order my coffee," I respond, unable to delay my caffeine fix any longer.

When I have a very tall paper cup of coffee in hand, I sit with my friends, chatting about nothing serious. It feels blissfully normal. When Thea announces she's needed back at the clinic, I let them know I'm heading to my shop. We say our goodbyes and Thea and I walk outside together.

Her gaze narrows at me, making me a little self-conscious. "How are you feeling? Not to sound like a cliched healer, but you look a little peaked today," she observes.

I sigh. "I'm just worn down. Not much of an appetite. I'm ready to have my house back to myself, and it's only been a couple days."

She gives me the side-eye. "Kick that undeserving male out from under your roof. Healer's orders. I'll even write you a note."

"Maybe there's a potion I can take to repel exes?" I joke.

"If I could make that, I'd have a vacation home in every continent," she chuckles.

She walks me the rest of the way to my shop, then continues toward the clinic. During my shift, I spend the day alternating between helping customers and ordering inventory from our suppliers, mostly Whispered Folk, but some human as well. A few customers were uncomfortably nosy about my situation. Before I even had a chance to clap back with a *bless your heart*, Sunny was on hand to nip that in the bud right quick, calling me back to the workshop area for some urgent reason or another she made up on the spot. Luckily, it worked like a charm.

After work, I drive back to Ben and Cara's. They invited me and Clancy over for dinner. It's a welcome reprieve from hanging around the house. As I step out of my automobile, the clopping of heavy hooves announces Clancy's presence just as he rounds the corner. He waves enthusiastically and trots a little faster.

"Stars above, it's good to see a friendly face," he greets me while leaning his torso forward to give me a hug. "I've been fending off every variation of 'where are the warlocks?' and 'is that fae going to break out of its cell or get sprung by its fae buddies?' all day long. I know people are upset, but it's exhausting fielding questions all day that I don't have answers to. It'll be quiet for a day and then someone gets riled up and the cycle starts over."

"Niven won't keep the fae around longer than necessary," I empathize.

"It'll be a relief to have it gone, one way or another," he remarks darkly.

We walk up to the front door and Cara opens it when we knock. "I've been looking forward to this all week! Come in!" she effuses in high spirits.

Cara appears surprisingly recovered. Her physical injuries from the fae's attack are healed, her pale skin unmarred from the deep cuts she suffered. Her large hazel eyes look clear and untroubled, no sign in them that less than two weeks ago she experienced significant trauma and lost a dangerous amount of blood. Instead, she looks refreshed. Her outfit, a light pink pointelle knit dress, fits her beautifully, emphasizing her curvy figure that's looking even more buxom than when she first arrived. Her dark brown wavy hair is piled on top of her head. She looks at ease in Ben's house where she permanently moved after the fire. I really enjoyed having her live on the property with me. But I couldn't be happier that she and Ben are embarking on a new life together.

"The star jasmine growing on the ironwork really does look beautiful. And the fragrance! Lovely," I say to Cara.

"It was all Ben's idea. Luckily, I made some good memories on Samhain. That was one of them," she says wistfully. I pull her in for a hug. It was a good night until the end.

The rest of us settle into the living room while Cara opens a bottle of wine in the kitchen. Ben has a record playing, some old human musician who they both like. He shifts forward a large, reinforced bench designed for Clancy from a cleared corner of the room. Ben built it when he moved into this house after his grandparents passed away. Clancy lowers the back of his equine body onto the bespoke bench with practiced ease. I tuck my legs under me on a plush, oversized chair and get comfortable.

Cara comes back with glasses of wine on a tray, passing them around. With her own glass in hand, she sits on the sofa with Ben, who wraps his tail affectionately around her ankle.

"So, is that big blue son-of-a-bitch overstaying his welcome at your house? I told him to keep away from you. Let me know if he breaks his promise to me and Madge about not bothering you. I'll tell Bran at the inn to clean out a maintenance closet. He can sleep standing up." Clancy doesn't pull any punches.

"He seems to think he is now my knight in shining armor. It really puts a burr in my saddle!" Clancy guffaws at my pun. "He gave me pastries and a gift basket yesterday. Nothing too extravagant. But I don't want anything from him. Cara graciously took the gift basket off my hands."

"It was nice stuff. I don't mind wasting that guy's money," she quips. "Walt had said at our lunch the other day that you could try to date again. Maybe if he saw proof you've moved on, it would help get him off your back?"

"It's hard to say. I certainly don't pretend to know what motivates Norrell. Plus, no one in town really interests me in that way. I'm forty-two already. I know I'm not old, but I'm certainly not a young witchling with hearts in my eyes. I doubt I'll ever find another male who would make me want to try," I admit.

"I date plenty, so no one would bat an eye if you're seen on my arm," Clancy chimes in. "I will sacrifice my allergy to commitment and fake date you for however long you need. Just think about it. We could have fun going out as friends, but with the right amount of carefully orchestrated public displays of affection we could easily sell it."

I giggle at his enthusiasm. "We can't ruin your reputation as a Casanova with the females in town. Ashes, I should have asked Niven when he got here. We get along so well it could have been convincing. But the idea is not worth getting a bee in your bonnet about. The ruse would require too much duplicity to keep going. More than I care to engage in when we have so much else to worry about right now. Norrell is not worth the effort. Plus, I wouldn't want to embarrass Niven if anyone else noticed."

"No, that male is far too busy leading the investigation to be courting anyone while he's here. Though I guess you could stage him sneaking out of your bedroom so *Jack Frost* sees him. Niven would certainly agree to that," Clancy jokes, no doubt delighting in the notion of sticking it to Norrell.

"I'm not sure I want to add to the tension at the house." I sigh loudly. "You want to know one of the worst parts about having him under my roof? My cats adore him. They treat me like a stranger nowadays unless it's mealtime. I guess I'm not good enough company anymore," I intone sarcastically.

Ben replies matter-of-factly, "Cats are not known as human or Whispered Folk's best friend for a reason. A dog wouldn't do that to you."

"It's true. I set myself up for this. I should mention, it's not *just* Norrell. They have lit up like never before since everyone arrived. They started scratching at bedroom doors at night wanting to sleep in the guest rooms. But it's so infuriating that Norrell is their favorite. Aurelia made them sausage this morning, but they still went straight to Norrell. Those traitors constantly weave around his legs or jump on his lap when the opportunity presents itself. Too bad that even if I had my magick, I couldn't tell them he's not the prize they seem to believe he is. That he'll leave the moment things get tough," I gripe, hurt threatening to spill over as tears.

"Those little dinguses are choosing him over you? They need to remember the hand that feeds them." Clancy snorts in disbelief.

"Oh, the little princes don't care. They will do as they please," I say, not without a little resentment.

"Forgive me, Ada. I don't remember the names of your cats. I only ever saw them in passing. And then with everything that happened…" Her voice trails off.

"The boys are Earl Grey and Vanny, short for Vanilla Paws," I answer.

Cara's eyes light up. "You named them Earl Grey and Vanilla Paws?" She scrunches her hands to her heart. "Those sound like the names of cute internet cats!"

"Hon, you really think I don't watch cute cat videos like everyone else?" I tease.

"I wasn't sure if you'd get sucked into them like humans do. I don't know!" She throws her hands up and laughs.

"When the safety council disperses and I get my house back to myself, I will have you over to meet them properly. If you're okay with coming to the house, that is. I don't want you to do anything that will make you uncomfortable."

"I appreciate that. With the carriage house gone, I think I'll be fine. I can't let my fear get the better of me," she says, squeezing Ben's hand and giving him a tentative smile. He leans in to kiss the top of her head.

"Despite everything, I miss that carriage house. Some days I walk outside and I'm surprised by that big empty space," I say, grief clawing my chest.

"Do you know if you're going to rebuild? Come by my office and I'll help you draw up plans for a new carriage house or guest house when you're ready. No charge, just helping a friend," Ben offers. His company, Guardian Construction, has expertise in all types of construction projects.

"Thanks. I haven't decided yet. Barely had time to think at all, to be honest. But I appreciate it," I tell him with a melancholy smile.

"Are the guests asking too much of you? Can we take care of anything for you while they are here?" Ben asks, sounding concerned.

"No, it's been alright aside from Norrell. They don't need much of anything. They're all so busy anyway, I hardly see them. I'm trying to spend more time at the shop, get everything squared away while I'm... blocked. But I think I have everything handled at home too. I raked the leaves and debris in my yard by hand the other day, a good arm workout so I've discovered," I say, trying to lighten the mood.

"Oh, I just started a raised bed garden in the backyard, and I can't believe how many muscles it works that I didn't know I had. I cheated just a pinch and used some magick fertilizer, so the vegetables grow out of season. It's early in the process, they're still sprouting, but I've loved it so far. Tending to the garden is so relaxing. Very zen for me. Once we have our first harvest, I'll bring some over!" Cara gushes.

"I think it's been helpful during your recovery, my belle," Ben remarks, his eyes searching Cara's.

"Yeah, it really has," she agrees, her eyes turning bright.

As the night progresses, everyone solicits little ways to help me. They are so wonderful, and I'm honored to have such good friends. But I'm still left betwixt and between. So much hinges on my magick. It'll be smart to plan for a life without it regardless. The world is moving on without me, and I shouldn't let myself fall too far behind.

CHAPTER 9
NORRELL

"You can't be serious," Niven challenges into his phone. From the staircase, I cannot hear exactly what he is being told, but the caller sounds agitated. "I'll be right there." My eyebrows rise as I enter the kitchen. Niven seems caught off guard by the call. He smirks to himself, shaking his head as he stares out the glass doors at the back garden.

"Did trouble find you already this morning?" I ask wryly.

"Wouldn't you know, it did. But things just got a lot more interesting," he confirms, his gaze flashing to mine. "Sometimes they surprise me, especially when I haven't even finished my first cup of coffee. Norman Weatherby turned up just now at the gas station outside the wards in a stolen automobile. He claims he's defected from the other warlocks. Wants to turn himself in."

"Sounds like a break in the case," I reply, cautiously optimistic.

"It is even if turns out to be some sort of elaborate setup by the warlocks," he answers. "We can't be too careful until I have him under compulsion. You can block magick, right? That's what you yetis do?"

"Something like that. I sense the source of magick and draw it away from the wielder or the spell they cast," I answer hesitantly.

"And you're good at it?" he questions with a gleam in his eye.

"Very," I confirm, curious where this is heading.

"Excellent. You'll be my backup. I'll finish my coffee and we'll hit the road," Niven says with a broad grin. Like he is anticipating having some fun.

We get into Niven's borrowed automobile to drive to the gas station outside the ward, where members of the Monstera Bluff coven and some of Niven's colleagues wait for us. Security is tight. Travel through the sealed ward is now granted manually, as the enchantments within community members' travel amulets are no longer compatible with it. Witches stationed just within the ward open a section momentarily to grant us passage. We park near the building's front door. There are several other automobiles in the parking lot. It seems like a crowd has already arrived. I am not sure how I will react to seeing one of the perpetrators of this violence against Ada. For his sake, he better hope I keep a level head.

As we step into the disguised building, several witches dressed in uniform eject one by one from the travel portal. Niven greets them along with his team who I saw at Ada's interview. They surround an old, graying, human-looking male with a bloated, ruddy face who sits slouched in a chair, his hands in magickal cuffs behind him. He hardly looks like a threat, but sometimes the most dangerous are skilled at concealing it. My hands feel fidgety, ready to slash his throat if the opportunity arises.

"Well, someone decided to grow a conscience. You were only a few weeks too late to make it meaningful," Niven chides the male, whose hunched posture looks guilt-ridden. "It looks more like you got sick of roughing it."

"I never thought they'd take it so far. The plan was just to get seats on town council. Then everything spiraled." He sounds as pathetic as he looks.

"You're not in a position to inspire any trust in your words, so you're going to submit to my questioning now," Niven commands through clenched teeth. The male has the intelligence to look frightened. Though as soon as that expression crosses his face, it slackens as Niven's compulsion takes hold.

"Where are Dalton Atticus and Ralston Samuels?" Niven asks, not wasting any time.

Empty of expression, the male answers, "When I fled, they were staying in an abandoned fishing shack only a few miles down the coast. They seek out weaknesses in the ward every day."

Niven's brows knit in anger, though his hold on the warlock's mind does not falter. "What is their plan if they find a weakness?"

"Ralston wants his revenge on everyone who wronged him. Cara, Clancy, Ada, the rest of town council. They're trying to summon a Malefic to help them through and exact their revenge. They're practicing invisibility spells to help them go undetected while they ambush their perceived enemies. They brought a collection of their enchanted weapons with them," the warlock responds ominously.

Weapons? This sounds like they have been planning something for a while, way before the human female showed up. "Then what will they do?" Niven presses.

"Try to leave the town in ruins. And then they'll go somewhere they can take over a human's land, use their magick to get anything they want. Everything they deserved from this town." The warlock's lifeless words send a chill down my spine.

"Did any of you tell the fae to target Ada's magick?" He pushes the warlock even further, based on the beads of sweat now collecting on the male's ugly face.

"No, Ralston told it to dispose of Cara and anyone who got in its way. Spare no one," he confesses.

After several more questions trying to get a better idea where the two remaining warlocks are holed up, Niven releases Norman Weatherby from his mind control.

"I want to apologize to Ada and Cara. Could I tell them before I go?" the warlock begs. The nerve of this insufferable male. Even I can tell he is not that sorry. Ada is staying protected and safe behind the ward. Niven scoffs, making it evident he agrees.

He levels a look of indignation toward the idiotic warlock. Gesturing at the guards, he bites out, "Take him away. Put him in solitary until I have time to question him further." As the guards pull the warlock to his feet, Niven turns to me. "Can you drain his magick so he can't put up a fight? I want him nice and docile for my friends at the prison."

"Gladly," I confirm. It takes little concentration to find his source of magick where it concentrates deep in his chest. I do not see it so much as feel it when I use my abilities, like I become a magnet that attracts magick. I pull it from him slowly at first, and then in one big tug. The warlock's body spasms as I do so. When the last of it is gone, he gasps for air as he crumples, though he is caught by the guards' firm grip on his arms before hitting the floor. Unwilling to display any more of my abilities to the group, I let it dissipate into the wild magick that flows naturally in the atmosphere.

As the contingent that just arrived from New York shuffle the warlock through the travel portal, one of Niven's assistants sniffs derisively in their direction. "They've really joined the dark side."

The other one barks a mirthless laugh. "No Whispered Folk community will let them in. They've basically turned into Malefic themselves."

Once they have gone, Niven lets out a long sigh and scrubs his hands up and down his face. "That was too easy. The male barely put up a mental fight. He was so weak-minded. No wonder he was so easily swayed by them. He can barely think for himself."

"Those plans sound dangerous. We must treat them like a serious threat," I warn him, anger toward the warlocks seeping into my words.

"We are. Those warlocks can't stoop too low. I don't want to give them any opportunity to deal more damage to the town or to Ada," he assures me. He pulls out his phone, and after a motion asking me to hold on for a moment, turns away from me. "He's just through the portal. We need eyes on the nearby rivers and the edges of the ward for the other two. Abandoned fishing shack about three or four miles south. Bring in the flyers."

I huff a laugh at the description. They must be a special team of winged Whispered Folk.

"Apologies, just wanted to get the ball rolling on this search. They'll be through the portal within the hour," Niven explains. "Why don't I drop you back at Ada's before I head to the constabulary to fill them in. We need to be ready for any possibility."

As we get into the automobile, he pauses before starting it. "So it's really that easy. You just took his magick?" He shakes his head in disbelief. "It's rumored your people are capable of it, but *ashes,* who could have known it was so effortless. It looked like you knocked the wind out of him without lifting a finger."

I nod. "I am one of the most skilled in my clan, mayhap among all the yetis as well. His magick was not particularly complicated, nor was he trying to defend himself. But, yes, it is easy as you say. And I did not take his magick, just released it."

"But you *can* take it?" he detects astutely.

I grunt in the affirmative. "I do not absorb it myself or gain anything from it. But it is harnessable in other ways."

"You store it somehow, I'm assuming? It makes more sense now that your clan chose to live in that frozen tundra where the Malefic like to go," he observes.

I hold out my wrist, where a leather tie with several clear quartz beads wraps around it. He hums in understanding.

"The Malefic amass deep wells of magick even while approaching the North Pole where it is so highly concentrated. Clear quartz absorbs it well when we draw from them. It holds an immense amount of magick and remains stable, more so than other materials. It is also easy to procure," I reply, carefully choosing my words.

"I wonder if the fae is doing something similar to Ada. Continually draining her magick. But what for? Does it feed its own?" His voice is not accusing, just contemplative. It mirrors my own thoughts when I learned what happened to her. His dark green eyes narrow at me. "What does your clan do with all that magick it acquires from the Malefic?"

I consider how to explain our use of it. We do not share this information with outsiders, but now is the time to start. The elders say Whispered Folk would seek to take it away from us if they knew the extent of it, that we could be perceived as a threat to magick wielders. Truthfully, they do not want to have to share their vast stores of magickal energy. That is why they insist we keep it secret.

"We use their concentrated magick as an energy source. It transformed our entire community when we made this discovery. Our people figured out how to create a sort of electrical grid from it. We transfer small amounts of that magick into anything electrical or electronic, and it supplies the energy needed to power those. We created artificial suns to grow food. It powers lights, appliances, and computers. Anything that uses electricity. It works especially well with rechargeable batteries. And once we transfer a small amount of that concentrated magick to them, those devices will continue to absorb more from our vast stores of magickal energy on their own. Our current supply is so immense that it will last us centuries, even if we never hunt a Malefic again."

Niven is speechless for a while. He wipes his hands along the sides of his face like he is in shock. "Ashes, your people have figured out how to move it through conductive materials. You created a new renewable resource. That's fascinating. I wouldn't have thought that was possible. I would love to see how that works someday." After studying me for a moment, he asks, "Would you be willing to assist me when we interrogate the fae? My team and I have been working out the safest way to do so. I think you're our best bet. And I wouldn't mind seeing how you store its magick. No spell needed, just moving magick around. That's extraordinary. I wonder if I could even detect it in such a concentrated form."

My head tilts as I ponder his request. I do not relish putting on a show for him. But getting close to that fae gives me the best chance to help Ada. Plus, I may be granted the undeniable pleasure of ending the vile creature. "Alright. I will help," I tell him.

"Thank you. It means a lot you'd help the team like this. Even in confinement, we want to take every precaution. We worry about defending ourselves against one of its spells even in its weakened state."

"It will never cast a spell again. That fae is no match for me," I reply.

His eyes widen in surprise. "Alright, well, this day just keeps looking up."

When I return to Ada's, I call my brother Elgar who is acting as clan leader while I am away. "How goes these last few days with the clan, brother?" I greet him.

"No surprise, the elders are still unhappy. But what else is new?" he responds, chuckling, knowing well how frustrating they can be.

"Have they reached out to the other clans to ask about any knowledge of a fae spell that steals magick? Any old stories they might know from their clan history?" I ask.

Before I left, I requested they do this as soon as possible to help figure out what the fae may have done to Ada. I have not yet received an update from them.

"Not to my knowledge, but I would not be surprised if they simply are not telling me. They have been cagier than usual these last few days," he admits.

"They have been acting that way for some time now. But ignoring a direct request? I am the leader of the clan. This was not a suggestion," I grouse, frustrated by their inaction.

"I will do everything I can to push them. In the meantime, focus on helping your mate as best you can from there. I will call you as soon as I know anything," he allays.

I thank him for his help before we hang up. Their negligence leaves a bad taste in my mouth. I try calling my uncle and then my cousin. Neither answer. I send both a quick text reiterating my request. Something tells me I am being ignored.

To take my mind off the stress of my clan, I explore Ada's house to take note of what needs to be done. Towels and sheets fill the hampers in the guest bathrooms. Her linen closets are stocked so everyone can replace them as needed. No one has taken the initiative to run a load of laundry, I noticed earlier, even though we have been living in her home for over a week at this point. I fill the washing machine with dirty towels to start the load in her small second story laundry room. A second basket will be thrown in after this first one is done.

The others have been cooking or fending for themselves for meals. But they have been remiss in fully cleaning up after themselves. Dishes pile up next to the sink from the breakfast Aurelia made this morning. I unload the dishwasher and reload it with the dirty dishes. I handwash pans and wooden utensils that seem like they need it. It all takes less than twenty minutes, which makes me even more annoyed at my fellow guests' laziness.

The cats wind around my feet while I wipe the counters, perhaps looking for scraps. "You did not get any sausage this morning?" I ask them, dubious.

Earl Grey meows a response I do not understand.

"Alright, little ones." I grunt as I bend over and pick them up, one in each arm. "Where does your keeper store your belongings? You two look like you could use a brushing." Their coats are short but lush. I have no doubt Ada goes to great lengths to keep them healthy.

Walking around the empty house, I look in corners and shelves for any hint where their supplies could be. I remember a junk drawer of sorts in a credenza that her parents kept in their living room. Ada retrieved items from it countless times all those years ago. It is still there I believe.

Upon opening the drawer after setting down the cats on the nearest sofa, I spot the brush right away, sitting on the edge of the drawer marking its frequent use. I take it and sit down with the cats on the sofa. They take turns walking over my lap, curling their tails into question marks as they do. When the first swipe of the brush slides across Vanny's back, a fur clump immediately shoots over to the corner. Ah, one of those dust collector charms the witches create. No wonder this house looks so clean. I continue brushing both, alternating between cats as they both seem to enjoy it immensely, and the fur hurls itself to that corner, keeping it off me and the sofa.

Once the cats' coats shine, I scratch their cheeks and rub along the bridge of their noses until they decide they no longer want attention from me. They chase each other out of the room and gallop up the curved staircase in the foyer.

Delicate footsteps on the sidewalk shift my attention away from the cats. Those light, protracted footfalls are unmistakable. My ember is tall for a female witch and her legs are long. The quiet open-and-shut of the door is characteristic as well. To less attuned ears, she would be nearly silent. Her physicality is graceful and poised in a way that I always found ethereal. Though her good humor and kindness ground her to this earth.

She startles, her hand flying to her chest, when she notices me sitting in the living room. "For being so big, you are unusually quiet." She exhales. "Is anyone else here?"

"The boys were in here with me until a minute ago," I answer calmly. "No one else is in the house."

She eyes the brush sitting next to me on the sofa. "They let you brush them?" The question sounds like an indictment of my character.

"They did. Both seemed to enjoy it. Vanny was purring," I recount.

Ada shakes her head in disbelief. "At least someone is glad you're here." She starts to leave, but pauses, saying through gritted teeth, "You can't waltz in here and act like everything's peachy. I don't like you. I don't want anything from you. Don't buy me anything else. I know you lied to me the other day about the gift basket. I'm done with your lies. And with you." Her expression is cold at first before turning dispirited.

When I nod my understanding, her head dips slightly and then she turns to walk away.

"Ada," I call out. She stops and looks back at me with tired eyes. "I am sorry I did not tell you."

"You never told me much of anything." She purses her lips. "I'm still not clear why you're here. But if you think I will forgive you and get back together, you are sorely mistaken. I'm not dumb enough to make that mistake twice." She resumes walking up the stairs and disappears into her room.

I pull on my beard, mulling over our interactions since I arrived. It was unwise not to fess up to the gift, but I wanted her to enjoy it unconcerned with who it was from. I will not do that again. I will have to be more considered in my efforts. There is much I can do that is not gift-giving. Chores are not gifts, so I will continue those.

Walking into the salon—or the grand ballroom as Ada liked to call it when I swept and dipped her around the room in our early days here—I continue my assessment of the state of her house. The room is dark, though. Walking over to one of the tall windows, I pull the curtains aside and look out at the porch and her front lawn. The view reminds me of the day I try, and forever fail, to forget. It has haunted me for fifteen years. Pacing across this room, listening to my brother's heavy words, demanding I sacrifice my future with my mate to save the future of my clan. Part of me died that day when I weighed the burden and chose my clan over my mate.

I left my warmth and compassion for them in Monstera Bluff that day too. Right here in this spot, in fact. I will never forgive my uncle's failures that forced me to go back without her.

Fifteen Years Ago

My phone buzzes in my pants pocket. Looking at the screen, my younger brother Elgar's name appears. I walk into the salon and shut the doors as to not disturb Ada, who has been cleaning out her mother's workshop for hours. Though I suspect she is lost in her memories and not getting much done. It is understandable. It has only been a few months since her parents' deaths. Each day is still filled with grief. Answering my phone, I greet, "Hello, brother. How goes the day?"

"Not well. I have no easy way to say this, but Uncle Harlok was gravely injured. He will have to step down as the Huntmaster," Elgar begins, sounding weary.

"Will he live?" My voice is thick, shocked by the news.

"It is likely, though he will be physically impaired when he wakes up. He may never walk again," he answers. He draws in a long breath before continuing. "It was bound to happen sooner or later. He was too old to hunt in such a small party, but he was too stubborn to listen. That side of our family is all the same. Utterly irresponsible. His party encountered several revenants traveling together, an unusual encounter they were unprepared for. Now he is wounded, in a coma. Our healers say his recovery will take months if not years."

"Was Torman with him?" My voice shakes.

"For better or worse, no. Our cousin rarely hunts now. He dodges all responsibility, and his father looks the other way. Now he is busy trying to take up his father's mantle, making the proclamation that it is his right to govern in his father's absence. But he is still unpopular. The hunters are already deeply divided. Some are refusing to go out at all. They refuse to elect our cousin. And I cannot blame them. But they do not want to give me the job either. They say that I am too young, too untested even though I have led hunts for years. There will be civil unrest until you get back here," he speaks adamantly.

"Fire of the frost! My mate is here. I was already told by Harlok and the elders she would not be welcomed into the community. Elect one of those stubborn hunters then if they think you are not fit for it. I am not returning anytime soon," I say with conviction as I stare out the window. Bright afternoon sun shines on the mess of flowers in front of the house, so different than the harsh Arctic terrain of my home.

"There is no one better suited for the role of Huntmaster of the True North than you. The other hunters will never agree on who among them to elevate. They bicker enough as it is. Distrust is rampant. To ask them to grant one so much power over the rest will cause a riot. The clan will suffer. You are still our best hunter and now one of our most studied in the ways of the Malefic. They will rally under your rule. You may be the one thing they agree upon, other than their dislike of Harlok and Torman," Elgar argues.

"By the bluest glacier, this cannot be the only way. There were plenty of hunters of all ages capable of being Huntmaster when I left," I reply.

"Norrell, you have been gone for three years. Tensions have grown since then. Torman's laziness has drawn the ire of the hunters. Harlok's refusal to bring him into line has caused the hunters to become restless and angry. Most are calling for you by name to return. They looked up to you for so many years. The elders believe it is the only way to bring our clan back together," he disputes me.

"What about Father? Can he take Harlok's place until you are deemed ready?" My desperation is evident. The plan sounds weak even to my ears.

"No, that wild work of frost would go nowhere, believe me. I thought of this and already spoke to Father about it. He is even older than Harlok and has not hunted in many years, as is standard for that age." His voice sounds haggard, full of regret.

"Then I will agree only if I can bring her with," I declare.

"Only the blue hag of winter knows why, but it would sow the seeds of chaos even deeper. You cannot bring a witch here. Mother and Father accept her. I do too. But we are of a very different mind than the rest of the clan. She will only suffer from their prejudice, their aversion to anyone possessing magick. They will be cruel. Do you want her to bear such a life? Be alone in a hostile environment, unsure of her safety the moment your back is turned? Your union with her will end by necessity if you bring her here," he states sadly.

"They would never. As my mate, they would have to show her respect." My voice booms in anger.

"And what of a child? What if your child is a witch and not a yeti? Will you subject your child to such an environment?" he reasons, his voice trailing off to almost nothing. We are both breaking under the weight of these expectations.

"I..." I am at a loss for words. It would take many years, perhaps decades, for their minds to be changed about magick wielders. I could not do that to Ada. Any child we may have. It would not be fair to trap them there.

"I am so sorry, brother. Believe me, I do not want this for you. Your path away from the clan has been forged through your own making and should be honored as such. You should never be asked to give it up. But the future of the North Clan is at stake. Our numbers are so low that we would not survive a rebellion. We would be fighting ourselves while the Malefic Folk grow drunk on power unabated near the True North. It would be the end of everything as we know it." Elgar sounds defeated.

"The elders..." I try to reach for any alternative. "They must have a plan. They could be the ruling body."

"That is not our way. They advise and not always unanimously. We need a leader." The words land like a heavy weight.

"I will be a shell of a male without her. This will cost not just me, but all of us, if I do this." The grim reality sinks in. Any hope for the future dwindling fast.

"It will. We live by bluest reason. There is no other choice. Do what you must. The clan will not be at peace until you come back." His voice sounds as hollow as mine.

My mind races with the possibilities of integrating her into our clan, their bigotry be damned. She could prove to them that magick wielders have a place in our society and that no harm will come to us with connection to outsiders. Ada's heart is kind and pure, surely they will all recognize that and eventually accept her. She would be a good role model to them. Ada would be glad to help me with this. Show them that magick-wielding Whispered Folk are different from the Malefic that we hunt. She could never be mistaken for one. My chest constricts as I consider how long that could take. Harlok, when he recovers, and many other elders would fight every step. Poison the well against her. Years of shunning and browbeating would cure her of those precious qualities.

Dread pools in the pit of my stomach. Even if she did not live here in Monstera Bluff full-time, she could visit whenever she wanted. The journey is long, but if she stayed here for weeks at a time it would not be such a burden. The shop could be managed by someone else. But if we were to ever have a child… How could I justify being absent from them so much of the time? How would the clan react to a child who may very well be a witch? They would treat them horribly, like an outcast, just like their mother.

If I do not bring her to our settlement, how often could I leave and visit here? A few weeks a year at most. Even with an expiration date on my leadership, she would have to wait for me, put her life on hold, be a single parent, for many years until my brother or someone else can step in. Though this scenario might be easiest for her, what kind of mate is gone most of the time?

In that moment, I realize I can never tell her why I must go. She would insist on coming with me, though it would be a prison sentence for her. She would gladly let go of everything in her life to be lonely. Under constant watch, constant threat. I would never trust anyone beyond my immediate family with her. Not even my uncle or cousin. Especially not them. They would eagerly cast her out for the Malefic to find.

I love her too much to trade her happiness for mine. The thought of her facing so much pain—shrinking her life to shield herself from some crusty, old yetis who may have to all die off before she will be treated with any degree of civility—makes me sick. The pain in my chest grows as different scenarios race through my mind. All the ways they would cut her down until there is nothing left. Her innate joy ruined. That light that burns so brightly within her snuffed out. I would not deserve to be her mate if I knowingly put her through that. In truth, I already put her through too much. I never deserved her.

Collapsing into a chair, my head falls into my hands. My clan has put me in an impossible position. It is not fair to me. And it is even worse for Ada. Pain radiates from my chest into my limbs, my head. It is unbearable. But it pushes me into a decision. As soon as I know what must happen, the pain is replaced by a hollowness. Everything that makes life good has been cored out of me with the realization of what I must do.

She will have a happy, full life in this community, a place where she is so deeply loved and admired. Her future children deserve a peaceful, loving life. Her friends and family will continue to lift her up when I leave. Her future is promising if I am not in it. The choice comes down to whether I destroy myself or both of us. The answer feels right now that I have made it. She stays.

With an unwavering resolve, I run upstairs to pack, shoving some clothes, books, and electronics into an oversized duffle bag. I must go now. If I spend another night with her, I will never leave her arms. And then my clan will fall to ruin. I do not know what would happen to my family. What would happen to the world if the Malefic had no barrier to reaching the True North.

I will make this a quick clean break for both our sakes. If I can convince her I am a ruthless, heartless, terrible male, there is a chance she will love again. Move on to someone who would never give up the honor of being loved and cared for by her. I will never move on. Never get over her. Ada will always be my entire world.

Stepping away from the window and the memories of that awful turning point in my life, I consider Elgar's advice to focus on helping my mate while I am still here. I feel compelled to, regardless. The clan has been an afterthought this entire week. It is a relief. Devotion to Ada feels so right, in a way that leading the clan never did. If she only allows me into her orbit for this fleeting moment, I will make sure she is well taken care of.

Wandering toward Ada's workshop, I crack open the door. The memory of her face as I broke the news to her explodes into my mind. Shocked. Crushed. Betrayed. Like her world had truly ended in that instant. Mayhap it felt like it had. It did for me too. But she has thrived here since. I cannot regret that.

Unable to face my shame any longer, I put distance between me and that room, crossing the hallway into the kitchen. It gives me the strength to push past the bad memories. I must focus on the present. Her kitchen is clean already, so I step out of the house to her back garden. It is evident that whatever magick she utilized to control the growth of the grass and landscaping has long since depleted. It has been looking more overgrown by the day.

The walk downtown is swift. The gardening store has much of what I am looking for to manage the lawn. I will start on it at first light tomorrow. It is one less thing to manage when so much else weighs on her shoulders.

When I walk up to the property, carrying my newly acquired tools, I skirt the edge of the house to hide them at the back of the garden. Hopefully, if I work while she is asleep or out of the house, Ada will not observe me out here.

Returning to the house, I wash my hands and head straight to the laundry room. With one load of laundry completely done and now folded and placed in the linen closet and the second in the dryer, I return to my room to read until the laundry buzzer sounds. As always, my mind is on Ada. Pondering all I know of the fae and their powers. There must have been something in the hundreds of old tomes I read, especially those in the academy library. It just is not coming to me yet.

After I fold and put away that second load of laundry, I wander downstairs to see if the cats have been fed their dinner. Ada must still be napping. She has not left her room since we briefly spoke. Their bowls look the same as this morning. I wash them out quickly in the sink, including their water bowl. Ada keeps their food in one of the lower kitchen cabinets, so I squat down and inspect any difference in their cans of food. As if they have a sixth sense, the cats sprint toward me, purring and trying to climb into the cabinet around the short stacks of cans.

"Any preference?" I ask with an amused grin. Two sets of round eyes look up at me. Vanny chirps once and then they both run over and sit in front of their clean bowls, ready to eat. They must not be picky. I grab two cans, pulling off the lids and pour them into the bowls. The cats somehow manage to purr and eat simultaneously, making little vocalizations as they open their mouths to take each new bite. An unbidden laugh escapes me at their enthusiasm. These furry little creatures are growing on me.

CHAPTER 10
ADA

Norrell's broad, pelt-covered back sticks out like a sore blue and white thumb from the view out the kitchen window. He leans over a messy bed of flowers and shrubs at the edge of my garden. Neat piles of pulled up weeds and encroaching grass are spaced out showing he's already worked his way across a good deal of the lawn. The sun rose not that long ago. So either he's the world's fastest gardener or he came out here when it was still dark out. It would have to be the latter, unless he's had practice in someone else's garden. Of course, if he has, that's not my business.

By the look of his progress, that task was long overdue. The irony is that it's something I had often done by hand, a meditative task that blanked my mind from anything else except finding every small and hidden weed looking to invade my herb garden and flower beds. But now with Norrell out there toiling away, all I see is endless chores ahead of me that I can't keep up with since the attack.

Magick makes that back-breaking work so much easier. I command the wind to blow the tiny leaves and acorns fallen from the mighty live oaks into a refuse bag. The grass stops growing after reaching a certain height. Flowers stay in bloom all year round.

But this is *my* house, *my* mess, not his to clean up. It's presumptuous of him to do any of this without even asking me first. As if he has a right to it. And I'm certainly not going to work out there alongside him, as if I approve of his presence here like some twisted portrait of domestic bliss. It's high time to call the inn again to check on their vacancy. The moment a room is available, I'll kindly but firmly tell him it's time to leave. He's already proven I'll be unable to keep the wolf from the door without the ease that magick brings. Ashes, I basically invited the wolf inside along with Norrell. I'll need a small fortune I don't have to hire people or buy enough magickal products to maintain everything. Landscaping, gardening, cleaning... It feels like I'm starting from scratch. But at least my hosting duties will be over soon enough. He'll be out of my house and my life for good. And I can manage these tasks on my own terms. And if I can't, well, maybe that's my sign to move on from here.

The fight in me deflates almost instantly. What would it look like if I lambasted him for pitching in? Only he has the power to turn me into an ungrateful harpy. I don't like that such a side of myself comes out so easily in his presence. Life will be different from now on, and I'll have to figure out new ways of living. But the last person in the world I want support from is him. He'll be gone soon. Until then, I must keep myself in check to show that I'm truly over and done with him. He shouldn't be able to provoke such a big reaction in me.

Using my reflection in the glass as my guide, I comb my fingers through my hair and tighten the belt on my house robe to make myself more presentable. As the days wear on, it's harder to remain so formal in my own home—lacking any privacy beyond my bedroom, always having to look put together despite my worsening bone-deep exhaustion. I'm still in my admittedly conservative pajamas this morning. I was too tired to get fully dressed for the day so early. I had mistakenly assumed sneaking downstairs in the wee hours would allow me some time to myself.

As I open the door and step outside, he cranes his neck to look back at me and then slowly pulls himself up to stand, carefully brushing the dirt off his hands and his brown pants. It's an unusually humid morning for mid-November, the air already making my skin clammy at the brief contact. Sweat beads down his forehead and chest, a sign of his hard work and his incompatibility with the sultry southern climate, though it looks entirely too good on him. It always did. An inconvenient and thoroughly unwanted heat swirls low in my belly, having nothing to do with the weather.

"Um... thank you for weeding the garden. I'm making breakfast, would you care for some?" I ask woodenly, my eyes looking everywhere but at his gaze.

"I would. Thank you, Ada," he answers evenly, watching me intently, patiently. He breathes in, slightly opening his mouth like he's about to say something more but instead leaves the silence dangling between us. It makes me uncomfortable, but I'm unwilling to fill it with meaningless pleasantries.

I jerk a nod and whirl around, stepping back into the kitchen and closing the door with a resounding thud. I cool off instantly in the air conditioning, much needed after any interaction with him. That male gets under my skin entirely too easily. It's impossible to remain aloof around him. Not that I ever could. Never in a million years would I guess that his support would be more unpleasant than his coldness. This good guy act will crumble soon enough, and he'll show himself to be the cruel male I know him to be.

Deciding to take my frustration out on some unsuspecting eggs, I open the fridge and remove a carton, along with links of chicken sausage, which were delivered along with a box of produce by Taurus Farms a couple days earlier. They included a "get well soon" note, which was mighty sweet of them. They're a wonderful operation, supplying almost every restaurant and café in town, not to mention the farmers market. Little did they know their eggs would be cracked and beaten to an inch of their life like some kitchen-oriented rage therapy.

I forcefully break the eggs against a bowl, relishing each crack. Of course, it sends half of a shell flying to the floor. Vanny, my perpetually underfoot shadow, races for it, like it's one of his toys, batting it under the table. I quickly follow him, arms lowered, trying to scoop up the eggshell before it gets broken into pieces and harder to clean up. "No, Vanny!" I scold, hurrying toward where he's bent over in a hunch, ready to pounce on it.

As my foot is about to land on my next step, I screech in surprise as

Earl Grey races underneath about to get stomped on. Abruptly wrenching myself to the side to try to miss him, I land hard on the edge of that foot, pain shooting like lightning through my ankle. "Ow!" I croak as the now radiating pain causes me to stumble. I fall forward onto the floor, twisting my ankle even more as I land awkwardly despite my attempt to catch myself with my hands.

"Fire burn it to ashes!" I curse. I can't believe this is happening. I've never been a klutz. But life has me so unbalanced lately, I shouldn't be surprised something like this was in store.

I gingerly touch my ankle and flinch as I realize that's a terrible idea. I'm not sure what to do. I landed in a sort of pigeon pose, with my front leg bent to the side and my back leg far behind me. I push myself onto my butt, grunting in agony, and carefully swing my back leg around, avoiding the kitchen table. As soon as I do, the door opens and I hiss in pain as the cats race over my smarting foot and ankle to get to their new favorite person as fast as their little legs will carry them.

"Ada, I heard a commotion. What happened?" Norrell asks as he lunges forward to examine me.

"It's not even worth explaining," I gasp out, with a dismissive wave of the hand toward the two hellions, now on their best behavior, the very picture of obedience, as they watch us with interest.

Norrell reaches toward my already-bruising ankle, and I instinctively recoil from his touch. Horrible, spasming pain drives a shrill yelp from me for my trouble.

"Stop, do not move," Norrell implores, spreading his hands with his palms out in emphasis.

"Don't touch me," I wheeze, as I cup my hands above my ankle, like that could prevent it.

"Ada." He draws out my name, reminding me of moments better left forgotten. "You twisted your ankle, mayhap sprained it. I need to carry you to a sofa and call the clinic."

"No, just... give me your hand and pull me up. I'll be able to make it there on my own," I argue, trying to negotiate the least amount of touching possible.

"That is not going to happen. You cannot walk on that leg. And it is too far to hop all the way there. Please let me help you," he insists earnestly, sounding upset that I'd rather attempt it on my own than accept his assistance.

I'd crawl if I had to. Anything to keep away from him.

Finally, I look at his face, appallingly close to mine, meeting his worried ice blue gaze for an instant too long. I see too much in them, it's unbearable. My eyes wander to his furrowed brows and the vertical frown lines between them on his forehead. He didn't have those before. They don't necessarily age him. They look heavy, like he's borne the weight of something for too long.

I'd have helped him carry it, if he'd have let me. It's an intrusive thought in this dumb situation, as true as the sentiment may be. But he didn't want me to. I shouldn't care about some lines on his face and what may have caused them.

"Fine. But then I'm calling someone to take me to the clinic. Please just take me to the living room," I capitulate, my words clipped. I rub my face in frustration, willing away any tears.

"Thank you." He sighs, sounding relieved.

"What do you need me to do?" I demand, my voice bitter to my own ears. I just want to get this over with.

"Hold on to me while I pick you up," he offers calmly, unmoved by my tone.

"Pick me up? Absolutely not!" I scoff. Being in his arms is too much to handle.

"I promise I will not jostle your ankle. Just hold on while I lift," he urges, not paying me any heed as I look at him in wide-eyed shock.

"Stop!" I protest with a weak attempt to push him away. It falls on deaf ears as he hooks his brawny arms under me, gathering me close. He lifts slowly and smoothly as promised, like I'm weightless, no strain at all. A rich loamy scent from the garden mixed with his own note of spice I never forgot fills my nose while I'm awkwardly pressed against him. Struggling hurts my ankle, so I'm forced to remain still.

Allowing him to do this feels like defeat. I don't need to be reminded of his strength and agility. Memories rush into my mind. He was... is... physically magnificent. Completely breathtaking. And being in his arms was once the best feeling in the world.

"I'll put you down so you can elevate your foot and then I will bring your phone." He speaks in hushed tones, like I need soothing, as he steadily guides us out of the kitchen and into the foyer. He turns us through the double doors into the living room. His cradled hold keeps my leg nearly motionless, like he glides us across the house. Still, I've clutched desperately at his neck the entire time, scared my foot would knock into something. It doesn't, of course. He's excessively careful as he bends his knees and lowers his arms to place me down onto the sofa without any impact or bounce. After he slides his hands out from under me, he grabs pillows from the matching brown leather sofa facing opposite this one and positions them under my ankle, carefully piling and adjusting them to raise it higher.

"Where should I look for your phone?" he asks, again as promised.

"It should be in the kitchen. Probably on the counter," I respond, my voice resigned, the fight worn out of me.

When he leaves the room to get my phone, I take a moment to right my house robe so less of my pajama set is showing. In no time he's back, handing me my phone and then taking a seat on the other sofa with only a coffee table between us.

My mind blanks as I consider who to call. It's hard to think past my throbbing ankle. First, I try Walt, who doesn't pick up. He and Acton may be on an early morning hike. They're both early birds and it seems like Walt requires a daily communion with nature as much as Acton. Tapping the corner of my phone on my chin, I wonder who a trip to the clinic would inconvenience the least. Niven has a borrowed automobile, but I think he's still asleep upstairs and I don't want to disturb his rest. Ben's truck doesn't have enough room for me to stretch out. And Cara isn't strong enough to lift me. As I think, Norrell studies my form laid up on the sofa, not quite clinically, but with obvious care.

"Would someone from the clinic be able to come here?" It's a sign of how well I knew him once that I can tell it's a genuine question, not sardonic in the least even though it's a painfully obvious one—something I didn't even consider in my frazzled state.

"Yes, that's a helpful idea. I don't know why I didn't think of it. Thank you. For all of this," I say self-consciously as I gesture toward my ankle. Of their own accord, my eyes return to his, which blaze with emotion despite his otherwise calm demeanor.

"It was no trouble. I want to do this for you." The sincerity in his voice makes me ache. Its familiarity assails my heart. Everything is too raw right now to scrutinize this sudden burst of sentimentality.

A ghost of a smile touches my mouth, but I quickly rein it in. A slight nod instead is enough to acknowledge him. Forcing my eyes back down to my phone, I call my friend Thea, a healing witch at the clinic. She should have been an obvious first choice since she's been checking in on me regularly, both as a friend and in her professional capacity, but my mind is not cooperating.

"Hi Ada. So glad you called! I was just thinking about you and was going to check in later today. How's it going this morning?" she greets me cheerily.

"It's been a real fiasco. I had a cat-related accident and injured my ankle. When it rains, it pours." I pout, though belatedly I can't decide whether I should let Norrell know he is very much a part of this flash flood.

"Let me guess, it was Vanny circling your feet?" She snorts, knowing the boys well.

"No, but he started it. Vanny got ahold of an eggshell and Earl Grey wanted in on the action." My mouth twitches into a wry smile, and I can't hold back a bark of biting laughter I've been holding in since it happened. "I think Mother Earth has it out for me."

"Hush, I'll be over in about fifteen minutes. I'll take care of that ankle and you'll be just fine," she reassures me.

After we hang up, I try adjusting myself on the sofa but pain spikes through my lower leg at the tiniest movement. Norrell leaps up as I whimper, but I hold out my hand gesturing for him to stop. He stands there, hands on his hips, looking ready to do something. Hopefully it's in another room... on the other side of the house.

"Maybe you could finish breakfast while I wait for Thea? She should be here soon. Eggs and sausage are on the counter. Minus an eggshell somewhere on the floor. There's bread for toast too. Go ahead and make whatever sounds good to you," I suggest, hoping he'll take the bait if he's still on this infuriating kick to lend a hand.

"I would be glad to. Is there anything I can bring you in the meantime? Anything you want to do?"

This sickly-sweet act makes me want to gag.

"No, I'll be about as useful as a one-legged male in an ass kicking contest until she gets here. I'm just going to stay put until then. I'll be good as gold soon enough." I attempt to smile but end up grimacing. This situation is agonizing in so many ways.

His eyes stay fixed on me for an eternity before he leaves the room. Now that I'm blissfully alone, I carefully flop back on the sofa, trying to relax and forget about the radiating pain. Closing my eyes and counting down the long minutes until Thea arrives, the discomfort cuts through the noise in my mind.

I need a plan, a way to keep my dignity intact while my interloper houseguest playacts his nice-guy routine. I shouldn't put up such public resistance to his *pitching in*, his superficial gestures, his unflagging agreeableness. It just makes me look cantankerous. Instead, I need to look as though I appreciate it... be a little more cordial at least. I can't stomach the thought of being truly friendly, but I'll do my best while always remaining guarded. Be pleasant without letting him in. It'll pay to remember that bees with honey in their mouths have stings in their tails.

If he keeps this up around the house, it strikes a few items off my to-do list. And that energy saved can be redirected into keeping my eyes wide open for a misstep, any fleeting glimpse of his true intentions here. He's slowly ingratiating himself back into the good graces of some around town and within the safety council, but he isn't fooling me. I'll discover his ulterior motive and expose him as the pretender he is.

A door opens somewhere upstairs, ending my pain-induced rumination. Goodness me, here comes another witness to my embarrassing predicament. Probably more than one since it's getting on in the morning. I bite my lip, staying silent, as Tallie marches down the staircase and through the foyer in matching pink leggings and bra top. They contrast brightly and beautifully with her moss green skin. Her curved eyebrows shoot up as she spots me laid out on the sofa.

"Ada! What's going on? Are you alright?" She rushes over and squats down next to me, eyeing my elevated foot.

"Wasn't my best morning," I try to make light.

"Do you need anything?" she frets, leaning in for a closer look at my purpled ankle.

"My friend is on her way to heal me. Let's hope she's quicker than a hiccup." My wry laugh fills the room.

"I just thought to myself I should ask if you want to join me on my run. But I guess I'll be going solo today," she remarks, flashing me a regretful look.

"Do an extra lap for me." I wink, letting her know there's no hard feelings. I wouldn't have gone anyway, but I won't ruin her illusion I'm some sort of avid jogger.

"Hope your friend gets here soon and that you feel better," she says with a whoosh of breath as she straightens to her full height. I shoo her off since I don't want to keep her.

I attempt to read a few emails on my phone to distract me. Luckily, Thea lets herself into the house, and I can quit pretending like I can get any work done in this state. "Hello! I'm here for my house call," she trills from the foyer.

"I'm in the living room!" I call out while pushing myself back up to a seated position, gritting my teeth at the mistake.

"Oh my, Ada. I can already tell you've done a number on that poor ankle. Black and blue are not your best colors," she jokes as she steps into the room and sits on the coffee table.

"I'm inclined to agree with you." I snort.

"Let's get this over with then. I may not get you back to a hundred percent today, but this will surely feel much better," she assures me. Her large dark brown eyes flash with sympathy.

I cringe when she reaches for my ankle. Even the light contact aggravates it. She brushes over my skin lightly, summoning her magick and murmuring quietly to herself as she concentrates on her spells. Her hands heat up my already hot, swollen ankle as the magick weaves through me. It's an uncomfortable sensation at first like exposing a burn to the scorching midday sun. The pain steadily ebbs, and the swelling noticeably reduces. She doesn't stop until the discoloration turns from blackish to purple to green to yellow, healing before my eyes. When she's done, she smiles at me and moves her hands away.

"Give it a test run! But don't actually run, please," she encourages with a chuckle as she scoots over to give me space. Guess I really won't be going with Tallie anytime soon.

Still resting on the stack of pillows, my ankle swivels without painful resistance. Like she said, it's not completely healed, but it's close. Sitting up straighter and swinging my foot off the pillow, I place it gingerly on the ground next to the healthy one. So far so good. She holds out her hands to hoist me up from the sofa. My ankle takes my weight well enough. After a few steps, I feel confident I can walk without difficulty, only minor discomfort.

"So much better! Thank you, Thea. You're a lifesaver," I gush as I turn around and walk back toward her.

"Oh, don't be silly, this was nothing. But you're quite welcome. I'm so glad you called me. You may not be fleet of foot quite yet. The ankle looks good, and the sprain is mostly healed. I knitted together the partial tear in your ligament, but it still needs a few days rest to fully recover. I'm on my way to the clinic after this for my shift. I'll deliver some pain relief salve afterward. In the worst timing ever, the last of my jars at home ran out the other day and I haven't restocked. Promise me you'll use this as an excuse to laze about and take it easy today? Maybe read a good book and drink a glass of wine later to relax? In fact, I'm officially prescribing it."

We're both giggling as we embrace in a brief hug. Her delightfully spiky black hair tickles my cheek as she pulls away.

"Thanks again, and I'll follow your advice to the letter. I've already picked out the book," I declare.

"The saucier the better!" She winks as she steps out the door onto the porch. We wave goodbye as she hops in her automobile to drive to work.

After shutting the door, I slump against it, relief coursing through me now that there's only a dull ache in my ankle, hardly noticeable at all. Footsteps from the kitchen startle me, reminding me of my plan. I dub it Operation Unsteady the Yeti. Mayhap it needs a better name in the future, but for now that's what I've got.

No sooner than I've pushed myself away from the door, do I see his form darken the entry to the kitchen. "Breakfast is ready. I had not realized your friend would heal you so quickly. I was about to ask her to join us. I made more than enough. And I do not believe anyone else will be coming down soon," he observes as he turns his head toward the stairs, listening for signs of life and evidently finding none.

"I haven't seen anyone but Tallie, and she's out for a while. Thea works quickly. She's one of our best healers. Don't feel bad though, this was a detour on her way to work. She probably couldn't have stayed. Someone else will appreciate the food," I respond with a shrug, my tone matter of fact.

"How is it? Your ankle? Do you need help to the kitchen?" he asks solicitously as he joins me in the foyer, his gaze sweeping downward at my healed ankle. It takes all my willpower not to roll my eyes.

"No assistance needed, thank you. I need be careful with it for a few days, that's all." I offer a faint smile, putting my plan into place.

He narrows his eyes as they fix on my mouth and then back up to meet my gaze. It's hard to tell what he's thinking. But it seems to work. He nods and smiles back at me with a flash of sharp white teeth.

"That is good news. We should eat before the food gets cold," he says, using a casual hand to gesture for me to go first.

The aroma of breakfast wafts toward me before I even reach the threshold. And once I do, the kitchen smells divine. It sparks a longing in me, to a time when this house was full of life. So much love and happiness. When was the last time someone cooked just for me in this kitchen? It's hard to pinpoint, but likely it was fifteen years ago in the days leading up to, mayhap even the day of, his return to the North Clan.

Fifteen Years Ago

My mom left her workshop in such disarray. She expected to come home to it. It wouldn't have crossed her mind I'd have to clean out this space without her. She would have eventually organized her work in that system that only made sense to her. I turn over an old pendant, still brimming with her magick. When my mom worked on it, did she cradle it in her hands like I'm doing now? It's illogical, but holding each one, brushing my magick against the last vestiges of hers, makes me feel like she's still here. But this was just her work, stock to add to the family shop I was helping her run, nothing inherently special. So why are they now so important to me? Part of me never wants to sell them. Horde them in this room forever. The other, more rational, part of me thinks they're clutter covering up a useful workspace. Grief is funny like that. Suddenly everything and nothing holds meaning.

Every time I attempt to clean it up, I lose myself in years' worth of childhood memories of sitting next to her, watching her work, fascinated by all the tools, equipment, and strange objects strewn about. As messy as it looked to me, she always knew where everything was.

When I was old enough to begin practicing spells, we spent many mornings tinkering and experimenting with silly enchantments as she taught me how to make them. We created one that gave us bright rainbow-hued hair, weightless and floating in all directions, while we wore it. Another one made everything taste like bubblegum.

Any progress I thought I'd make today halts as I try shaking loose every detail tucked away in my brain. Even though it's been a few months since I lost her and my dad, it's hard to see the point in changing anything here. This space was hers. It should still be hers. I don't know when I'll ever think of it otherwise. I don't know if I want to replace these memories with new ones without her.

A noise in the hallway draws my attention away from the enchantment still clutched in my hands and toward the doorway. Norrell steps inside, stony faced, his eyes strangely lifeless. He has stuck by my side since my parents died. A strong, stoic companion whose love helped prop me up when I was ready to crumble apart in grief. For all the issues we had the past couple years, he has been unfailingly supportive in this.

"Time must have escaped me. Sorry, my love. I think I'm done for today," I say with a watery smile. I set down the items in my hands so I can wipe my eyes. I came in right after Norrell made lunch for me, but the low light from the window shows many hours have passed. I shuffle over to hug him. He returns it woodenly, hardly even touching me. I stare at him, baffled, as I release him, stepping back slightly on account of his tepid response. Is he angry at me? Did I forget something important? I've been in my own head lately and haven't been as attentive as usual, but he's never acted like this before.

"I have news. I was called by my clan to return home. Permanently," he speaks in a stilted voice. Not his usual cadence.

"Oh," I gasp, nearly shocked to silence. "When shall we leave?"

"I leave now. I am already packed. I am sorry, Ada, but I am going alone." He's acting possessed. This isn't like him.

"We're supposed to go together. We already agreed we'd visit," I remind him, my voice rising in panic.

"We did, but plans change," he responds, utterly emotionless.

"When are you coming back?" I ask desperately, my hands moving to his chest, caressing him, trying to soften him.

"I am not." His clipped, cruel answer sends me shaking, my hands now trembling on his shoulders. His hands circle my wrists and move them between us so I'm no longer touching him.

"*What?* What do you mean? What does that mean for us?" I gulp, my voice weak behind the growing lump in my throat.

"It is for the best that we part ways forever. I am sorry, Ada. I never intended for this to happen." He looks above me, distance in his expression, as he callously tells me this. My heart stops in my chest.

"But why? What did I do?" I clamor for answers, my voice breaking as I start to sob.

"It has nothing to do with you. My place is with my people, and I must go back. For good. We were always doomed to fail. Our worlds are too different. I should not have led you on." His words sound rehearsed.

"That's *nonsense*. We agreed to spend time with your family. To figure out our next step. If you need to go back for a little while, or even a long while, go ahead. I'll wait for you. We'll figure out the distance. We can still speak every day until you return or when I'm able to join you. My parents... my parents... being gone... doesn't change that. I can leave here. Leave this house. You mean more to me than anything left here. We can make our own future. Don't throw this away. I love you so much. You're my mate. My everything. I can't live without you," I argue, raising my voice even as it quivers uncontrollably.

"I made my decision," he asserts in frightening calm.

Why won't he listen to me? He can't leave! I need to hold him. Kiss him. Make love to him until he sees reason. I try to break my hands free from his grasp, but he firmly locks them in place like he can read my mind.

"I am no longer your mate. Your commitment to me is dissolved." His eyes shutter with an impenetrable barrier. His icy, detached tone leaves no room for misinterpretation. I've lost him.

"Don't do this! It doesn't make any sense. You're not telling me something. What happened there? Is your family okay? I will help you figure it out! Anything you need! I can't lose you," I wail, hyperventilating and nearly breathless.

"I will always treasure our time together. But this is goodbye. Forever." His eyes lower to my mouth and linger there. His body draws into me slightly, pulling the faintest gasp from me. At the sound, he stiffens up again, restoring that distance between us. Before I can find my voice again, he abruptly raises my hands, still joined with his, and kisses them hard with a barely suppressed fervor he hasn't shown in this entire conversation.

My breath hitches on a sob, making me gulp for air. He doesn't look at me as he drops my hands. I reach for him out of instinct, but he steps back briskly to avoid me. And then he turns around and rushes away.

I try to catch up to him, but my shaky body won't cooperate. "Don't go!" I beg, openly sobbing as he reaches the door. He doesn't even look back as he walks out of my life.

When I fall to the floor, there's no impact. Just nothingness. Like I'm sinking through it. The blinding pressure in my head pushes away the world, all that's painful, distorting and muting everything outside my mind. I lose all sense of reality, my tether to it severed now that I'm completely alone. There's nothing left for me there anyway.

Norrell's a ghost now. Another ghost in this house, haunting me the rest of my days. Until I'm a ghost too.

I discreetly wipe a tear from my eye as I step into the kitchen. Norrell set the kitchen table exactly as we used to when it was the two of us here. Our respective plates, his piled much higher than mine, sit in front of our preferred seats. The sight makes my stomach lurch, throwing into focus the last time he did this. It *was* the day he left. I would have given anything at that moment for him to stay. Now I'd give anything for him to leave. There's a bitter irony in that I'll have to analyze later if I'm going to get through this meal in an agreeable mood. Maybe even a touch pleasant if he's lucky.

Taking a seat, I'm surprised to see an omelet on my plate along with the sausage links. He must have dug through my fridge for the vegetables and cheese. He brewed coffee, too, and poured some in my favorite mug. How did he know?

"Thank you, this looks delicious," I tell him honestly. I cut a small bite of the omelet with my fork. It tastes as good as it looks.

"The vegetables in your crisper looked so fresh. I had a hard time choosing what to use," he remarks.

"Probably from Taurus Farms. You might… not remember them," I say unthinking, my correction sounding awkward.

"If they were at the farmers market, I probably would," he answers smoothly.

"They are. It's still going," I confirm.

"A nice tradition in this town," he observes around a bite of food.

My eyebrows raise slightly in surprise. This sounds like small talk.

"I guess that means you don't have them in your settlement?" I venture to ask.

"Ah, no. Our market is a little different," he answers enigmatically.

I shrug, unsurprised by his non-answer. "That's too bad."

Both cats laze next to each other in a sunny spot on the floor, idly watching us, like it's been an uneventful morning. I'd reprimand them if I thought it would do any good. I know better. Instead, I roll my eyes at them.

"Those two are more trouble than they're worth sometimes," I say without any real teeth, pointing my fork in their direction.

"It looks like they wore themselves out playing with that eggshell before I took it away from them," he says with a frown, drawing my eyes to the shape of his lips, a dangerous place to look.

Graceful clip-clopping down the stairs announces Cyrinda's imminent arrival. Luckily, there's some food left in the pans for her. She saunters in, already dressed and made up for the day like she has big plans.

She eyes the sausage and eggs with displeasure. "Is this all there is ready to eat? Well, I wanted to go downtown anyway. Get a shot of espresso. Maybe a croissant," she says flippantly as she walks over to the table.

Her gaze homes in on Norrell's chest. "You've got a little dirt on your pelt. What have you been up to?" she observes dryly, sounding suspicious of him.

Norrell's lips twist into a wry grin, like he's humoring her. "Yardwork. Figured Ada would need some help around the house since she is putting so much energy into hosting us. I bought a whipper snipper yesterday. I will get started with it after everyone else has woken up."

My mouth gapes open, perplexed since I told him not to buy me gifts. Would that even count as a gift? "You did? Why would you do that? And do you mean a weed eater?" I question him while trying to tamp down my complete exasperation.

"I've always called them weed whippers. Whipper snipper makes no sense," Cyrinda interjects, sounding haughty. She's really elevated this whole notion of "taking sides" to the next level.

"I guess we're all kinda right. It's just a piece of machinery anyhow." I offer them both a placating smile to try to smooth over this semantic disagreement.

"Not really," she balks and marches out of the kitchen.

Norrell blows out a long breath. "She has not warmed up to me."

It conjures memories of how he would bend over backwards for people, no matter how inconvenient. Well, everyone except for me that is. I'm sure her blatant dislike of him sticks in his craw. "She could start an argument in an empty house. Don't take it personally. But I don't think you're ever going to get on her good side," I observe with a shrug.

Like I figured, he doesn't look pleased by this. It seems that quality hasn't changed in these long years apart. I continue eating my breakfast and try not to let myself dwell on it.

"I ran into your Uncle Walt on my way to the garden shop yesterday. He looks hale and healthy for a human male his age. I hope he and Acton are well. He did not seem like he wanted to talk," Norrell notes. I'm unsurprised. Walt's eyes were always wide open to Norrell's shortcomings. He saw much of it before I did. His words at the time when

Norrell left, *We are washing our hands of him*, still ring true. I'll do Norrell the favor this once and not rub it in. But if Walt ever decides to give him an earful, that's his issue to deal with.

"He is. We've all grown long in the tooth I suppose, except for Acton that is." I huff a small laugh at Acton's seemingly eternal youth.

"Long in the tooth. That would be an apt description for me. My tusks are longer than they used to be. Yours look the same, not that your dull square teeth could be mistaken for tusks," he jokes with an amused grin. It doesn't exactly land. I'm not sure how to feel about him trying to act so familiar with me.

"Your tusks do look a little wilder," I agree, trying not to stare at his mouth too long. "But yes, they're both well. Living life to the fullest now that Walt is retired. They always have camping trips planned to regional forest preserves and national parks. I keep... kept... Acton in steady supply of glamor charms for their travels. When they're home, they hike almost every morning. I'm not sure Walt's fully let go of his old job. He likes to keep an eye on the condition of the trails, especially along the marsh where it sometimes floods."

"From what I remember, that sounds like him. Community-minded," he says, looking thoughtful.

We fall into silence as we finish our meal and drain our cups of coffee, making us both aware of the sounds emerging from other parts of the house. Taking my last bite, I subtly push the plate away from me. Norrell stands up and takes both of our plates to the sink and starts washing them. I get up to pour myself more coffee.

"Thank you. Do you want more?" I ask, shaking the pot a little.

"Please," he answers automatically. "So, when is that farmers market again?"

I look over at him, surprised. "Tonight, actually. It starts an hour before sundown so everyone can attend."

"Were you planning on going?" he says the words carefully.

"Um, I was..." My voice falters.

"Then you will need someone to assist while your ankle is still healing. I will go with you," he declares as if it's a given.

I stiffen. I don't want to spend even more time with him than I have to. "I'll be fine on my own."

"No, you will need someone to carry your bags. You cannot risk aggravating your ankle," he persists.

"I can carry my bags. They're enchanted to be weightless. I'll be fine, I just won't buy very much," I object, my voice sounding insubstantial compared to his.

"Buy as much as you want. They will weigh nothing to me regardless of an enchantment, but they will still be bulky. I will drive us in the Wagoneer because you should not walk very far. We will go when it starts," he decides presumptuously.

I draw back. My chest pounds wildly in panic. Is he serious? He's proposing to go somewhere together in public? Where people might see us and assume we're together again? That would draw way too much attention. It would be a disaster for me.

"I don't think so," I manage, my voice thick with unbidden emotion.

"You cannot walk there. And you should not drive. The movement of your foot on the pedals would not be good for your ankle. I do not see another way unless you want to skip this week," he says pragmatically as he dries our plates, still watching me all the while. I do, in fact, need to go tonight. This is so unfair.

I can't trust my voice, so I just nod.

CHAPTER 11
ADA

My day is spent resting like Thea instructed, sticking mostly to my bedroom to avoid Norrell. It figures, the moment I put my plan in place, he decides to accompany me out somewhere. Under the guise of *helping*, of course. Moon and stars, I should know better than putting myself in such a stupid position. Plans should not be made while under the influence of a great deal of pain.

I plop down on the stool at my vanity, an assortment of pots and spray bottles of potions in front of me I've brought home from my shop. I eye myself critically in the mirror. My hands squeeze and stretch at my cheeks. I'm beginning to look as dull as I feel. Weeks without magick are taking their toll.

Twisting the cap open and scooping out a dollop with my finger, I smooth a rejuvenating serum across the skin of my face and down my neck. It gives the skin a healthy, youthful glow. Its effects compound over time to look even better. The magick works immediately. I look refreshed, but I still feel low on the inside. Next, I spray a shine and volumizing potion into my long, straight hair. My natural dark red color looks flat and my white forelock, courtesy of Mayweather genetics, seems frizzy even after applying the spray.

My fingers comb through my hair one last time. There aren't

enough beauty products in the world to fix this right now. Since i's nearly time to leave, I change out of my lounging clothes into a pair of navy-blue twill wide-leg pants and a cream knit short-sleeved top. My foot and ankle are still a little swollen, so I gently pull on a pair of tennis shoes, loosening the laces on the right shoe so it's more comfortable. I want to look casual and not at all like this is some kind of date. A shudder runs through me just thinking about it.

He is still so handsome it hurts to look at him, the most attractive male I've ever seen. His beard lends extra gravitas to his already dignified face. He looks more mature than before but looks can be deceiving. Maturity doesn't alter the fact he cruelly walked away from me, his ex-mate. Former mate. Whatever we are. It's so unusual there isn't even a proper term. It'll be good when he's gone. I'll no longer need to deal with these thoughts.

I head downstairs to gather everything that I'll need. The large cloth bags are stashed under the kitchen sink. I stuff a few cardboard containers inside that I intend to return to a vendor. The cats watch me as they wait anxiously at their bowls for dinner. I chuckle at their habitual impatience and grab two cans from the cabinet. Their little faces crowd the bowls as I scoop the food into them. With that task out of the way, I check my fridge and pantry, making a quick list on my phone of everything I need.

The front door opens, and from the rhythm of the footsteps, I can tell they're Norrell's. Planning to meet him in the foyer, I move toward the kitchen doorway, only to almost collide with his broad frame. He takes hold of my upper arms, halting me so I don't march face first into his chest. I look up at him, slightly dazed by the abrupt contact. He must have been walking faster than I realized.

"Careful, my..." He clamps his mouth shut and drops his arms as I take a reflexive step backward. "I am sorry," he corrects himself. "I did not mean to run into you."

I refuse to let him rile me up. I have an idea of what he was going to say. It nearly sends a shiver of longing through me. "That's alright. No harm done," I respond with a tight close-lipped smile.

"Are you ready?" he asks. His eyes search mine uncomfortably.

"Yes, let's head out." I school my face and gesture for him to lead.

He holds the front door open for me and follows closely behind as we walk over to the Wagoneer. Walking isn't painful, but I'm moving slower than usual. Digging through my purse, I pull out my keys and hand them over to him. It's been ages since I've ridden in the passenger seat. It's an odd feeling being in such close quarters with him again. He starts the automobile and pulls out onto the street like it's been a matter of days and not years since he's driven it. It creates an odd feeling in the pit of my stomach, nostalgia for that happier time mixed with resentment that he can jump back into my life so seamlessly. My house, my cats, my automobile. What's next? Not a chance it will be my bed.

The street in front of town hall teems with vendors. There are usually twenty-five to thirty each week, many selling their wares here in lieu of a storefront shop. We're out of retail space downtown. Luckily, the new development currently underway past Howling Road will offer more opportunities for those who want to expand outside of the farmers market.

Norrell parks the Wagoneer as close as he can to the market. The short ride was quiet, but not as awkward as I feared. When he cuts the engine, he motions for me to wait and runs to my side to open my door and help me out. My mind struggles to find a reason not to take his proffered hand, to bat it aside and step out of the car by myself.

So I don't fight him on it. I told myself I'd play this game. When my hand clutches at his larger, calloused one, he almost envelops it fully in his fist. The hold provides enough leverage so I can gently lift myself out of the automobile, avoiding any pressure on my ankle. I snatch my hand away the moment I'm upright. The sensation of our joined hands was too familiar for my liking.

"Let's start at this end," I tell Norrell as I motion toward the side where we're parked.

I peruse each vendor, stopping periodically to look at new items on their tables. Not only do I intend to shop today, but I also want to talk to the organizer about a booth for Sunny and her cosmetic charms and potions. It would be a good opportunity if she ever wants to run her own shop one day. She's been so helpful to me, especially with everything that's happened.

Gathering this information on her behalf is the least I can do. I haven't mentioned it yet because I'm not sure whether the organizer is accepting new vendors right now.

Norrell holds my bags, which are still mostly empty. I buy a lot of my groceries here. Those vendors set up at the other end of the market. He stands to the side while I browse a table full of tea blends. Since the season is slowly changing into colder weather, I compare the labels of some of their spicier winter varieties.

A choked noise from Norrell's direction startles me.

His head snaps to the side with knitted brows, and his mouth hangs open in shock. From behind him, I see manicured fingers dance down his shoulder. Marieke, a selkie who for a time was frequently seen on Clancy's arm, steps out from behind Norrell and gives him her most seductive grin with her full red lips. Norrell looks scandalized and takes a step back.

"I didn't realize such a big male would be so shy. Don't worry, I know just how to bring you out of your shell." She giggles, pushing her long shiny black hair behind her shoulder.

"That will not be necessary," he stammers.

"I don't think I know you. Are you in town for that long meeting? I'm sure you're feeling awfully lonely," she presses, reaching out to lightly trace her fingernails down his arm.

He pulls away again sharply, stepping onto the street. "I am not interested," he reiterates, his tone even more rigid.

She shrugs and saunters away, her curvy hips swaying in her tight dress. "Your loss," she calls out witheringly over her shoulder.

Despite her forward overtures to males, Marieke is not unlikeable most of the time. She just enjoys male attention... a lot. But my jaw clenches and my eyes burn suspiciously as she walks away after coming on to Norrell. My patience for her is wearing thin right now. I've stood here stunned and unblinking watching the entire exchange. Norrell seems as taken aback as I am. His eyes finally flash to mine with a troubled look.

"Ada, I had no idea that was going to happen," he sputters. His hand reaches out to me, but he pulls back before it touches me, closing it into a fist and dropping it to his side.

"That's Marieke. Go ahead and talk to her if you want," I grouse.

"No, she is not the female for me," he practically snarls. Something feral blazes through his eyes as he tells me this. His face leans closer to mine and our eyes lock. When it dawns on me that he may try to kiss me, I fling myself away before I do something stupid and let him. My memory snaps back to that moment in the foyer so long ago, pleading for him to stay. His cold, emotionless face as he left the house told me everything.

"Oh, I wouldn't know what your type is anymore," I retort. I'm being flip, but I can't play nice right now. There goes my plan, couldn't even last a day. A pained expression crosses his face. I ignore it and tromp past him to the next vendor.

Sensing him on my heels, I speed by a couple more as fast as my ankle will allow. He isn't relenting and keeping pace only a few steps behind. Spinning toward him and forcing him to an abrupt stop, I put my hands on my hips and glare. "This isn't working for me. Just take me home," I grit through my teeth.

"Please, let us talk for a moment first," he urges.

"You won't want to hear what I have to say," I warn him.

"I do. Rage at me. Do not hold back. I deserve it," he insists.

My shoulders slump and my head bows as I try to hold back the tears that fill my eyes. I can't do this here. Or anywhere for that matter. My utter humiliation forces me to walk away from the crowd forming at the market, always so observant.

"It's best if we don't." I'm suddenly very tired.

"I disagree," he says fiercely, following in step with me. "Do not hide yourself away because of some brazen female I have no interest in."

"That's not it and you know it," I argue.

"Then what is it?" he entreats, sounding genuinely rattled.

My ankle grows sore as I pick up speed. When we get to the Wagoneer, Norrell opens the passenger door for me, and I propel myself inside before he can assist.

"Take me home," I demand, unable to bring myself to look at him in the driver's seat.

"Please tell me what is on your mind," he pleads. "Do not hold back."

"You don't get to ask anything of me, Norrell. That's what's on my mind. You don't get to look like you want to kiss me. That this charade with you staying at my house is pointless pageantry on your part to make yourself feel better. You left me at a time when I needed you the most, plain and simple. You threw our life away and I'm still not sure why. Was my grief too much for you? Did I not give you the attention you wanted?" I chuckle mirthlessly. "Don't bother answering. Frankly, I don't care. I wouldn't trust anything coming out of your mouth anyway. I want you gone for good when these meetings end. You aren't getting me back. I deserved a better mate than you. I deserve to be happy and free of you forever!" I explode, pointing my finger at him aggressively.

I'm winded by the end of my tirade. My chest feels squeezed and my heartbeats punch uncomfortably against my ribcage. I've never raised my voice like this to anyone before.

"You have always deserved better than me. But let me do right by you this one last time, and then I promise to leave you alone forever," he vows, sounding deeply serious.

"One last time? No. We are done and have been for a very long time. I don't owe you anything," I argue.

"You do not ask for help because you want to be strong for others. But you need it right now while your magick is gone. I am here in Monstera Bluff for *you*, Ada. You should not deal with this alone," he counters, emotion thick in his voice.

"I have help. I have my family, Walt and Acton. I have my friends. They help me anytime I ask," I defend them. It's ludicrous he thinks no one has done anything for me. That he's somehow my only savior while I'm downtrodden.

"But how often do you ask? Do they know the extent of what you go through every day? Do they understand what being cut off from your magick feels like?" he points out.

"I ask! And they know it hasn't been easy," I counter.

"Then where are they every day? Why did they let you host guests in your home? Why did they let me stay there and not force me out?" He sighs loudly. "They do care about you greatly. I will not argue that. But you need someone who is dedicated to looking out for you every day."

I bark a sardonic laugh. "You think that'll be you? That barely happened during our relationship. I was never your priority. That improved for a little while after my parents died. But then you abandoned me. Up and left with no explanation!"

That silences him for an instant. A shamed expression crosses his face. "That is the truth. I did those things. If it helps, consider this my penance for all those times I wronged you when I should have taken your feelings into account. It was thoughtless of me. There was no excuse," he whispers hoarsely.

I shake my head at the nerve of him saying these things to me. Too little too late. "Fire and ashes, I don't want your penance. This doesn't absolve you of anything you did in the past. Go to the grave knowing none of this will make me forgive you. You are doing this for *you*. Not *me*."

"Mayhap, but by the bluest glacier I will make sure your magick is restored, Ada. Leaving you was the biggest mistake of my life. I know you do not want to hear it, but that is the truth. I will spend the rest of my days making it up to you," he says somberly.

I roll my eyes. It's easy for him to say that when there's nothing between us. When he has no actual responsibility toward me. My answer is simply, "No, you won't." I fall silent after that, letting it show the loudness of my anger. He still hasn't started the automobile, I realize, keeping me stuck here in some half-hearted attempt to force me to talk. I look out the window, away from him.

He sighs, finally breaking the quietude that dangles precariously between us. "I am so sorry for everything I put you through. My behavior as your mate—being inconsiderate of your time and feelings—has no excuse. During these long years, I reflected on my actions. I remember your sadness mayhap even more than your joy. It struck me that I was raised to live in service of my clan. And so, I continued with what I knew, even though Monstera Bluff is not a clan. There were no such expectations placed on me. My obligations are different here and especially so with a mate. I should have recognized that at the time, but I was too naive."

I shrug. It doesn't really matter why anymore. We were not teenagers when this happened. He was a grown male aged thirty-two. It was a choice he made.

His breath stutters, overloud in the small space. "When I left, I was convinced that the clan was about to devolve into civil war. That may well have happened from what I saw when I returned. But my biggest regret was not trusting you to understand what was being asked of me. They needed me to lead them after my uncle was severely injured, but they would not have accepted you as an outsider and magick wielder. I should have forced it, made it a condition of my return. Come up with a timeline to hand over leadership when another hunter was ready to accept it."

Though my eyes are still glued to the window, looking at nothing, I sense his unbreaking stare, the subtle leaning closer as he speaks.

"I wish I was smarter then. I see now that I did not have to listen to the elders and let you go. I should have fought harder and trusted you to choose for yourself. It was going to be complicated. Likely too messy for you to ever agree to. But I should have at least asked. I am so sorry I did not. I will carry that regret forever. To the grave and into the next realm, Ada. It was unforgiveable. I do not even want your forgiveness. I do not deserve it, and nothing I do now will change that. But you deserve to know the truth. It was never your fault. It was me and a series of foolish assumptions and choices I made. Each one compounded your suffering." His voice wavers, growing thin by the end.

"You should have told me." My voice sounds hollow. "I would have understood the situation, no matter how difficult it was going to be. Did you ever stop and think that my life as a Mayweather in this town is not much different? The constant expectations? The weight of family history? We would have figured out a way forward together. You would only ever share the bare minimum about your family, your clan. I didn't need to know everything about your people. Something like this though, I would have grasped exactly how serious it was. It's like you didn't even know me. But the past can't be changed. That ship sailed so long ago it's out of commission."

"You are right. I want you to know, now. In case it helps you move on," he acknowledges.

I shake my head. He thinks the sun rises just for him. "I figured you were from a high-born family since you were sent to the academy. But I had no idea you were a prince of the yeti or some such. And now their king. It shows how little I knew you. How little you trusted me," I scoff.

"I suppose I am their king in a way, the Huntmaster of the True North. But it must be earned and agreed upon by all the hunters of our clan, it is not a birthright." He pauses to rub his eyes and sigh miserably. "You did know me, Ada. My uncle being the clan leader at the time was nothing but an accident of birth. One that put me in your path, but otherwise spoke nothing of who I am. It only dictated my obligations. No one has ever known me as well as you. I have never opened up to anyone else like I did to you. Even my family, my brother who is my closest friend, have only seen a part of the real me," he argues.

"That sounds unhealthy," I say impudently, trying to mask my emotions. I burn to know more about the clan, but I would never ask. He brushed off any attempts I made in the past. I've learned my lesson.

"It is," he admits. "But no one in my clan has earned that right."

"You should return to them. It sounds like they need you more than I ever did." There's cruelty in my words, but nothing he said has merited me going easy on him. All of it is selfish and self-serving.

"They do not. It was the gravest mistake to ever think so," he replies fervently.

I hum an acknowledgement, making my annoyance clear. Even if it's true, there's no going back on it. He created this situation for us. He can deal with the guilt. Especially since this explanation makes me feel worse in a way. He gave up on us needlessly. I don't understand it and likely never will.

Finally, Norrell turns the key in the ignition and pulls out to drive us back to my home. My ankle hurts again, and I don't have anything for it.

"Stop by the clinic first, please," I ask impassively.

He pulls up in front of the building, following the directions I give him. I step out of the automobile, not bothering to wait for him. Thea happens to come out from the patient area as I step inside.

"Ada! So sorry to keep you waiting on the pain relief salve. I hope it hasn't flared up again," she frets.

I smile kindly in response, not wanting to let her know that it has.

It's my own fault, anyway. "It's still feeling much better," I say, mostly true.

"Oh good! It was such a crazy day here. I couldn't break away until now. Just rub a small dollop around your ankle and foot anytime it feels tender. You shouldn't need it for more than a few days. But do call me right away if the pain noticeably increases," she instructs as she hands it over.

"Thanks, Thea. I will. Hope your evening is restful," I tell her as I wave goodbye.

"Yours too!" she exclaims brightly as the door closes behind me.

Returning to the car, Norrell eyes the jar of salve in my hand. "Does your ankle bother you again?"

"Yes, but it'll be fine," I respond blankly.

"I am sorry for causing you to overuse it," he says, self-reproach evident in his tone.

"Like I said, I'll be *fine*. It was stupid of me to come here. I should have just stayed in bed," I murmur more to myself than him. I rub my temples, where a headache is forming. It's long past time to go home.

"It was not stupid. Losing your magick has already changed your routine so much. It is understandable that you would not let an injured ankle hold you back from even more," he says.

I don't bother with an answer. I'm over this. And him. I'll fly off the handle if he pulls anything else. Closing my eyes and leaning back against the headrest, I will the rest of the car ride to be quick and quiet. He doesn't delay any longer and drives us back. This day has been one giant disaster start to finish. When I get home, I'm going straight to bed so nothing else can take me by surprise.

My body is stiff as a board getting out of bed. I must have slept funny. At least my ankle feels better. Thanks to Mother Earth Norrell will be out of the house this morning. He and Niven will be busy interrogating the fae. The thought of it being taken out of containment sends a chill down my spine. But Niven won't take any unnecessary risk.

In the cold, damp morning air, I try to touch the ward around my property with that pitiful mote of magick. It taunts me each day, but I still try. As ever, the ward is exasperatingly indistinct and out of reach.

After being forced to neglect the shop yesterday, there's no question I need to show up and put in a full day. It's unfair to Sunny and the rest of my staff to keep calling out. First, though, I need to stop by Walt and Acton's cottage. They live on the edge of town, near many of our town's shifters who want easy access to the woods. Their cottage is reminiscent of a log cabin, with an abundance of decoratively carved wood accents. As I pull up, Acton is bent over the lock on the door to their back garden. A tall wooden fence surrounds the entire garden. The door stands even higher with a rounded top and a sunburst shape cut out of it.

"Good morning, Acton!" I greet him as I walk over. "Is the gate acting up?"

"Mother Earth has seen fit to reopen our garden permanently. This latch has not caught since the rising heat of the summer," he croons in his soft voice. Walt built the fence some years back after young members of the wolfpack inadvertently trampled over a bed of exotic flowers.

"Well, if the humidity is causing an issue, I can... ask around in my coven if anyone would enchant it to open just for you and Walt. You wouldn't have to deal with the latch anymore," I suggest, commiserating with him. I could normally perform such a spell myself. But that's out of the question right now.

"Yes, magick to contain nature's bewitching beauty within. There's something apropos in that," he chirrups.

"Good, I know exactly who to call for this," I assure him. I peck his green cheek. It's as smooth and soft as a leaf, though his face looks more like skin than plant.

"Thank you, my gold-hearted girl. Walt is awaiting you inside," he dismisses me affectionately and returns to fiddling with the gate.

Rapping my knuckles on the front door, I call inside as I open it just a crack. "Hello, Walt?"

Walt opens it fully and motions me in. "Good morning, Ada! I'm so glad you stopped by," he tells me, punctuated by a kiss on the side of my head as he hugs me tightly.

"Thanks for letting me come over this early. I'm going to have such a long day at work, I wasn't sure when we'd have the chance to get together otherwise," I say apologetically.

"You are welcome here anytime. Can I offer you coffee? Tea? I made cherry almond scones if you want one," he offers.

"I'm not hungry, thanks. Coffee would be great," I accept with a warm smile.

"Just coffee for breakfast? Are you feeling okay?" The concern in his voice is unmistakable.

"I haven't been in the mood to eat recently," I answer with a shrug. It dawns on me that I haven't eaten since the omelet yesterday morning.

"You're not just hear for a social call. You want to talk about me running for one of the town council seats, don't you?" he postulates as he pours coffee into the empty mug in front of me.

I grin brightly at him. "You know me too well. As soon as the safety council wraps up, we need those seats filled quickly so we can get back to town business. I'll help plan your campaign, though you are the breath of fresh air that everyone needs a big whiff of right now. It won't take much convincing," I cajole. Every word of it is true.

He looks thoughtful. "I hadn't considered it until you brought it up at our lunch with Cara the other week. Do you really think I'd be suited to that? I'm human, after all. The townsfolk may not accept that on the town council."

I look at him like he's sprouted vines more magnificently than Acton. "Why not? Are there not humans here? We shouldn't let those warlocks' nonsense infect our thinking. Besides, you already worked for the town and transformed our parks here. Now Kiernan Lykander has taken over, and you helped instill that similar vision in him. You've already left a strong legacy. And you have so much more wisdom and insight to offer. I promise you will always have plenty of time to spend on your connection to nature. And all the connecting you do with Acton in nature," I encourage with a cheeky wink.

"Oh shush." He laughs playfully. "What do you expect when two outdoorsmen find love?"

"Well, I stand by what I say. You've lived here for half a century. I know you have opinions on how things should be run," I press.

"I suppose you're right. I'll put my hat in the ring," he concedes with a shy smile.

"Oh Walt, I'm tickled pink! We'll get to spend even more time together!" I clap my hands in glee.

"That's what I'm looking forward to the most," he adds, holding out his coffee mug for a toast. I pick mine up and we clink mugs, taking a long fortifying sip afterward.

"Did you see Acton outside?" Walt gestures his mug in that direction. "I will say that deliriously delightful dryad has been awfully obsessed with transforming the back garden. He's even looking into water features. Fish will be a step too far, Ada! I have to draw the line somewhere. I'll just insist we go kayaking if he wants to be close to aquatic life."

"He was looking at the fence when I got here. I didn't have a chance to peek at the back garden." I pause, grimacing. "I'm not sure about the fish either."

"It's not much to look at right now. Most of it's torn up to make room for his new design. We replanted anything native in the woods if we thought it might thrive. The rest we gave away to the neighbors. He has some grand design in his green noggin. I'm just letting him run wild with it." He smiles fondly and shakes his head.

"Moon and stars, you're going to have an entire eco-system back there. I can't wait! Send him over to my house next."

We finish our coffee and make plans to go over his campaign later this week. I know Clancy and everyone on town council will be on board. Hopefully the other two vacancies will be easy to fill.

Seemingly out of nowhere, Walt's expression turns troubled. He exhales raggedly as he folds his arms over his chest. "I worry with those two warlocks still out there. That they'll cause trouble for us if they aren't caught by election day. Even with Weatherby in custody, they've been smart enough to evade capture."

I bite my lip, unable to hide my own concern that they've cloaked themselves powerfully enough to hide from our law enforcement. "They'll slip up soon enough. They can't keep this up forever."

"Desperate and evil is a volatile combination," he observes, frowning.

As I get ready to leave, he puts a warm hand on my shoulder. He steps in front of me, his eyes studying me.

"You look depleted, Ada. Thinner than usual too. Believe me, I know you don't need another old man hounding you, but you look like you're running yourself into the ground. How are you feeling? Are you getting enough sleep?"

I sigh pitifully. "Sleep has not come easy recently. I just notice myself feeling low. Low energy, low spirits, you name it. I don't know how to describe it. There's been this nagging emptiness in me since my magick was taken."

"Is it that blue devil? I saw him the other day, but I tried to avoid him. Figured if I didn't have anything good to say, why say anything at all. But if I need to talk to him..." he starts.

"No," I interrupt. "It's not him. Or not *just* him anyway. We had a painful conversation yesterday, for me at least. I think for him too. But something else is going on. Maybe I'll go back to the healers clinic if I don't feel better soon."

"Did the conversation give you closure at least?" he asks in a gentle tone, knowing firsthand how broken I was.

"The opposite, in a way. He was still evasive like always, but he tried to tell me that he was forced to leave without me to lead his clan due to their politics. And that he regrets not telling me about it at the time and simply... leaving. Now he feels beholden to help me to make up for it. Ashes, the whole conversation made me feel more muddled than ever. I'm still so angry at him. He thought he knew what was best for me then. He's doing the same now. He hasn't changed as much as he thinks," I share with a wry smile.

Walt whistles low in surprise. "Oh boy, he went ahead and opened that can of worms." He did indeed.

There's already a line at the counter when I hurry through the door of my shop. Ashes, Sunny would have only just opened. Before I get sucked in to the day's work, I craft a quick email to the farmers market organizer to ask about the vendor application process. I wish I spoke to him last night. But that outing derailed right quick before I had the chance. Hopefully he'll have good news for me to pass along to Sunny if she's interested.

Finally, Sunny and I get the morning rush out the door. It gives me time to set out a display of winter-themed charms and enchantments that should be popular this month. The Warm Hug charm feels like just that, perfect for the colder months. No coat is necessary while wearing it. The Fuzzy Slippers spray insulates any footwear against the cold, leaving feet nice and toasty even while wearing sandals or high heels. The door chimes as I busily arrange the items.

"Ada! You weren't home so I figured I'd find you here." Aurelia's voice catches my attention, so I spin around to greet her.

"Oh, Aurelia! I think it's been a couple days since I've seen you." I exaggeratedly widen my eyes. "You don't even want to know what's happened since then. Well, yes you do, but I'll fill you in later. What can I do for you?"

"Of course I want to know!" She barks a husky laugh. "Well, I wanted to see your shop while you're here, and I finally have some time this morning to pop by. We had some long days of meetings recently, but they've been good so I shouldn't complain." She swivels her head, looking around the shop. "It's so lovely in here, Ada. You must be so proud of it. The décor is the right blend of moody and cozy, exactly what I'd hope for in a magick wielder's shop. I feel like I could sit in here all day and read a book."

"You are most certainly welcome to," I tell her with a wink. "You know, the shop has probably looked like this for a century. Luckily, it never fully went out of fashion." A laugh bubbles out of me.

"Well, I really am impressed by it. I better get back for the next meeting, of course, but I'll return at lunchtime to take a closer look at your wares. Maybe we can grab a bite together?"

"I'd like that," I tell her. We make plans to meet back up in a few hours.

When she leaves, I grab another stack of items to add to the display. As I return to the counter, a painful prick in my chest makes my steps lurch. I grab wildly at the counter's edge, suddenly weak and woozy. The charms in my hands clatter onto the floor. A few customers notice, asking if I'm alright. Sunny dashes over and tries to help me to the lounge area. The pain surges now, bringing me to my knees before we get there, taking Sunny down with me.

"Call the healers!" she shrieks to the customers as I slump into her, the pain overwhelming me. This can't be happening again! The fae must have escaped! Will it fulfill its promise to kill me this time? The edges of my vision blur as commotion erupts around me, but everything is hazy against the blinding pain radiating throughout my body.

"Stay with us, Ada! The healers are almost here." Sunny's voice rings in my ears, the last thing I hear as the world goes dark.

There's a din of scrambled voices in my head. My eyes are glued shut and it takes me a minute to unstick them. My vision swims as I look around to get my bearings.

"Ada, you're in the healers clinic," Thea says calmly from somewhere nearby. I blink and her face hovers over mine. "I administered a pain relief potion after I examined you. It must be working if you're back with us."

"What happened?" I ask in confusion, my brain still sluggish.

"You collapsed at your shop. Sunny said you were clutching at your chest and whimpering in pain. The fae's spell is at work again. The magick surges as violently as it did on Samhain night. It still resists healing." She sounds worried. "Rest here while I make some calls. Sunny's here too. I'll let her know you're awake."

She dims the lights as she exits the room. Only a dull lingering ache remains of the excruciating pain, but I'm too exhausted to care much. I think I'll just lay here for a while.

"Ada, I was so scared," Sunny quavers as she appears by my side. "How are you feeling?"

"Better," I rasp out. I don't want to distress her any further. "I'll be alright. Thank you for staying with me. You're a good friend."

"I couldn't leave you," she insists. "I care about you."

I manage a weak smile for her. "I care about you too. But I don't want to keep you here. Why don't you close the shop and take the rest of the day off."

She worries her lip, unsure whether to accept. "I mean it. The shop can wait until tomorrow. We could both use a break," I assure her.

"Alright. But promise to call me when you get home? Let me know if you need anything?" she urges.

"I promise." She wraps her arms around my shoulders carefully in a light hug, not putting any pressure on me. Her expression is still full of uncertainty as she waves one last time from the doorway before she heads out.

I'm not sure how much time passes, but with the combination of the darkened room and the pain reliever, I begin to nod off.

A deep rumbling noise startles me back to consciousness. I'm hardly able to piece together that it's Norrell's voice before he charges into the room with ferocious intensity.

"I came as soon as I heard!" he says in a rush of breath. "We just finished with the fae. *Fuck*, I should have known bringing it out of containment could harm you. I failed you again, Ada."

I can't suppress a resigned exhale. His melodramatics do nothing to improve my mood. If the fae's spell is responsible, this will happen every time Niven interrogates it. I close my eyes, trying to blot out the dread of finding myself between the devil and the deep blue sea. I wonder if one day I won't wake up again.

My eyes open again at the sound of someone else entering the room. Thea returns, her expression just as grim as before. "The worst has probably passed for now. We'll send you home to rest more comfortably in your own bed. Please take it easy today. I'll give you some potions to help you rest better, but don't hesitate to call us if the chest pains return." Turning to Norrell, she adds, "And next time y'all mess around with that fae, bring her here first."

"You have our word," Norrell responds solemnly.

"Focus on feeling better. I'll take care of updating everyone on your condition." She squeezes my hand gently as she helps me out of bed.

Norrell takes my keys from me and retrieves the Wagoneer still parked near the shop. When he returns with it, I'm able to stand and walk on my own, but Norrell hovers right beside me and helps me in.

Quiet and uncomfortable tension flares between us during the short ride home. When he pulls into the driveway, he hops out and rushes over to open the passenger side door. I take his proffered hand but let go as soon as I'm standing steady on my feet.

"Would you allow me to carry you inside?" he asks calmly, though his rigid posture makes it look like he's ready to spring into action at my next fainting spell.

"No, I'm fit as a fiddle. I can make it," I assure him. He's like a shadow behind me, sticking uncomfortably close.

"I'm going to nap on the sofa," I decide after considering my options. The comfortable spot calls out to me when my bed feels too far away up that long staircase. I refuse to let him carry me again.

"I will be here when you wake," he says from the doorway after watching me lay down, making myself comfortable. I lack the energy to respond and almost immediately drift off to sleep. Voices in the foyer wake me a few times, but the pull of sleep is too strong for me to hear much.

The sun is low when my eyes open again. I must have slept all afternoon. It did me some good. My mind is much clearer. And I finally have just enough energy to make it up the stairs. The door to my dad's study is open a crack as I walk by. I poke my head inside, and Niven looks up from the desk. His expression turns anxious when he sees it's me.

In a blur of motion, he's in front of me, hands gently grasping my shoulders. "Oh Ada, I'm so glad you're awake. There are no words... I'm so sorry. We should have known the fae's magick would still have such a tight grip on you. Next time, we'll take more precautions. Make sure you're safe. Had I known..." He sighs, his distraught gaze locked to mine. "Had I known, we would have figured out another way. We can't let this happen again."

I lean into him as he wraps his arms around me in a tender hug. "This can't stop you from your work. Next time, maybe someone at the clinic can knock me out first," I try to joke, but my voice sounds thin.

He pulls back to meet my eyes again. "I can't stand the thought of hurting you. Of this *thing* hurting you further. Your well-being is the most important thing."

"It needs to answer for its crimes. It wouldn't be fair to the community to stop interrogating it."

"But what's fair to you? How much more do you need to put up with?"

"What doesn't kill me..."

He looks appalled. "No Ada. That's patently false. You must think of yourself, your own well-being. If anyone expects you to martyr yourself, they are selfish fools. We can still investigate these crimes without bringing the fae out of containment. It's not all or nothing."

"Thank you for saying that. But now that we know what happens when it's awake, I'll make sure to prepare. It just makes sense. I'm willing to deal with this if it means my magick can be restored and the community can find peace again."

"I don't feel good about intentionally putting you in that position while not fully understanding the repercussions on your health. Let me explore other options first. We'll only do this again as a last resort."

Worry etches across his brow. The sight brings a sad smile to my lips. "I trust you. So trust me in return. Please don't let this affect your work. We can't let it win."

He nods, still looking conflicted. "This discussion isn't over. I'll talk to my team and figure out our options. No matter what we decide, I'll make sure we minimize the risk to you."

"That's all I ask." I squeeze his arm reassuringly.

I head to my room to change into something cozier than my outfit from this morning. Sitting on my bed, I consider just going to sleep. I could easily sleep through the night even at this early evening hour. But I can't shake Norrell's promise that he would be here when I woke up. I shouldn't care, but I do. It seems important that he keeps his word for once.

Determined, I walk downstairs again, my energy depleting fast, but there's still no sign of him. Did he end up leaving? Again? It would be apropos. I step out the front door, checking if he's outside. Looking around the front lawn, it's immediately noticeable someone tended it since this morning. Raked, weeded, edged. It looks almost picture-perfect. Norrell must have been busy out here while I slept. Fire and ashes, I'll need to thank him for his hard work.

When I go back inside, Norrell appears, walking down the stairs, shirtless as usual. He looks freshly showered. I stop in my tracks, staring at his brawny, powerful body, his pelt and hair still damp. His stunning form sparks a fierce longing in me. A curl of warmth settles in my core. I once knew what every inch of his body felt like. But that was ages ago. The thought cools my ardor a little.

Norrell studies me in return, his mouth pressed in a tight line. He walks over to me as I stand foolishly at the door glued to the spot. He halts directly in front of me. He raises an arm over and past my shoulders, leaning toward me. When I hear a soft thud, I belatedly realize he had to push the door shut behind me. I must not be as recovered as I thought.

"You are awake. When was the last time you ate?" he rumbles. His brows furrow as I crane my neck up to look at him.

"I had coffee today. And... well, then everything happened," I respond self-consciously.

"You did not eat dinner last night, Ada. Why are you not eating?" he challenges.

"I don't know. It wasn't intentional. I just haven't felt like it."

"Were you planning on eating dinner tonight?"

"Maybe later unless I fall asleep again first," I answer defensively. This is swiftly devolving into an argument.

Norrell's sigh is long and heavy. "Fire of the frost. Ada, that is unacceptable. I will cook dinner and you will eat it. All of it. You need to keep up your strength. There is no way you are you are getting out of this, not after ending up at the healers clinic like you did. I know you skip meals more often than you would ever admit to me. Come with me to the kitchen. Now. You cannot leave until you finish your plate," he scolds me like I'm a child.

My steps sound closer to stomps as I follow behind him. "Why does this matter to you?" I ask his sinewy back.

He abruptly turns and my face is inches from his chest. "Because this is not like you, Ada. You are strong and sharp. But you are weakening in front of my eyes. It is not just stress or a lack of magick. This fae has done something more to you. I will keep you healthy until we know what it is doing to you."

I scrub my hands over my face. I ache to find comfort in that broad, warm chest but I hold myself back. It's an illusion. He's not safe. But he's right though. Something is very wrong with me. "Alright," I surrender. "Please make me dinner."

When we enter the kitchen, the boys immediately swarm me, their purrs resonate like little motors. I fill their bowls and then obediently sit at the table while Norrell fetches ingredients from the fridge. I watch him in confusion. A lot of that food looks like it came from the farmers market. But I didn't buy any of it.

"Did you go back last night?" I ask incredulously. I can tell by his face that he knows exactly what I mean.

"I did." He nods. "It improved since the last time I was there."

My eyes roll of their own accord. "Yes, that's true. It doesn't answer why you went back?"

"Because I inadvertently made you leave. You wanted to shop last night, and I ruined it for you," he states plainly.

It's my turn to breathe a long, drawn-out sigh. "This." I wave between us. "Is too difficult to navigate."

"It does not need to be," he remarks as he rinses off some vegetables.

"I'm not sure what that means."

He sets the vegetables on the counter and turns toward me again. "I hurt you very badly, and that can never be erased. There is nothing either of us can do to change the past. But for right now, while I am here, let me in enough to take care of you. I will never ask for more."

"Honestly, I'm fine here on my own, just as I have been for years. I need to get used to this new way of life if this is permanent. Having you or anyone here is just prolonging the inevitable," I insist.

"Mayhap, but I am working with Niven to make sure it will not be permanent," he lets slip.

"What do you mean?"

He tugs on his beard before he explains, "When the fae's interrogation began this morning, it was primarily a test to see how far we could restore it to consciousness. It went as we expected. But that fae is still extremely powerful despite all their safeguards. It fights him at every turn, but Niven will pry out its secrets by force, no matter how difficult it is. And as quickly as possible to minimize the effect on you."

My brows raise in alarm. Niven didn't let on how dangerous the situation was for them. "I wasn't aware. He told me he me he wouldn't risk my health just to interrogate it. But I told him that's a risk I'm willing to take."

"At some point very soon, the council will disband and everyone will return to their homes to enact the new safety and security measures they agreed upon. Niven and his teams will remain until their job is complete. So will I. They need me for my ability to dispel the fae's magick. The only reason I am helping him is to make sure we force the fae to tell us how to break the spell. I will see you through this, no matter what," he declares. His eyes alight on me and I can see the weight of his promise in them. A shiver whispers down my back.

"Okay," I acquiesce, unsure whether it's wise. But if Niven needs him, I'll put up with it. "You can stay until this is over."

"Thank you for this gift, Ada. I will make sure you do not regret it." His eyes search mine, but I look away, pretending to be distracted by the cats.

Wisely, he doesn't push me any further. He proceeds to make dinner while the cats and I silently watch. It's a simple meal of pan-seared fish and roasted vegetables. As we eat, Norrell looks inordinately more pleased with each bite I take.

Guilt and weariness nag me as we sit next to each other in silence, so I force my eyes to his. He immediately puts down his fork and gives me his full attention.

"Thank you for dinner. And for the yardwork. I noticed it earlier. I'm not sure how you managed after the interrogation."

"Handling the fae this morning was not that difficult. Over decades, I took down dozens of them with my fellow hunters. They are incredibly dangerous, but so am I," he stresses.

When I finish the food on my plate, a triumphant smile curls his lips, drawing my attention to his tusks, reminding me how he'd run them sensually along my neck. I suck in a shaky breath as I remember the feeling of it.

"Very good, Ada," he praises in a low voice, sending a spike of arousal through me. Somehow my so-called plan has backfired. Now I'm the unsteadied one.

CHAPTER 12
NORRELL

"Let's make this quick, team. Ada's health is on the line," Niven instructs the room as we ready ourselves. Ada convinced Niven to move forward with questioning the fae. He and his team agreed, albeit reluctantly, that this opportunity is too valuable to pass up. I think they could have come up with something else, keeping her from suffering further. But since it is not my decision, I will do all I can to help Niven keep this session as short as possible.

The fae shrieks an unearthly racket as one of Niven's team releases it from containment. Even though we heard it before, the unpleasant screeching grinds excruciatingly in our ears.

The fae has been kept in an enchanted lockup that forces it into unconsciousness. Powerful wards surround the containment unit as well as the room, preventing any chance it could break free. Though these efforts still cannot stop the damage it does to Ada while it is uncaged. The fae magick is twined within her. She is in the healers' safe hands right now as we interrogate it for a second time.

Upon its initial release, the fae seems lethargic, though still ear-splittingly cacophonous in its altered state. Slowly it will fully regain consciousness. My senses are alert, feeling for the intensification of its magick. It is not nearly strong enough yet to strike out at us, but I never let down my guard. That is one of the first lessons taught to hunters in my clan, especially around the fae.

A young female witch from Ada's clan, Darla Rallis, asked to join us today. Niven told me she is a Seer who has visions of the future. One of them brought Ada's human friend Cara here last month, who the fae set its sights on. Darla's magickal talent is rare, much like Niven's. Unfortunately, she did not see the fae's involvement. Niven told me she feels tremendous guilt, and so she is here to help however she can. I sympathize with her. She stands silently in a corner, her amber eyes glued to the fae.

The fae's swirling yellow eyes grow steadily brighter. When its power draws to the fore, spiking alarmingly in strength, I swiftly absorb the magick into the clear crystal attached to my bracelet, rendering the fae's fight impotent. The explosive screeching starts up again in anger. Its shadowy mass is like a black hole, destructive and hungry. I cannot begin to fathom what this creature would look like in its own realm. It bucks against the magick holding it, trying to break free. The wards remain strong against the fae's weakened onslaught.

The fae's incorporeal nature helps it shapeshift, but it also allows the ward to keep it small while Niven interrogates it. According to the witches who were at Ada's that night, it had ballooned nearly as big as the carriage house before they weakened it enough to place the first of these wards around it.

Maintaining my concentration on the fae's surges of magickal energy, I siphon an incredible amount from it. Far more than I would believe possible with all the wards containing it. I nod at Niven letting him know he can begin and then return my focus onto the fae once more.

Niven stands a few feet in front of the fae, studying its wispy, undulating shape, taking measure of it and determining where best to focus his abilities. At last, he draws himself up, and stares straight into those yellow orbs. Niven's eyes darken, his pupils expanding wide as he locks into the fae's consciousness and infiltrating its mind. As he does so, the orbs seem to lock in place and nearly solidify. Niven and the fae look almost equally possessed.

"What spells did you use when you touched Ada Mayweather?" Niven begins.

"Powerful ones that have no translation into a language you can understand. Her magick had so much flavor, so much complexity with its ancient pedigree. It was delicious knowing I was the last to taste it. But she is just a witch and no match for me. Her ethereal spark was so easy to dim under my power. Once I tainted it with my magick, it was mine for the taking. And I will keep taking it. Until nothing of her is left," the fae responds, nimbly avoiding the answer Niven seeks.

Fire of the frost, the fae's voice is unsettling, like dozens of individual voices speaking in unison. Sometimes one will come through louder than the rest. Only the blue hag of winter knows why. Niven's team didn't find a pattern for it during our first session with it. Cara and Ada heard only one, the same deranged sounding, higher pitched masculine voice. Mayhap it alters the tone to strike the greatest amount of fear in its opponents.

Undeterred, Niven continues his questioning. "How are you taking Ada's magick?"

The fae laughs maniacally, a mid-range masculine sounding voice taking lead. "You misunderstand, witch. I do not take her magick. Her magick may be the only reason she still walks this realm and I have not claimed all her ethereal spark as my own."

Niven's brows knit in concern, as he guides his own magick to further seek the truth from the fae. "You're taking her *ethereal spark*?"

"Yes, her ethereal spark among the realms in this universe. You measly little witches refer to it as life force because you could never understand the realms like I do. There is so much hidden from feeble minds like yours. They are vast and infinite," the fae responds, sounding smug. "I feel her, little by little strengthening me, settling into me. Do not think to get rid of me, witch. I knew exactly what I was doing, tying her ethereal spark to mine. It was so easy to do when her coven created a convenient distraction. You will kill your precious Ada along with me, if you dare try. When my ethereal spark dims and sends me into the next realm, so does hers even if I have not yet taken full possession of it. It is obvious what she means to you. Such a pity you find yourself in this predicament."

That malicious threat alone tempts me to test its assertion. But instead, I steadily redirect its magick as it swells, even if the fae is trying to bait us into losing control. Niven still needs to get us answers on what it is doing to her. It is nothing I have ever heard of.

"Are you able to absorb anyone's *ethereal spark*?" Niven's tone grows even chillier as he determines the extent of the fae's power.

"Only on Samhain. The first burst of her ethereal spark that night was enough to sustain me for decades, I was almost drunk on the potency of it, like divine ambrosia. The rest is mine to take. It is what she deserves for interfering that night. The little bird should have burned in her nest. Now the witch will give me what I am owed." The fae's voice rises to almost a shout, with two or three feminine voices loudest among the chorus.

Niven seems to assess the fae after that outburst, his jaw clenching in anger.

"What would sever her *ethereal spark* from yours?" Niven asks carefully.

"Not so clever, are you witch? A counter-spell, of course. But I do not know how, and so I cannot tell you. I only take lives. I do not give them back. Extinguishing the Mayweather line will be so delectable," it taunts in a booming low voice offset by a piercingly high pitched one.

"How long will Ada survive your spell?"

"She may have years, but she will surely fade until then, down to nothing. I wish I could see it myself, all her suffering. But oh how I feel it the more I take," the fae intones melodiously, shifting into a child's voice. It giggles, as if it plays a silly game. Mayhap it is, to the fae. It is a disturbing dichotomy that will sear into my memory forever.

Niven looks as unsettled as I feel. The fae messes with us despite his best attempts to control it. But every word that leaves its mouth is the truth, as bad as it may be.

"What can we do to slow the process of her decline?" Niven questions through gritted teeth.

"Slowing it down will just make it more painful for everyone. Better to let me have her now. But if you insist, only the comforts of a good life will help stave off the effects. Healthy food, quality sleep, high spirits, true love. But that little witch has been left all alone for so long. I could feel it when I finally touched her. She will be mine soon enough," it threatens, the full chorus of voices returning.

It aims its jab at me, even if unknowingly, striking at my very soul. I cannot suppress a growl escaping from deep in my throat. I will do everything I can to save Ada from this despicable creature.

"Looks like I chose wisely with that witch. How lucky was I to pick the right one? She all but handed herself over to me. Her death will be sweet as can be," the fae sings in a strange little tune.

Niven gestures to his assistants to strengthen the wards around the fae and encase it again in its containment. I gradually slow my pull of the fae's magick until it is fully warded again. Niven's face falls as he turns to me. He shakes his head in frustration and gestures for me and Darla to join him outside the room.

His entire body shudders. "That felt awful, abhorrent, like an oiliness in my mind I want to wash off. The fae tests my magick. It was a challenge to force any truth from it. Its mind is twisted, beyond anyone I've ever encountered before. Fae are not of this realm, of this I've never been more certain."

"We need your coven to research magick that can stop the fae from taking her *ethereal spark*, whatever the fae called it. We need to remove whatever connection the fae established between them," I snarl. "And then it needs to die."

"We will. I'll make some calls to our experts today. This fae is full of surprises, it seems," Niven says with a grimace.

"Your experts have not helped at all yet. Time is of the essence, Niven. You leave her fate up to some faraway witches who know nothing about fae," I bite out.

"They know the stakes. Believe me. If Ada starts feeling its effects more acutely, they'll come up with ways to help her until it's possible to break the connection. I don't want it to sicken her or reduce her lifespan either," Niven gnashes at me.

"It already has, if you have not noticed. She is growing weaker and not eating very much. It is obviously because of this spell," I point out, growing angrier by the minute.

"Have you considered breaking up the spell inside her? What if we tried that now that we know what the spell is doing?" he argues.

"I dare not try to pluck it from her. It has infected her, intertwined with her vital organs. The damage to her could be catastrophic. I cannot risk it." My hands squeeze into fists, wishing I could punish the fae with them.

"Then we need to follow the fae's advice to the letter. *Healthy food, quality sleep, high spirits, true love.* Only two of those can be guaranteed. High spirits and true love are... abstract. And I personally don't think *you* will be able to help Ada achieve those." Niven sneers.

I snarl at his nerve. "*She* is my priority. You are too busy with this *council* to give her the attention she deserves. But I am there every day, taking stock of what she is dealing with. I see what you do not, and I make sure she has what she needs."

Darla looks thoughtful while we argue, ignoring us in favor of her own thoughts. "We should try to find out where the fae are coming from and why they're here. It will resist, but any clue is worth finding out." The abruptness of her question cools off the heated words slung between us.

"I will try another day," he responds to her, sounding doubtful. "We will be lucky if I can force it to divulge anything useful. Much of it may be hard to interpret. Fae minds are so different than ours. Undoubtedly their realm must be as well."

My gaze travels between Darla and Niven. "It mentioned 'extinguishing the Mayweather line'. Do you think it had anything to do with Ada's parents' death?" I ask, dreading the possibility.

Niven sighs. "I honestly don't know. We will follow that line of questioning next time. I'm not sure I can take more of it today," he answers honestly. "But I know in my bones there's more that damnable fae is still hiding from us. It thinks it has the upper hand. But we won't let it."

"Did you See anything while the fae spoke?" I ask Darla.

She thinks for a moment, her hand on her chin. Her eyes have a faraway look when she finally speaks. "My Sight was not clearcut during the interview. But I have this certainty that hope will follow in the new year when old paths converge again. It seems important to Ada's future."

Niven's curious eyes flash to mine. "A lot of old paths have converged since we arrived."

Both Niven and I return to Ada's house before she's due home from the clinic. This conversation will be difficult, but we cannot keep this new information from her. She needs to know what the fae is doing to her and what is at stake if we cannot help her in time.

I prepare our dinner, conscious of the *healthy food* directive, a hearty chicken and wild rice soup with plenty of vegetables. Fresh bread and butter as well. This seems very nourishing. But what would that fae know of nutrition for a witch? No matter, we must try everything possible.

I meet Ada in the foyer when she arrives. Her eyebrows shoot up when she sees me. Admittedly, I must look silly wearing her apron. But I did not use a big enough pot for the soup, so it kept splattering uncomfortably hot on my abdomen.

"Who knew pink was your color? Are you making dinner?" she asks, an unexpectedly light tone in her voice.

"Of course," I say with a small smile tugging across my tusks. "You deserve a hot meal after a long day."

"Wow, you're still trying to spoil me. I'm fully able to cook for myself," she remarks without any teeth.

"No need while I am here," I insist. What I do not mention is that I would stay forever and do this every day if she would allow it.

Niven descends the staircase. He must have heard us. His face is drawn. It is obvious he is not looking forward to this conversation any more than I am. But we need to figure out a plan.

"There's a lot to talk about over dinner," he admits to Ada.

"I see. So you *are* buttering me up." She looks concerned.

"No, dinner would have been made for you regardless. But we have a lot to tell you," I break it to her gently.

She follows mutely as we head to the kitchen. I already set the table for us, a pitcher of lemonade and the sliced bread waiting for them. I ladle piping hot soup into bowls. Niven and Ada take their seats, murmuring their thanks as I set the bowls in front of them.

"You have me on pins and needles. What is going on?" she presses.

Niven and I share a look before he turns his attention back to Ada. "We found evidence of the fugitives today. One of our trackers, a gargoyle, stumbled into a magickal trap a mile south of the ward along the coast. It tore up his wing pretty badly. He'll recover and gain an impressive scar from it, but the magick in the trap was tricky. Way too advanced for a couple of warlocks. It was likely fae. It took some time to release him."

Ada gasps. "That must have been awful," she commiserates.

"But that's not even the important update. Today I began questioning the fae about what he did to you. The process is a challenge. It takes a lot of concentration, and my ability to compel honest responses from it has a short time limit. It's nothing like using my abilities on Whispered Folk. Anyway, this is my long-winded way of saying we've only begun to scratch the surface. But what it said today was alarming."

Ada looks increasingly concerned. "What did it say?"

Niven's brows knit and he rubs his hand across his mouth. "The fae isn't stealing or blocking your magick. It's stealing your life. Something the fae called *ethereal spark*. I talked to some of our experts today, and we would call it life force, though they seem to mean the same thing. I remember some of this from studying older magick at the academy. It isn't common terminology among witches today. We think about it in simpler terms of aging and mortality. If I remember correctly, life force moves between realms. This fae has somehow claimed a piece of yours on Samhain and is slowly siphoning more. And now your lives are tied. If we kill the fae, it says it will kill you too. It was under compulsion to speak truth, and I'm sure it was."

Ada stares at him, tears shimmering in her eyes. "Am I dying?"

"We will not let you die from this." The words burst from deep within me. Never have I spoken with more conviction.

"The fae told us how to slow down the siphoning. Eating and sleeping well. But also keeping your spirits high and experiencing true love will help. It was an oddly helpful recipe to live a good life spewed from such a hateful creature. But it seemed sure of this, even if it wouldn't or couldn't tell us much more a magickal remedy for you," Niven explains.

"We are still looking for a way to separate you from the fae permanently. We will never stop. Do not despair." I cannot let her believe anything else.

"So why is my magick gone?" Ada rasps.

"Your magick is helping to slow it as well. It mentioned that it isn't draining your magick. That it could have taken more of your life force that night if your magick hadn't prevented it. Mayhap your magick is being used up fighting against this siphon it created in you. I suspect the ward may still be protecting you as well," Niven speculates.

Her expression slackens. She sits back in her chair, her shoulders sagging, and wraps her arms around her middle. "I've been tired lately. Lacking an appetite. But I figured I was feeling low about living without magick. I've never heard of anything like this other than a spell that would just outright kill someone."

"He wasn't just trying to kill you. Mark Hansen's murder was as it seemed, as was his attempt on Cara. But he wanted to absorb your life force for some reason. I suspect the spell helps make the fae nearly immortal. It said the spell can only be cast on Samhain. It must require the natural boost of magickal power that day to achieve such a feat," Niven says grimly.

"So what do I do?" Ada looks alarming pale, and she clutches her arms tighter around herself.

"I will continue to take care of you and the house, so you have fewer worries. We will take long walks to keep you strong. You will continue to spend time with your friends and family. We will make your life comfortable, so you do not over-exert yourself. Everyone will be happy to lend a hand until we find the right magick to fix this mess," I describe, having already planned for much of this even before today's new information came to light.

"I don't want to be treated like a child," she whispers.

"No one thinks you are a child," I instantly reply, slicing a hand through the air. "You have loving friends and family who would do anything to help you."

Ada exhales raggedly, rubbing her wet, reddened eyes. "It's hard to accept, especially if I don't know how long this will go on. Or if it will eventually kill me."

"As long as it takes, Ada. Please don't push us away," Niven pleads.

She nods, a small gesture, but her agreement shows her trust in us. And how immensely scared she must be.

Later that night, I call my brother and tell him to widen his and the elders' search to include any known magick or artifact that can transfer life force from one being into another.

"Life force?" Elgar says incredulously. "That sounds much more serious."

"It's already affecting her. We need something to stave off the effects. Have the elders shared anything from their search?" I already know the answer. He would have told me immediately if they did.

"No," he grumbles. "They are being as unresponsive to me as they are to you. Something is wrong. They meet in secret, according to my sources. Others have noticed how reclusive they have become. It worries me, Norrell."

I sigh, running an unsteady hand through my hair. "Ask Mother and Father to approach their families to try to get any information about what they are doing. This concerns me too, but I am not abandoning Ada again."

"I would not expect you to. They will help me investigate," he confirms.

Not wanting to miss any possible avenues, I dial Dean Esmeralda Jurado's number next. I have not spoken to her since she told me about Ada. No doubt she has been kept updated, but she will appreciate hearing this new development from me.

"Norrell!" she exclaims happily. "I'm so thrilled to hear from you again. Are you still attending the safety council? I hear it's wrapping up."

"Hi, Esmeralda. Yes, I am still here though I am no longer attending their meetings. They moved onto practical security measures to protect their havens and people. That is no longer my concern," I explain.

She huffs a laugh. "Well, I'm sure anyone can see you're not there to discuss the ins and outs of multi-layering wards. How has it been going?"

"It has been complicated, which is surely no surprise to you. I assisted Niven and his team with the fae. They could manage without me, but at much greater risk. Niven needs to be fully focused on finding answers. The fae told us some disturbing information today. It is stealing Ada's life force. Somehow it is still able to absorb it from her while in containment. It is worse when we must bring it out. It sickens her when we do so. This fae is unbelievably powerful. Mayhap even more than the ones we occasionally find wandering the Arctic," I recount.

"That sounds dire, Norrell. I won't sugarcoat it," Esmeralda remarks. "I've combed through our archives the past few weeks focusing on the loss of magick. I'll keep it up. There may be more out there about stealing life force. That is a term used in old texts describing passing through the realms. It's unusual in our contemporary lexicon. This fae may be quite ancient if it knows such spells. They have probably been long forgotten by witches or hidden away for good reason. It's a despicable use of magick. I'll redouble my efforts. The library will have something, I know it."

"Thank you. You are a true friend to her."

"Stay strong for her, Norrell." Her parting words stick with me.

After finishing a few final tasks in Ada's front lawn, I step inside to find Ada and Aurelia reading quietly in the living room, curled up on opposite sofas, each with a cat on her lap. Aurelia reaches for her mug of tea while she eyes me entering the room. Earl Grey blinks awake momentarily at the movement.

"You look cozy," I observe as I stand in the doorway.

"They followed us in here after breakfast. Vanny finally wanted my attention again after Aurelia's lap was already claimed." Ada scowls exaggeratedly at the cats.

"What are your plans for today?" I ask them mildly. I do not want Ada to feel like I track her every move, though I do.

"I'm just getting my daily dose of this love bug until I'm due at today's meeting. I should be off soon. If only I could stay here with the boys." Aurelia pouts theatrically and begins to coo affectionate nonsense at the cats.

Ada sighs. "Nothing much. I took the day off work. But maybe that was a mistake. Work might help me forget everything that's going on. It might be harder to face it all… here. Being at home… is not the most peaceful place for me right now."

I would draw her up in my arms if I could. But I know that is the problem. I say instead, "I understand. I put you in a difficult position."

Her expression softens slightly. "Yes, that's part of it, but not all of it. I'm not as upset by your presence here anymore." That is a huge step forward that I should take care not to jeopardize.

Aurelia grows noticeably quieter as we speak. She abruptly stands, the cat now in her arms. "Earl Grey and I have some important cuddling to do before I get ready. So we are going to head upstairs now." A blush creeps into Ada's cheeks as Aurelia flutters her fingers in a little wave before stepping out of the room.

I wait until Aurelia is out of earshot before I respond. "I knew it would be upsetting to see me after everything I did. I am sorry for costing you your peace in your own home. When I heard, especially how it happened, I had to be here. It felt like my presence could turn the tide."

She eyes me dubiously. An understandable reaction considering our past. "That's awfully convenient for you. Well, Niven seems to think you're indispensable now. I'll take that for the ringing endorsement it is."

"How about we take a walk along the beach today. It might help clear your head," I suggest.

She gazes down at Vanny who has settled into his long morning nap. "Alright," she agrees as if she's speaking to him. "Let me change and we'll head out." She gingerly moves him onto the cushion before standing up. He does not seem to notice.

When she returns to the foyer wearing a different outfit, she pulls her long garnet hair back with a tie. Her white forelocks streak symmetrically across the sides of her head. It has always been a compelling contrast. I let my gaze linger on her thick hair and the delicate lines of her ears and neck now exposed to me. She wears a loose light sweater and linen pants that cut off at the ankle.

She hands me the keys to her Wagoneer, another good sign. It is a short drive to the cleared-off parking area next to the dunes. We walk in step, though wordlessly, as we take the path to the long sandy beach. We used to come here on the occasional morning and beachcomb during those two wonderful years here together. Sometimes we would find fossilized shark teeth, colorful spiraling whelk shells, and sun-bleached sand dollars. Even the occasional live starfish we would try to rescue when it was stranded by the lowering tide. I could jump right back in to that closeness with her, though I do not hold out hope it is the same for her.

Watching the waves crashing toward shore, she quietly comments, "I think Cyrinda, Tallie, and Aurelia are leaving soon. The council is quickly wrapping up. They're all anxious to get home. You and Niven are welcome to stay as long as you need to."

"That means a lot to me, thank you," I respond evenly. It makes me immeasurably happy to receive such an invitation.

"Aurelia may miss the boys as much as they'll miss her," she notes with a chuckle.

"I will give them extra love after she goes," I assure her.

Her eyes scrunch as she smiles unguardedly at me, a sight I haven't seen in fifteen years. "They'll appreciate a warm lap to cry on," she jests.

"I spoke with Dean Jurado last night. She says hello," I mention.

"Esmeralda. She left me a message after …" Ada trails off. "I forgot to call her back. I hope she's well. I haven't kept up with her as much as I meant to since the academy days. You've stayed in touch with her?"

"Periodically," I clarify. "Her mentorship was so valuable to me. I did not want to leave that behind completely."

"Oh." Ada sounds crestfallen. Walking back through my words, I see why. "I'm sure she was glad for that."

"Ada, I did not mean…"

She sweeps her hands in front of her, interrupting me. "Sorry, I'm just being sensitive."

"Do not apologize for how you feel. Call me out when I say something thoughtless," I try to reassure her.

"We'll never get anywhere if all I do is call you out," she disagrees.

"We will, regardless," I tell her honestly.

She purses her lips. "It isn't doing me much good to dwell in the past. It brings me more sadness than anything else."

"You should not let it. You have a life full of meaning and many friends to share it with."

She smiles wanly, looking down at her bare feet treading over the sand. "In some ways, yes. In others, not really."

"Ada," I nearly groan her name. Her eyes fly to me. "I should have never pursued you, knowing what could have happened. What did happen. I was too consumed by you to pull away. It was entirely my fault. I should have protected you from it. Kept you free of me to find and be happy with someone else without all the pain I caused."

"I don't know if there would have been someone else. Not really. It's been a long time, Norrell. I haven't met him yet if he was out there. I would have been open to it. You didn't totally break me," she says joylessly.

"You were it for me. Always. No other female ever interested me. My heart and soul were already claimed. There was no room for anyone else, ever. Not in my heart, not in my bed," I admit.

"I don't want you to think I would send you away if you had a life after me," she challenges. "You took over leadership in your clan. Certainly, that comes with expectations."

"Mayhap for others. But I warned them who they were getting to lead them if they forced my hand," I reveal.

"Who did they get?" she wonders.

"A male with no warmth or sympathy for anyone or anything else. One who will do his job ruthlessly to make up for the guilt he carries every day. One who will not be cowed into any further demands from anyone, even the elders. Especially them. It was my punishment to them for what they forced me to do as much as it was punishment to myself," I describe in accurate detail.

"That doesn't sound like the male I knew, even if he didn't treat me very well some of the time," she remarks.

"No, he stayed in Monstera Bluff with my heart," I confess.

"Norrell," she says softly, chastising.

"It is the truth," I reiterate.

"I've been angry at you for so long. But I wouldn't have wanted that," she divulges.

"It is what I deserve. I will never be able to fully make amends."

Her brows knit. "Don't put it on me like this to forgive you," she counters.

"No, I do not want or expect that. I am mad at myself and the path my life has taken," I clarify.

"I can understand that," she empathizes. "I never thought my life would look like this either."

"I will stay for the long haul to help you through this. Whatever it takes. My clan can fester for all I care at this point if they are unwilling to accept my brother's leadership." It is a truth I have realized since coming back here. The life I want is not there. They are not my people anymore. *Your people* should not want you to sacrifice yourself.

Her expression turns introspective, her gaze returning to the horizon. We walk a while before she speaks again. "There's a lot we will both have to come to terms with. It'll take more than a few pretty words to hash this out."

"I am here for as many conversations as it takes," I vow to her.

The remainder of our walk is much quieter. We stop periodically so she can dig her toes in the sand and watch a pod of dolphins breaching above the waves. We are at ease with each other again and the stroll becomes companionable. After finding a few flawless shells Ada cannot leave behind, we eventually turn around and return home to make lunch. There is a lightness between us that has been missing since I arrived, marking the turning point I have been longing for since I reentered her life.

CHAPTER 13
ADA

"I can't wait to sleep in my own bed again!" Bittersweet emotions flood me when Tallie informs me that she, Cyrinda, and Aurelia are leaving tomorrow. Living under the same roof for so long bonded us, hopefully for life. I wouldn't say the past few weeks flew by quickly, but this announcement takes me by surprise.

"I'll drink to that! Though three weeks of horribly boring meetings was worth the trade-off to spend time with you delightful females," Cyrinda says in an uncharacteristically snark-less manner.

"Did you already break into a bottle of champagne, Cyrinda? You sound downright sentimental," Aurelia teases her old friend, who scoffs at her in return.

"I think we're all a little punch drunk after so many all-day meetings. I haven't had to do anything like that since my school days," Tallie whines.

Aurelia clasps both of their shoulders, lightly shaking them. "We got through it. Our communities' wards will be stronger than ever. And we'll go home with new and effective security measures to put into place. Feel good we're protecting our future," Aurelia reminds them.

"Ew. And you accuse me of breaking into the bubbly already?

You're being the ooey-gooey one right now," Cyrinda playfully defends herself.

"Speaking of bottles and bubbly, are we ready to get some drinks? How does Call of the Wild sound?" Tallie asks.

"You just want to stare at Hal's biceps one last time before you leave," Cyrinda says knowingly. "No judgment. I don't mind a side of beefcake with my cocktail either."

"So what if I do? Who better to know and appreciate a fine orc specimen than another one," she says touching her shoulder and making a sizzle sound. Aurelia and I giggle at her. Cyrinda clucks her tongue.

The three lead me on a quick walk downtown to Call of the Wild, clearly a well-worn path for them.

The afternoon sun shines brightly through the windows onto the dark wood-clad interior of Call of the Wild. This place does not believe in overhead lighting. Other than candlelight and the orange glow of their fireplace, it gets very dark at night, even for a witch's eyes without casting a darkvision spell. *When in the dark without sight, let me see like there's warm light.* So I'll be claiming a small hoard of their tea candles if we're here for more than a couple hours.

Unsurprisingly, Hal slings drinks behind the bar along with a werewolf from the Wolf Pack. They own and operate the pub, which helps fund their activities and programs. Celeste Longclaw, one of my fellow town council members, waves to me from a barstool as we sit down at our table. It's then I notice we have a direct line of sight to Hal. These ladies never fail to make me laugh. Even though at times I was frustrated by the lack of privacy while hosting them, I will miss all of them immensely when they're gone.

"I'm tempted to stay down here through the winter, Ada, but my mate would miss the snow. Winter is already in full swing Upstate. Brr, it makes me cold just thinking about it. You wouldn't mind a seasonal houseguest if I never needed to escape it, would you?" Aurelia quips.

"Not at all! You know you're as welcome as the flowers in May. Though if you are interested in eye candy, and I'm talking to all of you, Bran at the inn has turned into a tall drink of sweet tea. He's a bit younger than me. His family has always lived on my street. I can't help but still think of him as the little kid who'd tag along with me and my friends." I smile to myself as I recall his big puppy dog eyes, which to be fair, as a barghest, were somewhat genuine.

"We took stock already. He was quite popular with some of his unmated guests, though he remained respectable and professional, to their dismay. So disappointing." Cyrinda sighs her words.

Tallie listens with half an ear as she surreptitiously ogles Hal, who seems to be flexing a little more than usual, at least to my eyes. He's not usually such a flirt, but he must be hamming it up for her in good fun.

"Mother Earth to Tallie," Cyrinda waves her elegant hand in front of Tallie's face. "Someone's got a little crush."

Tallie shrugs, smirking at us.

"Let the female have a little fun," Aurelia tuts, waggling her eyebrows.

"I suppose, but we are having ourselves a farewell ladies' night. She can look but not *look* if you know what I mean. At least until later," Cyrinda says, aiming a wink at Tallie.

"I have a feeling we'll use our portals a little more after this council ends. It beats flying six hours to visit the west coast," Aurelia reflects.

Cyrinda takes umbrage. "Frankly, I'm offended you talk about coming here for the winter, Aurelia. I have a perfectly good house in sunny Los Angeles you can stay at." She crosses her arms in an exaggerated fashion and pouts at her.

"Is the invitation open to anyone?" Tallie wonders. "I wouldn't mind seeing the sun a little bit in the winter. It gets downright dreary in Cascadia."

"I suppose you've grown on me enough to let you stay." Cyrinda rolls her eyes playfully. "Sometimes it feels like I need to escape the sun. So, this better be a two-way street."

"You like to pretend to be a city gal, but at heart you like a slower pace of life surrounded by beautiful nature more than you care to admit." Aurelia gives Cyrinda a knowing look.

"Mayhap, but if one of you isn't there" —she points her finger at us —"I wouldn't be caught dead near the woods. Yuck, there are so many bugs," she complains with a shiver.

"You talk like a live in a cabin in the woods. I live in town!" Aurelia exclaims, laughing at Cyrinda's words.

"Close enough. You live next to a path to the woods. That's basically the same thing!" she defends.

"You love it," Aurelia intones, nudging Cyrinda with her shoulder.

"Sometimes. When I'm sick of the city that is," Cyrinda relents with a dramatic sigh.

"That's how I met this ludicrous female. She *needed to get away from it all* but ended up in a town full of bear shifters like it was some yoga retreat." She smiles fondly at her friend.

"Don't pretend your town doesn't have a yoga studio that overlooks a bluff. I'd call that a retreat," Cyrinda argues.

"I'll be sure to pass that business idea along," Aurelia says thoughtfully.

"I suppose. Unless it gets too popular and I'm forced to book months in advance. I like having my own secret getaway. If half the Whispered Folk world found out, I'd be *very upset*," Cyrinda insists.

"That would be a good problem for us to have. Don't worry, there's always room for our favorite sharp-tongued faun. You're basically part of the clan at this point," Aurelia croons to her, reaching out and pinching her cheek. Cyrinda playfully bats the hand away from her face while cracking up.

"Ashes! You don't have to blab all my secrets." Cyrinda wheezes as they poke at each other, their behavior reminiscent of siblings.

When they order a second round of drinks, I opt for sparkling water with lime instead. Alcohol is going to my head a little too quickly these days, though I could always stop by my shop to pick up a hangover cure potion. But I do feel pleasantly loose after this one drink.

"So it'll just be you in the house with Niven and Norrell starting tomorrow. They've become surprisingly friendly in the last week. I wasn't sure if that was in the cards for them. Niven didn't seem to be a fan at first," Tallie notes, turning her attention to me.

I rest my chin in my hand as I consider her question. "Yes, they find common ground in the work they're doing together. I'm not sure they'd necessarily be friends in other circumstances. Neither of them open up that easily."

"I'll extend my stay a few days if you need a buffer against Norrell. I would never leave a female in the lurch like that," Cyrinda says very seriously.

"Oh, I know you wouldn't, especially if you could get in a few more good jabs at him," I chuckle. She winks at me in response. "Things are easier between us. But it's still a new horizon, and I don't know what's on the other side. At first, I thought he was all hat and no cattle, but his support feels genuine now. Mother Earth knows he's running all over hell's half acre keeping up the house for me. At times, it can be hard to accept. I don't relish being the damsel in distress."

"Aw, listen to you sounding like a little Southern belle. No wonder he's head over heels for you," Tallie remarks, a smile in her voice.

"Is it *his* help or any help?" Aurelia wonders.

"Both, I guess," I answer honestly. "I've been self-reliant for so long. And now my life is turned on its head. That loss of independence is as difficult a pill to swallow as the effects of this fae curse. It's one more thing taken away from me."

All three of their expressions turn pensive. Cyrinda puts a comforting hand over mine on the table. "You've got this. It's not a failure to ask for help when you need it. Though he better not mess up. Niven may have given him the benefit of the doubt, but he's still on my shit list. Remind him I have my eye on him, even from afar." Her tender tone only slightly softens her pointed words about Norrell.

"I don't think anyone wants to attend a pity party tonight, so instead let's toast to new and lasting friendships," I exclaim, holding up my glass. Everyone raises theirs to mine.

"To badass babes leading Whispered Folk into the future!" Aurelia rhapsodizes.

"To independent females unafraid to take what they want in life," Cyrinda adds.

"To all the fun we'll have invading each other's homes," Tallie jokes.

We clink glasses and take a sip. I have a feeling we'll remain friends long after this council is behind us.

♡ ♡ ♡ ♡ ♡

After finally connecting with the farmers market organizer, I compiled everything needed for Sunny's booth application. I've worn a smile since I opened the shop this morning, eager to show her when she arrives.

Sunny walks in, bright and bubbly as usual, her beaming smile lighting up her face as we greet each other. When we have a break between customers, I ask her to sit with me, unable to hide my excitement.

"What's going on?" she asks lightheartedly. "You look almost giddy today."

"I have some fun news to share," I begin, as we take our seats. "You're under no pressure whatsoever, but I have everything you need to become a vendor at the farmers market. I want to keep selling your potions here, but that will open even more doors for you if you want to run your own shop in the future."

Her jaw drops and she looks stunned. "Mother Earth, I guess I hadn't thought about going for it yet! I still have time left in my apprenticeship. Are you sure you wouldn't mind? I don't want it to affect your shop at all," she frets.

"Absolutely not! Don't worry about me or the shop. Your apprenticeship will continue and you can adjust your hours however you need. You'll be a hit at the market. The organizer says you're a shoo in. It'll be a good stepping stone for your own shop someday," I assure her.

"Thanks, Ada. You're the best! I'm so lucky you're my mentor," she gushes as she leans over and squeezes me in a big hug, rocking me back and forth in her enthusiasm.

"We're friends above everything else," I remind her. "I can't wait to see what you're going to accomplish."

When I leave work that afternoon, Norrell meets me to walk over to Walt and Acton's house. Walt and I worked together to design the campaign posters he picked up from the printer's this morning.

"Did Walt come up with a slogan?" Norrell asks curiously, having already heard bits and pieces of our phone calls over the last few days.

"Walt barely needed any help with that," I tell him, laughing at the memory of Walt's and my last conversation. "He chose 'A vote for Walt is a walk in the park.'"

Norrell chuckles heartily. "That suits him."

When I told Walt that Norrell would be joining us this afternoon, he was upfront about his hesitance to include him. Walt still hasn't warmed up to Norrell, and I don't blame him. My feelings are still *thawing* as well. But eventually Walt relented since Norrell seemed very serious about not just coming with me but also lending support to the campaign. I made sure Walt understood that, and he seems to have accepted that he can't actively ignore Norrell any longer—a big leap forward for Walt, who is as loyal to me as they come.

Walt and Acton are waiting outside, posters in hand. He immediately hands half the stack over to us, looking pleased as punch. "They did such a fine job at Inkling Press. See how bright this green is?" he raves, pointing at the lush shade of green framing the edges of each poster.

"It's eye-catching!" I agree.

Walt grins at us. "I'm tickled pink that we're doing this. I never thought of myself as a man who would run for office. I always figured myself to just be a civil servant who tries to spend his days outdoors. But I can't ignore Ada's good ideas," he enthuses.

"There are countless virtues I could extol about my mate, but he is too modest to receive my boundless praise," Acton chimes in affectionately.

"Oh, Acton, you know just how to make me blush," Walt says sounding adorably flustered. "Why don't we walk downtown, and we can each take a side to poster up the street. Then I'll treat everyone to dinner afterward."

We split up, and Norrell and I uneventfully visit the first few shops along our side of the street, asking to affix a sign in the window. I've quickly grown tired, walking to Walt and Acton's house and then back here again. Norrell notices my struggle and holds out his arm for me to take. I tightly wrap my hand around the crook of his elbow, locking myself to his strength. He guides us down the sidewalk, essentially holding up most of my weight. It doesn't slow him down a bit.

The heat of his skin is a shock to the system, warming me all over in ways I wish it wouldn't. His physicality was always so alluring to me, both sexy and comforting. He made me feel like I could let go and he would carry me through anything. Well, he showed me that it was just a fantasy. Still, it's hard not to let that feeling creep back in again, to fall back into old habits.

When we reach the tailoring shop In Stitches—always a busy place to accommodate Whispered Folks' many sizes and specifications—the owner, a soft-spoken elfin named Finch, comes out from the back room to greet us. His eyes widen at the sight of Norrell.

"Why Norrell, I haven't seen you in an age. It was so long ago, but I don't believe I properly thanked you for helping with my deliveries after I broke my foot. I was about ready to hobble all over town dropping off those garments. I've never forgotten your kindness. Please accept my very belated thank you for helping me when I needed it." There's genuine warmth in his voice.

"No thanks necessary, Finch. It was no trouble at all," he tells the elfin kindly.

Finch's pink-hued skin deepens in color as a blush blooms on his cheeks. "I'm glad to finally be able to tell you. I wasn't sure if I'd ever see you again. Now, what can I do for you both," he asks, his eyes shifting between us curiously.

"Walt Sutton is running for a town council seat. Would you mind if we put a sign in your window?" Norrell says, keeping a light tone. We've both been mindful to not pressure anyone, though so far everyone has been enthusiastic about it.

"Anything for him. Walt is a true gentlemale. I haven't seen him around as much since he retired several years ago," Finch replies. "Tell him he has my vote!"

"We will. And I'll remind him to stop by and say hello," I add, earning a toothy grin from Finch.

After adhering the poster to the window, Norrell and I wave goodbye and then continue down the street.

On the next block, we reach the door beneath the pink Pearlhouse Pastries sign. The head baker Marius Pearlhouse, whose family owns the bakery, is cleaning out one of the ovens. Mars—as his friends call him—

and I go way back, but I haven't seen him in a while. Norrell hasn't mentioned him, so he may not have either. As we approach the counter, Mars jerks toward us in a clumsy manner, at odds with the agility I know him to possess, jolted by the shock of seeing Norrell.

"Moon and stars, I scarcely believe my eyes. Norrell Snowstrider? Is it really you?" he asks incredulously. "It's been years! I was gutted when I heard you had left." His eyes dart between us speculatively. "And the two of you had parted ways."

Mars and Norrell became friends while he was here, even socializing somewhat regularly. The tarasque steps out from behind the counter and embraces Norrell, a large leonine paw tipped in long claws smacking his back affectionately. It amazes me how his unexpectedly nimble hands create pastry masterpieces each morning, using his claws so expertly and delicately. He holds Norrell by the shoulders now, taking a long look at his old friend. "I thought I'd never see you again. What brings you back?" Again, his eyes flash quickly to mine and back. "And how long will you be staying?"

"It is so good to see you, Mars. I have sorely missed our friendship. I returned a few weeks ago to attend the safety council and am now assisting the team investigating the attack. There has not been much free time yet, to be honest, but I will have more now that the council has gone home. As for how long I will stay..." Norrell hesitates, *his* gaze now searching mine momentarily as if I have the answers. "I will be here for some time, it seems. Much of it depends on the investigation. We should plan a time to catch up." He carefully sidesteps talking about me, which I'm thankful for.

Mars's large golden eyes shine and his wide mouth splits into a delighted grin, making his rugged face, a blend of leonine and human features, look almost boyish. A feat when many consider his appearance —with a long reddish-brown mane that extends from his head to around his collar bone where his skin turns to scales—to be intimidating. "I would love nothing more, old friend," he replies.

They exchange phone numbers and agree to figure out a date to meet up soon. When we ask Mars if we can put up a sign, he takes a small stack, promising to circulate them for us. "It's about time he runs. I've seen few as committed to the well-being of this town as Walt. You may be one of the few exceptions," he tells me with a friendly wink. He stops us before we go, piling a box full of pastries for us and handing us a couple bags as well, one for the box and one for the rest of our campaign signs. We gratefully accept them as we leave.

Stopping and chatting with people at the businesses and shops along the next few blocks eats up nearly two hours. When we reach the square in front of town hall, Walt and Acton follow close behind, their experience similar. "Well, you run for office and suddenly everyone wants to talk your ear off about the changes they want to see. I haven't even been elected yet." Walt chuckles, shaking his head in good humor at the situation. "Guess that's what campaigning is all about!"

"They sense your inner goodness and know you to be an honorable male worthy to entrust the town's future into your care," Acton lilts in his airy voice.

He blushes at Acton's praise. "Or maybe I'm just an old familiar face," he teases. "But thank you for your sweetness, Acton. I continue to be the luckiest man in the world to be your mate."

Norrell's mouth tips up into a smile as he watches them, and I realize mine has done the same as my eyes move back to my uncles, still deliriously in love after fifty years.

"So," Walt says with a light clap of his hands. "How does Midnight Mystic sound? Acton wants to try their new bee pollen smoothie." He puts his arm around Acton, settling a hand on his waist while pulling him into his side.

"Sounds great," I agree. "I've been so curious about it too!"

Walt marvels at all his signs in the windows along the street as we walk back to the coffee shop and café. They're unmissable with their cute slogan in big print.

Midnight Mystic has a full menu catering to nearly every Whispered Folk diet. I always enjoy seeing the food Acton orders since I never quite know what to expect.

Though we arrive during the dinner rush, we're still able to get a table, claiming it with our leftover campaign posters and then order at the counter. I order spiced pumpkin soup with a side of fresh baked bread. Norrell orders a beef and vegetable pot pie with a side salad. Looking at him, I would have figured him to be much more carnivorous than he is. But long ago he told me his people somehow grow fields of vegetables and grains in the expansive underground cavern they live in.

When we sit down, Walt sizes up Norrell more directly than he had earlier. And frankly I'm surprised he hadn't said anything sooner. "So, we haven't spoken since you came back," he starts, sounding hesitant. "I'm not saying I forgive you for what you did, but I'm glad to hear about everything you're doing for Ada since you've returned. And for your help today. I feel a little out of my element with this upcoming election, so I appreciate the support."

Norrell inclines his head. "You are welcome. If there is anything else I can do, just name it. And I have not forgiven myself either, so I would never expect it from anyone else, especially her beloved uncles," he responds, his voice turning pensive. "A lifetime of good intentions may never make up for that one terrible decision that led to my profound betrayal. And I will live with that knowledge for the rest of my days."

Walt looks at me for a long moment and sighs, rubbing an unsteady hand over his mouth. It's a difficult topic and I'm sure the expression on my face reflects my own range of emotions.

"It shows maturity that you understand the impact it had on Ada that you had the audacity to leave her. When you did. I'll follow Ada's lead on this, but it may take some time for me to come around again," he admits plainly. It looks like it pains him to say such a thing to someone he once cared for. Acton surreptitiously rubs a soothing hand along his back.

"I understand. I failed Ada. And you and Acton by extension of that. Leaving her meant I left her family as well. I am eternally sorry. I hope to earn your respect again one day," he says, his voice unexpectedly thick with emotion.

It's a crazy notion, considering everything, but I want to comfort both males, even though it's clear they need to work this out between themselves. Walt took the abandonment very personally since he embraced Norrell as a nephew, though that hadn't blinded Walt to his shortcomings as a mate to me. Acton was also upset, but he never expressed his heartbreak as outwardly except to comfort me.

Watching us, Acton adds, "Seasons of change bring out the best and worst of those in its midst. We shall let this metamorphosis play out until we cast any more judgment."

"That's wise counsel as always, Acton. If my situation is the metamorphosis, I feel like I'm turning into a slug rather than a butterfly. But I do feel like a well-cared-for slug, if that makes y'all feel better about things," I note with an easy laugh.

"You are not turning into a slug, my dear. They do not go through a metamorphosis," Walt gently corrects me.

"Anything is possible at this point," I joke, trying to lighten the mood at the table. Putting everyone at ease again will go a long way in helping repair their connection.

"You are already as vibrant as a butterfly floating on gossamer wings," Acton reassures me.

Before I can respond, a server stops by with our food. Everyone's dinner looks and smells delicious. I lean over to take a whiff of the bee pollen smoothie, a frothy concoction of sap from various trees as well as natural sugars, pollen, and honey. The combination smells pleasant, like it would make a nice scent for a candle. It is topped with pollen flakes and a sizeable chunk of raw honeycomb that Acton immediately plucks out of the glass and takes a big bite of.

We finally ease into more companionable conversation after our first few bites of food. I ask Walt who they ran into on their side of the street.

"Well, when we went to the garden store, they basically stole half my stack! Between all we've bought there and at their nursery, I guess we're their best customers lately, what with the big back garden overhaul project. They offered to hand them out to customers!" Walt slaps his knee and laughs at the sheer silliness of it. "I didn't have the heart to say no."

"Well, they know how to keep their customers loyal!" I guffaw.

"The dance academy wants to host the election night party. They said they've been my biggest fans since I helped them organize recitals in the parks for their students who fly. I was too flustered to outright accept, but I told them I'll consider it. That's too much, right?" Walt questions.

"I remember how beloved those were," Norrell chimes in. "The young students had tremendous talent."

Acton cups Walt's cheek in his hand affectionately, turning his head so they gaze at each other. "You have been a north star to many, even if you would never give yourself credit. Let them celebrate you, my overly modest mate." Walt and Acton share a knowing smile and a peck on the lips.

"Then I believe we'll have ourselves a party!" I gush, clapping my hands in glee.

CHAPTER 14
NORRELL

Niven stops me in the upstairs hallway as he emerges from his room, Ada's father's study where I often spent hours in long conversations with him all those years ago. There is a gleam in Niven's eyes, like he is primed for something.

"The warlocks' hideout has been sighted finally. Their cloaking spell must have flagged for long enough that one of our flyers spotted it before disappearing again. If they had help with their escape, it seems to be running out. I bet we'll get them within the next forty-eight hours. We're keeping a close watch on that location, trying to pick up any magickal signatures. My team and I will escort them through the portal as soon as they're in custody," Niven explains animatedly, sounding fired up to question the attempted murderers.

We walk downstairs into the kitchen together. Niven starts the coffee while I unload the dishwasher and set two mugs on the counter. Then I fry some eggs and put bread in the toaster. Niven sits at the table, flipping through his notebook and begins writing intently.

"In case we need to leave quickly, there's a lot I must accomplish in today's session with the fae. Ashes, between how much of my magick it drains and how it affects Ada, I need to make sure we're as short and to the point today as possible," Niven says, not looking up at me, still taking notes.

"We need to find out how to separate it from Ada and then we should rid our realm of it. The fae are always unsettling, even after dealing with many over the years. This one is beyond the pale," I answer, taking the pan of eggs off the burner and plating them with the toast. I prepare a plate for Ada, who will be downstairs shortly. She will go to the clinic again this morning and then hopefully be able to work at her shop afterward if she feels up to it. Though the effect these short interrogation sessions have on her still fills me with dread.

When I set down Niven's and my plates and pour the coffee, he breaks down his plan for the morning. Most of the session will again focus on Ada and the fae magick stealing her life. There is added pressure since he could be gone for a while depending on the outcome of the warlocks' interrogations. And then the Yuletide season arrives.

The interrogation starts earlier than usual and with an even greater sense of urgency. Niven called Darla Rallis to join us again. She eagerly agreed and is in the room with us. As we have done for weeks, the team of witches lifts the wards as the fae is taken out of containment. I search for its pool of magickal power, letting it awaken and draw strength until it becomes threatening.

Niven's focus locks in, his pupils expanding and darkening his green eyes as he wrestles for control of the fae's mind. When he is satisfied, he begins the questioning. "Do you steal the *ethereal spark* of others every year at Samhain?" His use of the fae's phrasing seems purposeful to elicit a better response.

The fae sounds more unhinged the longer we question it, like it loses its mind the longer we keep it warded. It is unconscious while in containment, so to the fae, this must feel like one long series of questions.

"Yes! Yes! Decades from each one before they perish. My life will be eternal!" the fae shouts gleefully in two voices, a child-like squeak and a wispy but distinctly masculine one.

"Alright, that answers another question I had," he says to the room. "Does it matter if the victim possesses magick? Does that make their ethereal spark more potent?"

The fae giggles wildly. "I always savor the magick before it is gone. It takes extra effort to fight through it to get to their ethereal spark, but the payoff is sublime. It draws out the sweetness in their pain. And to be the last one to relish their magick before it extinguishes forever, it is glorious. It makes their ethereal spark so much stronger, particularly if the creature is powerful. Ada was one of those rare treats I will remember fondly *forever*." The fae punctuates its point with a chorus of soft and musical feminine tones.

"Why do you have to fight through their magick?" Niven presses, his physical stance turning as aggressive as his tone.

"Because it wants to preserve ethereal spark at all costs. Magick has an instinct to survive as much as the life form that wields it. That is the only challenge I must face when I snatch it for my own. The magick will fight and fight to banish the spell, but mine is stronger. It *always* wins," the fae warns in a menacing tone delivered by that childlike voice again.

"What can reinforce that ethereal spark and let magick do its work to try to extricate your spell?" Niven has found that following the fae's line of thought helps him dig for more detailed information. His magick seems to control the fae more smoothly with that approach, flowing with the twists of its mind rather than against it.

"More ethereal spark, so much more. Both magick and ethereal spark resist my pull, but once my claim on it has started it is nearly impossible to stopper. It takes more ethereal spark and magick than one creature can possess to break my spell. No one has *ever* survived it," the fae sing-songs eerily in a deep bass vocalization.

"Are there known artifacts or relics that can boost Ada's ethereal spark or magick enough to break your spell?" Niven asks, squinting in extreme concentration. He seems particularly focused on this question.

The fae attempts to seize its magick, as if about to cast a spell, but I absorb it well before it can do anything. It is desperately resisting this question. "Not many are known to me. They are all fae made, gifts dropped here long ago from another realm for the fae to use. Those who took possession of the ones you seek store them high in the sky where the Whispered Folk rarely go, where there's plenty of wild magick to fuel their incredible power. The Banner of Life will grant ethereal spark from one into another. But it is known to kill those it pulls from if they are too weak. The Forged Ruby is the only substance that can absorb magick from one being and transfer it into another in a useable form. This gift has only been sparsely granted to this realm, so do not think you can easily find it." The fae laughs maniacally in a trio of feminine voices.

I notice Darla leaning back against the wall behind her, her eyes vacant and wide. She remains upright, so I am not overly concerned about her. The witches standing near her seem to have their eyes on her. As a Seer, this may be a normal occurrence.

Niven's magick crackles with intensity. I can feel it rushing from him into the fae. "Did you or other Malefic Folk have anything to do with the deaths of Whitt and Estelle Mayweather?"

The fae's many voices cackle loudly, the echo bouncing off the walls unnervingly. "We take great joy in disrupting the Whispered Folk. If one was nearby, it surely would have tried and succeeded. How many poor unfortunate Whispered Folk have lost their lives in tragic ways? Oh, I would start looking back to seek out the patterns. They are sure to be there," the fae answers enigmatically.

Niven motions for his assistants to contain the fae again, so I yank away its remaining magick and direct it into the chunk of clear quartz on my wrist. The amount of magick it holds from these sessions is already substantial. It is not yet full but will be soon.

Darla is coherent, though she is now pacing, swaying on her feet a bit. I offer my arm to her. She takes it to keep out of the way of the team as they restore the robust wards around the fae.

When they finish up, she turns to address the room, though her eyes still look glazed. "Apologies for my reaction. It took me a while to snap out of it. My vision showed me a frost-mailed warrior journeying against the bitter, blustery winds with tools of salvation on his back. Two items so rare, their values are incalculable and matchless in this realm. It is you, Norrell. You must find them," she says at a sluggish pace at odds with her urgent tone.

She must still be recovering from her Sight. One of the other witches runs a hand a few inches away from her form, murmuring almost silently. Darla looks steadier and offers the witch a hint of a smile.

Niven's eyes, now returned to normal, search mine. "Do you know what that means?"

I nod hesitantly, still contemplating everything the fae and Darla have said in this session. "Mayhap. There are a few other yeti clans with mountain ranges in their territories. It would not surprise me if a clan kept these artifacts hidden away in a mountain cave if they are *high in the sky* where wild magick is stronger," I conjecture. I find myself absently scratching at the pelt on my chest and force my hands down again.

"I take it your clan wouldn't know for certain?" Niven questions. His expression matches the grim undertone of his words.

A mirthless laugh pours out of me. "No, we would not. Our clans are nearly as secretive with each other as we are with other Whispered Folk. It is why we always had a self-contained settlement. As a rule, our kind are extremely distrusting if you cannot tell."

"Can you make contact with them?" he asks.

"Yes, my clan will be able to. Whether they respond is another matter."

As soon as I step outside the constabulary, I call my brother. I do not expect anything has changed since I last spoke to him. The elders are stonewalling both of us. Clearly, they have no interest in helping a witch, even on my orders. But now it is clear that a clan somewhere holds the key to Ada's survival.

"Brother, how goes your days with your mate? I hope she fares well," Elgar greets me.

"She does for now, but I can see her growing more tired every day. Have you learned anything from the elders?" I ask, trying not to let on my desperation.

"Nothing. It is impossible to get those old fools to focus on anything but themselves. They are proving themselves to be a liability to our clan. They only act in their own best interest," he grunts.

"They have become noticeably more self-absorbed since our uncle joined. He is still bitter over his loss of power. He grows more out of touch with reality with each passing year and seems to be bringing the rest of the elders with him," I gripe.

"Have you learned any more from the fae?" He knows all that has come to pass in the other sessions.

"We did. I have a lot to tell you. And even more to ask of you." I sigh, readying myself for the long story. As I recount everything the fae divulged and the vision it sparked in the Seer, he anticipates where I am going with it.

"Say no more, I will accompany you wherever these artifacts are located. I will call an emergency meeting with the elders first thing tomorrow so we can start searching for them. I will let you know the time so you can call in and order them to act like the doyens they purport themselves to be," he promises.

"Push those pompous old fossils to get answers. The time to play nice is over," I growl.

Elgar grunts in agreement. "Their insubordination and secrecy make me fear that the treachery within Monstera Bluff is not so rare an occurrence."

Those elders better not hem and haw for too long. We need to reach out to the other clans as soon as possible to find out where these tools of Ada's salvation are located.

I call my uncle, cousin, and a few elders who seem more level-headed than the rest, none of whom pick up. I send more text messages, pressing the issue, but I doubt this will sway them to care. None of my other communications to them in the last few weeks have. They always have the same excuses.

When Niven meets me outside a few minutes later, we agree to debrief while eating lunch at Midnight Mystic. We barely walk a block before there is a wave of confusion in the streets. As if choreographed, witches near us in the street freeze or stumble, all affected by some unseen force. Then they whirl around as if looking for something. Several more stagger out of storefronts.

One of them spots Niven, yelling, "It's the ward! It's under attack!"

Another witch jogs over to us. "All of us who feed our magick into the ward are able to feel it, but it's never grown this intense before." He pants as he holds his head in pain. It is a small mercy that Ada cannot feel it right now.

We jump in Niven's borrowed automobile. I take the wheel, peeling down the road, taking us as close as possible to the location where the witches say they felt it. Niven barks orders over the phone to his teams, both the investigators and the trackers.

I drive the automobile as far offroad as possible, until we run into marsh. When the tires struggle on the softening ground, we abandon the vehicle and continue on foot. Murky, muddy ground slows our steps, slurping noisily at our feet. Niven curses as he nearly loses a shoe.

"Grant us passage over the terrain as if we're on solid ground," he snarls, shoving his foot back in the mud-covered shoe.

His spell on our shoes works immediately and we quicken our steps, though the thick grass and vegetation remain an obstacle.

Two figures, likely the warlocks, stand in the distance near a strange disturbance in the air. Wards are not meant to be seen, but this blood red hole must be burning through it, forming a doorway almost large enough for the figures to squeeze through. Their bodies are partially hidden behind it as we approach, though we hear their heated words to each other. One yells at the other to hurry up. The other tells him to quiet down and let him focus. The opening spreads at an alarming rate. They must have some powerful magick at their disposal if they can break through the ward so easily.

New voices sound from behind and above us. Witches from the coven and the tracker teams have quickly caught up. I do not let that distract me while I search for the magickal source supporting the spell. Alarmed at its strength, I cry out, "It is fae magick! Watch out!" I urgently absorb the unbelievable amount of magick powering the spell, but I can barely keep up. The potency of this spell is way beyond anything the warlocks should be capable of on their own. Dozens of witches around us start casting their own spells, presumably fighting against this blight slicing through the ward.

None of our efforts make a dent in its slow spread. Within seconds, the warlocks push themselves through, a subtle haze surrounding their forms. It is a protective spell, from the looks of it. They are about to unleash something deadly.

"Protect yourselves!" Niven shouts into the fray, coming to the same conclusion. The more putrescent and sinister looking of the two steps forward and tosses up a glowing yellow orb. Rushing into action, I push my abilities to the limit, further than ever before in my life, wrenching strong swells of magick out the orb to weaken it. There's no time to transfer it into the clear quartz. I let it go into the atmosphere. Even the leak of its magick is so potent it feels like being exposed to a sudden rush of fumes, making it hard to breathe.

The orb pulsates and it is clear time has run out. It will detonate at any moment. With everything left in me, I tear away the strongest root I can find that binds together the orb's foul fae magick. Hopefully it will weaken the worst of the spell.

In the blink of an eye, I am blown several feet backwards as the orb explodes, shooting energy outward in all directions, the force of it like a bomb. The wind knocks out of me, even though I land in marshy sludge. The cushion probably saved me from worse injury.

Wheezing in breath, I lay there for several seconds, weak but whole. It is a struggle to get up once my breath catches again. The flyers—gargoyles, gryphons, and other winged Whispered Folk on the tracking team—all fell from the sky. They slowly push themselves up from where they dropped around me, looking muddy and scratched, though mostly unharmed.

Before it strikes me to locate the two warlocks, Niven's voice rises behind me, exhausted but steady, "Grasses weave into sturdy rope and bind those with wicked hearts." The marsh vegetation surrounding the two warlocks surges unnaturally high and swirls like several mini tornados, weaving sections together from the ground up. When they resemble long, thick lengths of rope, they wrap around each of the warlocks like mummies from human history. Their furious screams muffle as the rope circles around their faces.

Niven, still sitting in the mud, flops backward onto his elbows, fatigue catching up with him. I stagger over, lowering onto my haunches. If I dare sit down, I might be too tired to get up again. "Good work," I tell him as I check him over for injuries.

"I could say the same of you," Niven scratches out, chuckling softly. He takes my outstretched hand, and I slowly pull him up. He wobbles on his feet, so I hold steady him while we make the slow walk back to his automobile after checking on everyone else. Those who were furthest back from the blast rush forward to help those hardest hit and to make sure the warlocks are incapacitated. Luckily, Niven's spell on our feet still lingers, otherwise we would not be getting out of here on our own.

"I called it, didn't I?" Niven jokes from his bed next to mine in the crowded healers clinic, his voice still sounding rough. I turn my head toward him, confused by his statement. "We didn't even need those extra forty-some hours."

I grin, understanding him finally. He certainly called it. It is a relief it ended as quickly as it did.

Before I can respond, Ada's melodic voice sounds from within the clinic, making apologies as she rushes through, weaving around healers and visitors crowding the space. She is wild-eyed as she approaches us, like she expects the worst.

"I came back as soon as I heard what happened. I had only just left here when everyone felt the ward," she utters as she stops between our beds, sounding winded. My poor mate must have jogged here. Hopefully she was not worried for too long.

"We are alright," I assure her, reaching out to pat her arm before I even realize what I am doing. To my surprise, she takes my hand in hers and squeezes it tightly. "We just needed a light healing tonic to help with some bruising."

Her eyes dart between me and Niven, as if she is assessing for herself whether I tell the truth.

"We've seen better days, but after a long night of sleep, we'll be fine," Niven confirms, patting her other hand she placed on his shoulder. "The warlocks are in custody finally. A team of guards just arrived from New York to escort them through the portal. It'll be my pleasure to make their interrogation long and thorough." He cracks his knuckles in a cliché gesture, making Ada laugh.

"Will you have to leave soon?" Her melancholy voice pulls at my heart.

His smile fades. "Yes, sometime tomorrow. I'll probably be gone until after Yule. But I promise we'll spend some time together tonight before I go."

She will miss having him here. And no doubt she is worried about her health. I give our joined hands a little squeeze in return, hopefully sending some comfort back to her.

CHAPTER 15
NORRELL

The latch on the front door softly clicks open and closed. The cats, already fed their evening meal, stampede into the foyer meowing their greetings to Ada. "Hello boys. Missed me today, did you?" Ada's lilting voice floats from the other room.

When she walks into the kitchen, she looks tired enough that she needs to sit down. "Tough day?"

"Not particularly, but no matter how long I sleep I never feel rested." She sighs while shrugging half-heartedly.

"Since it is the two of us now, I am making one of your favorite meals. Carbonara," I tell her, hoping it will lift her spirits. Niven left first thing this morning. Ada accompanied him to the portal to bid him farewell until he can return. I could tell it left her shaken. Everything has wrapped up except her absent magick and the life slowly draining from her.

"You are?" she exclaims, clasping her hands toward her chest in delight.

"Of course, I had not forgotten," I say lightly, not wanting to ruin the moment.

"I haven't had it in so long," she says dreamily.

I'm unable to suppress an enamored grin. "I am happy to change that."

I tell her to wait in the living room, where she can curl up on the sofa while I make dinner. It is a simple meal I perfected all those years ago. It does not take long to brush up on the few but rapid steps needed to make carbonara well.

When the dish is done, not even thirty minutes later, I fill two wide bowls with it and join her in the living room so we can eat on the sofas.

"Wow, thank you so much, Norrell," she squeals as I hand her a bowl. She immediately twists the fork into the noodles and scoops a heaping bite in her mouth. She hums her happiness as she chews exaggeratedly.

I chuckle at her silliness, part of her I have sorely missed. It warms me to see it again. "I did a good job it seems."

"Mmm-hmm!" she agrees, her mouth still very full of that first bite.

Watching her eat fills me with deep contentment. I love making her happy, which can be as simple as making a much-loved meal. But there is so much more I wish I could do.

As we both dig in, the cats decide they will be more successful at begging if they split up, one of them claiming each of us. Vanny paws at my arm occasionally, rubbing the side of his face on me affectionately, as he begs for food. I do not give in, despite how cute he looks while doing it. I am unsure if she would want me to encourage him. After a few more bites, an eternity for the cats based on their reactions, Ada finally dips a finger into the cheesy, eggy sauce and offers it to Earl Grey. Immediately sensing his brother has succeeded, Vanny jumps to the coffee table and then positions himself on the other side of Ada to get his taste. Ada giggles as the boys lick the sauce away.

"So scratchy," she murmurs as their little tongues move frantically and their purrs rumble endlessly. "They seem to love the meal too."

After we polish off the meal, I stand up to take both of our bowls to the kitchen. As she hands me hers from across the coffee table, she reminds me, "Sunny is coming over tomorrow before her shift to check on the enchantments. It shouldn't take too long. Don't be surprised if you see her walking around. And the day after that is the election. I can't believe the time has passed so quickly!"

My eyebrows raise in surprise. "I did not realize it was so soon."

When I return from putting the dishes in the dishwasher and wiping up the counters, I sit down again on the sofa opposite Ada. "I will probably be working outside much of the day. So, Sunny will be free to do what she needs," I assure her.

"She's learned almost everything I can teach her, well, what I *could* teach her before everything happened. I'll be sad when her apprenticeship ends. Even if my magick doesn't come back, it'll end next fall. If she wants to, I could recommend her to some colleagues who have similar specialties. But she seems ready to strike out on her own. There's such artistry in her magick. Mine is so utilitarian in comparison," she laments with a rueful laugh.

"I do not see it that way. You cast complex spells. It is why the charms and potions in your shop are in such high demand and why businesses here need your services to transform their materials into higher quality ones. Half of the materials used in that new development on Howling Road were spelled by you, I heard," I remind her. She studied so much during that year at the academy after we met. Her magick was already in high demand by the time I returned to my clan.

She sighs, worrying her mouth into a thin line. "*Were* spelled by me," she corrects. "Not anymore."

I pause a moment to collect my thoughts. She watches me patiently, still knowing me well enough to recognize the look on my face when I have something to tell her. "Some progress was made yesterday while interrogating the fae. Niven asked me specifically to talk to you about it based on what we learned. Darla was with us again. She had a vision this time, not just a hunch like before. The fae told us about two artifacts, both of fae making, that could expel the fae magick left in you that connects your lives. One can transfer life force between living beings and the other transfers magick. They sound dangerous, which is why they are hidden away. But Darla's vision showed me traveling with these artifacts somewhere cold and snowy as I bring them back here."

Her eyes widen and her shapely mouth is pressed flat, looking unduly worried. She stares at me for a long moment before asking quietly, "Are you leaving too?"

"Not yet. But at some point, I must retrieve those artifacts. I am not sure when that will be. My brother is talking to the elders about our need to obtain these artifacts if they are held by another clan. Their assistance in retrieving these will not be mandatory," I tell her resolutely, so she does not worry about something else outside of her control.

"Fire and ashes, that all sounds so dangerous, Norrell!" she frets, rubbing her arms again.

"Nothing I cannot handle. It will be more of a negotiation than anything perilous," I assure her, telling her a sanitized version of the most plausible truth. She does not look convinced. I am glad my mate cares so much for my safety though...

That thought almost undoes me, but I carefully blank my face in front of Ada. She is not my mate, as much as I wish she was again. Fire of the frost, that is a dangerous line of thinking right now. Too hopeful that I can overcome the long years of pain I inflicted upon her. The pain I witness in her every day.

As if the cats sense the shifting mood, Vanny climbs over Ada and stretches across the sofa with his feet pushing against her leg. Earl Grey hops over to me and curls into my side, a welcome distraction right now.

Diverting her attention away from the fae's words and Darla's Sight, I change the topic to something for her to look forward to. "What would you like to do for Yule this year? I will help you start planning for it." My voice is too bright, and I know she will see through this tactic.

At first, her eyes narrow in suspicion but her face quickly softens, like she knows what I am doing and accepts it. She tilts her head, looking into the distance. "I'm not sure about Yule. With everything going on I hadn't thought about it. I don't even know if I'll be involved in the coven's rites this year." She closes her eyes and tears line her lashes as she opens them again. "Usually, I invite Walt and Acton to celebrate with me. Sometimes friends from my coven will join as well. Ben and Cara might want to come over if they don't have something planned with Ben's parents. Though Ben's parents would be welcome too..." she trails off, looking embarrassed. "Sorry, I'm getting ahead of myself. I can figure out invitations by myself. Do you think you'll still be here?"

"I do, but only if you want me to be," I answer honestly.

"Yes, that would be nice," she confirms softly. Her lips curve into a gentle smile.

"We will make it a Yule to remember, whether or not you can join in the rites," I comfort her.

"I'll hold you to it," she responds playfully, though it strengthens my resolve not to let her down.

"Gladly." I will bring her vision of this year's celebration to life however she wants it.

Her smile fades a little. "You've made big promises in the past that you couldn't keep. I hope this time will be different."

"I did, and I am sorry. I always thought the measure of a male was helping those in need. It is, but not in the way I went about it. I was immature and could not see the nuance of the situations I put us in. I should not have done so at your expense. It made me a bad mate."

Her expression grows wary. "I wish you listened to me when I asked you to be more considerate of my time. Of *our* time together. But I don't think you ever understood what I meant."

"No, I did not. I was too rigid in that belief at the time." I exhale roughly. "That last Yule we spent together, I should have been here when you and your parents returned from the early morning rites. Even though the neighbors' stove broke that morning, there was no need to spend hours trying to fix it. They could have called someone else or paid to have a handyman come out. But I had blinders on, that if I did not immediately drop everything to help someone who asked for it, then I was not worthy of living here."

"Why would you think that?" she interjects, tears filling her sad violet eyes.

"It makes no sense, I know. But it was instilled in me by the clan, and I was convinced it must be true here as well," I explain dolefully. "My priorities have been so misguided my entire life. I only feel like I have truly woken up since coming back here."

"I know you didn't intend to hurt me all those times, but you still did. It made me feel so insignificant that you would put the time and comfort of anyone, even acquaintances and strangers, ahead of mine. I wish—" Her voice hitches, "I wish that last Yule hadn't been tainted by my anger at you. It made it hard to enjoy the day. Had I known it was my last one with..." her head drops. "Well, I just wish it had been different." She swipes at the tears trailing down her cheeks.

"I am so sorry, Ada. I would go back and change everything if I could," I murmur, my voice hoarse with emotion.

"I know," she says wanly.

"Walt will have no problem winning a seat. I wouldn't be surprised if he gets the most votes overall," Ada whispers to me. I am inclined to believe it even based on our experience with the campaign posters.

"I can hear you, sweet girl," Walt says as he nudges her shoulder with his. "Thank you for your confidence, but let's not get ahead of ourselves." She sticks her tongue out at him in response, drawing a chuckle from him.

While we stand in line at town hall with Walt and Acton to cast their ballots, Ada explains to me that it is a ranked choice vote where the ballot asks the voter to rank the seven in order of preference and the top three with the highest level of preference will win seats. I never had a chance to vote when I lived here, so it is all new to me.

Polls are open from noon until midnight on each chosen election date in Monstera Bluff to ensure that everyone has a chance to vote. Walt is among a group of seven who are vying for the three empty seats on town council. Since the town is small enough, each council member represents the entire town.

Walt and Acton are handed their ballots first. "Wish me luck!" Walt jokes with a lopsided grin before they head toward the separate voting area. When Ada receives her ballot, she follows in the same direction, and I walk outside to wait for them. We will have dinner and then go to the election night party hosted by the Twinkle Toes Dance Academy, who adore Walt, based on the dozens of campaign posters they papered on their storefront. The party starts at ten at night, so that it will still be in full swing when the election is called within an hour or so of polls closing. Most who attend will bring their own celebratory beverages, but some drinks and snacks will be provided. Ada already dropped off a few donations to add to their offerings.

Walt is keyed up at dinner, fidgeting an uncharacteristic amount.

Acton and Ada do their best to calm his nerves. "I'm not sure I can even eat," Walt mumbles into his menu at our table at The Roaring Wood.

The hour is much later than any of us usually have dinner, but the place is quite busy tonight. The election seems to have kept many out later than usual. Some acquaintances stop by our table to wish Walt luck. He smiles and thanks them, exchanging a few words with everyone, but his body language betrays his nerves.

"We'll have confirmation of your win in just a few hours, Walt. It'll be here before you know it, I promise," Ada tries to soothe him.

"A healthy dose of nerves shows how strong your heart beats for this community, Walt. Now you must trust you have a place in their heart as well. They won't disappoint you," Acton intones in his soft-spoken voice.

Walt picks at his dinner, but the rest of us partake in the restaurant's delicious food. Even Ada, who still has not been eating as much as I would like, finishes more than half of her salmon in a creamy sundried tomato sauce. Acton easily finishes his salad of flowers drizzled with sycamore syrup and sprinkled with bright shards of candied goldenrod pollen.

"You are an hour closer to learning that you have won a seat," I tell Walt, trying to sound upbeat as we leave the restaurant to go to the Twinkle Toes Dance Academy for the party.

"It can't come soon enough," he bellows melodramatically, though he winks at me light-heartedly afterward.

Ada laughs merrily at his exaggerated outburst. "The time will fly once everyone starts talking your ear off!"

A sizeable crowd greets Walt as we arrive in the large practice room, spacious enough to hold an event this size. The atmosphere is energetic. Friends and neighbors socialize in clustered groups, with animated and lively conversations happening all around us. Some young students from the academy perform their routines as entertainment. A few couples even engage in an impromptu ballroom dancing lesson, twirling around the room just for the fun of it.

Many of his old friends and coworkers are there. With Walt's job as the head of the parks department and Acton's popular landscape design business, which he has slowed down since Walt's retirement, they are well known and liked around town.

A young troll, tall and bulky with long dark green hair, reservedly says hello to us in a low but quiet voice. "Wyck Pyewacket! I'm happy as a clam that you're here! It's been too long," Ada greets him enthusiastically. He smiles bashfully in return.

"Good evening, young man. I heard you improved the software that's tallying the votes," Walt notes sounding impressed.

"Well, it wasn't so difficult. Just a few tweaks to make inputting the data quicker. The calculation itself was already pretty fast," he stammers, trying to downplay the praise.

"Both of you need to get *on* your high horse. You are both far too humble." She laughs at the two males.

"Oh, I don't know about that," Wyck demurs, a blush darkening his cheeks.

Ada playfully shakes his outsized shoulder. "See what I mean?" she remarks.

Not long after, a brown-coated wolven strides up, extending a paw-like hand to Walt, who takes it in a firm handshake.

"Best of luck tonight, sir," the wolven says deferentially.

"Thank you, son. I thought my public life was over when I handed the department to you. But here I am back at it, and at a party for myself, no less." Walt chuckles self-consciously, embarrassed by the attention.

"We'll be all the better for it. Plus, I look forward to working with you again. We've got to keep them on their toes," the wolven jokes.

Walt turns to me, gesturing back at the wolven. "I'm not sure you've met. This is Kiernan Lykander. He worked on my team for years and then took over as the head of the parks department when I retired," he introduces us.

"Norrell Snowstrider," I state, grasping his hand in hearty handshake.

"Nice to make your acquaintance. Walt is the best mentor I could have asked for," Kiernan extols. "This is another good excuse to keep up with our weekly lunches. I think we're going to have a lot of fun with the upcoming projects I have planned." He aims a knowing smile at

Walt who returns it just as fervently. It seems he handed over his department to a fitting successor.

It is late and Ada is visibly tired, though she tries to fight through it to stay the duration of the party. She leans into my side. I support her by wrapping a hand around her hip to take some weight off her feet. The feel of the curve of her body against mine is bliss. The memory of it does not do justice to the real thing, like her body was made to fit against mine. My attention never wavers from the softness of her body and the cushion of her hip under my hold.

When she sags even further, I reluctantly ask Walt to grab her a chair. I would hold her in my arms, but I know that is only a dream right now. When she takes a seat, I position myself next to her in case she needs anything.

Clancy joins us around midnight, letting us know the results will be tallied quickly. He frowns as he sees Ada sitting in the chair, clearly tired. He then fixes me with a level stare as if I have something to do with her exhaustion. I hold myself back from making a face at him and instead look on as Walt, Acton, and Ada talk to another friend who just arrived.

Clancy's phone rings and he steps away from us. When he hangs up, he trots to the front of the room and loudly clears his throat.

"The results are in!" Clancy announces. The small crowd hushes to hear him. "The new town council members are Walt Sutton, Bo Aelfric, and Iara Calder! Congratulations to the winners, and especially to our good friend Walt!" Clancy sweeps his arm to Walt who is still standing beside us. The crowd erupts with applause and cheers.

An unmistakable flash of surprise crosses Walt's features, like he cannot believe he won despite everyone telling him he would. He faces Acton, who pulls him into a crushing hug, his heightened emotions causing a few wayward vines to snake across Walt's back. Ada jumps up from the chair and joins them, wrapping her arms around them both.

"Do I go up there? Should I say something?" his muffled voice asks them.

Ada's tinkling laughter travels through the air. "Of course! It's your moment."

Walt stumbles toward Clancy, who shakes his hand vigorously and claps him on the back. He then turns around toward the crowd with an awestruck expression on his face. Ada is still laughing, wiping a happy tear from her cheek. She angles her face toward me, so bright-eyed and elated that I am struck by her natural beauty all over again. She leans in for an unexpected hug. My body melts around hers, as I wrap an arm around her lower back and another behind her head, tucking her into my chest snugly but not too tight. I do not want her to feel trapped. She soon shifts so that she stands next to me again but leaves one arm clasped on my shoulder from behind. My hand returns to the curve of her hip, bracketing her to me as she stands for Walt's speech.

Walt's voice is endearingly shaky, overcome with the emotion of the moment. "I gave my best years to this town. But I think I have a few more left in me," he says to more cheers and whistling. "Thank you from the bottom of my heart to everyone in this community. You've embraced me wholeheartedly over the last fifty years. This town means everything to me. I promise I'll show up every day doing my best to keep this cherished place strong and thriving. I will never stop nurturing that trust and support you've always shown me. I'm the luckiest man alive. I want to thank my niece Ada, who gave me the idea to run for office. And of course, the love of my life, my mate Acton who never wavers in his support for me. I owe this amazing life to him."

Ada brushes a streak of tears from her cheek as Walt wraps up his short speech. I squeeze her hip as I smile down at her, happy for her and Walt. She looks up at me tenderly and laces her fingers over mine. We stay like that until Walt thanks the crowd again and the party disperses.

CHAPTER 16
ADA

Cara comes over when I have the house to myself one Saturday morning. Norrell is out at Walt and Acton's doing some work on Acton's back garden rainforest project, probably involving heavy lifting.

When she steps inside, she has the same wonderstruck look on her face as she did the first time she saw it. "Can I tell you again how beautiful your house is?" She leans in for a hug, but as soon as we let go, her attention returns to the grand details of the foyer. It's her first time back here since Samhain.

"Hon, you can say it until you're blue in the face. I don't mind a bit," I joke. "Come in and sit a spell."

When we settle into the living room with coffee and freshly baked buttermilk biscuits with strawberry jam, the boys join us as I'd hoped, probably because of the food. I promised Cara I'd finally introduce them.

"Are these the famous Vanilla Paws and Earl Grey?" Cara murmurs to the cats.

"Yes, these are the *infamous* fluffballs. Traitors to the bone," I accuse lovingly as I pick up Earl Grey off the floor and set him on the sofa next to Cara. I take my own seat on the sofa opposite.

"You are so cute. Who could stay mad at you anyway?" she croons as she scratches under his gray chin.

"So how is everything going at Ben's and your place? Do you feel settled in?" I'm curious about her honest response since we're alone.

"Yes, it was the easiest part of the whole situation. Ben offered to redecorate or get new furniture if there's anything I don't like. But why would I change anything? He has fond memories of the furniture and dishes he inherited. Plus, I barely have anything to my name, so a fully furnished house is a dream come true. I don't think he believes me yet. But we're getting there," she says with a quick burst of laughter.

"He just wants to make sure you're happy. He'll like it if you put your own touches on the place since it's your home now too," I reassure her.

"Yeah, he probably would," she admits. "I keep telling him I want to put up Christmas decorations, but he always reminds me it's *Yule*, not Christmas. And it starts a few days earlier on the winter solstice and lasts for twelve days. But the first day is the big festive celebration I associate with Christmas. I swear I'm trying, but maybe that'll be a good start. It's lucky I was never into Santa Claus and all that kitschy stuff. I've always loved having a tree, but beyond that I've always preferred subtle decorations."

"We do celebrate with trees," I clarify in case she didn't know.

"Oh yes, Ben told me. We're getting one tomorrow. I can't wait!" she says giddily, doing a little dance in her seat.

"Norrell asked if I wanted to celebrate this year. We haven't had time to talk much about it, but I should remind him later today," I mention as much to myself as to her.

"Are you celebrating with him? How is *that* going? I can't believe he's still in your house." Her dubious tone breaks me out of my drifting thoughts.

"It's better. We've come to a sort of... understanding... that he wants to take care of me while I'm struggling. At one point under the haze of pain when I twisted my ankle, I tried to bargain with myself that I was going to be nicer to him just to try to figure out his underlying motives. Like I was some kind of spy." I can chuckle about it now, but the concern hasn't fully left me.

Her hand flies to her chest. "Did he find out?"

"Are you saying I'm bad at being a spy?" I joke. "I'm not sure. If he did, he didn't say anything. My brain was fried like a piece of chicken when he arrived, I swear. I didn't trust him a lick. I still don't, if I'm being honest. I worry that these good deeds he's doing for me are all glitter and no gold. How could I ever fully trust him again after hurting me so much? I'd always wonder if he's just going to leave me again."

Her expression turns sympathetic. "Do you even want him to stay?"

"I don't know. He is still the hottest male I have ever seen. It drives me crazy. Even now when we touch..." I sigh dramatically. "But that's irrelevant. He finally told me he left me because his clan pressured him. So why wouldn't that happen again now that he's their leader? Where do I even fit into that? I just don't see how it ends well for me. Ashes, there's too much else to worry about. I may not much time left, anyway."

Her eyes turn overly bright at my reference to the fae's spell. "You don't know that. Darla had another vision, right?"

I offer her a tight smile. "She did, but we don't know where those artifacts are located or if they will work. I just need to plan ahead for every outcome." I don't point out that Darla's vision of her left out a lot of very important details, just like this one. Anyway, Darla does not deserve any bad feelings. She can't control what she Sees.

Cara notices my discomfort and nods sympathetically. "Does Norrell seem different this time around? Like he's grown emotionally?"

My head cocks to the side as I consider her question. "Yes and no. He was so infuriating at times when he lived with me those two years. He'd break plans with me on a whim or be extremely late if a stranger asked anything of him. And they had him pegged as a people pleaser. I swear they flocked to him asking for help. He never turned them down. It was so disrespectful to me. He was a nice, helpful male to everyone but his mate. Everyone said I was so lucky to have him. Well, no, I wasn't," I grouse.

Cara's eyebrows rise high on her forehead. She may not have known the full extent of it.

I take a deep calming breath and continue. "He's still like that, helpful and giving with his time, but no longer at my expense. He checks in with me and my schedule. He admitted to what he did and sees why it was wrong. Now he's here for me every day, doing chores around the house, making sure I'm feeling alright. It never occurred to me I would need looking after, not really. Everything is more difficult without my magick, but he recognized that I wasn't feeling my best even before I did. I just thought I was depressed." A wry laugh escapes me.

"That sounds like progress," she observes, trying to sound positive.

"It is. But he has very real obligations to his clan. I won't ask him to choose. And I'm not going to wait for him, either. I'm not *that* female... anymore at least. Look what it got me last time," I argue. My lips press into a grimace as I remember how naïve I was when I asked him to move here, not that he wasn't eager to do so.

"Did you wait for him before?" She looks appalled.

"No. I wasn't holding out hope he'd come back, if that's what you're asking. I could tell he was done with me. As to whether I've had lovers since then? Well, no. I haven't."

Cara's jaw practically hits the floor. My shoulders shake with laughter.

"I had enough heartbreak to last a lifetime. I don't need another entanglement to go awry, especially after I was elected to town council a few years later. I was asked out plenty. But it just seemed too public and messy to date here as a Mayweather. My mom didn't know my dad until she came here for an apprenticeship. It's why I thought meeting Norrell while I was at the academy seemed so perfect. Plus, I wasn't crazy about any of the males here. And that's on *me*, not *them*. There are many truly wonderful unmated males here. I just already know them too well."

She still looks baffled. "You mean no sex in *fifteen years*?"

I cackle at her horrified tone. "Cara, I will let you in on a little secret about magick. I'm sure you know that battery operated sex toys can be quite satisfying in their own way. Well, magickally enchanted sex toys take it to the next level and beyond. Ask Ben about it," I divulge with a playful wink.

"I think I might have to!" she says dazedly. "Did you know that *tails* are a thing?" I hoot with laughter. Her cheeks turn a delightful shade of red as she realizes what she blurted out. "We'll save that conversation for another day. But it was quite the surprise!"

"Whispered Folk are known for their *special equipment*," I joke.

"You're telling me!" she exclaims. "I understand holding public office and not wanting your love life scrutinized. But from what I've heard Clancy dated around a lot. And he's the mayor!"

"Clancy is cut from a different cloth, though I appreciate how he has no qualms about it. His dating habits were more *zealous* before he took office. Plus, the females mostly flocked to him. He didn't do much chasing, in that sense. They know what they're getting into—or not—with him," I muse.

Her face scrunches a little in concentration. "Maybe if you're still uncertain about a future with Norrell, then there's no need to worry right now whether he will go back. Just take it a day at a time. See if your feelings change organically. If it turns out you can't move past everything he did to you, that's alright. You will eventually part ways again. But if you start to want more, then cross that bridge when you get there. He may be willing to stay for real this time. But that doesn't matter until you're sure," she counsels.

"Well, how did someone so young grow so sage?" I accuse jokingly.

"You learn a few things when you've been in a truly terrible relationship followed by an unbelievably amazing one," she titters, clasping her hands to her chest.

"I'll take that to heart," I promise her.

She worries her lips while she watches me. "I was really depressed after everything that happened with Mark. He and his family were horrible to me. When I had to leave Chicago, I left behind everything that was familiar to me. I was alone in a new city and scared for my future. Mark took almost everything. My pride, my home, and my career were methodically dismantled by him. And it had a lasting effect. I was so sad and mentally beat down that I just couldn't get myself to eat sometimes. Obviously, I was really depressed and mourning my old life." Her sad eyes roam over me. "Do you think anything like that is going on with you since Samhain? That's a lot like losing your old life too. Someone took it from you just to be cruel. And now every day is filled with reminders of painful memories."

I nod empathetically. "I imagine that's part of it. With this fae business and losing my magick and Norrell showing up again, I've been a hot mess. And my future here is up in the air, if I'm being honest. Losing my magick has stirred up a lot of old, unresolved emotions. And it's been harder than I thought. I was slipping away without even knowing it. I didn't go out, I wasn't eating. It's still hard for me to bring myself to do so sometimes even though I love socializing and eating good food. Doing both at the same time is my very favorite hobby! When Norrell figured this out, he made it his mission to get me to eat full meals every day. I swear he'd feed me himself like I'm some kind of chirpy baby bird if I'd let him. So, if I'm looking spindly lately, it's not been for lack of food!"

She grins at my description of Norrell's behavior. "You know, I've put back on several pounds since I moved here. My wardrobe fits better, funny enough. But more importantly I feel better too. Ben likes that. And the extra pounds. He, uh, voices his appreciation quite a bit," she laughs, squeezing her hips with her hands.

"I believe he does! Ben has never acted this way toward anyone except you. I'm sure he loves seeing you healthy and happy and curvy. That male thinks you hung the moon!" I enthuse.

"I suppose he does," she responds, blushing furiously.

"Because it's true!" We both laugh and it seems to melt away some of her modesty. Her blush fades and her expression turns thoughtful. "I heard you just got back to work this week. How'd it go?" She had been out during the entire month of November, taking a break from her job as the new city planner to recover and relax after the Samhain attack. Most town hall business had also been suspended for a time because of the safety council.

"Really well. I'm glad to be back. The month off was probably unnecessary after a couple weeks of recovery, I won't lie. But it turned into a sort of honeymoon for me and Ben. That time together helped clear my mind of the fire and even all the bad things that happened earlier this year. I never had time to process any of it. I was in survival mode for so long. Anyway, after my first project got off the ground so quickly, I'm ready for more. About that..." She pauses and chews her lip for a moment. "There's something I want to bring up with you concerning my plans for the town. It involves bringing someone in from... the outside..." she trails off, sounding a little guilty.

Cracking up, I clap my hands in delight. "It's probably someone very specific?" I guess.

She exhales loudly, flinging herself back against the sofa and jostling Earl Grey, who looks offended to have his slumber disturbed.

"Sorry little man," she apologizes with a long pet down his spine. "Yes, it's a specific someone. My best friend Rose." She puts her hands up in a pacifying gesture. "It's not what you think. I'm not just asking because she's my best friend and it sucks keeping secrets from her. She's a very talented transportation planner. Since the town is growing, we need a reliable bus system sooner rather than later. It wouldn't be too difficult to fund, even with the initial expenses of purchasing buses and hiring her along with drivers and a small support staff. It'll be way more effective if we can lay the groundwork before the Howling Road development is complete. I'm sure there are plenty of people moving there who will convince themselves they'll need to buy a car to drive downtown. I want to prevent that. We don't need more cars here. I'm about to sell mine, to be honest. I really don't need it."

"That will be a big project for the town, but certainly worth it, especially if you include her in your proposal to town council. If you're worried about her accepting us, then we may need to talk about how you should break it to her. When she sees you happy and thriving, it may calm some of her fears of Whispered Folk," I consider.

"I worry about that too, obviously. It's a shock to the system." She waves at herself since I witnessed her fear firsthand when I introduced her to the town. "But she seems upbeat about everything else I've been able to tell her. She's ready to leave her job. And to be honest, she would probably only leave Chicago and her unbelievably awesome apartment for me. I need to consider her mom, too. She'll have to be moved into another assisted living facility close to here so Rose can easily visit. I'm getting in over my head. I need to ready my pitch to her as much as I do to town council." She sighs loudly in exasperation.

"You're already proving to be a good friend thinking ahead like this," I assure her.

"I hope so. I don't want her to hate me after she finds out the full truth." Cara grimaces, shaking her head in uncertainty.

"She won't. Do you *hate* me or Clancy?" I tease.

"No! Keep that word out of your mouth. I could never!" she scoffs lightheartedly.

"Then don't be so worried. She may surprise you." I give her a knowing smile. Cara claims she didn't take it well when she learned who lives here. To my eyes, she took everything in stride, publicly at least, much better than I could have even imagined.

"Alright, I'll try not to." She blinks exaggeratedly like she's trying to clear it from her mind. "There's so much else to do first, I shouldn't fixate on that right now. I'm so excited that Walt is going to be on the town council. I called him yesterday to congratulate him. I think my next presentation will be so much easier." She moves in another excited little dance on the sofa. I can't help but join in her enthusiasm.

"The meetings will be easy as pie from now on. The town is in good hands again. The three new council members should have run long ago," I agree.

"I was able to vote in the election. I couldn't believe it, being so new here. But Ben and Clancy assured me I'm an eligible voter. The only person I knew on the ballot was Walt, so I asked Ben who he was going to vote for to help me decide. Those are the three he wanted to win too," she remarks.

"Hon, this is your home now. Your voice matters as much as everyone else's," I assure her. I hope she knows how lucky we are to have her.

♡ ♡ ♡ ♡ ♡

"Norrell, we should get a tree tonight," I tell him from over my laptop screen as he comes into the kitchen. When he got home not long ago, he went straight upstairs to take a shower. He was sweaty and smeared with mud after a long day at Walt and Acton's. It looked like they really put him to work, though he isn't one to complain. Nor do I believe that landscaping is all that strenuous for him since he is as strong as an ox.

"Alright. There is a tree lot near town hall. We'll pick one out together. Should we go after an early dinner?" he suggests.

"That sounds nice." I can't help but grin. I love decorating for Yule.

He pulls out ingredients to start cooking while I sit at the table. I offer to chop vegetables, but he shakes his head and gestures for me to stay, looking affronted that I'd dare ask. I roll my eyes good-humoredly but stay put like he asks and continue working on my laptop placing orders for the shop.

Most of my Yule decorations were magickally shrunken for space and stored in a closet since last year. Luckily my tree stand is in the attic ready to go. I'll have to ask Sunny to bring everything else back to size the next time she's here. Still, there's plenty else we can do tonight to start decorating the house.

The tree lot is busy when we arrive, unsurprising on a Saturday night, but there are still plenty of nice trees to pick from. The town usually starts to decorate in earnest around now in early December. Norrell parked the Wagoneer nearby, but he's had his arm around me the entire time—something he's initiating more often—like we've had to walk some great, exhausting distance. I'm fine right now, especially since I took a nap this afternoon after Cara left, but I don't mind the wall of warmth he provides.

"I hope they have some balsam firs left. Those smell the best," I comment absently, scanning their selection.

"It smells like they might," Norrell remarks. The scent of the freshly cut trees fills the air as if we're standing in an evergreen forest.

We finally spot their balsam firs, and I can't help but gravitate toward the tallest, fullest, most stately tree. It would fit perfectly in the living room. All the trees are enchanted so that they won't drop needles for at least a month to last through Yule. It keeps them bright and fresh, too.

"Mother Earth, that was easy. I think we've found it." I turn my grinning face up to his as I sweep my hand toward the tree.

"A good choice," he agrees, his large hand squeezing possessively around my hip. His touch feels dangerous. "Should I tie it to the roof and then pick up everything else we need?"

"Alright," I breathe raggedly, betraying far too much.

His expression turns longing as we gaze at each other. I loop my arms around his shoulders, closing the small distance between us. He leans in and presses a lingering kiss to the top of my head. His other hand finds its way to my back, rubbing up and down my spine in a comforting gesture. I feel blanketed by his warmth, like it's the safest place I could be. Though that is a fiction I've already fallen for. I need to remember that.

Breaking away from our embrace, I guide us toward the counter to pay for the tree. Norrell handles taking it to the Wagoneer while I pick out bundles of boughs and pinecones to decorate with. We drive to the grocery store afterward to pick up rings of dried apple and orange slices the store has already prepared for the holiday, as well as bags of fresh fruit and other supplies. He places a gallon of cider, spices, and fresh cranberries in our basket. He seems to already have a plan for the evening.

By the time we return home, I'm already eager to start decorating. In the past, I've invited Acton and Walt over to help. But this year is different for so many reasons. It seems important that Norrell and I do this together. Like sharing this tradition again after so long marks a meaningful change between us, as scary and complicated as that is to imagine.

I open the front door for him as he hauls the tree inside. I then dash over to hold the stand firm to the ground while Norrell slides the tree into it. I tighten the metal prongs that hold it in place. With only a few adjustments, the tree stands perfectly straight. After returning from washing the sap from our hands in the powder room downstairs, we stand back, admiring our lush, festive Yule tree.

"Beautiful," I murmur. He hums his agreement, though I catch him out of the corner of my eye watching me instead. My face heats under his searing gaze as I turn toward him.

"Ada," he groans as his hands cup my jaw, rubbing the roughened pad of his thumb along my cheek with such gentleness. When it seems like he might lean down to kiss me, he pulls me into his body instead, resting my head against his chest. I sink into him, slinging my arms around him low on his waist, holding him just as fervently. Though he makes no other movement, I can feel the hard ridge of him against my belly, hot and hungry. It sparks an equal hunger in me, a fiery pressure coiled in my core. I'm conflicted, knowing my attraction to him is unwise but craving how good he can make me feel in the moment.

"My ember, tell me to stop," he begs as his hands squeeze and pull at my flesh, working their way down my backside. He has not called me his ember in a long time. It stirs long-suppressed emotions, a driving desire for intimacy.

"Don't stop." My voice cracks with my assent, a decision made in the heat of the moment. If I told him to, he'd respect my decision and fully back off. Mother Earth, I so badly want to feel good for a change. He's the only one who can make me feel the way I long to right now, bringing me some solace when everything feels so hopeless.

He hoists me up, his arms supporting me under my rear. I wrap my legs around his middle, bunching up my long skirt to my waist in the process, aligning our overheated cores. I subtly work myself along him, unable to control myself. He growls low into my ear, nipping the sensitive skin. His filed down claws press gently but excitingly into my hips as he holds me up. He carries me all the way upstairs to my bedroom. When he nudges the door closed, I expect him to lay me down on the bed. Instead, he pushes me up against the wall, grinding the hard bulge in his pants against my core.

My legs can't reach the ground to give me any purchase. They dangle in the air when I unhook them from his waist. I'm at his mercy to give me relief. I moan at the loss of control, clutching wildly at his hard chest and broad shoulders. The sound spurs him on, as he nibbles up my neck until finally our lips crash together, his kiss full of so much pent up passion. He's gentle at first, almost reverent as he brushes his lips lightly, tentatively on mine, like he's trying—and failing—to contain himself and savor the moment. It's at odds with the rest of his body that has primally pinned me to the wall. When his control breaks, his tongue plunges deep into my mouth, the sweetness turning to heat as it dominates mine.

When he comes up for air, he pulls his hips back slightly, still holding me up by one hand, and reaches between us with the other to unbutton his pants and tug them below his hips. He reaches into his boxer briefs and pulls out his full, thick length, a slightly darker blue than the rest of his skin and as heavily veined as I remember. He tucks the waistband under his large, fuzzy testicles. As I watch, he grabs hold of the front of my panties and rips them clean through, exposing my wide-open heat.

"I dreamt of this sight for years. The prettiest pink flower just waiting to be pollinated," he groans as he stares at my pussy.

I feel my channel pulse at the lewd words. My breaths grow more ragged as my need reaches new heights.

"Your pussy likes the sound of that. She is begging for me," he rasps. His hand guides his cock and rubs its tapered head up and down my pussy and circling my clit, coating it in a thin layer of his come that's already streaming from the wide slit that runs across his hefty cock's tapered head. "Are you ready, my ember? Ready to be filled by me?"

"Yes, I need all of you deep inside me," I whine.

He hums raggedly. "Good girl, telling me what you need." He taps the head directly on my clit to reward me. It sends shockwaves through me, like I could come from that alone.

We both watch as he drags his cock downward, finally lining himself up at my entrance, and pushes in. He stretches me wide open as he slowly enters, every bulging vein dragging across my inner channel. I whine despite myself. I nearly forgot how much there is of him. My pussy feels so tight and full inside as I get closer to taking all of him. There's no feeling like his entire rigid cock inside me, the exquisite fullness of it. When I've taken him to the root, he fully pins me to the wall with his hips alone. My legs still hang in the air, bracketed on each side of his waist.

"I need to see all of you," he commands, letting go of my thighs, he takes hold of the bottom of my sweater and guides my arms through the sleeves to take it off. He follows that with my bunched-up skirt, which I help shimmy out from behind me and then he pulls it over my head as well. My bra is next, tossing it onto the pile on the floor. "So much better. There should be nothing between us as I make you mine again."

"Yes, I'm yours Norrell. I always have been," I cry, needy and ready for him to move. Mayhap I shouldn't admit that to him, but I can't take it back now.

"Ada, there has only ever been you. Once I met you there could never be anyone else. Do you understand? My body is yours. My heart is yours. You are it for me. Always have been. Always will be," he states firmly, honestly, staring deep into my eyes, making me understand the truth of what he is saying.

"Give me everything," I beg on a ragged breath.

"Forever," he growls as he circles his hips, grinding his cock inside of me.

I keen at the unbelievably deep feeling of him, rubbing my inner channel with the grooved texture of his cock. He plucks at my nipples, bringing me close to the edge already. "Mother Earth!" I sob, overwhelmed by the sensation. Still grinding and circling, tunneling into me, he brings the tip of a callused finger to my clit and rubs it lightly. Bright white flashes behind my eyes as I jettison into my orgasm, crying out Norrell's name.

"Take your pleasure on your cock, good girl. It is all yours to fill you whenever you want," he murmurs into my neck as he licks a stripe to my shoulder. His warm hands slide steadily up and down my arms, soothing me as I recover.

"Would you fill me even more?" I ask, still catching my breath.

"You want my seed deep inside your pussy?" he confirms playfully.

"More than anything," I exhale.

"Hang on, my ember. I cannot hold back any longer," he warns. His hands grab my thighs again, holding me up as he slowly drags his cock in and out of my channel. I moan at the alternating sensation of full and empty, repeating endlessly.

There's a feverish light in his eyes as his hips cant briskly, stroking into me at an increasing speed. My channel starts to clutch at him as I grow closer to another orgasm. It makes the drag of his cock inside me even more pronounced. Pleasure swarms up my spine. Soon, I'm writhing upon him almost as wildly as he bucks into me.

"Touch yourself, my ember. Come on my cock one more time. I feel your pussy squeezing me like you are almost there," he orders.

I move one of my hands that had been grasping desperately at his shoulders and bring it between us to circle my clit. The instant I do, I start moaning and gasping uncontrollably. Norrell growls deeply, the vibration traveling down to his cock, stimulating me further. It drives me over the edge a second time, and I thrash unrestrained against him with each wave of my orgasm.

"You are mine, Ada!" he snarls as his cock thickens and pours out, splashing his come deep into my channel. The rhythm of his hips stutters and slows with the last few spurts.

I wrap my legs around his waist, keeping him inside me, as we gaze at each other unreservedly while our breathing slows. "I meant every word of it, Ada. I love you more than life itself. You are mine, forever, and I am yours. I am never leaving you again," he declares fervently, his eyes searching mine.

His words sound genuine. They are everything I longed to hear after he left, even when I knew it was foolish of me. Even when I finally realized a male capable of such cruelty toward me didn't deserve me in the first place. Fifteen years have cured me of the desperation I once had for them. Words alone hold very little meaning now. Maybe he'll never be able to atone for it, but I need this... him... right now in this moment. I want his affection despite knowing I'm making myself vulnerable to him again. I don't know what the future will hold for me. But Norrell is too intertwined with my life to ignore what's happening between us. Though I can't yet bring myself to tell him that I love him. I never stopped, even when I hated him too. That's a small piece of me that I still need to protect.

"I believe you," I whisper. It's not a declaration of anything on my part, but I can feel the breath leave his body in relief. He wraps his arms around me and kisses me slowly, reverently, now that the tension between us has burned off for the moment.

He walks us into my attached bathroom toward the edge of my tub. He helps me step into it, and when I'm steady, he pulls his softened cock from me, unplugging me. His copious come slides out of me and down my leg. He takes a couple tissues from a box and slowly wipes away the streak. He hands me another clean one before throwing out the used tissues. He motions toward the linen closet in the bathroom and I nod. He opens it, takes out a washcloth, and wets it at the sink.

"Open your legs, my ember," he asks in a low voice. I widen my stance and he gently wipes between my legs with the warm, wet washcloth.

"I am sorry about your undergarment. I will buy you new ones," he chuckles.

"Buy me ones you find sexy," I suggest slyly.

"Everything is sexy on you," he responds in a sinfully deep voice, sounding more like the Norrell I used to know.

After helping me out of the tub, we get dressed again. I change into a new pair of panties, throwing the torn scrap away. He carries me down the stairs bridal style this time. I nibble at the crook of his neck to tease him. He chuckles deep and satisfied. "Ada," he sighs my name. "I do not want to tire you out before we have a chance to do everything we planned."

"We can do both. Plans are overrated," I assure him, giggling.

"Later, my ember," he promises. "Now, it is time to decorate."

He sets me down gently on the sofa, making sure I'm comfortable, and then goes outside to bring in the bags left in the automobile. I'm sure I resemble a wet noodle, sprawled out like I am, feeling more languid and relaxed than I can remember. It's glorious. I want to feel like this all the time. His declarations still give me pause, but even silly old me knows better than to trust anything said in the heat of the moment. He can say he's *mine*, though I'm not *his* the way it seems he wants me to be. I won't confuse this physical release with being mates again, no matter how tempting those pretty words are. I'm not too old to have a little fun during whatever time I have left in this realm, especially if he's enthusiastically serving it up on a silver platter.

After putting the grocery bags in the kitchen, he returns to the living room to light a log in the fireplace. "I will heat the mulled cider on the stove. Then we should start with the decorating," he announces.

"Can I help with the cider, please?" I ask, batting my lashes, which probably just makes me look silly.

His expression turns playful. "Of course," he relents. "You can hunt for the rest of the spices we need."

In the kitchen, he pours half of the gallon of cider into a large stock pot and then gets to work coring and slicing the fresh apples. Next, he thinly slices an orange crosswise keeping the peel on. At his suggestion, I pull the allspice, cardamom, and sugar from their shelf and put them next to the cloves and cinnamon sticks we purchased earlier. I set out my measuring spoons as well so they're ready for him.

It takes only a few minutes for him to add everything to the pot where the cider is now simmering. It already smells fantastic even though it should sit on a very low heat for at least an hour to fully blend all the flavors.

I pop into the workshop and grab some twine, wire, several types of ribbon, scissors, glue, and other tools we'll need to start decorating the living room and the tree. Norrell helps me pull a long length of twine from the bundle. We sit on the floor in front of the fireplace and space out large decorative bows of thick velvety ribbon across the length of the twine. They are separated by the dried slices of fruit with a thinner ribbon woven in adding a little space and color between each slice and looping around the twine. The ends of each thinner ribbon hang decoratively from the edges of where they're wrapped around the dried fruit. Once we're happy with the placement, we glue the bows and ribbon into place.

The boys have fun playing with the excess ribbon and twine. While we work, we wave it around for them to chase until they're so tired they settle into opposite corners of a sofa for a nap.

After nearly two centuries of Yule celebrations in this home, someone long ago discreetly affixed small hooks underneath the mantel of the gray marble fireplace. I attach each big bow to a hook and let the fruit slices hang lower between each one. The result looks cozily homespun and the dried fruit slices are fragrant in the soft heat from the fire.

By the time that's finished, our cider is ready. Norrell and I return to the kitchen where he ladles the piping hot beverage into mugs for us. We return to the living room, sitting next to each other on the sofa not occupied by the cats. We look at each other with what feels like new eyes and clink our steaming mugs, taking a small sip afterward while maintaining eye contact. It's delicious. It tastes like Yule in a cup. I hum my appreciation, and he leans in for a brief but breathless kiss. The spice of the cider lingers on his lips.

We sit together and watch the fire, slowly sipping from our mugs. When they're empty, Norrell and I move on to our next craft. We glue a thin ribbon to the bottom of the pinecones, creating a loop we can hang on our tree. Then we use more of the ribbon and decoratively wrap the cones or place bows on them, gluing them in place. We create about thirty ornaments in all, the entirety of the bag, each only taking a minute or two to create once we get into the rhythm of it. Norrell and I work together to hang them on the tree.

After refilling our mugs of cider, we start on the last decoration of the night. We begin constructing a wreath with the fragrant bundles of trimmings we bought along with the tree. My scissors are spelled to cut through anything, which is useful when I'm making enchantments. Luckily the magick is still strong as I use them to cut a long piece of wire. We then form it in a circle and add another short loop at the top so we can hang it on the front door. Over the wire circle, we lay groupings of boughs at a decorative angle, overlapping them without any gaps. We attach each grouping as we go using twine and glue.

When we finally complete the circle, the patterned angle we laid them at fits together well enough that the starting point isn't visible. Lastly, we use that thick velvet ribbon to create a large bow, which we glue to the top right of the wreath and let the ends of the ribbon hang long. I cut an inverted V shape at both ends to complete the wreath.

We walk out to the front porch and carefully hang the wreath on the front door. It's obviously homemade, but I wouldn't change it for anything. Norrell is satisfied with the result too, looking at it with a twinkle of pride in his eyes. I lean my head on his shoulder as he wraps a brawny arm around my waist. This wasn't how I planned the night to go, but it turned out perfectly.

CHAPTER 17

ADA

The midday sun glints off the copse of trees ahead on the winding, wooded path. It's our destination, the graveyard established by my coven over two centuries ago. When Norrell suggested a walk this morning, I asked him if we could visit my parents' graves. It's been too long since I've visited. I haven't made this journey since before Samhain.

Norrell strolls alongside me, carrying a picnic basket with a lunch he put together for us. I grip the crook of his arm as we walk. Right after my parents died, he would accompany me on this familiar trek. Sometimes he would carry me back when I was too weak with grief to manage on my own. But since then, I usually visit this place alone, though sometimes Walt and Acton join me to pay their respects to their best friends they miss so much.

Speckles of sunlight shine on the grass as we approach my parents' tree. The towering pines around us block much of the light. The graveyard has grown into a forest, each tree marking a witch or mates from the coven who have passed on in Monstera Bluff. After setting down the basket, Norrell brushes some debris off the grave markers placed on their tree, then rubs a finger lightly over my parents' names.

"Hello Estelle. Hello Whitt. It is good to see you again," he murmurs.

Tears fill my eyes at the greeting. I don't want to interrupt him while he lingers in front of it looking lost in thought, so instead I spread our blanket and sit down on it. My gaze travels up the tree, already stretched so tall. My parents remain so dear in my heart, it will no doubt be the tallest tree here one day.

Our mood is subdued during the picnic lunch. Norrell lays his hand on my knee while I take slow bites of our sandwiches. "Do you still speak to them when you visit?" he asks quietly.

"If I'm alone, I talk about the shop or what is going on around town or... if something is bothering me. The same things I talked to them about when they were alive. I haven't been here to tell them about... Samhain and everything that happened since then. But maybe they know somehow." I shrug self-consciously and hide my misty eyes while I take another bite.

"I am glad you still do this. They treasured your close bond. It is a worthy tradition to memorialize them," he responds.

"I always think about how they would respond if they were here. What advice they'd give." I smile wanly at him. "It guides me more than I should admit."

"You are as kind and caring as they were. That is what guides you. Always has." He exhales deeply. "Estelle and Whitt are often in my thoughts. I am glad I knew them, even for that short time. I am a better male for it."

"They loved you," I remind him.

"I loved them too," he says wistfully. "May I come back here with you again?"

"I'd like that." I squeeze my hand over his where it rests on my knee.

We hold hands on our walk back. The radiating heat of his palm feels comforting on my cold hand. They're always freezing nowadays. I guess that means I should hold hands with him more often. Close to where we parked, I spot a thick fallen branch in a clearing, split into several pieces. I tug Norrell with our locked hands for him to follow as I veer toward it. He gives me a quizzical look but goes along without complaint. He eyes me as I stop and look down at the branch.

"Do you think we found our Yule log?" I ask.

His eyebrows raise in understanding. "It will be perfect."

SECOND CHANCE MAGICK

♡ ♡ ♡ ♡ ♡

With the sun poised to peek over the horizon any minute now, I shuffle my feet in the wet sand as the rites are about to begin. Everyone seems to be making last minute preparations, but I hover near the edge of the large group without anything to do. On this morning every year, my coven gathers on the beach to witness the sunrise over the Atlantic when it will shine for the shortest period. It's the winter solstice as well as the start of Yule, and we are here to perform our rites and celebrate the renewal of the sun, as each day will grow longer and the sun will rise higher into the summer solstice. I've long ago memorized the lengthy passages we always recite, they never change, but I'm unable to sense the usual rush of magick flowing around us as we progress through a series of spells that we speak in unison.

We release the darkness of the old year and stand vigil for the rebirth of the sun. O shining sun, guide us through the darkness of the long night. May your light continue until your own long day.

Watching my fellow coven members perform the usual rituals, the detachment nags at me, since I'm forced to remain an onlooker without a magickal contribution. It sets a disheartening tone for the day.

I drive home from the beach as soon as the rites wrap up. Usually, I'd stay and socialize with my coven. But I'm not in the mood, with them at least. I've been looking forward to everything else Norrell and I have planned for the rest of the day.

The aroma of Norrell's cooking greets me as I open the front door. He's making roast beef, buttermilk-brined roasted chicken, and scalloped potatoes. He agreed to let me manage the vegetable and salad. I decided on broccolini with pine nuts and parmesan and a citrus endive salad. Both are fairly easy, even if we're cooking for a crowd. We bought rolls and rum cake from Pearlhouse Pastries yesterday. The holiday items were spelled to stay fresh a little longer, so they cost a small amount more than usual. But convenience is worth it.

I whipped up a special meal for Acton last night. I had to confer with him on the recipe. I wouldn't want to risk including something he can't eat. The seaweed-based gelatin with orange blossom essence, dried orange blossom petals, and birch sap looks surprisingly elegant in its flower shaped mold.

We have a full house coming over in about two hours. I head straight to the kitchen to give Norrell a sweet and searing kiss before I go upstairs to change out of my ceremonial robes. It was a cold morning at the beach, so I bundled up beneath them.

Walt and Acton will come over first to exchange gifts. And then a bit later everyone else will arrive: Sunny, Thea, Cara, Ben, Ben's family—Nicolas, Lillian, and Lucas—and even Clancy is stopping by for lunch before his family's celebration in the evening.

Our guests will bring a few dishes as well. Lillian made her famous Bûche De Noël, which I've been especially excited for. It should be quite a feast.

While in the kitchen making the salad dressing, there's a knock on the door. The morning has flown by so quickly. I open the door to Walt and Acton, both grinning, holding a surprisingly large box and a smaller, standard-looking one.

"Mother Earth, your gifts are not nearly so grand!" I chuckle as I lead them inside.

Once Walt sets down the big box near the tree, he gives me a big bear hug. "Happy Yule, my sweet girl."

Acton reaches toward me once Walt finally releases me. "Happy Yule, Ada. I cherish our tradition of observing the holiday together," he says warmly as he looks down at me and affectionately pats a plush, mossy hand on my cheek.

Norrell joins us in the living room. "Happy Yule!" he wishes them, giving them hearty handshakes.

"The house looks beautiful, Ada! So festive!" Walt raves as he looks around. "Did you put up even more decorations than usual?"

"Mayhap a few more. Norrell did most of the work," I admit. After Sunny came over to resize my stored decorations and festive tablecloths, we adorned the house in earnest. We added the white twinkling lights to the tree and hung several dried wreaths I've collected over the years around the house. My Yule altar candles and candle plates were set up in a few spots like the living room coffee table and the dining and kitchen tables. Sunny strengthened the enchantment I placed on them years ago preventing the cats from getting near the flame, the same one I also used to enchant the fireplaces to keep them safe.

We ended up purchasing more fresh trimmings and other festive items. We placed fresh evergreen garlands on the top of the fireplace mantels and along the stair railing. Mistletoe hangs above a few doorways. We also dressed up the Yule altars by adding evergreen trimmings, acorns, pinecones, dried citrus slices, and holly berries around them.

"Should we open gifts?" Walt asks enthusiastically, rubbing his hands together in front of him. This is his favorite part of Yule. He loves watching people open gifts.

We sit on the living room sofas and Norrell passes out the gifts one by one. "Open yours first, Acton," I insist.

He smiles shyly as he carefully unwraps the small box. His face lights up as he pulls out several packets of rare heliconia seeds, a tropical flower he had talked about adding to the rainforest garden he's still busy designing. "They will be a centerpiece in our garden. Thank you, truly," he says delightedly.

"That's not all!" I tell him as Norrell jogs to the salon. He comes back with two pots of a dark red variety of the flower.

"Ada, Norrell, this is a bounty of beauty. From the bottom of my heart, thank you," he sputters, taken by surprise.

"You're next, big guy!" Walt states, motioning toward Norrell. They've grown close again in the last few weeks. It's been touching to witness the progress.

Norrell pulls his box from under the tree. His eyes light up, casting a surprisingly youthful look on his otherwise rough-hewn face. "By the bluest glacier, I love this text. It is an incredible historical account. I have not read it since the Academy. I never found another copy," Norrell says thickly as he holds up a worn but intact copy of a very old book titled *A Compleat History of Magicks in the North*.

"We thought you might," Walt responds with a burst of laughter. "I had some help finding it—not from Ada, I might add, she had no idea—but I'm glad I managed to get it in time before Yule. Expedited shipping straight from New York City. It was a close call."

That gives me a very good idea of who helped him, though I don't voice my guess while I beam at the three of them who continue to animatedly discuss the gift.

"Ada, that behemoth is yours!" Walt exclaims as he points at the oversized box. Norrell brings it over and sets it on the coffee table in front of me.

As I open it, Walt's expression is practically euphoric. He lives for this. Watching him like this is its own gift. "Oh, Walt, Acton, you shouldn't have," I blurt out, shocked at the extravagant present. Pulling away the wrapping paper reveals a pricey looking stainless steel espresso machine with a milk frother.

"I thought you might have worked that little old coffeemaker to its last leg after hosting that large group. Time for an upgrade!" he delights.

"I will think of you every time I use it, meaning every single day," I chuckle. "Thank you both so much."

"Last but not least," Norrell remarks brightly as he hands Walt his gift—several wrapped together.

"It's like you read my mind every time," Walt cracks up. "I've been thinking about upgrading these. How did you know?" He holds up the fancy waterproof camera and the water filtration system effective enough for survival situations but meant for off-grid camping, one of their favorite activities.

"I listen to your stories when you return from camping trips. I bought those over the summer!" I acknowledge, laughing at his genuine reaction.

"A star chart? Oh, that will make the nights during our trips even more special," he says wistfully, unfolding the beautiful and detailed maps of the seasonal night skies.

Norrell and I agreed to exchange our gifts later, just the two of us, after we have the house to ourselves again. Now that we're done gift-giving, Walt and Acton join us in the kitchen while Norrell and I continue cooking. Walt makes hot cider today. He calls it *wassail* because he says it sounds fancier for the holiday. *Cider is an everyday drink*, according to him.

In no time, the rest of the guests show up. Cara and Ben hand me a farro salad with apples and cranberries before they settle in the living room. Lillian, Nicolas, and Lucas are right behind them with their Bûche De Noël offering.

Sunny and Thea arrive together with a tray of immaculately iced gingerbread male cookies. They've been spelled with a little magick so their delicately iced faces wink and smile. I hope they don't take Cara by too much surprise. She still gets adorably flustered by magick like this.

Clancy brings his joie de vivre and a sweet potato pie from Pearlhouse Pastries. He is many things, but not a talented cook, so I happily accept the conspicuous pink box. He also brings in his bench from Ben and Cara's house, which Ben drove over in the back of his truck, so he has a comfortable seat at the long dining table.

When dinner is ready to be served, Norrell lights the Yule log in the dining room fireplace. After bringing it home from the woods near the graveyard, we gathered some fallen greenery from the lawn and used twine to wrap it around the thick piece of wood, binding some leftover evergreen twigs to it as well. We set it in the fireplace yesterday in anticipation of lighting it today.

As we sit around the table and watch Norrell, we all wish each other a happy Yule as the flames catch the tinder he put on the grate beside the log. Thea stands beside his kneeling form and whispers a quick spell so that log burns for an extended period. *Warmth for comfort. Glow for beauty. Burn until the festivities end.* I've always appreciated the practicality of her spells. It's useful in her sometimes face-paced role as a healer.

Lillian bubbles with anticipation at the feast laid out on the table. "All of this food looks amazing. Thanks for hosting us, Ada. We appreciate all the hard work it took you and Norrell to prepare this." Everyone expresses their agreement and thanks as we pass the dishes around the table and fill our plates.

"I'll hand it to you, yeti. You have kitchen skills. I hope you made a lot, because I eat like a horse," Clancy jests around bites of food.

"Thank you, Clancy. In the settlement, if we wanted a good meal, we would often have to make it ourselves," Norrell acknowledges.

"He's taken over the kitchen, and I don't mind a lick," I exclaim.

"Well, I'm glad he's doing his part to take care of you, Ada. Seems like he took those friendly reminders to heart," Clancy remarks, winking at me.

"Congrats, Walt, on the win a couple weeks ago. With all the new blood on town council, you're going to have a packed house again for your meetings. I stopped attending when Ben took over the business, but I might have to start up again at the next meeting in a couple weeks," Nicolas says from across the table.

"Nicolas looks forward to holding court during the public forum at the end of each meeting like he used to," Lillian jokes, smiling affectionately at her mate.

"I'm looking forward to the friendly discussion and banter again. It had been sorely missing for a time," Clancy chimes in, shaking his head.

"Hear, hear!" Nicolas agrees.

"You'd have thought the meetings were political," Walt adds drily. "I'm glad to help change that."

"It still keeps me up at night how close we came to disaster. That we're not even out of the weeds yet with that fae lingering in containment. And still no cure for Ada. I don't think I'll get a full night's sleep for a while yet," Clancy admits, the look in his large brown eyes softening when they meet mine.

"We stalled out on progress and Ada suffers for it. It is frustrating to just sit and wait," Norrell concurs, his expression turning dark.

"It's eye-opening to realize how much damage some deranged, power-mad warlocks could do in such a short time. We'll be dealing with the fallout for a long time," Thea laments.

"At least there's hope again for our community with the new town council," I chime in, not wanting the dark cloud hanging over us to put a damper on our celebration. "Monstera Bluff will be stronger for it." What I can't say to them is that I may not be here much longer to see it.

"A silver lining was that Cara was only subjected to one meeting of torment," Ben says ruefully. "And that she didn't pack up and leave that very night."

"Well, someone told me how they really felt and changed my mind," she admits with a bashful smile on her face.

"Who knew Ben was such a charmer?" Lucas quips and claps his brother on the back. Ben had been gazing affectionately at his mate, but he twists toward his brother on his other side and flicks him on the shoulder in return, cracking Lucas up.

"How long are you in town, Lucas?" I ask, curious because he came home for a week right after Ben and Cara were injured on Samhain.

"Turns out I felt really homesick after I left last month." He chuckles self-consciously. "I wasn't planning on it, but I figured I'd request an extended leave this month. My bosses knew I had left for a family emergency. They're so impressed with my work, *naturally*, so they told me to work remotely the entire month of December. I've been busy hanging out with family and old friends, taking advantage of this time at home. I'm not looking forward to going back next week if I'm being honest."

Clancy perks up. "I knew you'd be back for good!" he announces smugly as he rubs his hands in front of him. The two of them are almost as close as brothers since Clancy was a regular fixture at the Garde-Pierre household during his entire childhood.

"Well, not *quite* yet. In the next year or two," Lucas clarifies. "I have a lot left to learn. My bosses are exceptional engineers. They've been excellent mentors too."

"We're glad to hear this. He's been away for so many years. All my boys will be together again," Lillian adds with a happy sigh as she smiles fondly at the males. She has always treated Clancy like a third son.

"I can't believe you're not chomping at the bit to come home." Clancy chuckles at himself. "But I am glad you weren't part of Niven's tracking teams. We had a few gargoyles here. One got stuck in a fae-made trap set by the warlocks. It wasn't pretty."

"His team brought him in during my shift. The damage to his wing resisted healing for quite some time. It took several of us using an incredible amount of healing magick to mend it well enough so he'll fly again," Thea replies, shaking her head. "It's lucky we didn't see too many other patients that day because we were almost spent."

"I might be the only gargoyle in New York City who isn't on one of those teams. They're the only other gargoyles I've met so far. They're a tough bunch. An injury won't stop any of them for too long," Lucas remarks.

Clancy nods. "I joined them for a time when they were conducting sweeps after the warlocks were caught. They stayed behind for a few days after Niven Whitehall left and made sure there weren't any other nasty surprises left behind. I wanted to see for myself where those warlocks holed up and that everything was put to rights. It was squalor. Any magick they had used to spruce up the place had worn out already. There were a few items left behind obviously supplied by the fae. They were packed up and taken to New York for safekeeping. Good riddance," he recounts.

"Ashes, we had a terrible time fixing that hole they made in the ward," Sunny adds with a roll of her eyes. "Sounds a lot like that gargoyle's wing. The fae spell the warlocks used was like an infection. We had to cut it out of the ward to close it again. It almost reminded me of surgery!" As she speaks, she ties back her long dark hair adorned with a new enchantment for the holiday. The red, green, and gold streaks glimmer in the light.

"All of us in the coven who are of age have been casting magick into the ward's new security measures. It's been difficult to fit them to our existing ward. None of us want to start from scratch though, so we've been making it work," Thea says.

Much of this is new to me since I can't join in. It stings knowing all of this has been going on without me.

"I've learned more about wards and travel amulets this past month than I ever thought I would," Sunny agrees, blowing out a long breath.

"We'll all rest easier when it's done. The town appreciates everything the coven is doing," Clancy chimes in. "I'll be glad to get back to business as usual at town hall, if there is such a thing. I could use a boring day for a change, and I'm sure you could too, Cara. Though I know you're working on something big. You have been positively buzzing. And it's not about something boring like traffic patterns or zoning." He smirks in her direction.

She shoots me a desperate look before smoothing over her expression. "I don't know what you mean, Clancy. Maybe I've just been excited about the mating ceremony. It's only a few months away," she stammers.

Lillian's silver eyes brighten at her mention of the mating ceremony. "Isn't that just the best idea?" she gushes. "Benny really is a romantic."

"The right female needed to bring out that side of him. Like father like son," Nicolas says, grinning like a fool at Lillian. Cara's blush deepens as she flashes me another look.

"Oh, let me bring out the gingerbread cookies! I almost forgot," Sunny announces, dashing to the kitchen. When she returns, she sets the spelled gingerbread males unfortunately close to Cara.

"Oh no. No no." Cara's eyes bug out. "I can't eat one of these like this. How do I make it stop?" The cookie she points at winks and smiles at her. She snaps her hand back and holds it to her chest.

Ben cracks up, and the rest of us follow suit. He picks up the cookie and holds it in front of her plate. "It's not alive, same as those turnips at the festival. It's only magick."

Cara's shoulders shake in silent laughter, tears forming in her eyes. "Make it stop," she chokes. Ben takes mercy on her after dancing the cookie around her plate a bit. He snaps it in half, and the spell is broken. "Oh thank goodness." She sighs with relief and then takes a bite out of one of the halves. "These are really good when they aren't moving!"

The feast is a success, with everyone content and full at the end. The rest of the afternoon is spent socializing. We take our wassail and other drinks into the living room to sit more comfortably. The guests begin departing just before dinnertime. Thea, Sunny, and Clancy have other celebrations to attend. The Garde-Pierre clan leave soon after.

When it's just the four of us again, Walt and Acton insist Norrell and I take a seat while they clean up the dining room and kitchen, doing dishes and putting away the leftovers. It's a very kind gesture toward Norrell who probably would have ended up doing the bulk of it. I'm tired and unsteady on my feet after the long day, I wouldn't be able to help much anyway.

As we sit on the sofa with the cats curled up on either side of us, Norrell leans in and presses his warm lips to mine in a tender, exploring kiss. "Happy Yule," he murmurs as he rests his forehead on mine.

"I can't wait to give you your gift," I purr as we stay in that intimate pose for several minutes, resting our eyes and reveling in the closeness.

"Don't you two look sweet as pie," Walt ribs us gently when he and Acton return to the living room. "We should get out of your hair. It's been a long day, especially for you two."

"If you're sure..." I begin, but Walt good-naturedly waves his hand to stop me.

"We are. You two deserve a nice quiet night together. You both made Yule very special for all of us." We say our goodbyes, and they head out after putting their gifts in Walt's automobile.

"Are you tired, my ember?" he asks me, rubbing along the back of my neck.

"Yes, but I'm not ready for bed yet." I bite my lip as my hungry gaze sweeps over him.

His chuckle is low and knowing. "I will distract the boys with dinner. While I do that..." He pauses, plotting, as he eases off the sofa. "Be a good girl and think about all the naughty things you want me to do to you."

"What if I want to do something to you?" I wonder aloud, sounding playfully innocent.

"Yule is all about the spirit of giving, so I know we will both get exactly what we want tonight," he rasps with growing hunger in his voice.

Norrell is only gone for a couple minutes. He shuts the two sets of doors in the room so we have privacy. I pat the sofa beside me. Obediently, he sits and pulls me onto his lap for a long, languid kiss.

Slowly nuzzling down his neck to his chest, I slide from his lap, settling with my knees on the floor between his own. I look up at him through my lashes, smirking as I unbutton and unzip his pants. He lifts his hips, letting me slide his pants and briefs down to his ankles, then pull them off. He's fully naked and glorious in front of me. I admire the heat in his eyes as my hands knead up his muscled calves to his thick thighs, all covered in a heavy pelt, soft and supple to the touch. His straining cock twitches, leaking a string of white onto his belly where it rests.

His hard swallow is loud as I draw my hands around the base of his girthy, veined cock and lean forward to take it in my mouth. My tongue darts out to lick at the wide slit, already bubbling with pre-come. My tongue swirls around the tapering head teasingly as I stroke him lightly. When my gaze lifts to his again, he watches me with hooded, hazy eyes. He groans as our eyes hold while I bob my head up and down, working my mouth and hands in tandem around him. Not wanting him to erupt too soon, I slow down again, licking up down his shaft, nuzzling into him and gently cupping his testicles. When I want to work him harder again, I suck several inches of his cock into my mouth, hollowing my cheeks in the process.

"Ah, my ember. Just the way I like it," he moans. I can feel his muscles bunching in his legs where I rest my arms, trying not to spill yet.

His hands finally move to my head, guiding the rhythm as I return to sucking and bobbing my head, keeping pace with my hands circled around the root of his cock. When his blunted claws scrape over my scalp, I know he's close. I gradually increase my speed, and his hips begin rocking of their own accord. His snarling vocalizations grow louder until I can feel his cock judder and thicken in my mouth. His eyes roll back as long spurts of salty come jet out of his cock into my mouth. I do my best to swallow everything down while still working him through his orgasm.

When his cock softens, I carefully slip him free from my mouth, licking at his slit to make sure it's clean. He leans forward and pulls me onto his lap. "Such a naughty girl giving her gift first. Now it is your turn. I will be sure to give you an extra special one," he promises, his voice rich with need.

He guides me backward on the sofa, pulling my knees over his shoulders. Sliding a hand under my low back, he lifts me up slightly and pushes my dress up to my waist. He hooks the edge of my panties on one of his tusks and pulls it down my legs. With my feet now on his shoulders, he carefully guides my panties around them and tosses the scrap of fabric behind him. Leaning forward again, my knees around his shoulders, he inhales deeply into my pussy.

The first touch of his tongue to my clit sends shivers through my entire body. But I can tell he wants to explore first. He slowly licks inside my labia, tasting me. Moving to the entrance of my pussy, he laps up the wetness that accumulated while I was sucking his cock. I'm aroused just by the sight of it. His nose rubs insistently against my clit as his tongue works its way inside me. In response, I dig my heels against his back for leverage and grind my pussy against his hungry mouth, earning me an appreciative hum that vibrates his face against me.

"Yes, Norrell, yes! Keep going," I wail as his nimble tongue propels me closer to my peak. His tongue skates upward again, landing on my clit. He sucks on it as he lifts my lower body fully off the sofa. Instinctively, I cross my ankles behind his head to lock him in place. He pulls a desperate, needy whimper from my throat as his finger presses inside, making way for another digit in wet, steady strokes.

"Moon and stars, that's it," I moan. I'm about to come already. I feel my channel clamping around his fingers. When he crooks them, rubbing behind my clit, the orgasm bursts from my core, plunging my entire body into a state of bliss. Tears gather in the corner of my eyes as I gulp down shaky, shuttering breaths.

My legs rest on his back as he continues to hold up my body, only my upper back and head rest on the cushion. Norrell slowly pulls his fingers from me with an embarrassingly wet squelch. I watch as he sucks them clean while still staring raptly at my pussy.

"That was incredible," I breathe. "I don't think I can move."

"There is no need. I will hold you," he replies, distracted.

"But we still haven't exchange Yule gifts," I exclaim with an incredulous chuckle, my hands covering my face.

He hums in contentment, nibbling absently at my inner thigh while his eyes are still glued between my legs. "I do not need anything else."

"No, it seems you don't. But I want to give it to you anyway." I giggle.

"In a minute," he replies. His breath is hot on my pussy as he breathes me in.

Watching him while he's entranced by me, his eyes finally dart to mine about a minute later. He presses a firm, final kiss to my inner thigh and lowers me down gently. I smooth down my dress but don't even bother with my panties. Norrell stands to pull up and button his pants over his still swollen cock. The fabric barely contains the bulge.

He bends down and reaches for the two boxes left under the tree and sets them in front of us on the coffee table. When he joins me on the sofa again, I hand him the gift I wrapped for him earlier this week. After tearing through the wrapping paper with a blunt claw, he slowly opens the small box. His expression gentles when he sees the thick leather bracelet intricately woven with clear quartz beads to create a pattern. It's a surprisingly masculine piece of jewelry. I knew it would suit him when I saw it and ordered one with the quartz he likes.

"Thank you. This is an amazing gift, Ada. I will never take it off," he says sincerely. "Help me fasten it." He offers me his wrist. I secure the leather bracelet, making sure I can still slide a couple fingers underneath, so it doesn't rub against his skin.

Norrell hands me my gift, flat and rectangular in shape. I'm puzzled as to what it could be. I slowly unwrap it and then open the box. Inside is an old, slightly tattered leather-bound notebook. When I open it to the first page, I gasp in a sharp breath. It's my dad's handwriting. My jaw drops as I stare at it in wonder. I'm truly speechless.

Norrell explains, "When I spoke with Esmeralda Jurado last month, it made me wonder if your father had any academic submissions in the library. I texted her a few days later asking if she could do a quick search for me during the years he spent there for his apprenticeship. She found several typed, formal documents he had filed with them. But then she happened to come across this journal in the language studies section. Something he later probably typed up and submitted elsewhere."

My mouth flops open and closed. No sound comes out. Norrell takes pity on me again. "Esmeralda told me he went to some far-flung places to immerse himself in rare Whispered Folk languages during his apprenticeship. While he was there, he kept academic field journals with observations about his experiences. This was from one of his trips. Dean Jurado scanned it, so they have a replacement copy but shipped the original to me for you to keep."

A sob tears from my throat. "This is unbelievable, Norrell. I can't believe this still exists and you found it. That it's in my hands. I had no idea it was there," I babble, nearly inconsolable, throwing myself into his arms. "Thank you."

"My ember, I am glad it is finally where it belongs," he murmurs while his soothing hands sweep up and down my trembling back.

CHAPTER 18

NORRELL

My ringing phone wakes me up in the dead of night. Luckily it does not stir Ada, who is still asleep next to me in her bed. She sleeps longer and deeper to fight off the fae's spell as it steals her life. It is no surprise she slept through the noise. Creeping out of the room after silencing my phone, I quietly answer the call from the unfamiliar number in the hallway as I walk downstairs.

"Hello?" My voice is still groggy.

"Norrell, this is Tallan Frostweaver," says a frayed voice on the other end of the line.

"Tallan? Why are you calling me at this hour?" He's an elder in my clan, having held a seat on the council for many years.

"I have not slept in over a month. Night or day means nothing to me anymore. I thought if I come clean to you finally, mayhap that will change. Or at least unburden my conscience when I find myself in an early grave," Tallan rambles. He is a calm presence on the council. One of the few in its current form. Whatever is going on is already concerning.

"Tell me what you want to say," I instruct him coolly.

"When your brother Elgar asked for our help the first time, we stayed silent. Played dumb. All agreed we would not get involved. We did so again when the true picture of your mate's suffering became clear," he claims.

"Are you saying the council of elders is outright refusing to help me?" I try to clarify.

"Yes, that is exactly what I am saying. Harlok, your uncle, kept secrets from you. Made all of us keep secrets from you for years. Secret histories and relics that you should have been made privy to as our Huntmaster. He claimed you did not deserve that knowledge when you so reluctantly took on the role. That the next Huntmaster would be a leader who would finally deserve them. And in the meantime, we would keep this information quiet," he explains.

A deep, thundering headache forms behind my eyes. I ignore it for now and try to focus. "Which of these secrets would help my mate, Tallan?" I ask directly, trying to keep the anger out of my voice.

"The relics. The two the witch pulled from the fae's mind. The two that the Seer foretold," he reveals solemnly.

"*We* have the relics?" I roar, not caring whether I blow out the eardrum of this addled old male. "And you kept this from me for a month? Fire of the frost! You helped this disgusting fae, an enemy to our kind, genuinely suck the life out of my mate for an entire month longer than necessary while you wrestled with your morals? You should be ashamed, Tallan! All of you! She will die without them!"

"I do not want her to die, Norrell. We already took her from you once. I could not let the fae succeed in doing so again," he mumbles in a small voice, sounding deeply ashamed.

"You are going to tell me right now where those relics are. And then you are going to call my brother right away and tell him exactly what you told me, followed by every other secret you kept from me. I do not care about any of them except these two relics," I demand through gritted teeth.

"Alright. It will be done. And mayhap I will find peace again." He exhales shakily into the phone. "There is a cave to the far north in the Arctic Cordillera where no Whispered Folk or human would ever dare stumble." He proceeds to tell me in great detail the path to this treacherous mountain cave where these powerful relics were stashed away centuries ago. I commit every word of it to memory.

Immediately I text my brother, who responds in a remarkably short time that Tallan has indeed called him and they are meeting imminently. It is the middle of the night there as well, so I do not believe Elgar is taking any chance in letting dear Uncle Harlok and the council of elders block that information any longer.

Next, I call Niven. I nearly feel bad that I will likely wake him up, but I realize he would be upset if I did not in this situation. "Norrell, what happened?" Niven answers.

"I know where the relics are. *My* clan had them all along. An elder finally had a crisis of conscience and told me. After an entire month of Ada needlessly suffering. I am livid. Only the blue hag of winter knows how hard I will come down on every one of those lying cowards, especially my despicable uncle who kept this from me." My voice is still sharp and angry. I pace across the foyer as I try to control my rage.

"Good, they deserve it. Go get those relics and come back as soon as you can. I'll arrange the travel portal to get you as close to your settlement as possible. The local coven will assist you on the rest of your way there and back. Be at the portal at seven sharp. That's only a few hours from now. Pack what you need. And then tell Ada you love her and you'll be home again soon with everything we need to save her," he advises.

Running back upstairs into the dark bedroom, I gently rub Ada's shoulder to wake her. "My ember. I am sorry to wake you, but this is urgent," I murmur softly, not wanting to startle her.

"Norrell? Is everything okay?" she croaks, not fully awake, and reaches out to hug me.

"Yes, but there is urgent news," I reveal.

That gets her attention, and she sits up abruptly, looking alarmed. "What's wrong?"

"I know where the relics are. I must retrieve them. But that means I will be gone for a little while. Hopefully only a couple weeks," I assure her.

"Why that long? Where are they? Will you be safe?" she frets. She clutches her hands to her chest.

"I will be safe. It will be like going on a long hunt, something I have done plenty of times before. A full team will be with me, including my brother, who I trust wholeheartedly. But the trek to the cave where my clan hid the relics will take several days in each direction, even with our snowmobiles and mountain climbing equipment. And then I will come right back to you and make sure that fae magick never touches you again," I vow.

"Your clan?" she asks in disbelief. Her eyes grow wide.

"My clan. And may they rot for how much harm they put us through. I am done with them forever," I say, never surer of anything in my life except my love for Ada.

Ada looks stricken as we wait for the portal to open. Her face is paler than usual and new worry lines etch deeper around her eyes. "Come back to me, Norrell. I..." She pauses with a rush of breath, like she's trying not to cry. "I love you. So much. I don't think I can live without you," she confesses.

Though I have expressed my love for her many times, she has not returned it until now. It is the first confirmation that she may still feel as strongly for me as I do for her. It leaves me breathless. With so much on the line, it amplifies my concern that this journey will be fruitless, that I will completely fail my mate again despite the Seer's vision.

Pulling her into me, I nuzzle her cheek so my lips are close to her ear. In a low voice, only for her, I whisper, "You will never have to. You, my ember, are my entire reason for existing. You will be safe and protected in my arms forever. I love you, Ada. I will return to you as quickly as I can."

Her body trembles with silent sobs as we take solace in each other's arms for these last few moments together. "Stay safe for me. Don't take any extra risks," she pleads in a reedy voice edged with fear I wish I could kiss away. My eyes fill with tears that my mate has misplaced worry that my safety is tantamount to hers.

One of her coven members quietly approaches telling us they must open the portal. I cradle her face in my hands and press my lips to hers with such passion it will stay with me the length of my journey.

Determination overrides my sadness as I step through the portal to begin my travel northward. When I come back with the relics, free from all obligations to my clan, the rest of our lives can begin. The long trek to my clan's settlement is arduous, but at least I know from experience what to expect. The witches waiting for me on the other side of the portal in Toronto accompany me to the northmost human settlement through a series of flights to increasingly small airports. From there I make my own way on the Old Path, one that we keep marked and passable for trade purposes, to the North Clan settlement.

I kept my brother updated at every step. He and I will have a long conversation about handing the title of Huntmaster of the True North to him. Technically, all the hunters will have to agree. But no one holds a candle to my brother's drive and skill other than me. There can be no recycled argument that he is too young for the mantle of leadership. He is now forty years of age. Much more mature than I was when I took over at age thirty-two. There will be no pushback this time.

The path grows more defined, cutting through the harsh landscape, the closer I get to the settlement. It could still easily be overlooked by someone unfamiliar with it. Yeti do not require the easy footpath that a human would. Our feet are toughened and nimble. Our bodies made for this harsh environment. My brother Elgar, the spitting image of me except for his slightly taller stature and dark gray eyes, meets me far enough down the path that the settlement is still out of sight.

"Brother, it is good to see you. I am glad you returned so quickly. I have learned much since we last spoke. Though none of it will likely surprise you," he says bleakly.

We embrace briefly, our usual show of sentiment, though I know that we hold more affection for each other than anyone else in our clan save our parents. Our parents are now getting older. They both stepped back long ago from the hunt and never pursued seats on the council of elders. They are happy in their retirement. As brothers, my father and Harlok could not be more different. I am glad my parents had no part in this deception, though I know they would not have allowed such a thing to occur to any leader on principle alone.

"Harlok's sway over the council of elders is stronger than I thought possible. He has subtly led decisions on the hunting groups, giving easier runs to the kin of his supporters. It is disgusting. We will have a generation of undertrained hunters and all the ramifications that it brings if this continues. Not to mention another group will be worked to the bone just because their families are not politically connected," Elgar states bitterly. The elders have long overseen the hunting groups in order to prevent such blatant favoritism as this. Obviously this approach was naïve.

Harlok. My dislike for him grows with each passing year and with good reason. He is an embittered old male who now walks with a cane after he was gravely injured by revenants fifteen years ago. The ripple of chaos his sudden departure from power caused could only be quelled by a strong leader. Me, apparently. Taking a seat on the council of elders is a privilege. There is no shame in coming to an age that would qualify someone to become an elder. In fact, it is expected of former Huntmasters. The position is meant to be aged out of, which is why we have our elders to help guide us through those transitions. Unlike Harlok, most choose to end their reign gracefully. They realize it is their time to step down before it is challenged by an unwise hunt or by another skilled hunter seeking to oust them.

In addition, he has always encouraged our worthless cousin to undermine me. I guess it was by design. No doubt he is doing the same to Elgar now. And as a result, Harlok undermines the stability of our clan. He has yet to accept that his son Torman will never prove himself worthy of the position. He spoiled Torman and never held him to the same standard as others. And my cousin inherited the worst of his father's narcissistic traits. Torman always wanted the easiest path, never bothering trying to become a great hunter or skilled tradesman for our clan.

"Harlok's actions do not surprise me. How easily the other elders fell into line does," I confess somberly to Elgar. "The corruption runs deeper than I thought possible. Past generations of elders would turn in their graves if they knew about this. If Tallan Frostweaver could be swayed so easily, the rest are just as compromised."

"The council of elders holds no value to our clan anymore in the current form. They are a liability for us, in fact. We cannot trust any of them to oversee their own reform, rooting out their corruption from within. We must wipe the slate clean and appoint a more balanced and principled group of elders to sit on the council. It will be hard for some to swallow, but once we make public what Tallan has told us, the clan will be on our side. It is detrimental to too many hunters and their families to let it continue," he argues.

When we return to the settlement, we waste no time calling an immediate clan assembly. We will not let the council of elders poison the well any further. Some groups of hunters are away on long hunts. But their families are still here, and they will not take kindly to the news we are about to share.

My brother and I stand in the public square, where the roof of our cavern reaches its highest point, at least ninety feet high, and gradually slopes lower a mile in each direction until it meets the cavern floor. Public buildings surround the open space of the square. Our structures were constructed mostly with stone, mortar, and clay repaired countless times over the centuries. Wood is less common since trees do not grow this far into the Arctic Circle. Artificial suns light the entire cavern, powered by the magick we absorb from Malefic Folk. The cavern itself is a natural wonder that our forebears settled millennia ago. Though what little the clan tolerates of magick, we had it magickally reinforced long ago and it continues to hold without issue.

The crowd grows large straightaway. This is an unusual occurrence. Some hunters congregate near us, looking concerned and not a little disgruntled. "Norrell, have you returned for good? Or are you abandoning us again for a witch?" one spews with unearned cockiness, spitting on the ground in disgust.

I level him with my own withering gaze. He is one of those benefitting from Harlok's stranglehold over the hunter assignments. No doubt there is a strong current of disrespect and bigotry among that group. They are in for a rude awakening.

"Brothers and sisters of the clan," I begin. "Elgar and I have grave news concerning the council of elders. They have been conspiring for many years, not only to undermine the leadership of the Huntmaster of the True North, but also the egalitarian opportunities given to the hunters in our society. For years, they have granted the easiest, safest hunts to those who garner favor with Harlok and the rest of the elders he pulled into his schemes. He works to undermine the very fabric of our society, the foundation of our clan's ways."

Elgar, who has always been more at ease with public speaking, steps forward and elaborates in excruciating, undeniable detail how this was done and why. Much of this information came from Tallan directly, who also provided evidence to back up his claims. Two other elders who in the past had been trustworthy, or so we thought, came forward similarly once Tallan told them he confessed everything to Elgar.

The insolent hunters who stood near us earlier have conveniently vanished from the crowd. No doubt escaping the public shaming. But their names will still be dragged through the frosted bedrock as enthusiastic participants of this treacherous favoritism.

As Elgar thoroughly demolishes the reputation of Harlok and the council of elders, Harlok and Torman storm into the square. "They lie! I have done no such thing. Yes, we kept information from Norrell Snowstrider, but only because he was never worthy of leadership! He swooped in and stole power for himself! He wanted to change the old ways. So we did not let him. We have strayed too far from our era of heroes! I alone am working to bring us back to our prime. Under Norrell, we are growing weak, breaking with the heroic ways of our past. He has put the interest of filthy magick wielders and Whispered Folk above our own since my reign ended," he shouts in a frenzy, spittle flying from his lips.

This unhinged declaration does not sit well with the crowd, whose chatter intensifies during his speech. "You make us weak, Harlok!" A voice yells from the crowd. "No hunters should be coddled!"

"Send your own weakling son on a month-long hunt, Harlok. See how he fares in the rough so far away from his family," clamors another.

The jeers continue, turning into chants against Harlok and the elders. Those in attendance, including Harlok, quickly leave the scene when it's clear that no one believes him.

When the crowd calms again, Elgar resumes his speech, elaborating on how he has agreed to take over my position permanently once he receives the votes needed from our hunters. He will have to wait to make it official until the rest of the hunters have returned. But in the meantime, he will continue to act in my stead, as I am stepping down from the role of Huntmaster of the True North. The noise of the crowd swells after the declaration, but it seems supportive.

He sighs roughly, his disgust with the council of elders written on his face. When he finally resumes his speech, he lays the situation bare. "A layer of black, putrid frost formed over this corrupted body. The council of elders is hereby dissolved, and the members lose their title as well as the respect of the clan. They are all disgraceful. A stain on our history. The council will be formed again in time with elders who are committed to upholding the true values of our clan. And we will formalize the scheduling of the hunts and make the process public. We will also introduce programs to train hunters from all backgrounds who are interested in leadership on the hunts as well as working toward the role of Huntmaster of the True North. Our society hinges on these opportunities made available to all of us. Our heroes of the past were not kings and queens, but extraordinary hunters from all walks of life. We will not tolerate the gatekeeping of power to only those who are most connected. It is a cycle that perpetuates systemic deception and inequity."

The crowd responds enthusiastically. Many surge forward to speak with me and Elgar, vocalizing their support for these ideas, many wishing they had been implemented decades ago. If nothing else, I hope that Elgar has been put in a good position to lead them into a better future. One that I relish leaving behind.

That night, we gather in our family home. Elgar and I leave first thing in the morning to retrieve the relics. A large group of capable hunters volunteered to accompany us. While most still do not trust other Whispered Folk, they want to join us on principle in light of the elders' wrongdoing.

My parents embrace me tightly as I step inside, the first time I have seen or spoken to them since I returned. We did not take any risks before calling the meeting, not even telling our parents, in case it inadvertently spoiled the element of surprise we needed to act quickly and decisively.

"Son, we are so proud of you. Both you and your brother are a credit to our clan," our father praises us as he clasps my shoulders affectionately.

"This is all such a shock," my mother says. Her body sags into mine as we hug. "It makes me sick how close Harlok came to compromising our entire clan."

"Mother, father, before we talk about everything going on with the council, I need to tell you I am moving to Monstera Bluff permanently. Ada has always been my mate. That will never change. We will be together again," I tell them firmly.

My mother nods her head in understanding. "We agree you should stay there. We are so grateful you have found a second chance with her. We know how much the separation from her hurt you. It hurt us nearly as much to see the constant sadness in your eyes."

"You have done more than your fair share of duty to the clan. Go and be happy with your mate. We will miss you, but most of all we want you to live the life you want," my father affirms.

"Thank you," I sniffle, my emotions heightened after a tremendously long, trying day. "I will miss you too. But I will not bring Ada here, ever. I will never fully trust the clan to treat her respectfully. But I want you to visit us whenever you wish. I will arrange everything to make it easier for you."

"We will," my mother confirms, her voice unusually tender. "We look forward to meeting her one day soon."

At the appointed time, the group joining our expedition meets in the public square, ready to set out on the long journey. We anticipate running into groups of Malefic Folk, so we are treating this like a long hunt into our territory's wilder works of frost. It will be challenging for all of us, but we are ready. Those joining me and Elgar hunger for the opportunity to prove themselves. Most are those who were forced into the worst hunts for many years. They are seasoned and reliable. It surprises me to see a few who benefitted from Harlok's system, though they assure me they want to separate themselves from it. I trust they also be valuable to us.

It takes many arduous days to reach the cave. As Darla foretold, I am the *frost-mailed warrior* from her vision. The weather does not let up the entire time. I am encrusted in snow and ice the entire journey there. All of us are. But no one slows their steps, understanding the gravity of the mission.

The cave itself is unremarkable except that its giant maw opens about a third of the way up a mountain, following an inhospitable path that requires us to climb steep, sheer rockfaces with our tools, and at times just our clawed hands and feet. The cave is deep enough that the relics are kept well out of the elements. Their fae magick pulses around us in unimaginable power. No wonder our ancestors hid them away so thoroughly. If relics like these are needed to reverse the fae's spell, I shudder to think how powerful it must be. Ada is unbelievably strong to have fought it for this long.

"Here they are, brother. Some of our clan's darkest secrets," Elgar observes sardonically, eyeing the relics with some trepidation. I don't blame him. We are all viscerally repulsed by them.

"What are they?" one of our younger hunters cuts in.

There are several relics hidden here, but we will retrieve only the two mentioned by the fae: *The Banner of Life* and *The Forged Ruby*. Tallan gave us their descriptions, so we can identify them. The Banner of Life looks like an elegantly crafted crown. No doubt that says a lot about who it was intended for. The Forged Ruby does resemble a ruby, though its inconsistent color is lit from within, showing both darker and yellower variation inside the chunk of red gem.

"Proof the fae are an abomination," I respond to the young hunter, who has kept his distance from them the entire time.

Elgar and I secure the items in our packs, wrapping and cushioning them carefully for the long journey back. We camp for the night close to the mouth of the cave, the currents of fae magick emanating from the relics setting all of us on edge.

The trek back to the settlement is fraught with more Malefic confrontations than we had on the way there. They are drawn by the strong aura of magick surrounding us as we carry the relics. They are nothing we cannot handle with a group of our size and strength, but we are all weary from the long trek.

It is a relief to arrive back at the settlement several days later, though I am anxious to return to Ada. The journey took eight days in all, a long stretch for even seasoned hunters. Elgar and I rest and recuperate for the night before we begin our journey to Monstera Bluff. I call Niven the moment I enter the settlement. He has already arranged for the same witches to accompany us back to the Toronto portal safely. Niven does not want to leave anything to chance now that we have the relics. Ever since the fae mentioned that Malefic could be responsible for more Whispered Folk deaths than previously thought, he and the witches are on high alert for any threat.

Exactly as planned, the Toronto coven witches meet us and bring us uneventfully back to the portal. When Elgar and I step through the strange, soupy miasma, a large, welcoming crowd greets us on the other side. Ada jogs toward me immediately, wrapping her long, slender arms around my waist. She looks frailer than before. The stress of my absence may have accelerated the effects of the fae spell. Hopefully she will never have to worry about that again.

"Ada, my mate. It is such a relief to hold you again," I murmur into her hair as I mold her to me. I was able to call her briefly to let her know I arrived that first day and then again yesterday when we returned from the cave. But those two brief days I spent at the settlement were such a blur of activity I barely had time to speak with her.

She reaches up, running a soft hand along my cheek and jaw. Her gaze seeks mine earnestly. "Moon and stars, I was so worried for you," she quavers, tears filling her eyes. I lean my face down and tenderly press my lips to hers. Her face fits perfectly between my tusks with her delicate features.

Niven and a small group of unfamiliar witches are also here to meet us. When I finally survey the room, Elgar stands in a corner, still looking shaken from walking through the portal. I cannot blame him. It never gets easier.

"Ada, please come and meet Elgar," I ask as I lead her to my brother, whose eyes blink rapidly, mayhap still trying to wrap his mind around the fundamentals of the portal. He has not often had reason to leave the settlement other than to hunt.

Ada holds out her hand to Elgar who grasps it immediately like a lifeline. "Ada, it is my honor to make your acquaintance. Please know that our clan forcing Norrell away from you will be the biggest regret of my life. What it did to him... and to you. I humbly ask for your forgiveness," he says, unusually subdued and genuinely contrite.

Tears fall from Ada's eyes as he speaks. She quickly dashes them away and draws closer to me. "Thank you, Elgar. I appreciate your apology. I'm glad to finally make your acquaintance too," she replies with a watery smile.

Niven steps over to us, greeting me and introducing himself to Elgar. "I don't even need to ask if you have the items. I can feel their foul magick already," he shudders.

We gladly hand over the packs to him and his team. He introduces us to the unfamiliar witches. They are experts in magickal artifacts.

"Your clan knew what it was doing hiding these away. Mother Earth knows how they came to be in Northern Canada, but these do not belong in our realm," one of them states to me and Elgar, his eyes wide as he holds the unwrapped Forged Ruby.

"What is the red one made of?" I ask, jerking my chin toward it.

The witch murmurs quiet words to himself as he turns it over in his hands. "Painite," he answers eventually. "Probably the rarest gem in this realm. Its extreme rarity leads me to believe this substance originates in the fae realm. Mayhap it conducts their magick better than materials here." After briefly inspecting the relics, the witches pack them away again.

We ride in a caravan of automobiles through the ward into Monstera Bluff. Ada drives me and Elgar. She tells me a little about the time I was away, that Walt and Acton moved in temporarily to keep an eye on her. Sunny, Thea, Clancy, Cara, and Ben came over a few times to do some chores and keep her company.

The automobiles pull into the parking area at Ada's house. The witches, including Niven, will stay at the inn. They arrived last night right after I informed Niven we had returned successfully. This meeting at Ada's will allow us time and privacy to form a plan to use the relics. Niven's team, who were here previously, are waiting for us. The biggest surprise, though, is that Esmeralda Jurado waits with them.

"Dean Jurado?" I exclaim in confusion as I approach her. Her dark hair is streaked with silver and is cut a little shorter. Otherwise, she looks the same.

"Norrell! You didn't think I'd miss the excitement of breaking a fae spell?" she jokes as she leans in for a hug. "But in all seriousness, I spoke with Niven last week and he asked if I wanted to come here and help when you returned."

"I cannot believe it," I sputter, still shocked. "I have not seen you since Ada and I left Sparklight Academy."

"Well, some of my favorite former scholars are here to save the life of another one. I couldn't miss out on that. I'm here for you, whatever you need," she voices in earnest.

"It brings us great comfort," I tell her honestly.

We go inside, where Walt and Acton are already setting up a table with catering in the large salon. They both envelop me in a giant hug. "Thank you for saving our golden-hearted girl," Acton says tearfully.

"We are nearly there," I assure him.

"Her spirit has already been restored seeing you safe and sound again." His airy voice sounds unmistakably relieved.

A small crowd from Ada's coven arrives several minutes later. When the entire group settles in, Niven calls for everyone's attention.

He looks around the room. "We have both artifacts, one for life force and the other for magick. I am opening the discussion with our experts on how to use these artifacts to break or force out the fae spell cast on Ada."

One of Ada's coven members stands up immediately, interjecting before anyone else starts speaking. "I'm not the expert you're asking for, but the magick part may be easier. The entire coven has volunteered our magick for the artifact. As much as needed, for as long as needed."

Ada's expression brightens, and she mouths a "thank you" 'to the witch, who nods in return.

One of the relics experts looks pleased by this news. "A glut of magick should work well for this type of artifact. Drawing from strong sources similar in nature to hers will likely make the effect on Ada more potent. It will better absorb into her own magickal signature," she remarks.

Another expert, the one who identified the rare gem, also pipes up, "If Ada's magick is being sapped constantly fighting the spell, an over-supply of magickal energy pushed into her will help fight it off, just like strengthening the immune system to fight an infection. That said, it might be the most effective to also push ethereal spark, as the fae called it, back into her from the other artifact to not only offset what has been lost but also to strengthen her physically to aid her magick in fighting the spell."

Niven's expression sinks. "But whose life force would we take? For all we know, it could kill someone instantly. It is fae designed after all. We do not know the strength of life force or the lifespans of those who created this item." He nods his head toward the relic sitting on the table near him. "You think whoever wore that crown cared if it killed the being it was stealing the life from? I don't. We can't ask anyone here to potentially sacrifice their life," Niven argues.

There's some shuffling movement in the room at this grim realization. Acton stands up and faces Niven. "I have already lived a lifetime, and I have another to spare. I will do it," he says quietly.

"No, Acton! I can't risk losing you!" Ada blurts out.

Turning his head, he smiles at her and then at Walt, a gleam of something determined and sure in his eyes. "You won't," he finally replies. "My life has more meaning with you in it. Maybe I can't risk losing you. Besides, we don't want you to return to your teenage years." He hums a small laugh. "So if there's any of my life force left after you recovered what you lost, I want to give it to Walt."

Walt gasps and raises his hands to his mouth. He shakes his head *no* while staring at Acton. His willingness to be the test subject spurs multiple conversations around the room, chattering about minimizing the risk and attempting smaller transfers of life force in the initial attempts.

"Acton, I can't agree to this. I can't agree to something that is designed to harm you and shorten your lifespan. It doesn't matter if your natural lifespan is longer. It's because you're a dryad. My body is not designed to live centuries. Yours is." Strong emotion laces Walt's voice.

"This is mayhap an opportunity no one has had in many centuries, millennia even. I could not live those long extra years at the end of my life in good conscience if we do not take this opportunity. It may not work at all. But at least we will have tried," Acton explains, his position unwavering.

"I'm not sure if I need to even ask you, but are you sure, Acton? You give your consent to let our experts attempt to take some of your life force to give to Ada and potentially to Walt as well?" Niven confirms.

"Yes, I know it's what I must do." His serenity upholds the truth of it.

Niven studies him closely, and a smile curls the edges of his mouth. "Let our experts examine these relics further. We will attempt to use them tomorrow afternoon, barring any unforeseen circumstances like a sudden decline in Ada's health. Then, once that process is complete and we are confident that Ada has recovered, we will finally deal with this fae. I'm sure we all share in the relief knowing its days are numbered."

The meeting continues, but its focus shifts toward examination of the relics and discussion of how best to use them. The experts believe the fae could command the magick as they wore or handled the items, as the Banner of Life is clearly a crown. It would also likely mean fae are corporeal in their realm, unlike in ours. Niven asks me and Elgar to join them while the witches carefully test their power.

He purses his lips at the relics. "Do you think your abilities could control their flow of magick? You may have a lighter touch with them than any of us," he says gesturing to the other witches with us.

Elgar and I share a look. His eyes narrow in concern. "What would you have us do?" he asks.

Niven nods in understanding at Elgar's confusion. "Ada will likely be unable to command the crown, as she does not have magick to use it. We would like one of you to monitor the flow of magick from this relic as one of our experts tries to absorb life force from Acton to transfer into Ada. It will likely be safer for Acton that way."

Elgar is unpersuaded. "This relic is powerful. Too powerful for any of us to use safely. Norrell and I could absorb some of its magick now to try to weaken it to the point of injuring but not killing the dryad on contact."

My mood turns grim. He is right that the power contained within this relic is not meant for Whispered Folk to control. "Do we risk breaking it?" I point out.

"Yes." Elgar sounds sure. "It is unusable in this form anyway. It is a death sentence."

"There is truth in that," I agree, though it is only an educated guess. But Elgar's observation is correct. The guilt would be crushing if Acton was harmed.

"Ready?" Elgar asks me while pulling a piece of clear quartz from his pocket.

"As ever," I say wryly. My bracelet from Ada still circles my wrist.

This is a much more delicate process than we are used to. I concentrate on the source of power in the crown. Elgar is doing the same beside me. The magick within it is complex and layered, like several spells have enchanted it, though I have no idea what they individually do. To keep them intact, we work to draw out the magick slowly enough that we weaken but not disrupt the balance of the individual spells. Doing so could nullify the relic's power.

Elgar shifts next to me. "Pull back. We risk the enchantment."

"Good call. We are almost there," I say through my clenched jaw.

Finally, I draw back as well. The magick within the item is diminished to the point it will not kill anyone on contact anymore—an improvement.

Niven's gaze moves between us. "Is it safer now?"

Elgar shrugs. "It is still dangerous. But we risk breaking it if we take any more. It requires an extraordinary amount of magick to support it."

Niven nods in understanding. "If one of us could activate it, do you think you could control the level of magick flowing from it while it's being used? We should try the gem first. Something a little less deadly."

"We can try. It may help us understand the crown better," I agree.

Esmeralda raises her hand. "Me! Go ahead and try it on me first," she enthusiastically volunteers.

I eye her dubiously. "Are you sure? This will be unpleasant."

"I'm your guinea pig. Lay it on me," she confirms.

Niven nods hesitantly, eyes darting between me and Esmeralda.

The expert steps forward and picks up the Forged Ruby. "Ready?" he asks both of us. "This is completely untested. I've used relics before, but they're all a little different. If I'm being frank, this may knock you on your ass, Esmeralda."

Both of us voice our agreement. The rest of the group steps back to give us plenty of space, though a couple are positioned behind Esmeralda to catch her if she falls. The glow inside the red gem pulses malevolently as the witch whispers some words that seem to activate it. "Just telling it my intent to drain her magick," he tells the crowd.

His focus returns to the gem and Esmeralda. I sense the source of power stretching itself. It is easy to differentiate Esmeralda's magick from it. I draw from the threads of the fae magick as they extend from the enchantment into Esmeralda and direct them into the quartz around my wrist. When she shudders and starts to sway on her feet, the witch whispers again and the glow of the gem returns to its normal state. The two nearby witches rush to her side and help her to a chair.

"Wow, that's strong stuff!" she declares. "The fae weren't messing around when they made that. It took less than a minute to drain most of my magick. I feel exhausted, but not ill. This isn't something I'd want to do every day, but I'm okay." She holds her hands out in a reassuring gesture.

Niven comes over to her and pats her shoulder in a friendly gesture. "Thank you, Esmeralda. This test will make tomorrow go that much smoother. Would you like any coffee or water? Some food?"

"No, I'm alright," she assures him. "Just no strenuous activity for me the rest of the day." She gives Niven a lighthearted smile and a thumbs up that he returns.

Niven addresses the group again. "Alright, I'd say that was successful. Tomorrow we'll absorb magick from the rest of the coven, whoever is willing to help. We need a strong burst of it to flow into Ada. The power of her entire coven if possible."

The witch who volunteered them earlier takes out her phone. "What time do you want them here?" she asks.

"We'll take them in shifts starting at eight in the morning. We'll take every step of this very slowly. We don't want anyone to get hurt," he announces.

The witch nods and turns around to make a phone call.

"Well, it looks like we'll have a lot of guests tomorrow," Ada jokes as she walks up beside me.

"Everyone wants to see you healthy and recovered." I wrap my arm around her shoulder and pull her close.

"I know. I'm grateful for the lengths everyone has gone for me. And especially you. Thank you," she says, her voice muffled by the pelt on my chest, where she rests her head.

Ada, Walt, Acton, and I move into the kitchen to talk. The witches and Elgar are still fussing over the relics, figuring out the least dangerous way to use the crown. We leave them to it as Walt and Ada need to discuss Acton's decision.

Walt takes Acton's hands in his and gazes at him. Acton leans forward and rests his forehead on his mate's. "My bluebell, this is decided. My selfishness dictates it. I want both of you in my life as long as possible."

"Acton, petal, what if it hurts you? I couldn't stand it if anything happened," Walt argues.

"There is great reward in this risk. The yetis and witches are very capable. They will not let it get to that point," he maintains.

"It seems like the magick boost will enough," Ada insists.

"It may not. Even the fae believed both would be needed to cure you of its evil spell. It was compelled to tell Niven the truth." Acton is undeterred.

"Nothing to do with the fae and their magick is straightforward in this realm. But Niven is confident in what the fae revealed," I add.

"What even is *life force*? Is it the body's natural aging process? This is all too theoretical for me. I don't want to change who I am or who Ada is," Walt worries. "Is it something unique and fundamental to each of us like a soul?"

Acton carefully considers his response, tilting his head in thought. "My small amount of magick is tied to Mother Earth and the nature she commands, the life that grows from the ground and everything it nourishes and creates. What I've come to understand is that the origin of life and magick within all of us and everything that is known as life force is not unique, like the human concept of a soul would be. It's another building block of nature. Ours is the same, I just have more to sustain me over a much longer lifetime. Even the fae shares it, so it seems."

I will relate this explanation to Niven since life force seems an archaic topic even among witches. It is a small comfort knowing witches must have long ago shunned this topic and any attempts to manipulate it within themselves and others.

"I don't like it, but I know I won't change your mind," Walt says ruefully, pulling Acton into an embrace.

"Don't worry overmuch for Acton," I soothe Ada. "I will make sure nothing happens to him. I would break the relic before I let it harm him."

Her eyes look sad when they meet mine. I crowd her against the kitchen counter where she was leaning, wrapping my arms around her possessively.

She nods her head into my shoulder. "It still makes me nervous, but I trust you."

It is all I can ask for.

Walt and Acton go home soon after to spend time together. They need privacy to speak more openly about the potential outcomes, which are certainly very scary for Walt. Ada is exhausted, and I help settle her into bed. The witches stay well into the night, as they plan for every possible risk tomorrow.

Elgar pulls me aside once they leave. "I am impressed by everything I have witnessed today. This community has rallied to help your mate... Her uncle is sacrificing some of his own life for her... I am glad we were able to trek into the mountains to find these. It was a small effort for such an important outcome. It is an honor to have played such a part," he says on a tired sigh.

"She downplays her deep connection with her coven and those who love her. But there are so many who would go to great lengths for her, as we saw today," I expound, thinking of the last couple months.

"There is a line in a book that stuck with me. *Deep roots are not reached by the frost*. This hardship reveals the strength of their love for her," he muses. "It brought you back to her, after all this time. It also brought you back to yourself. I have missed that male." My brother does not hold his tongue.

"It did bring me back," I concede. "Something would have eventually. I'm not sure how much longer I could have gone on without her.

But this was my chance to prove to her what she has always meant to me."

"I see why you like it here in Monstera Bluff. I always wondered what your life was like here. But once you came back to the clan, I knew you did not want to talk about it." He looks away with a mix of emotions on his face. "I need to take a walk to settle my nerves. Thinking about what we face tomorrow makes me uneasy. I do not know whether sleep will find me tonight," he acknowledges.

"I do not think it will find me either," I confess.

CHAPTER 19

NORRELL

The purple smudges under Ada's dulled eyes would worry me more if this were a different day. They will brighten once we have cured her of this fae spell. Esmeralda is going to keep her company and help her around the house until the relics are ready. The arrangement takes away some worry since I will be busy the entire day leading up to this.

Her coven members arrive in shifts to not overcrowd the house. Several healers from the clinic, including Thea, are on standby, making sure that the witches are healthy after donating their magick to the Forged Ruby. Elgar and I work side by side the entire time, helping to control the amount of magick drawn from each witch. Nearly all of them have the same reaction as Esmeralda. It makes them a little woozy and unsteady on their feet. But they recover quickly after having some tea or juice and a bite to eat.

Each draw of magick is quick, taking no more than a minute. Within a few hours, we work through the entire stream of volunteers. Like the healers, Elgar and I have not expended much of our own abilities yet to ensure we are ready to fully harness them later. The gem, the Forged Ruby, is now pulsing heavily on its own, the amount of the witches' magickal energy inside it staggering. It is much greater than what I would draw from dozens of fae, so I am confident this will be enough to overpower and expel the fae spell.

Walt appears calmer today when he and Acton arrive in the afternoon. Acton must have soothed his frayed nerves. He does not make choices lightly, so I trust that he will accept the result, no matter how it turns out.

When we meet again in the salon, the healers set up three portable gurneys. Walt eyes them warily, letting on his remaining undercurrent of anxiety. The healers lead Ada, Walt, and Acton to them. They choose to sit for the moment. I stand next to Ada, holding her clammy, weak hand. A light sheen of nervous sweat covers her brow. She worries for herself, but mayhap more so for Acton. I rub my warm, steady hand along her back.

While I tend to Ada, the witches talk through their plan one last time to coordinate their use of the relics. I will manage the Banner of Life on Acton and then transfer the life force into Ada first and Walt second. Simultaneously, Elgar will help the other witch unleash the full force of magickal energy into Ada. In doing so, the witches believe we can prevent the waste of any of Acton's life force.

Even I begin experiencing a case of nerves as we make our final preparations. I need to tamp them down and be fully focused on the task at hand. Niven signals to me that they are ready. I press a lingering kiss to Ada's lips and then join the witches. Walt and Acton briefly kiss as well and then lie back on their gurneys.

Acton nods at me, telling me he is ready. The witch whispers his spell, commanding the Banner of Life to pull life force from Acton. The magick trickles out at first, but I do not let down my guard. The onslaught will be sudden, fierce, and deadly if left unchecked. As I suspected, its full power bursts forth, commanding a deep pull of Acton's life force. I immediately absorb as much excess magick as I can, decreasing the potency of the relic to stymie the flow of Acton's life force to a small stream. Acton loses consciousness but otherwise looks healthy and unchanged. The witch immediately speaks the counterspell, severing its connection to Acton. As planned, the healers wheel Acton away and minister their healing magick to him.

The magick in the crown feels unstable now that it brims with life force, like it could trigger at any moment. All of us get into position around Ada. The power blazing within the Banner of Life instantly explodes, flooding straight into her. I drain down the pulse of fae magick after it hits her with a heavy dose, enough to fill her cheeks with a healthy glow on her skin that has been missing since I returned.

Elgar tempers the current of magick into Ada, slow and steady, but it seems to be working. Ada's body goes stiff as a board, every muscle pulling taut and her eyes widen in shock… until they roll into the back of her head. Her whole body slackens as she loses consciousness except for the occasional violent full body twitch that sets off alarm bells in my mind. I jerk toward her, needing to reach my mate to make sure she is still breathing, still with me.

"Stay back!" Elgar snarls, tearing me out of my haze to reach her. He is right, this must be so painful for her, an ocean of magick crashing into her, that she passed out. I cannot stand in its way even if my instincts scream otherwise. I force my attention back to the crown and the witch holding it.

"Ready?" he asks, turning his attention to Walt.

"Do it," I respond immediately.

The crown is still replete with life force. The amount we poured into Ada made up for what she lost and more. I have no concern there. But this leftover glut in the relic could be lifechanging for Walt. I hope so, anyway. With another set of softly spoken words, the witch and I work together to thrust the remaining life force safely into Walt. His eyes are closed, and I cannot tell if he is conscious. The transformation is fast, shedding decades of age in a matter of minutes. The deep lines on his face earned over the years become visibly shallower and many disappear completely. His chest and shoulders fill out and broaden. His silver hair turns a dark blonde and fills in thicker.

Once the relic is emptied of life force, the witch and I share a look of near disbelief. "This is power beyond anything I imagined. The crown scares me if I'm being honest. I've never used a relic this powerful," he says breathlessly, looking pale.

"If this is what it can do after we weakened it yesterday, my ancestors made the right choice hiding it away in a remote mountain," I concur.

Walt looks incredibly healthy now that the transfer is complete, though he lays unmoving on his gurney. Thea breaks away from the group surrounding Acton and pulls Walt's gurney to the side to check his vitals. I turn my attention back to Ada. Her ribcage is heaving with deep, forceful breaths. It is a favor from Mother Earth that she is not awake to feel this magick violently coursing through her body.

There was much of it from her coven contained within the relic that Elgar and the other witch are still pouring it into her nearly ten minutes later. Her overall complexion is much improved. Her cheeks and lips are a healthy radiant pink and the lines that exhaustion carved around her eyes have disappeared. Within another minute or two, the gem's blazing light finally dims as it empties.

I rush to Ada's side, wiping the sweaty hair from her brow and gently clasping her hand. Her eyes flutter and slowly open. "How do you feel, my ember?"

"Better than I look, I'm sure," her voice scrapes. She tightens her grip on my hand.

"You look well," I assure her.

She smiles calmly, still gazing up at me. "How are Walt and Acton?"

"Better than we thought possible. You will be surprised when you see Walt," I tell her, a smile in my voice.

"A good surprise?" she asks.

"A very good surprise," I confirm.

Thea comes over to check on Ada. They share a tender smile as Thea runs her hands above Ada's body. "You're looking so healthy, Ada. That's a very good sign. Let's make sure that fae spell is fully gone," Thea remarks as she hovers her hands over Ada's abdomen and chest. Another healer joins her. They intend to be completely thorough in making sure the spell has been broken. I no longer sense any fae magick within her. The beauty of her own magickal signature shines again. I hold my tongue even though I believe this has been a success. I want the healers to declare her cured first.

The rest of the healers assess her and then confer with Niven. The other witches wheel the gurneys next to each other again. All three of them are now awake and smiling. Ada's eyes light up and her jaw drops when she finally sees Walt's transformation.

"You're a kid again," she gushes as she holds his face in her hands.

They both giggle wildly and embrace, rocking back and forth in happiness. When they finally break apart, he laughs self-consciously. "Not a kid exactly, but I feel really good."

The three of them hop off their gurneys and Ada leads them to the fireplace where a mirror hangs over it. Walt leans in close, examining his face, poking and rubbing at it. "Well I'll be. I look like I'm about twenty-five again. Not much older than when I met Acton," he declares.

"You are my handsome mate at any age. I look forward to watching you grow old again," Acton murmurs as he stands behind Walt and wraps his arms around his shoulders.

"You still haven't aged a day," Walt notes, leaning back into his mate. His light expression quickly grows concerned. "How do you feel? Did it hurt? That had to be hard on you."

"I fell asleep right away. But when I awoke, I felt as I did this morning. It was the right thing to do, Walt. My heart is content," Acton assures him.

"Thank you for the gift of many more decades together, my petal. I look forward to each one," Walt purrs, turning in his arms and nuzzling into Acton's neck.

I take Ada by the hand and walk her over to Niven. She looks so much stronger and healthier than she has since I arrived. I am unsure if she is physically younger than she was, but her health has been fully restored and mayhap even enhanced.

A grin splits Niven's face. "Moon and stars, you look fantastic." His voice is full of staggering relief. They embrace, and two months of pent-up fear and stress appear to melt from Niven in that very moment. When he pulls away, he holds her by the forearms and studies her, seeming to search for any sign that the relics did not work. Tears fill his eyes as he looks up at her face again and he subtly sniffles. "The healers have good news."

Thea comes by and gives both of their shoulders a quick friendly squeeze. Her expression beams. "There are no more signs of the fae spell. It seems to have been broken like Niven's team had hoped. We will wait until tomorrow to officially give you a clean bill of health. But we're very optimistic," she explains. "Why don't you try to cast a spell. Let's see how your magick is doing."

Ada shuts her eyes, squaring her shoulders. After a few moments, a dreamy expression settles over her features. "May the magick of our ancestors protect this home and keep away those who would harm it." She pauses, opening her eyes again. "I feel the ward. My parents' magick. I can strengthen it again." There's a smile in her voice. A sense of peace in her I have not witnessed in many, many years.

She abruptly spins toward me, and a peal of laughter erupts from her. "It's back!" she cries out. "I can't believe it!" She springs into my arms, wrapping her legs around my waist. She laughs, unrestrained and gleeful. It is contagious. I swing her around, laughing with her between our sweet kisses, releasing months, if not years, of pain and heartache. Finally, I settle her against me. She still giggles into my chest, the warm air caressing my skin through my pelt.

"I'm so relieved," Thea exclaims, watching us. "Even if you don't feel like you need to, take it easy tonight. You've been through a lot today."

Ada turns her head to look at Thea, still resting it on my chest. "I will, but I feel amazing," Ada delights. "Thank you for everything."

"I barely did anything. It was all them." She motions between me and the witches, who are chatting with Elgar.

Elgar looks over at us, exhausted and spent. I feel the same, though attempt to hold it together. Ada unwraps her legs from me and slides down my body to stand on her own. She pulls me toward the group. Their mood is joyous and their voices sound light and easygoing, a welcome change from the tense atmosphere earlier. They turn their attention to Ada as she approaches.

"From the bottom of my heart, thank you all for your help today and through the weeks you've been preparing for this. I can never fully express how grateful I am." Ada's voice hitches raggedly. "You all saved my life. I'll never forget it." She fights her tears, but they flow freely in relief.

"Every minute was worth it, Ada. We're all so happy it worked," Niven assures her, speaking for the team.

After many more comforting hugs and earnest words of praise and congratulations, the witches clean up the salon. The healers shrink the gurneys and put them in a case they set against a wall, out of the way. The healers then talk to both Walt and Acton, who both still look dazed by Walt's physical transformation. The sparkling smiles on their faces as they listen to the healers' words confirm they are both in good health.

Walt and Acton approach me and Ada after their conversation with the healers ends. "We're heading home. I can hardly believe that this is real. I'm a simple man and this has surely blown my mind," he quips self-deprecatingly. "I need some time to let it sink in."

"I can hardly believe it myself," she empathizes.

"My girl, we are so unbelievably happy you're free of that awful fae. It was hard to watch you grow weak. I can only imagine how it felt," he whispers as he pulls her into his arms.

"I don't know if I'm your girl anymore. I think I'm your elder," Ada jokes, laughing tearfully into his shoulder.

"You will always be my girl. I'm still an old man at heart even if I don't look it. Now I know how Acton feels," he says with a bark of laughter. He winks playfully at his mate over the top of Ada's head.

"Your body reflects your heart and soul once more, endlessly young and full of adventure," Acton responds.

After they leave, the witches follow soon after. They announce their decision to head straight to the pub to celebrate. The second wind blows them in that direction after a long, stressful day. Elgar collapses onto a sofa in the living room, depleted after managing the relics for so long.

"You two rest, I'm going to make dinner," she declares as she practically skips through the doorway, a lively spring in her step.

"I will not make it through dinner. I am still recovering from the hike to the mountain and back, and I barely slept last night," Elgar groans, his head lolling backward on the sofa.

"Eat a snack and then head upstairs to bed," I offer.

"Thanks, Norrell. That sounds good," he responds, struggling to keep his eyes open.

Jogging into the kitchen, I find Ada humming and dancing around as she sets out ingredients. "Slight change of plans," I say as I come up behind her and press a kiss to her neck, "Elgar is off to bed. The cats are still upstairs. It is just the two of us."

She leans back into me, then playfully spins away as she puts a pan on the stove and then dances toward the pantry.

I grab a banana from the counter to give to Elgar. When I walk in, his eyes barely blink open. "Oh, thanks," he remarks groggily as he takes the banana. Making quick work of the peeling, he shoves it into his mouth and places the peel into my outstretched open palm. He pushes himself off the sofa and shuffles toward the stairs.

Returning to the kitchen to throw away the peel and help Ada, I cannot help but shake my head and laugh at my brother. "That male tired himself out today. He will be dead asleep the moment his head hits the pillow."

A frisky gleam lights her eyes. "Oh really? You don't think he'll be downstairs at all?"

Following her line of thinking, and liking it, I respond, "Not a chance."

She stops in her tracks and turns around. "Interesting. Well, I have some ideas about what I'd rather do than make dinner," she says in a husky voice, biting her bottom lip seductively as she looks me over. "You were gone for so long, we have a lot to make up for."

My dick stirs just beholding her. She looks so healthy and vibrant, the way I always remember her. Hopefully, now that her appetite is back, her curves will fill out again, giving me more to squeeze. I love palming her ass and thighs when she is on top of me.

"I missed you too, my ember. I want to show you just how much," I growl.

She hooks a finger over the top of my pants and tugs me forward so that I press her into the edge of the countertop. I am already hard, so I grind against her, letting her know I am ready for anything she has in mind.

"How do you want it? Slow and soft or quick and hard?" I murmur, trailing my fingertips up her arms, across her shoulders. Up her neck to cradle her head in my hands, brushing my thumb across her lips. She catches it in her teeth to give it a little bite.

"I want it hard. I need you right here, right now," she whines.

"Anything, my mate. It is yours," I promise easily.

I lean down, pressing my lips to hers in a searing kiss. Hungry for her, my tongue opens her mouth to find hers. When they meet, I groan into her, longing to devour her. I want her to let me in everywhere.

"Take me here, Norrell, please. On the counter. I can't wait any longer," she begs breathlessly as we come up for air. She clutches at my pants, trying to pull them down.

I lean my torso away from her long enough to unbutton and slide them down my legs, stepping out of them as they fall to the floor. She shimmies a little and her panties land on top of them.

"I like it when my good girl is eager for my cock," I tell her with a dark chuckle. "You make it even more swollen and ready for you."

"I need to feel you splitting me apart, Norrell," she says desperately, clawing at my shoulders and chest.

"Does your pussy need to be pounded with my fat cock?" I tease her.

"Yes, always," she moans. With that, I lift her up by her backside and position her at the edge of the counter. I circle my cock around her spread open heat, making sure to pay extra attention to her clit. She squirms and gasps as I ready her.

She pulls her dress over her head and unclasps her bra. When she's fully bare to me, I lean in and suck one of her nipples and circle the other one with my thumb. I love her breasts. The small round globes are always so sensitive, especially when I use my mouth. She cards her fingers through my hair as I pull away from her nipple with a loud pop and move to the other one.

"I'm dripping for you, my mate. Please fuck me," she commands.

I growl as I give one last lick to her nipple and pull myself fully upright again. I line up my cock with her slit and rock into her, filling her all at once. She cries out, grabbing onto the back of my head for support. My hands curve around her bottom, kneading her softness, to anchor her as I fuck into her in fast, deep strokes. She moans my name loud enough to wake the dead, mayhap even our dead asleep guest upstairs. She only quiets down when my mouth finds hers again.

Thrusting my tongue in time with my cock, she whines and keens through our kisses. She rubs herself against me frantically, the sign she is close to coming. Moving one hand between us, I circle my thumb around her clit until her channel clenches my cock, making the already tight squeeze a challenge to push through. In just a few more strokes she falls apart around me with a scream muffled by my mouth, as I use both my tongue and my cock to invade her.

The rhythmic pulsing of her channel pushes me into my own orgasm. The warm, incredible release of it starts in my cock, spreading low in my abdomen until it rushes through the rest of my body. Returning my hand to her hip, I gather her close so I can empty myself as deep inside her channel as possible.

Even after my orgasm is over, I continue to slowly grind into her hot, soft depth, luxuriating in the feeling of being inside her. "Was that good for you, my ember?" I ask.

"So good. Exactly what I needed," she says with a dreamy sigh.

Ada's violet eyes sparkle in the morning sun. She turns fully toward me from her side of the bed, her head still on her pillow with her gorgeous long dark red hair spilling out behind her. I tuck a piece of her white streak from her forehead behind her ear. She grabs my hand and holds it with both of hers between us.

"I haven't felt this good in a long time," she murmurs in a voice full of wonder.

"You look good, too," I joke lightly, waggling my eyebrows.

"Even right now with bed head and bad breath?" she questions with a delicate snort.

"I always think so. You are the most beautiful sight in the world," I tell her truthfully, staring into her captivating eyes.

She giggles as she whispers, "Static charge my messy hair and stick straight up in the air."

Immediately her hair puffs out, like a wild red cloud. She scrunches her face and sticks out her tongue, as if this goofy look would change my opinion at all. I chuckle as I attempt to smooth it down, but the strands repel away from my hovering hand, a wave rippling and parting her outrageous hair with each movement. She cackles as I draw patterns in the air to see how fast I can make her unruly strands move.

"Static, static, go away, come again another day." Her smile is contagious as she voices her counter-spell, and her hair gently falls to her pillow and over her face. As she combs her hair out of her face, her giggling gives way to sniffling. The happy smile on her face falls. "I can't believe my magick is restored." Her voice wobbles. "I felt so different without it. Like I was living a half-life." Her breath stutters and tears gather at the corners of her eyes.

"You do seem more like yourself again," I say reverently. Intertwining our hands again, I bring them to my mouth to kiss hers.

"When I lost my magick, I lost everything. It was the only thing I had left." Her brittle voice struggles between her sobs.

"You have so much. You always have. Now your magick is back for good. And so am I if you will have me," I whisper.

"What if this is a fluke? And I wake up tomorrow without it? What if I wake up one day without you?" Her uncertainty breaks my heart.

"That will never happen again. Both your magick and I are here to stay. Not even a fae can change that," I answer.

"But what's here for you? Why is this time any different?" she quavers, watching me through her wet lashes, tears still streaking onto her pillow.

"I am different. But I do not want to just tell you in words. I will work every day to show that to you," I pledge.

"But I don't need anyone to take care of me anymore. My life will return to normal," she rasps.

"Just because you can survive without it, does not mean I should not support you, pitch in whenever I am able, make you feel valued and loved. I liked helping around the house, Ada. I loved cooking for you. I will continue doing that even now that you have recovered."

Her breathing starts to even out. She scrubs the tears from her face and then stares into my eyes again. With a wet huff of laughter, she says, "Some of it will be a breeze again with my magick, but I won't turn down anything you want to do. Thank you." She kisses my hands the same way I kissed hers.

We lay there for a few minutes while her tears subside. "I should check on all the enchantments in the house today. And the fountain. Moon and stars, I miss the ritual of it. I can't wait to get back into the swing of my normal life again." Her wistful tone convinces me her mood is lifting again.

"It is more than that, Ada, I want to be there for you, always. For everything. To love each other and live our lives together as mates. Build the life we dreamed about. The one I thought I ruined fifteen years ago." It only skims the surface of all I have planned. Of all the ways I will show her I love her.

"I want that with you too. My life was missing something vital without you. I'm looking forward to the future in the way I haven't been able to in a long time." Her voice is soft, but sure. I cup her jaw in my hands and bring my lips to hers. Our kisses are slow and unhurried, like we have a lifetime for it.

My phone vibrates, interrupting us. "You should see who that is. It might be important," she murmurs between kisses.

When I reach for it on the nightstand, a text from Niven pops on the screen. "Niven asks if you could stop by the clinic today for a final checkup. Then I need to meet him at the Constabulary station one last time," I say as I scan the message.

"This is finally it?" she asks, sounding hopeful. She still does not want to hear about the fae, so I omit the details.

"This is it. All of this will be over and behind us. Completely. And then we will celebrate."

When we arrive at the clinic a little while later, Thea and one of the other healers in attendance yesterday scan her with their healing magick. Both agree the fae spell is still truly gone and she is in perfect health. They cannot stop smiling the entire time.

On the way to drop her off at home, we stop by Pearlhouse Pastries. She stares at the pastry case like there is some hidden mystery inside. It seems this habit will never change, and I do not mind a bit.

"Go ahead and order your usual," I observe.

"Am I really that easy to predict?" she scoffs playfully.

"No, I just know you so well, my mate," I say, loving the sound of that word, as I snake an arm around her waist. I nuzzle behind her ear as she giggles and twitches against me until I stop.

"I think I *will* have my usual. And not because you suggested it," she says primly.

"Of course not," I respond, sounding as if I would never think such a thing.

The young employee comes over to take our order. "One raspberry chamomile frangipane croissant and a latte, please. He'll have a maple bun and a black coffee."

The constabulary station seems more crowded than usual. There's a buzz in the air, relief as well as a sense of justice that the fae will never be allowed to harm anyone else in this realm. Niven's team is already there, waiting for us.

"Elgar, glad you're joining us. I feel better with both of you here so we can get this done quickly and cleanly. But I have a few more questions for it before we send it on. I'm holding nothing back," Niven states.

As usual, the witches lower the wards surrounding the containment unit and slowly open it to bring out the inky cloud that makes up the fae. Niven's eyes lock into the fae's unsettling yellow orbs for the last time.

"Why are the fae showing up in this realm?" he inquires forcefully, seemingly drawing an immense amount of power into the question, one that Darla the Seer had wanted answered.

"Your realm has so much wild magick that ours does not. In mine, the most powerful among us harness it for their own use, not sharing. Though if we prove ourselves worthy servants, some of us are rewarded and sent here to hoard yours since you Whispered Folk are too weak and stupid to use it all yourselves," it answers, the voice dipping lower in pitch as it goes.

Niven's lips thin in response. His entire body goes rigid, as if any movement would detract from his single-minded focus. "How do you travel into this realm?"

"We have our own ancient relics that allow us travel to this realm and others. You could not begin to fathom how we rule the realms. We are deities while you are insects under our feet," it describes, its bassy tone full of disdain.

Elgar must not be able to help himself as he mutters, "You do not even *have* feet." I crack a smile, but I maintain my focus on funneling the fae's magick away from it.

"Tell me about the Whispered Folk you have killed." Niven pushes on.

"There are so many puny, defenseless Whispered Folk to torment. They should learn to be afraid of the shadows," it says smugly. "Sometimes I sought them out. Sometimes I just stumbled upon them. A wolven out for a run. A troll alone in a cave. A vampire out on her own hunt. A shifter living in a towering city. A kraken resting too close to the Arctic shore. A satyr on a moonlit frolic in the woods. A witch who wandered too far from the fire on Beltane. There were others, so many others. Too many to remember over the centuries I spent here."

Without looking away from the fae, Niven remarks to the room, "Take note of this. We'll investigate them later." He pries more information out of the fae about the victims, where he found them and when.

"The shifter could be that PI in Chicago," observes one of his assistants.

"Agreed," Niven replies. He then turns his full attention back to the fae. "Are you sure you didn't kill Whitt and Estelle Mayweather?"

"I did not kill them, but it was well known among the fae. We keep track of your world to strike at its heart anytime we can," it warns, the voice rising in pitch again, sounding young and feminine.

"I'm tired of this vile thing," Niven spits. "Norrell, do the honors."

"Gladly." I drain its immense magick, the very essence of this creature, slow and drawn out, prolonging its decline as it absorbs into the clear quartz pieces in the bracelet Ada gifted me. Elgar stands by in case it attempts to lash out at us with a sudden burst of power. But I have kept it weak and nearly defenseless the entire time on purpose. It screeches and whines in a cacophony of disturbing voices until it finally fades from existence. It has no body, so there is nothing left, as if it never existed. Its demise is a sight Elgar and I have seen many times, but the witches seem to be shocked by it.

"Fire and ashes, you'd think a thing like that would go down in a blaze of glory. Not a tiny wink out of existence." Niven laughs, sounding relieved.

"Only the blue hag of winter knows how much of a fight they put up in the Arctic. Those fae are preoccupied with seeking power," Elgar says sardonically.

"I'm not surprised. This one was wily. It presented a real challenge to my magick," Niven responds shaking his head.

The three of us walk out of the room as his assistants finish up in there. Feeling the need to get some fresh air, we step outside and stand in the sunlight as if it can burn the shadow of the fae from us for good.

"Working with you was good, Norrell. You too, Elgar, even though we only spent this short time together. Your skills are useful, but I don't need to tell you that. If you're not opposed to it, I'd like to hire you to join me on short assignments every so often. Nothing that would keep you away from your mate for long. We deal with Malefic Folk from time to time, nothing near like what keeps your clan busy in the Arctic. Your abilities would make our investigative work so much easier. No need to answer me now. Just think about it and get back to me," Niven offers, respect threaded through his voice.

"I might take you up on that," I reply. It is something to consider to keep my skills sharp.

"I already updated the town officials, but I figured you'd want to know too. The warlocks are being sent to the High Court. It's likely they'll all get life in prison. As we saw, they had some parting gifts from the fae, some of which they used on us that day. That orb would have taken them out too if you hadn't weakened it. They decided to attack that day when they discovered the power of the fae enchantments were waning. The fae knew what it was doing and wasn't going to leave them with endless power. So they wanted to hit us with as much as possible. Ashes, they are pathetic. Entitled, codependent, missing too many brain cells. Interrogating them was almost as sad as it was infuriating," Niven recounts.

"What truths did you force from them?" I wonder.

"Surprisingly, Ralston Samuels won his seat on the town council legitimately. His family lineage goes back a long way in this town. Maybe his ancestors were more likeable. He sat on the town council for quite a few years. His cronies Weatherby and Atticus cheated their way into their seats. They bought illegal cloaked magick from a fellow warlock—something they weren't even skilled enough to do themselves

—and used it on the ballots they cast to tamper with the vote count. We picked up that male too on his own charges. He had quite a bit to spill. It's a mess, frankly. But my part is done. They're the court's problem now," he explains with a satisfied smirk.

"How did Clancy respond?" I ask, truly curious.

"He told me he knew those election results were *horse shit*." Niven cracks up.

CHAPTER 20
ADA

Waking up rested, alert, ready for the day, it makes me realize just how much the fae's spell affected me. The last two and a half months feel like a fog that has finally lifted. Waking up to my mate lying in bed next to me makes it even better. Norrell has always been the love of my life. I trust he'll never intentionally hurt me again. His desire to build a life together as mates is sincere. I see it in his eyes and in his actions. I know he's a changed male.

When I go downstairs while Norrell is showering, it's quiet except for the boys, who were not happy about missing out on all the action yesterday. They meow grumpily for their breakfast, still annoyed that I shut them in a spare bedroom until the evening after everyone had left. They had everything they needed, but that doesn't matter. I know it'll take another day or two for them to forgive me.

After filling their bowls, I reach for the tea kettle out of habit. Stopping myself, hand in mid-air, I realize I don't need it anymore. My lips curl into a smile. I can make tea the normal way again. I take out my favorite mug and fill it with water. Then the words flow from my lips as naturally as if my magick never left me. "Water turn so piping hot as though heated in a pot." Simple and to the point. I drop in the tea bag and let it steep.

It's a silly, domestic thing, but feeling the magick around my house is comforting, like being wrapped in a warm blanket. I walk into the workshop, loud with the magick I've poured into enchantments, but there are still remnants of my mom's magick in the tools and worktable. I run my hands over them. A few happy tears spill down my cheeks. I'll never take this feeling for granted.

When my tea is steeped, I take it with me and sit in the back garden. I murmur my spell to strengthen the ward, the same one my family used for generations. "May the magick of our ancestors protect this home and keep away those who would harm it." The words have even more meaning than I ever realized. They did protect me and my home.

Taking my tea with me, I get up and wander the garden, admiring Norrell's handiwork. It's hard to picture going through this ordeal without him. I grew so weak by the end. As he told me earlier in bed, he's going to continue taking on his share of the work keeping up this big old house alongside me. If he finds meaning in it, he should continue with whatever work he pleases. This is his home too now. Though I can't help but use some magick to sweep away a layer of leaves and debris that have fallen recently.

"Collect the leaves and twigs that fall and bind them tight into a ball." As if a wild breeze blows through the yard, the layer sweeps into a neat little pile and magickally adheres together. I kick it toward the edge of the back garden into the trees on my property line. It'll eventually fall apart when the spell fades.

I walk around the side of my house to the front lawn. The tall, ornate old cast iron fountain gurgles peacefully. I should spend more time on my front porch again listening to its calming ambient sound. The enchantment on the fountain still feels strong, but I give it a boost anyway. It started out as a chore when I was a child, but it feels more like a tribute to my home and ancestors. "With cold clean water clear and flowing, free of leaves and dirt and never slowing." The water splashes and dances a little more vigorously down its tiers.

I slowly wander back inside. Norrell is downstairs and dressed, giving the boys much needed attention. "Ready to head to the clinic?" he asks.

He's smiling like a fool. I believe I am too. He chuckles, picking me up and twirling me around the foyer. When he finally sets me down, he kisses me thoroughly, so passionate and full of promise. I'm ready to live life to the fullest again, and I'm so glad it will be with Norrell at my side.

We knew the fae spell was gone, but it's a load off my mind to hear it officially from the healers clinic. All of this was a difficult price to pay to bring Norrell back into my life. But in the end, I came out on the other side with so much more than I started with. Mother Earth smiled upon me.

When Norrell drops me off after we visit the clinic, he and his brother are finally on their way to join Niven to make sure the fae never harms anyone else ever again. I'm glad. It was evil incarnate. Both Cara and I will breathe easier knowing it's gone for good.

My dad's journal, my Yule gift, has been sitting on my nightstand for weeks. I pick it up at night and flip through it. But I haven't had the energy to make any headway.

It's a crisp January day, perfect for a thick cozy sweater and sitting outside with a hot drink to finally read the journal. Sensing lingering hints of my dad's magick around the house as I take it downstairs puts me in the right frame of mind to absorb everything he has written. I want to get to know my dad again, and this journal will surely help.

Sitting on my front porch, a hot mug of tea next to me, I carefully open its leatherbound cover. My dad's neat script fills the pages. Its long skinny loops and steep angle are a solace amidst my parents' loss all those years ago. It still cuts deeply, but I am ready to move forward without the tunnel vision of grief. The journal recounts the month he spent living in a village of púca, a particularly mischievous and powerful type of shifter, hidden away along coastal Ireland. They liked to tease him, taking their favored animal forms when speaking with him. He wrote that it made learning the phonetics of the language a little more difficult than usual, but he had a lot of fun doing it.

The journal is a treasure. A brief glimpse into his life before he met my mom. They both loved to travel together, but for him it was a life-long passion. Mayhap I would have shared in it more had my life been different. With Norrell at my side, I could be a little more adventurous again.

When Norrell and Elgar return from the constabulary, they still look careworn, but noticeably lighter. Especially Norrell. This has been a long journey for him as well. Since Elgar is staying with us until tomorrow, we walk around town with him, showing him our favorite spots. It's a nice opportunity to get to know him since I'm not sure when we'll see him again. Hopefully it won't be too long.

The beach is our last stop we take him before dinner. I'm not sure that he's ever seen one like this before. "This sand is so much more pleasant underfoot than the gravel and mud in our territory," Elgar marvels. "You should be out here every day, brother."

"Who says I am not? I take nothing for granted here," Norrell teases, winking playfully at me. "It is also a refreshing change of pace to have a peaceful walk without any Malefic to bother you."

Elgar grunts his enthusiastic agreement. "The townsfolk have made this a cheerful and welcoming place, Ada. I see why it was always so dear in Norrell's heart," he tells me in unfeigned interest.

"It is. The town has grown a lot, but the heart of it remains the same. The vision my ancestors had for the town endures. My family has always been involved in its leadership in one way or another. I'm glad that their hope became a reality," I share.

Elgar nods, considering my words. "I never thought it would be possible for so many Whispered Folk to live together in such harmony. It gives me much to think about as I take over leadership of the clan. They need a solid push toward a broader definition of acceptance. The shake-up we just had will finally be the impetus Norrell and I sought for so long. It would do our clan good to host visitors more often, like those witches from New York City. Our clan needs more exposure to the world at large."

"You will accomplish what I never could," Norrell assures him. "You are the leader to bring them into the future. My heart was too frostbitten to lead them there."

"It is due to both of our efforts they will finally see that the world offers so much color and character, and that magick wielders are a large part of that," Elgar reasons.

From what I've since learned about the clan and their bigotry toward magick wielders, I agree there's nowhere to go but up.

♡ ♡ ♡ ♡ ♡

Glasses clink in celebration as our friends and acquaintances—everyone involved in breaking the fae spell—exclaim new and progressively more ridiculous toasts.

"To yetis! The fae's natural predators!" Clink.

"To Niven! The mind melter!" Clink.

"To Esmeralda! Fae relic tester daredevil!" Clink.

Esmeralda cracks up as the table cheers for her. She waves her hands downward, to calm them as they grow rowdier. "As mayhap one of the first to have witnessed their relationship, I want to propose a toast to Norrell and Ada, who have found their way back to each other," she announces as she lifts her glass. "May the moon and stars above bless Norrell and Ada in hearth, home, and love." It's a slight variation of a common but much beloved toast.

As everyone at the large table at The Roaring Wood lifts their glass for the toast, they hoot and holler for us. Norrell watches me with a contented smile on his face as they make a racket around us. Those hard lines between his brows finally look smoother and less stark, like a crushing weight on his shoulders has lifted.

Luckily, Esmeralda sits in the chair next to me, so I turn to her as the rest of the group carry on. "Having you here means so much to me. You have always been so supportive and caring. Staying in touch with Norrell, researching cures, sending the journal, and now being here, it's more than I could have ever asked for. Thank you," I acknowledge our deep appreciation of her.

"All of it was my pleasure. Mother Earth, I'm so glad to see everything turn out as it should." Her beaming smile could light up the room.

"Niven, this would not have been possible without you. Thank you for all you have done for Ada," Norrell tells him with a hearty clap to the back, their admiration for each other clear.

"I think I made out the best here. A valuable consultant. New and revived friendships. Another big case investigated and closed, earning me some much-needed time off. All compelling reasons to come back and visit. This place has been good to me," he says with a huff of laughter.

"A home away from home," Walt chimes in with his newly youthful voice. "You couldn't pick a better place."

"The collective heart of our community embraces all those who visit," Acton agrees.

"Hear, hear! To Monstera Bluff! Niven's home away from home!" Clancy exclaims, initiating another toast, setting off another round of clinking glasses.

"This town is a credit to Whispered Folk," Elgar adds as we take a drink.

"We hope to have you back again soon, Elgar. You're family now," Walt replies.

"I will return soon and bring our parents. They were not happy he was forced to leave here to take over leadership all those years ago. But the situation in the clan was fraught for so long. It was rotting from the inside out. Our parents always wanted to meet Ada and visit this place," Elgar divulges. "They are grateful to finally have that chance."

"Hopefully it'll be the first time of many," Walt encourages.

Esmeralda turns to me again. "What are you going to do now that you're feeling better?"

I deliberate for a moment. "Well, I still need to show Walt the ropes of town council. Our first meeting of the year is next week. He's the young up-and-comer on the council now," I joke, reaching out and squeezing his hand. He belly laughs, still sounding the same as ever. "As for the shop, I've leaned on my team a lot the past few months. It's shown me that Sunny is a natural leader in addition to being responsible and smart. Same with the rest of the staff. I'm considering stepping back to focus on my specialty again. I've been reminded of so many memories of my time at Sparklight Academy, I miss working in transmutation and alchemy every day. The challenge of it. There have been a lot of special projects I've had to turn down because of time constraints. It'll be good to reprioritize"

"Ben will be happy to hear it. I'm sure Guardian Construction will make good use of your magick," Clancy remarks.

"I've always felt bad turning down some of his requests, especially for his more aesthetic and creative projects," I respond. "So hopefully I'll free up time for him and others who need it." I pause and smile at Norrell, never getting enough of the profound love in his eyes when he looks at me. "Most of all, though, I look forward to spending time with Norrell and building our life together."

"I am the luckiest male in the world," he declares as he leans in for a quick kiss.

"He knows it too," Esmeralda teases.

"To Norrell! The luckiest male in the world!" a witch across the table calls out. A round of cheers and clinking glasses follow.

Clancy stares at Walt, rubbing a hand over his chin. "Walt, I can't get over seeing you as a young male. It makes an aging centaur feel positively ancient," he snickers.

"I may have to come out of retirement. Growing young again has presented some unique but good problems to have," Walt jokes.

"Who knows, I may get to hand the *reins* of the town over to you someday." Clancy smirks at his pun. "I should have long ago learned my lesson to expect the unexpected."

"To Walt! Proof that seventy is the new twenty!" Clink.

We go well into the evening toasting each other and everything we can think of. The tension I've felt since Samhain lifts with each one. I'm floating in happiness—and a bit of a buzz—by the time we head home.

The next morning, Norrell and I drop off Elgar at the portal outside of town. Niven and his team are there as well. They will accompany him back to the path that leads to the clan's settlement. A team of his hunters will escort him the rest of the way. After seeing the relics in action, they aren't taking any chance of letting them fall into the wrong hands. The yetis will return the relics to the cave immediately and leave them there, hopefully forever.

Norrell's emotional goodbye to his brother shows me just how much he appreciates him. They embrace, clapping each other hard on the back, taking their time before pulling away.

"Thank you, Brother, for allowing me to step away and resume my life here. I will never forget it." Norrell's voice is unusually hoarse. "Come back soon. You will always have a place to stay."

"Mother and Father will not let me stay away for long." Elgar huffs a laugh. "Anything you want me to bring next time?"

"Just my books. Nothing else holds any importance."

We say goodbye to Niven and his team. They've all grown fond of Monstera Bluff, but Niven especially. "You'll see me again before you know it," he assures us with a warm smile right before he steps through the portal.

♡ ♡ ♡ ♡ ♡

"You look great!" Sunny rushes over to me when I step into the shop for the first time since I was cured. "That magick must have been the fountain of youth! You're so fresh-faced and rejuvenated. How are you feeling?"

"So much better. Thank you for taking charge during all of this. I owe you a raise at the very least."

"I was happy to. I'm just so glad to see you looking like yourself again. Even better in fact!" she gushes.

"If you want to see a fountain of youth, you'll be quite surprised the next time you see Walt." I huff a laugh. "That will knock your socks off."

"He's a snack!" she exclaims, drawing out the vowels. "No wonder Acton snapped him up."

"I don't need to hear that. They're my uncles!" I grumble jokingly, covering my ears with my hands.

"Let a female appreciate!" she justifies with a playful wink.

"Alright, well, I had also forgotten how handsome he was, not that I ever saw him this young. I wasn't born yet," I concede.

After a few minutes catching up, she finally asks, "You said in your message you wanted to talk to me about something?"

"Now that my magick is restored, I thought we could revamp the rest of your apprenticeship. You know everything necessary to create the potions and enchantments we sell. We can leave the bulk of that to the rest of the team. So, I thought I might work with you more on my personal specialties of alchemy and transmutation. With your artistic skill, your magick will surely have creative and beautiful results when transforming one substance into another. I also thought you might like to learn even more about running a shop. I'll still oversee much of it, but I hope this might gain you some practical experience to make your transition into your own business even easier," I explain.

"I'm down. Let's start today," she agrees readily. "My booth will debut at the farmers market in the spring. I have a lot to learn until then."

That evening, Norrell and I meet up with Walt and Acton so I can share some hard-earned wisdom from my time on the town council. The warlock years were the worst, but it's never easy. Since I twisted his arm, I want to prepare him.

"Sometimes, they just want someone to listen to their problems. There may not be anything you can do but lend an ear," I advise.

"I had plenty of practice for years at the parks department. Townsfolk have a lot of opinions." He shakes his head.

"This is a solid piece of advice, so take note. Do not accuse Viran of falling asleep at the meetings. His eyes may be closed but his ears are wide open. He will call you out if he hears something he disagrees with. Clancy finds it unsettling. I think it's hilarious especially when it catches the constituents off guard."

"I could have sworn he was asleep half the time. I swear I've even seen him twitch like he was having a dream," Walt insists with a chuckle.

"He doesn't miss a beat. I'm not sure how he does it."

While I lift the curtain on the town council's secrets, I hear snippets of Norrell and Acton's conversation about his rainforest garden project, finally nearing completion. When Acton asks if Norrell has any free time to help the following week, Norrell looks like something has clicked into place.

"How has your landscaping business been going?" Norrell wonders.

"It has wilted as my days are more sweetly spent with Walt in his golden years. Now that we have been gifted another sixty years together or more, mayhap it is time to reconsider the business," Acton ponders.

"If you consider expanding, I would offer myself as a landscaper. I would enjoy spending the days outdoors and working with my hands," he offers.

Acton tilts his head thoughtfully. "That would spread rays of sunshine over the grayest of days."

Walt's head immediately swivels to their side of the table. "Well, if you're going to hire Norrell, then you should hire me too. It'll be a family business."

"Bluebell, there is no pressure to decide," Acton urges. "A new calling may be awaiting you elsewhere."

"Spending my days with my family sounds like a fine idea. I may once again have the body of a twenty-five-year-old, but my mind is still seventy-three."

I look between the three of them in disbelief. "Did you form another family business that fast? You three crack me up!"

The town council is understandably forgotten as they spend the rest of the evening making plans to expand Acton's business. It's touching to see their eyes light up in excitement as they come up with ideas, many which are quite extraordinary.

When Norrell and I get home, I bask in the feeling of having the house to ourselves again. Taking him by the hand, I lead him up the stairs. He obligingly follows. I walk us into our bedroom, finally stopping next to our bed.

"I want to ride your cock, Norrell," I purr as I pull my sweater dress over my head.

"It is always ready for you," he chuckles darkly, adjusting the growing bulge in his pants. "Where do you want me?"

"On the bed, naked," I command, pointing near the headboard. He slides his pants down his long legs, exposing his thick, furred thighs and his fat cock already pointing straight out at me. Kicking his pants away, he takes a seat on the bed and slides toward the headboard, putting a pillow behind his back to prop himself up.

As I slowly shimmy out of my matching lacy pink bra and panties set, I flick the panties at him. He catches them and draws them to his face, taking a deep whiff. I giggle when it sets off a rumbling growl deep in his chest.

"Come here and take a seat, my mate," he beckons me, slowly stroking his cock with the pre-come oozing out of him.

"Are you offering me the best seat in the house?" I muse, biting my lip as I watch him play with himself.

"It is reserved just for you," he quips.

I climb over his muscular legs and straddle his lap. His cock rests between us, smearing white onto my belly. Raising myself up onto my knees, I rub his cock along the outside of my pussy, focusing on my clit. As I do this, Norrell's hands grab and knead around the curve of my ass, even landing a light spank along one side and then rubbing soothing circles over the spot.

The tension grows in my core and I'm ready for his cock to ease it. Reaching between us, I finally guide him to my entrance, and we both groan as I slowly sink down.

"Bounce me on your cock, please," I beg him.

"I want nothing more." With his hands still under me, groping my backside, he lifts my hips up and down, controlling the pace that I'm fucking him so all I have to do is revel in the feel of him.

At first, it's slow and leisurely, drawing out the drag of the hard, protruding veins that surround his cock. Their bumpy texture feels exquisite moving inside me like ribbing. My eyes flutter close as I start to lose myself in the long, slow draw of his cock inside me. A hot mouth tugs at one of my nipples, making me pant as he sucks on it. His tempo speeds up slowly, gradually, and his hips thrust upward to meet mine, pushing him as deep inside me as he can go. Soon I'm truly bouncing, the motion springing me on the bed. My breasts jiggle and sway. Nonsense spouts from my lips. "Yes, so good. Keep going."

"Touch yourself, my mate. Use your pussy to squeeze me dry," he directs me.

I do as he says, using a finger to rub across my clit. I feel myself teeter over the edge, my pussy tightening and his cock pressing through the squeeze. It tries to suck him in and keep him deep inside me. I wail as his cock hits a new spot at the front of my channel. He keeps working that spot, right where I need it. I moan uncontrollably as pleasure shoots from my core like lightning through the rest of my body.

When the pleasure softens to a low buzz, he flips us over so I'm on my back. Throwing my legs over his shoulders, he fucks me hard into the mattress. "Take my seed as deep as it will go, my mate. Right where it belongs," he snarls as his cock thickens and pulses inside me, filling me with his hot come.

At the last twitch of his cock, he shifts backwards, pulling out his softening length and guiding my legs down to the bed again. When he pushes my knees apart, I feel his come sliding out as he repositions me. With his eyes focused on my pussy, he uses his finger and pushes it back inside of me and holding it there like a plug.

"Are you trying to keep it inside?" I ask playfully.

In a rough, sexy tone, he answers, "For now. But you will always be full of my come, my ember."

On a breezy late spring afternoon, in the lush rainforest garden Acton carefully curated, fueled by his imagination and tenacity to see it through, Norrell and I stand facing each other amidst the dense greenery and blooming flowers.

Cascading ferns, vines, moss and even monstera adorn every surface of the large, fenced garden, creating riotous, complex layers of textured greenery. Embellishments of colorful flowers throughout including hibiscus, orchids, and of course the heliconia we gave him for Yule were planted with care and artistry. We are transported into a dreamy vision of the tropics.

Long rectangular pavers placed lengthwise create walkways through the vegetation. They lead to a clearing under a tall pergola crawling with vines that only lets through a spray of dappled light onto the ground. Our closest friends and family join us there as we hold a small mating ceremony. We never had one the first time. It's fitting that we do so now, when our commitment to each other is strong and true in a way it never was all those years ago. This is our second chance. And nothing will keep us apart ever again.

Norrell brings my hands to his mouth to press warm, firm kisses into my palms. He lowers them, holding them between us, as the ceremony starts. Love shines in his light blue eyes as he stares into mine. They're all I can see as he promises, "Ada, you are the ember that melted the frost in my heart. It lit a fire within me that never dimmed, even when time and distance separated us. My love for you burns eternal. It grows stronger each day. It will warm you, provide for you, and comfort you, throughout the rest of our days. I pledge all of myself to you in this realm and the next."

If his gaze could penetrate my mind, he'd see that my love burns the same for him. "Norrell, your care and love are the greatest gifts of my life. You are the rock that I will always anchor myself to, a steady, strong force I can count on no matter what life may bring. I love you with every fiber of my being. I pledge all of myself to you in this realm and the next."

He'll forever be my yeti of the night.

EPILOGUE
ADA

Stella sits on my hip, sucking her thumb. She's tall for her age, like I was, but she's still a toddler. My little girl is growing up too fast. She's already getting heavy when I carry her. Soon I'll be teaching her spells. As we walk across the front lawn toward Norrell, I gently dislodge her thumb and hold her hand in mine. "Daddy's almost finished with the stairs. Are you excited to go play up there?" I ask her, pointing both our hands toward the project Walt, Acton, and Norrell spent over a month building. Well, years, considering the tree itself.

"Why is there a house in the tree, Mommy?" Her eyes are wide as she looks at it. She's asked this question many times. I hope Norrell doesn't hear her say it again, but his ears pick up everything. He shakes his head, but there's a crooked smile curling past his tusk as he descends the spiral staircase they ingeniously built. It's amazing what they accomplished, often after long days spent on their thriving landscaping design business.

"It's a treehouse. A place your daddy and uncles built just for you. We'll play in it together for now. And then in a couple of years, you and your friends can play there all by yourselves. We climb up these stairs to reach it."

"Aubin won't need to when he's bigger," she remarks with a tiny frown.

"In a few years he might not. But he can't fly yet, sweet pea. He'll have to use the stairs just like you for a while," I explain. Cara and Ben's son, Aubin, is a few months younger than Stella. They are adorable playmates, the best of friends, but sometimes she shows some sibling-like jealousy toward Aubin's wings, even though he's much too young to fly. "You will both have amazing talents. Remember, you will wield magick one day."

"I guess," she concedes. She doesn't look satisfied, but she's no longer frowning.

Norrell watches us from where he's testing the enchanted staircase's strength one last time before we take her up with us. "Alright, Snow Angel, are you ready?" Norrell asks.

I'm about to tell him to wait when I hear Walt and Acton step outside the front door.

"She's a beaut," Walt admires as they walk over to us. "I can't get over how you twisted those branches to create a fence around the platform." Acton volunteered his magick to help the now mighty live oak tree grow from a sapling to full maturity in only a few years. Taking the process slowly ensured the tree developed as strong and sturdy as possible. He also shaped its growth to hold a platform and treehouse without damaging the fork where the branches grow from the trunk. Only at that point did the three of them start building.

"The tree senses the profound changes in the earth where it grew. It eagerly fills that space with life again. Its noble purpose," Acton remarks.

When I was pregnant with Stella, a notion popped in my head that we should plant a tree where the carriage house once stood. From there, the idea of the treehouse came together when the four of us talked about it.

"That will be a well-loved tree, especially as Stella gets older. I think Elgar and his folks are going to love seeing it when they visit next month," Walt agrees.

"That's too tall for Mommy," Stella declares to them, gesturing toward the platform. When she's satisfied that her uncles heard her, she lifts her head to look up toward the top of the tree.

"It's perfectly safe. I used magick to make sure of it. We'll all go up together." I borrowed a spell to cushion any falls under the tree that the parks department uses at Howling Woods Canopy Park. I hope it's overkill, but Norrell and I agree we should keep it in place indefinitely.

"Okay," she blurts out, then squirms to get out of my hold. I put her down and she runs straight to Norrell. She's a daddy's girl at heart. He smooths her wispy white hair—the same color as Norrell's—out of her face and then holds her hand to help her walk up the spiral stairs.

"She had me worried for a second she wouldn't go up," Walt whispers to me. I hum my agreement, but her curiosity would win out fast enough. Especially if Norrell reminds her that he and her uncles built it for her.

"Moon and stars, I'm so glad you remembered," I tell Acton as he hands me our picnic basket I left in the kitchen. A little tea set and a bottle of juice are packed inside. All the necessities to host an afternoon "tea party" to celebrate the completion of the new treehouse.

"Knock knock!" Cara announces from the foyer. Aubin's soft voice mumbles something I don't catch while they walk toward the kitchen.

"Sounds like Aubin wants his own treehouse," Norrell whispers, his eyebrows raised.

"Well, this one is as good as his anyway." I crack a smile, remembering the last time he was here and couldn't stop staring at Walt and Norrell as they worked on it.

Ben, Cara, and Aubin noisily enter the kitchen, with Aubin impatiently tugging Ben's hand, trying to move him faster. When he spots Stella coloring at the table, he lets go and runs over to join in.

"Aubin's in a mood today. Terrible threes and all," Cara murmurs.

"We could play with them outside in the treehouse until dinner is ready," I suggest.

"He would love that. He hasn't stopped talking about it all weekend." The tension leaves Cara's body.

Something pokes my leg. I turn around and two sets of big, round baby eyes look up at me—one violet and one hazel. They must be ninjas, silently sneaking up on me like that. "May we play in the *twee*house now, please?" Aubin asks in his gruff little voice.

I press my lips together to hold back a giggle. He's already losing his baby teeth, and the big gap in front leaves him with the cutest lisp. I'll miss it when they grow back. "Mmm-hmm," I agree, nodding my head.

"Yes!" His lisp is on display again as Aubin gives a little fist pump. They dash toward the front door. Norrell and Ben follow them out.

"I know he's not human, but I can't get over how big he is already. And his teeth! Don't even get me started. I asked Ben if the tooth fairy should visit, and he didn't know what I was talking about." She chuckles, shaking her head. "There are days Aubin reminds me of a teenager, even though he's only a toddler. I can't even think about when he starts to fly." Cara exhales loudly, giving me a look.

"Their development can be faster than humans'. But time moves differently watching them grow up. Sometimes I still see Stella as a baby. Other times she's like a little adult," I agree.

"Are you thinking about having another?" she asks abruptly. Without letting me answer, she continues, "I do, often, but Aubin's quite a handful. Ben and I talk about it, and he tells me our son is a normal, healthy gargoyle, growing right on track. Ben is *such* a good dad. He makes everything easier. But wow, that little guy keeps me on my toes. No wonder Nicolas and Lillian waited a decade between kids."

"Don't forget about their honorary third son Clancy!" I remind her.

Her eyes go wide and her hand flies to her mouth, trying to contain the laughter bursting out. "It's a wonder they had a second at all," she wheezes.

We walk outside in time to see both Norrell and Ben swinging the kids around in circles by their arms. They giggle wildly as the momentum lifts them off the ground.

"Ready to fly up there?" Ben asks them when they're back on their feet. They shriek in excitement, jumping up and down in front of him and holding up their arms. Ben scoops up both, one in each arm and lifts off the ground, beating his powerful wings, easily carrying the kids' weight. He gently deposits them over the short fence made of twisty, leafy branches onto the platform. He hovers in the air, watching them as they explore the treehouse together. Norrell climbs the narrow spiral staircase to join them and talk to Ben, who has become one of his closest friends.

It's not unusual for Norrell, Ben, and Clancy to get together at Call of the Wild. Cara and I often join them too. Norrell loosened up more than I thought possible in the last few years. I'd even venture to call him social nowadays. He's built quite a group of friends. He's also close with Mars, Kiernan, and Hal. He's even able to persuade Wyck to come out on occasion. He regularly talks on the phone with Niven—even more than I do.

Cara and I watch them from below for a couple minutes. The kids' laughter and joyous shouts ring from inside the little structure. A smile stretches across Cara's face. "I think they'll spend a lot of time in there, especially as they get older," she says. "I would have *loved* a treehouse like this when I was a kid."

"They will. It's good for kids to have their own spaces. It'll turn into their club house or their hideout, whatever fits the bill that day."

Cara sniffles noisily. Alarmed, I turn toward her and put my hand on her shoulder. "What's wrong, hon?"

"Nothing. I'm being silly. Sometimes I have to pinch myself to believe this is my life." The happiness in her eyes shines through the tears.

♥ ♥ ♥ ♥ ♥

"Stella tired herself out playing with Aubin," I tell Norrell as we close her bedroom door and tiptoe toward ours. "I don't think she'll wake up until morning."

"I would not mind an entire night to ourselves," he says in a smoky tone and then lightly slaps my rear.

My hands fly to my mouth to hold in a squeal. "Neither would I," I whisper from behind them.

Once we're behind our closed bedroom door, I spin around, gazing at him through my lashes.

He crowds me against the bed, forcing me to lie back on it. Leaning over me, he brackets his hands on either side of my head, slowly lowering himself onto me. "You smell so good, my mate," he growls, rubbing his nose along the side of my face.

"I have a confession to make." His attention sets off sparks in my core, making it hard to focus. "I took a potion earlier."

He rumbles low in his throat. "What kind of potion?"

I giggle. "A fertility booster."

"Ada," he groans. "Is that the perfume I smell?"

"Mayhap." My attempt to be coquettish is unnecessary because Norrell is already grinding against me. "I have another confession."

He moans into my neck, where he nibbles behind my ear, letting me know his enthusiasm about everything I have to say.

"I have a potion for you too. The birth control antidote."

His kisses along my neck drift lower, turning sloppy and fervent. He pulls aside the collar of my shirt to expose more of my chest. "You wear too many clothes."

"Don't you want to take it?"

He abruptly pushes himself off me and kicks off his pants. "Where is it, my ember? I will put another baby in you before the sun comes up." He sounds like a male possessed.

I smirk, anticipating this very reaction, finding his obsession with breeding me so insanely hot. It was just like this the first time too. "On top of the dresser."

Naked and ready for me, his cock already straining and leaking, he unstoppers the vial and downs it in one gulp. "I will need to fill you all night long, my mate. Make sure this potion takes effect and that you are good and bred by morning."

"It works fast. But you should pump me full of your seed so many times just to make sure you breed me." My voice is breathless in anticipation.

"Take off those clothes. Fast. Or I will have to rip them off you." His wild gaze moves down my body as he tugs at his testicles, looking large and swollen as if he had taken his own fertility-enhancing potion. Happy to comply, I make quick work of pulling off my outfit followed by my undergarments. I wore a sexy, lacy set just for this occasion. But Norrell is too worked up to appreciate them, not that I mind a bit.

"Are you feeling empty? Right here?" He looms over me again, pressing his hand to my low belly. His obsession with my expanding belly and breasts grew along with my pregnancy with Stella. I'm sure he's picturing my body swelling with our next child.

"I need to be filled. Nice and deep."

"Do you want to carry my baby? Have my seed planted deep inside of you?"

I moan, already feeling my pussy fluttering. "More than anything."

"Open up, Ada. Your yeti is going into rut," he snarls. He knows how much I love when he turns primal.

I spread my legs, feeling the wetness of my pussy hit the air. He pushes his face into it and licks a stripe up my slit. "You are fertile, good girl. Ready to be filled with my baby." He lifts from me, a frenzied expression on his face. "Get on your knees."

Obediently flipping over, I look back at him from behind my shoulder and shake my backside to entice him. A large hand grabs my hip, the filed claws digging in with dull points, a little bite in my skin but not painful. Just enough of a grip to make me feel his total possession of me.

With his other hand, Norrell scoops up the string of pre-come leaking onto the sheets and rubs it along his cock. "Nothing is going to waste. Every drop of my seed will be in your pussy tonight." I'm about to lean back into him when he finally thrusts inside me, fast and deep. "Earn your seed, good girl. Squeeze it out of me."

His hips pump sharply into me. I try to meet him thrust for thrust, but the striations of those thick, bulging veins on his cock scrape so pleasurably inside me, and I'm having a hard time keeping up. His chest rumbles as I lose speed, and he hooks his arms under my shoulders and lifts me upright. The thick pelt on his chest and legs chafe deliciously against my bare skin, reminding me of his wildness and virility. One hand plucks at a nipple, the other circles my clit. I look down and watch his swollen cock, shining with our juices, pump in and out of me. His massive fuzzy testicles swing upward with each thrust. The sight of him breeding me is enough to push my orgasm over the edge. I close my eyes as the sensation takes hold, a flash of white behind my eyelids. "Give me your baby, Norrell. Breed your good girl," I wail.

As the words leave my mouth, he roars through his release, grabbing my hips again and forcing himself deep, shooting ropes of hot come right into the mouth of my womb. "Drink it in deep, my ember," he rasps, winded. "Soak in it until I fill you again."

He moves us backward, so he rests on his heels and I'm sitting on his lap. He keeps his still-hard cock inside me, plugging me up. One hand travels slowly over my waist, spreading his fingers across my stomach, as if his seed is taking hold this very moment, and then he slides it lower to my clit.

"My seed will be planted in your belly by the time I am done with you. My cock is not leaving your body until you are bred." He massages my clit as he whispers hoarsely into my ear. "How many loads will your pussy squeeze out of me tonight? How much of my seed will it hold until we are too exhausted to move?'

"All that you can give me," I keen, feeling the wind up of another orgasm as he pinches my nipple and runs a smooth tusk along my neck.

"My seed belongs to you, Ada. I will breed you as many times as you want." I want this second baby with him. Maybe another after that. "Come on my cock, good girl. Ready me so I can bathe your womb again."

And I do, many more times throughout the night. I lose count of my orgasms—his, too. And he keeps his promise to never pull out. His come leaks out of me, oozing onto both of us, despite his best effort. But he seems to take it as a challenge, though there's no doubt much of it stays inside me. We don't stop until the sky brightens the room, both of us sweaty, sticky messes, collapsing together onto our bed.

One morning, a few weeks later, I feel a little green around the gills soon after I wake up. When I tell Norrell, he grins from ear to ear, knowing exactly what that likely means. The smile doesn't leave his face the entire drive to the healers clinic. Unsurprisingly, my pregnancy test is positive. All that breeding talk we love certainly works like a charm.

About the Author

Katie Haypenny

Katie delights in a good story, especially when it weaves in a powerful dose of swoonworthy romance. After years of work in the corporate world, she's now putting her creative skills to better use. She's often found typing away on her laptop in coffee shops, pouring her heart into captivating tales set in a whimsical, made-up little place called Monstera Bluff. Currently, she enjoys life in picturesque Savannah, Georgia, where she shares her days with her husband. Find out about upcoming books and sign-up for her newsletter at www.katiehaypenny.com

www.ingramcontent.com/pod-product-compliance
Lightning Source LLC
LaVergne TN
LVHW012034070526
838202LV00056B/5490